On the ground before them,
cicadas seethe over Sadie.

The sight whisks away Detective Paterson and all she knows about calm certitude under pressure, leaving in the detective's place Vicky, mother of Sadie.

And Vicky almost freezes up. It's more like half a second of slow motion, when time grinds to a halt and what lies before her is truly revealed.

A writhing, chaotic mass the deep-blue color of a late-winter dusk. Pops of translucency, flickers no more substantial than heat shimmers. The instant impression of great numbers of tiny things in some senseless collaboration with a single-minded goal. The sight brings to mind ants overtaking a fallen meat scrap from a grill.

A swarm.

Praise for Andy Marino

"Marino has a good eye for genuinely disturbing imagery.... This novel hums with a terrifying momentum."
—*Kirkus* on *It Rides a Pale Horse*

"Marino draws readers in quickly...[immersing] them in a world of art, siblings, deadly intrigue, and a centuries-long nefarious quest."
—*Booklist* on *It Rides a Pale Horse*

"Marino is very willing to plumb the depths of human discomfort and nihilistic despair, revealing disturbing images that sear into the brain while showing how art, and sibling bonds, can both create and destroy."
—*Library Journal* on *It Rides a Pale Horse*

"A visceral, disturbing story about the power of art and ritual."
—*Paste* on *It Rides a Pale Horse*

"*It Rides a Pale Horse* is a bizarre thrill ride from beginning to end. Captivatingly surreal."
—*San Francisco Book Review*

"Marino offers horrors both existential and visceral. From a stunning opening, the sense of dread just builds and builds."
—M. R. Carey, author of *The Girl With All the Gifts*, on *The Seven Visitations of Sydney Burgess*

By Andy Marino

The Seven Visitations of Sydney Burgess
It Rides a Pale Horse
The Swarm

THE SWARM

A NOVEL

ANDY MAR|NO

REDHOOK

Copyright © 2024 by Andy Marino

Excerpt from *It Rides a Pale Horse* copyright © 2022 by Andy Marino

Cover design by Lisa Marie Pompilio

Cover images by Shutterstock

Cover copyright © 2024 by Hachette Book Group, Inc.

Author photograph by Stan Horaczek

Hachette Book Group supports the right to free expression and the value of copyright. The purpose of copyright is to encourage writers and artists to produce the creative works that enrich our culture.

The scanning, uploading, and distribution of this book without permission is a theft of the author's intellectual property. If you would like permission to use material from the book (other than for review purposes), please contact permissions@hbgusa.com. Thank you for your support of the author's rights.

Redhook Books/Orbit

Hachette Book Group

1290 Avenue of the Americas

New York, NY 10104

hachettebookgroup.com

First Edition: November 2024

Redhook is an imprint of Orbit, a division of Hachette Book Group.

The Redhook name and logo are registered trademarks of Hachette Book Group, Inc.

The publisher is not responsible for websites (or their content) that are not owned by the publisher.

The Hachette Speakers Bureau provides a wide range of authors for speaking events. To find out more, go to hachettespeakersbureau.com or email HachetteSpeakers@hbgusa.com.

Redhook books may be purchased in bulk for business, educational, or promotional use. For information, please contact your local bookseller or the Hachette Book Group Special Markets Department at special.markets@hbgusa.com.

Print book interior design by Bart Dawson

Library of Congress Cataloging-in-Publication Data

Names: Marino, Andy, 1980– author.

Title: The swarm / Andy Marino.

Description: First edition. | New York, NY : Redhook, 2024.

Identifiers: LCCN 2024013091 | ISBN 9780316563994 (trade paperback) | ISBN 9780316564014 (e-book)

Subjects: LCGFT: Detective and mystery fiction. | Paranormal fiction. | Novels.

Classification: LCC PS3613.A7485 S93 2024 | DDC 813/.6—dc23/eng/20240329

LC record available at https://lccn.loc.gov/2024013091

ISBNs: 9780316563994 (trade paperback), 9780316564014 (ebook)

Printed in the United States of America

LSC-C

Printing 1, 2024

For Bradley

PART ONE

FORT HALCOTT

1

Hoarder houses are like happy families: all alike. Detective Vicky Paterson holds her breath. There will be cat piss.

With a gloved hand she pushes the front door open as far as it will go. The old wood, swollen in the summer heat, creaks in its frame. In the bad light of the foyer she can see a canyon of stacked magazines, boxes of yard-sale kitsch, the glint of scattered doll eyes. A tangled mess of kitchen playsets, their plastic skillets caked in charred lumps.

Did someone actually use them to cook?

Vicky's eyes water. It's only a matter of time before she'll have to take a breath. Barely inside and particulate matter sticks to her skin. Her heebie-jeebies are no joke. Two swipes of menthol ChapStick under her nose and she risks an inhale.

Vicky knows this, right here, is the best it's going to get, just inside the door, a few feet from the Adirondack mountain air. One last glance at the two uniforms lighting cigarettes by the cruiser parked down the gravel path reveals queasy upset all over their faces. Rookies on the graveyard shift doing a wellness check, not expecting this.

Whatever *this* is.

Vicky shuffles fully inside. Her vinyl shoe covers make a

crispy sound in the wee-hours silence. Filth's in sedimentary layers on the floor: rat droppings, fur, dust, pebbles, beads, petrified food scraps, kibble. A single lamp is perched atop a tower of board game boxes, their labels faded and yellowed. Old-school Clue and Monopoly along with more obscure titles she's never heard of. One's called Jiminy Cracker Skin.

It's a miracle that electricity still runs to this place. Vicky supposes whichever relative called in the wellness check keeps the utility bills up to date. Without any kind of judgment, she wonders why this daughter or brother or niece didn't have the resident old lady committed.

Well, maybe they did. Seventy-two-hour hold in the overcrowded, underfunded psych ward and then pop goes the weasel. That peculiar combination of maddening stubbornness and heartbreaking mental illness that alienates folks with hoarder tendencies. The old lady's burning resentment that she was ever committed in the first place. The slow dispersal of fed-up friends and family. The cycle of ingrained habit and solitude that begets itself. The ruin. The junk. The cat piss.

Vicky moves slowly past typewriters and candles, holiday lights and nutcrackers. A crooked sign says BLESS THIS MESS, a heavy-handed detail no one will believe. Books and moist cardboard fused into unholy lumps, stuffed animals and clothes with yellowed tags attached—all of it conspires to render the hallway at a strange angle. Vicky feels like she's treading the deck of a ship listing hard to port. Nausea rises. She makes a mental note to ask the ME for some of that medical-grade menthol rub. ChapStick is useless. Ten million cats used this place as their litter box.

A muffled conversation drifts in. The uniforms outside, embellishing their war story. She turns a corner past a pair of end tables stacked atop an ottoman, all draped in cobwebs. She tries to remember the name of the Dickensian lady in the wedding dress in the crumbling mansion. The drama club at Halcott

Central did that play back when she was a teenager, and everyone was forced to attend an afternoon performance. It felt like it was six hours long.

Vicky turns another corner and squeezes through the middle of what was once a living room. Clear plastic recycling bags stuffed with odds and ends rise from an adjustable hospital bed. The light fades. The stench grows. A cold pressure grips her head, at odds with the stifling air. She clicks on her flashlight. The beam plays along old iron bed frames, soiled blankets, frozen dinners bought in bulk. The toe of her shoe catches on a rain slicker, and something scuttles across her path. She freezes, spooked, hand on her holstered Glock, until she hears the critter burrow deeper into the labyrinth. Her flashlight illuminates a rare section of exposed wall. At first it looks burnt. Then she realizes it's mold, black and speckled and moist. An oily sheen covers everything, as if the rotten drywall is sweating. She makes a note to ask the ME for a hazmat suit too.

Vicky moves into the dining room. An archway, perhaps once grand, is festooned with threadbare garlands. Here she stops. Her mouth opens—something she's been trying hard to avoid. She sucks in a breath. A new and pungent stench is in the back of her throat now, the cloying, hot-garbage odor of decay. The only smell on earth that delivers a synesthetic rush to her head, all the drab and muted colors of death popping like sad fireworks behind her eyes.

She smears more ChapStick across her upper lip and takes in the scene.

This perfectly square and windowless room has been cleared out, except for a long dining table that shines as if doused in lemon Pledge. Lingering patches of torn carpet cling to ancient linoleum. She makes note of the sheer effort it must have taken to remove a thousand pounds of junk from the room. This had not been accomplished in a single hasty visit.

The old woman is lying on the table, dressed in a clean floral housecoat. Her hands are folded across her stomach. There is no immediate indication of violence. What strikes Vicky about the scene is the total lack of that lurid snapshot quality of most homicides. Rage and terror in the rude angles of splayed limbs, fury scrawled across walls in great spatters of blood. Not here. Here there is funereal peace.

Vicky sweeps her light across the bare, decrepit walls, then the ceiling. No sign of a light switch or overhead fixture. No lamps either. She'll have to be careful. She keeps the light trained on the floor as she walks to the table, careful not to disrupt any errant debris. At the table's edge, she shifts the light to the woman's face. Mottled skin is drawn tight against the cheekbones. The lips are stretched into a grimace that Vicky chalks up to gravity, not pain. Her heart begins to pound. Eight years into her career in the Fort Halcott Police Department—the last two in Major Crimes—and still, the proximity to death gets its claws into her.

She can already feel tomorrow's cold sweat, waking to the hint of afternoon light slinking around the edges of her blackout curtains, the sinewy tenderness of the old woman's frail throat invading the corners of her mind.

But for now she has a job to do. Being alone in this place is unpleasant, but she's grateful for the chance to perform a thorough, solitary appraisal before someone careless disturbs her scene. She takes a video of the corpse from head to toe, panning slowly, following the flashlight. The mental notes tick themselves off. Snap judgments and fledgling theories arrive and she acknowledges their presence and lets them drift away. Vicky's *Buddhist shit*, her partner calls it. A leaf on the wind or whatever.

The woman's bald head captures her attention. There are no wispy strands of hair, but there is what appears to be soft stubble. Peach fuzz. *Shaved*, Vicky thinks. *With clippers.* No obvious signs of violence on the scalp, face, or neck. She notes again the spot-less nature of the housecoat, at least on the fabric that covers the torso. Fluids have begun to pool in the lower half. She pauses on the woman's folded hands. There's something odd about them. Vicky has to look for a long time before it hits her: All ten fingernails are gone. Not clipped or torn. Removed entirely. On a hunch, she pans down to the bare feet.

The toenails are missing too, nail beds pale and shriveled. No blood. The killer or killers were careful, almost surgical, in their precision here.

A sudden feverish rush forces her to grip the edge of the table. She lets the dizzy spell wash over her and waits for it to pass. Methodical killings aren't exactly a staple of Fort Halcott. New York's twenty-sixth largest city (population sixty-four thousand, just behind Schenectady and with a healthy lead on Utica) sees its share of robberies gone wrong, wannabe-gang killings, the odd domestic that escalates to murder, some darker-than-garden-variety drunken mayhem.

This is something different. The thought of a man standing right where she is now, bending over the corpse, taking his time with various grooming tools, cranks up those heebie-jeebies. She kills the video and pockets the phone. Then she takes a moment to raise the flashlight and aim the beam down the hall. Light settles into the nooks of the hoard. Plastic organizers draped in ancient linens. Curtain rods and fireplace tools. Hundreds of paperbacks. She dispels the notion that she's being watched.

All alone, Vicky.

Another sweep of the room reveals nothing new. There's only one more place to look. She kneels down to peek under the table.

"Dang."

Three small cardboard boxes are lined up in a neat row. Their flaps are closed but not sealed.

Down on one knee, she pauses. This crime scene is already doused in off-kilter energy. A profiler would call it *ritualistic.* This likely won't be the only killing. It might not even be the first. It certainly won't be the last. There's also an element of all this that's nagging her and has nothing to do with the death itself. She can't yet give this hunch form and meaning.

"Oh, dang it all," she says. Tentatively, with a gloved hand, she flips up the first box's flaps. She leans forward, ducking fully under the table, and peers in. Within the cone of light sits a nest of gray hair streaked with white.

So the killer shaves the old lady's head and tucks the hair neatly into a box like he's prepping an Easter basket with a bed of grass.

Her whole body is tingling, pins and needles in her fingers and toes. All over Fort Halcott, people are settling in for an air-conditioned slumber, cuing up late-night shows, raiding fridges for midnight snacks. Normalcy abounds. And then there's this.

She reaches for the second box and steels herself. She thinks she knows what it's going to be, but it doesn't make the process of discovery any less harrowing. Up go the flaps, and there's the small pile of gnarled, corroded nails. Thick and amber-colored, fungal in a way that breaks her heart. Not a drop of blood. A word comes to her and she wants to dismiss it but she can't. *Harvested.* At the third box, she pauses. Hair and nails. What else could be missing?

Her phone buzzes in her pocket. She ignores it. If it's the babysitter she'll call back in a minute. Her hand is poised over the third box.

"Just flippin' do it," she tells herself. Her fingers go to work. The light shines in. Her sharp intake of breath pulls foul air down her throat. "Oh no."

The box contains a bloodless pile of teeth. Only about a

dozen or so, which makes sense: The woman must be in her eighties or nineties.

Vicky straightens up. She lays a finger against the woman's lower lip and pulls lightly. The exposed gums are drained of color, the toothless ridges unmarred by signs of violence. Like the hair and nails, the teeth have been extracted with great care. She steps back and contemplates the scene. The feeling that she's overlooked something ratchets up. She takes another step back. A sticky softness tingles against the back of her neck. Swatting at her skin, she pulls long strands of dusty cobwebs away from her body. She flicks her wrist and they sail out into the humid air.

Bugs.

That's it. That's what's missing.

Judging by the condition of the body, this woman has been lying here for several days. The entire room should be a hell-scape of corpse-feeding insects. Yet there's not a single maggot clinging to the lips or nostrils. Not a single fly buzzing around the table.

Vicky backs away. She doesn't want to lean against the wall, doesn't want her body to touch any part of this house, but her legs feel weak. The anticipation that strikes her at crime scenes, when she knows just how the images will manifest as she sleeps, is amplified to shrieking levels in this place.

How can there be no maggots, no flies, not even one of those disgusting beetles that actually *feed* on maggots?

The walls are covered with spiderwebs, but not a single spider. In defiance of all forensics, pathology, and entomology that she is aware of, insects have completely vacated a room where a person lies dead. Vicky pulls off a glove, jabs at her phone, and lifts it to her ear.

"Victoria." Her partner's caffeinated voice comes on after half a ring. "You really should be here. You're missing out. Corner of Stanton and Wheeler, so, you know, the garden district.

They got the whole ladies' auxiliary handing out lemonades."
He pauses. "I'm shitting you, there's nobody here except the vic.
Get this, he caught four in the chest, center mass, like somebody
used him for target practice. We're looking for a real marksman
here. You know, I hate when they split us up. But this is what
happens when you hit peak summer killing season, we gotta
divide and conquer."

"I need you here, Kenny."

"Shit, you okay?"

"I need more eyes on this."

"Weird one?"

"You just have to see it."

"Ten four, they can roll mine up now anyway. You need
anything? Green tea? Granola bar? Methamphetamine in butter-
fly stamp bags?"

"Don't stop for any food, please, Kenny."

"I'm rushing to your side as we speak."

"I can hear you chewing already."

"That's gum. Over and out."

Vicky kills the call and texts her babysitter: *90% sure it's going
to be a late one. You might be on breakfast duty. So sorry!*

Kim hits her back immediately. *All good. The peanut's in bed.
We lost George and it was touch and go for a minute, but we discovered
him under the radiator in the front hall.*

Vicky smiles. George, the stuffed ladybug, her daughter
Sadie's favorite toy, the one she clings to at bedtime. She closes
her eyes and imagines Sadie clutching George to the side of her
head, claiming it's the only way she can hear words in ladybug
language. Vicky tries to swim inside the memory, but the menthol under her nose fades, the head-spinning ammonia of cat piss
rushes in, and she opens her eyes. Her flashlight beam is pointed
at the floor, so the corpse on the table is draped in deep shadow.

To live a long life and end up this way, Vicky thinks.

There was once a girlhood, laughter and beach trips, friends and gossip and charm and suitors. If someone could have shown the young version of this woman her sad house and horrible death, what would the girl think? Would it ruin everything, or would she dismiss it with a laugh and a flutter of her hand, something so far off as to be inconsequential? To have no bearing at all upon the girl at the boardwalk linking arms with her best friend and skipping into the wide-open night.

Vicky thinks of Sadie once again, sleeping soundly with George the ladybug. Then she shakes it off and goes outside to wait for her partner.

2

The crickets aren't supposed to be this loud. Will Bennett's got the windows of his RAV4 up. Still it's like a thousand insects are in here with him, crawling over the back seat. There's no way to drown them out with air-conditioning and music. He can't turn on the car. He can't do anything but sit and watch. And listen to the goddamn chirping drone.

He wonders if it's an upstate thing. If a city boy like him just isn't used to the noise. Used to it or not, it seems to Will that the good people of Fort Halcott would not stand for it. How could they live like this?

He unwraps another Starburst and trains his binoculars on the warehouse, a low-slung brick of a building with an empty row of loading docks. A single streetlight sends a lonely cone of light down onto the blacktop.

Will's parked on an embankment in a lot choked with weeds. Thick stems shoot up through cracks in the pavement. Behind him is the empty shell of an old fast-food joint. There are metal speaker boxes on poles for each parking space, the kind of retro 1950s setup where they bring you the food on a tray. Maybe even on roller skates. Fort Halcott's own Saturday-night malt shop, where the greasers and the preps cruise with their best girls. Or maybe just a Sonic that went out of business.

The warehouse he's staking out sits empty and silent. Will sweeps the binoculars away from the building. Just down the embankment is the access road that curls through the northeast part of town, where the residential streets give way to office parks and manufacturing centers. Posters on an empty bus shelter advertise last year's movies. A hubcap sits in a drainage ditch. Cattails sprout from a runoff swamp. He wonders if that's where all these crickets live.

Will lowers the binoculars. He works the lemon candy around the roof of his mouth. What's left of it sticks to the back of his front teeth. He should have picked up something else, something with chocolate and peanuts. The motel vending machine had Snickers. He imagines for a moment that he will turn his head and see that the fast-food joint has sprung magically to life. He can smell the cooking oil and grease. Lights shine as bright as a carnival midway. The other cars are long and low, and some of them have fins. A girl glides out on skates to deliver him pristine cheeseburgers and salty fries. She wears a paper hat. Her eyes sparkle in the light. When she gets close to his car, she smiles and his heart stops beating. He knows this girl. She's been waiting for him. But he can't roll down his window. Can't even move. Her smile falters.

THWACK. Knuckles on glass.

Will jolts upright in his seat. He blinks away vestiges of twinkling light. In the rearview the old restaurant is dark.

"Fuckface!" There's a woman's voice outside the passenger door. A shadowy figure stands there, radiating impatience.

Will unlocks the car and his ex-wife slides in and shuts the door behind her. Her black leggings and T-shirt are a match for his, more or less.

He fights the urge to lean over and give her a kiss. Old habits. "Hey, Alicia."

The former Mrs. Alicia Bennett reaches over the console to take the Starburst pack from his lap. "Nice dream?"

"I wasn't sleeping."

"Bullshit. There were visible Z's floating up out of your drooly mouth. It's not even *late*, Will. In stakeout time it's like noon." She unwraps a little square.

"Don't eat all the lemon ones."

"First of all, not a problem, because nobody likes those."

"I do."

"Yeah, 'cause your palate is pure old man. Your favorite candy is Werther's Original. When it's early-bird-special time at the diner you call an Uber and you're like, step on it." She palms a handful of Starburst and flings the pack back into his lap, aiming straight for his crotch. "We should've stopped at the 7-Eleven."

Will grabs his phone and pulls up his photos. He swipes through and stops at the smiling face from his dream. It's a portrait of a fair-haired woman in her early twenties. She's posed in business casual against a blank wall. There's something perfunctory about it. A corporate ID or a college key card shot.

Alicia leans over and affects a deep southern accent. "Violet Carmichael, as I live and breathe, how *are* you?"

Will makes the photo bounce as he does a posh rich-girl voice in response. "I've been positively *kidnapped* by a *freaky sex cult!*"

Alicia's face snaps to all business. She looks at him with those admonishing eyes. "Will. Be serious. This is a life-and-death situation here."

He takes one more quick look at Violet Carmichael's eyes and puts the phone to sleep. "You started it, but speaking of life and death, what did you see down there?"

"A warehouse."

"I knew there was a reason I asked you to come."

"It's honestly nondescript as fuck. Words fail me."

Will pauses. The buzzing cacophony sets his teeth on edge. "You hear those bugs?"

Alicia frowns as she unwraps another candy. "What, the crickets?"

"I can't believe they're this loud."

She shrugs. "Country living."

"Fort Halcott's bigger than White Plains. That's hardly the sticks."

She gestures out the window at what could generously be called nothingness. "Not exactly Atlantic Avenue either. Plus, there might be a quote-unquote *downtown* with a few office buildings, but the whole city's surrounded by the forest preserve. It's like they stuck Rochester in the middle of a national park or something."

"We were here the last two nights and I don't remember them sounding like this."

"Full moon."

"That's your answer for everything."

"I assure you it is not."

"It's always some astrological, Mercury in retrograde—"

"Don't say *always*. Nothing is ever *always*."

Will falls silent. This is an acknowledged problem for him when he gets worked up. They talked about it in couples therapy with Dr. Capaldi. Will does a quick breathing exercise to center himself. He lifts the binoculars to his eyes for due diligence. Still nothing going on at the warehouse. He lowers the binoculars to his lap and rephrases, working from a place of calm, respect, and clarity.

"It *sometimes* feels like you use things related to the stars, or astrology, to shut down whatever I'm saying. Like, it's a way of being dismissive without actually saying, *You're an idiot, I don't want to talk about this with you anymore.*"

"Like when you start to point out aspects of the scenery we're driving through when I'm trying to engage you in serious discussions *you* never want to have."

"Okay, but this is about the specific thing I just tried to bring up, not other hypothetical—"

"They're not hypothetical—"

"Dr. Capaldi said—"

"Car coming."

They both go quiet. The car turns out to be a Sprinter van, tall and boxy, heading up the access road from the south. It rounds a long, easy curve. Headlights roam the drainage ditch. The hubcap glints and disappears.

The van hangs a right off the road and heads up the driveway to the warehouse. The fence along the entry glides open on big metal wheels.

"Remote control," Alicia says. Will agrees, unless there's someone inside, a guard with a bank of monitors in a security room. She lifts up her night-vision camera with its telephoto lens. "I'm at a weird angle here."

Will ducks down in his seat. "Better?"

"Can you open the window?"

"It's like a bug war zone out there."

"Oh my God."

"I'll have to turn on the car to roll down the windows. It might get somebody's attention."

Without another word, Alicia opens the passenger door and scampers out to the edge of the embankment. Her body language is pitched at a forward lean, all productive energy and a lack of tolerance for bullshit. He senses a familiar flutter down by the Starburst pack and realizes with a bittersweet pang how much this aspect of her character turns him on. Will figures she left the door open on purpose. It's a petty move that he also finds arousing.

He keeps an eye on her silhouette and tries to acclimate to the insect noise. The bugs are throwing a rager down in that swamp. He doesn't know if it's some kind of mating thing or what. There's just enough off-key overlap to drive him nuts. It sounds like bugs have crawled inside his head to rub their wings against his brain. He wonders if it really doesn't bother Alicia or if she just doesn't want to give him the satisfaction.

Her scent lingers in the car: lavender hair stuff. The insects drone on. He raises the binoculars.

The Sprinter van is parked in one of the loading dock spaces. The dome light goes on inside as the doors open. A man and a woman step out—the driver and passenger. They're dressed in jeans and T-shirts. The woman slides open the back door of the van and a trio of kids piles out. Not *kids*, Will corrects himself. Early twenties. Like Violet in the photo her parents supplied. He scans their faces, barely lit by the dome light, and adjusts the focus. Two girls and a guy. He doesn't think Violet is among them but it's hard to tell. The woman slides the door shut. The light goes off. He switches to his own night-vision binocs: panoramic quad tubes, PNVGs. The actual view is disappointing. Like every other kid raised on action movies, Will had always expected a certain depth of field from night vision, like the daylight world but greener. The reality is more like tunnel vision with an odd flattening effect. He watches the trio of acolytes from the back of the van carry several large boxes inside the warehouse. Then all is quiet.

Alicia gets in and shuts the door carefully. The volume of the cricket song is barely halved.

"She wasn't there."

Will sighs. "Another fun call with the Carmichaels awaits."

The clients—Violet's parents—insisted on daily reports. Will bargained them down to every other day. These conference calls are miserable. Will feels like an asshole, finding new ways to wring dubious notes of progress from their methodology. It's not like he's lying about anything, it's just that the realities of this operation don't lend themselves to exciting updates. This particular cult doesn't have a single compound where they all live communally and do their composting and perform tantric rituals or whatever. They're embedded in the fabric of Fort Halcott. They've been here for years. Decades, maybe. They own all kinds of property buried in shell corporations. They're made up of the professional class. Will and Alicia follow leads that aren't linear. They snake all over town, doubling back, overlapping. Sitting and watching and eating vending machine candy. Their per diem dwindles. And while they're mired in a web, the Carmichaels grow more impatient by the day.

And these are not people accustomed to waiting around, or to helplessness, or to the feral kind of desperation that the vast swath of non-rich society has learned to weather. That hunger—for decent food, a good job, a full night's sleep—is an alien feeling to Ed and Fiona Carmichael.

You're supposed to be the best, Ed is fond of saying in sheer exasperation.

Will wishes he could tell Ed the truth: that he got lucky once. Lucky enough to establish a reputation and burnish it to high heaven.

"Tell them their precious Violet is probably having the time of her life," Alicia says, "and if they'd been more attentive and understanding, she probably wouldn't have joined a cult in the wilds of upstate New York. She would have stuck it out in grad school and moved back to the city to help administer her parents' various philanthropic foundations."

Will unwraps the last Starburst. "Maybe you can tell them that."

Alicia twists off the massive lens and cycles through her photos in the viewfinder. She turns the camera so Will can see.

Instead of muted green, her photos are a strange combination of sharper imagery and wacky colors: a vibrancy that brings to mind the way the Predator sees.

"New thermal imaging looks good," Will says with admiration.

"Courtesy of Ed and Fiona."

Will's thankful he had the presence of mind to call in his ex in time for Alicia to sweet-talk the client into more cash up front for expenses and equipment. He also has her to thank for their funky hipster motel, the Mountain View Lodge, a comfy tourist trap that beats the hell out of Fort Halcott's bastions of extended-stay sadness.

Together they cycle through photos while the crickets chirp on and on. The two women are the right age, roughly the same athletic build, but most definitely not Violet.

He closes his eyes. Christ, nothing is easy. In the darkness of his self-pity, the crickets shriek and shriek.

"Will!"

Alicia hits him on the shoulder. His eyes snap open. She points at the warehouse.

A bright flash lights the building from within. Then another. Staccato, off-time bursts that fill the three square windows set high in the wall.

Gunshots. There's no report from any firearm, but the sound could be dampened by thick warehouse walls. And the hellish chorus of crickets. Will reaches across Alicia's lap to open the glove box and remove the Sig Sauer pistol.

"Jesus, Will, let it be."

"No." He opens the door.

"Violet's not even in there!"

"We don't know what's in there," he says, stepping out onto the weed-choked blacktop. The day's humidity hasn't quite burned away, and he's instantly coated in a sheen of sweat.

Outside, the crickets are percussive, with a deep bass thump to their cries. The noise is incredible.

A moment later, Alicia is at his side, pulling on his arm. "Will, I'm serious." Her eyes are wide pearlescent circles in the night. "Don't go in there."

"I can't just sit here."

"You don't have to prove anything to me!"

He shakes free of her grip. "You think that's why I do things?"

"Dr. Capaldi says—"

"Fuck off, Alicia." He starts down the embankment.

3

Detective Ken Grimes lights a fresh cigarette from the smoldering end of his last one. He pinches it between thumb and forefinger and closes one eye as he takes a drag. His open eye settles on Vicky and narrows with disdain.

"Don't say it," he growls.

"There are mindfulness techniques you can learn."

He blows smoke into the night air. "They're all bullshit."

Three cruisers, an unmarked, and a van full of CSU equipment are parked in front of the old lady's house. The porch is taped off. A pair of crime scene techs file out, leaving one still inside.

Grimes is only a few years older than Vicky, but he's an elder statesman on the FHPD. The kind of man that's been a weathered, world-weary old guy since he was a senior in high school. The jokes are endless: Grimes in the cafeteria drinking chocolate milk out of a flask. Grimes taking on one last big homework assignment. Grimes being twice divorced before graduation.

Vicky lets him smoke. She doesn't prod him. He's just spent some time inside the house and now he's processing.

"Reeks in there," he says after a while. Half his lip curls as he exhales smoke. Remnants of a boyhood cleft repair operation that left some nerve damage. "It's always the cats with these people."

"Don't say *these people*, please."

"You know what I mean."

Vicky has to concede that in this case, she does. She tells herself that her heart can go out to the illness while still acknowledging that it does indeed reek in there. "I was thinking, back in that room—that lady had a life once, you know? I mean, at some point she was a young person with dreams."

"Could've been a young hoarder cat lady too." He bends over to stub out his cigarette then pockets the butt. Vicky has long become accustomed to her partner's general miasma of ashtray. He takes a piece of spearmint gum from the other jacket pocket and pops it in his mouth with his tongue out like he's getting his tonsils examined. He's quiet until he lands on what he thinks might be troubling her. "Sadie's gonna turn out fine, Vic. She's a good egg."

"She loves her uncle Kenny. But I wasn't thinking about Sadie."

"You'll meet a nice gal someday, just keep swiping."

"I wasn't thinking about *me*, either. You know, sometimes people can have empathetic feelings without having to center their own lives in everything."

"Jesus. You join the fun police too?"

"So what do you think?"

"About what, the boxes full of teeth and hair and nails? I think it's pretty run of the mill, open and shut. We can probably close the file."

Vicky looks off into the woods, lets her partner's mind spin off silently until he's ready for some real talk. She eavesdrops on two of the techs who are trying to look busy but mostly killing time. One says, "He hates watering plants but he wants a goddamn kid." She flashes to Sadie's sweet, sleeping face. Babysitter

Kim dozing on the sofa in the glow of the TV. She fights the urge to prod Grimes along on his journey toward earnest police work. She lets the sounds of the woods wash over her. Bullfrogs. A distant owl. About a million crickets.

"I think it isn't his first and it won't be his last," Grimes says after a while.

Vicky frowns. The crickets are *loud* out here. They sound like a screaming chorus. She pictures little bug mouths stretched into human-like howls of despair. The thought makes her shudder.

"I agree," she says. "But." She pops a sugar-free ginger candy in her mouth. "You don't think we'd have heard of something like this, if it's happened before?"

There are eighteen officers in the Major Crimes Division. Four of them investigate homicides. They're all clustered together in the same decaying institutional office. If a killing beyond the usual shootings and domestics crops up, the whole division knows about it.

"I know, I know." Grimes makes a gravelly noise, the acceptance of a bad memory. "All of Major Crimes oughta be juiced. Like the Winters kid. The whole building was running a fever."

Billy Winters, yanked into a Chrysler LeBaron in broad daylight up in the Royal Terrace Apartments, found twenty-six hours later with a railroad spike through his stomach, pinned to an oak along the trails behind Collins Park. Vicky lets a dizzy spell wash over her.

"That was the last incident that was even in the same ballpark," she says.

"Well, this sure as shit wasn't Silas Nedry."

The rest is unspoken. Nedry's dead, courtesy of Vicky's Glock. The only time she's ever fired her service weapon, and it's to give a child killer exactly what he wanted: suicide by cop.

"But Nedry *was* from Manitoba," Grimes says. "Which is my point. Plenty of psychos—sorry, Vic, *disturbed individuals*—are

nomadic. Can you think of a more sinister word than *drifter*? I
can't."

"We're getting ahead of ourselves," Vicky says. Profiling, theories, gut instincts, victimology—all of it is desk-bound work,
study and conversation and whiteboards and a-ha moments. She
doesn't want to waste precious time at the scene on premature
speculation. "What stood out to you in the dining room?"

"Probably the boxes of hair, teeth, and nails, if I had to pick
something."

Vicky opens her mouth to reply, then shakes her head. She
glances in mild annoyance at the dark woods. It's probably her
imagination, but the bugs are suddenly louder, like somebody
cranked up the volume.

"Do you hear those crickets?" she says.

"Those aren't crickets."

"Then what are they?"

"What am I, the bug police?"

"Kenny, I'm exhausted and I've got Kim at home with Sadie
on overtime."

Grimes chomps his gum. "They don't sound anything like
crickets to me, is all. I can't identify them, and yes they are loud.
I also know what you're fishing for. What is arguably weirder
than the shit in the boxes is the total absence of maggots or flies
in and around the corpse." He pauses. "Now I guess I *am* the bug
police."

"It's not possible," Vicky says. "Maybe if a body was trapped
inside a hermetically sealed environment, or a freezer, but we're
talking about *that* house. It's already a breeding ground. The
whole dining room should be crawling with insects." She pauses.
A thought forms, tenuously connected, but nagging enough to
voice. "I backed into this huge spiderweb while I was in there.
No spider, though. And I didn't see any roaches. These kinds of
situations always have roaches."

Grimes takes this in. "Maybe some kind of cleaning agent our guy used to wash the body. Something caustic that fucked up the breeding ground."

"Maybe," Vicky says. She's never heard of any kind of solvent that would have this effect, but anything is possible.

"Detectives!" One of the techs beckons from the edge of the sagging porch. She's fully suited up, hazmat-style, in a white plastic onesie, surgical mask, goggles, and gloves. "You might want to take a look at this."

"Nah, Frannie, we're good!" Grimes calls back with a cheerful wave.

Vicky turns her back on her partner and heads for the house. She crunches the last bit of ginger candy.

"Ignore him," she says to Francesca Morales, a veteran tech.

"I always do."

Vicky lifts the yellow tape and joins Francesca on the creaking, rotted boards of the porch. A floodlight's been set up, and the front of the house is bathed in a bright glow. An empty picture frame juts from a broken window. A chainless porch swing, long since collapsed, is piled with sun-faded cereal boxes.

Francesca motions toward the door with the camera dangling from a strap around her neck. "I lifted the vic's housecoat to document the torso." She pauses. "Did you look under there?"

"I didn't." It sounds odd to say this out loud. Like she's admitting to a small failure. A bout of laziness.

The tech hesitates, but Vicky knows it isn't tacit disapproval. Fran's body language, normally confident and graceful, is anxious and halting. "I need to show you."

Vicky follows her into the front hallway. The narrow canyons of sedimentary clutter rise to the ceiling. The smell assaults her nasal passages. A moment later, Grimes is plodding along behind her. The crickets are muted by layers of the old lady's hoard, but Vicky notes with some surprise that she can still hear their droning buzz. She thinks that Grimes is probably right. Crickets don't sound this angry, this pointed, this *mission-driven*. Crickets float and trill. These insects bellow and shriek.

They reach the dining room together. A pair of smaller floodlights have been rigged up so that the table with its corpse looks like a stage set. The old woman's flesh is nearly translucent in the brightness. Blue veins snake just beneath the skin. Vicky glances over her shoulder. Half of the massive spiderweb she backed into is still clinging to the wall. With the room lit up like a stadium, she confirms what she already knows: no maggots, no flies, no roaches.

Fran clutches the bottom hem of the old lady's housecoat, down by her knobby, scarred knees.

"All right," the tech says. She pauses. Then she whips the fabric back like she's ripping off a bandage.

"What the fuck?" Grimes exclaims. His hand reaches out, finds Vicky's shoulder. His fingers dig in. His other hand goes to cover his mouth.

Vicky blinks. She takes a deep breath, takes in the stench, and forces a steadiness through her body. At the same time she knows her dreams will spiral down into sightless depths with this desecration flashing like a strobe. This is something unprecedented, and as such it will command her nights for a long time to come.

"I don't know," Fran says, backing away from the table as if this new sight is giving off infernal heat. "I really don't."

Vicky wills herself to move in for a closer look. Grimes lingers at her back. The fact that he's gone quiet is deeply unsettling.

But she understands why.

The old woman's torso is a patchwork of fibrous flesh the color of Lipton tea. It's woven in some mad pattern, like a crosshatched pie crust gone horribly wrong. Pale, papery skin appears at odd intervals. Without touching the blemish, Vicky has an impression of its texture. Smooth and hard. A half-formed carapace. The blemish extends down the woman's left side and becomes a mottled mess as if it has dripped, unfinished, then hardened like wax.

This is not a postmortem mutilation. Vicky doesn't believe a human being could have done this. Not because of its depravity but because of logistics, methodology. What even *is* this?

"She had some kind of disease," Grimes says, sounding unsure of himself. "That flesh-eating virus. I don't know. Fuckin' leprosy."

"We need a pathologist here," Vicky says. "And a forensic entomologist."

"We need to burn this place down," Grimes says, "and salt the earth."

Vicky is glad for her partner and Francesca. She clings to human company in the presence of this aberration and tries not to think of the coming dreams.

She will certainly be alone in those.

4

Will finds Alicia's carefully snipped chain links around the east side of the warehouse. A hill rises at his back, beyond which the industrial edge of Fort Halcott dribbles out into wilderness. He pushes the fence. After a moment's give, the opening reveals itself and he slips though.

You don't have to prove anything to me.

This has nothing to do with you, Alicia. Their argument unspools in his mind. As usual in hypothetical discussions, he is articulate and reasonable. *It's the right thing to do.*

No. He shakes his head.

Helping people is the right thing to do. He adds a perfect little dig: *Always.*

He'll put an end to whatever is happening in there, and Alicia will see that he was right.

Will would like to see that guy she's dating, the lawyer—Will would like to see *Carter* rush headlong into danger. Dude would probably piss himself at the sight of muzzle flashes.

The thought of Carter shrieking like a small child at the merest hint of conflict makes his heart pound, flooded with gleeful adrenaline.

He jogs in a low crouch along the pavement that circles the

warehouse like a moat. The crickets thunder in his ears. He knows it's all wrong: Crickets don't *thunder*. Yet here he is, moving through the eye of a once-in-a-lifetime cricket storm. He shudders with the prickly sensation that there are millions of them all around him, flitting in and out of the shrubbery that lines the drab brick building. Screaming.

There's another bright flash in the windows, imprinting afterimages on the night. Yet even now, twenty feet from the building, Will can't hear the shots. Not even a muffled *pop*. Your basic 9mm can hit the decibel level of a jet engine. Either the soundproofing is heavy duty, the weapon is silenced, or the shots are drowned out by the ambient cricket noise.

Will reaches the building and sidles between hedges trimmed to military flattops. He straightens up with his back against the wall. A silhouette darts out of the blackness and rushes up to his side.

It's Alicia, breathing hard. "You're acting like a total maniac!" she hisses.

"So you want to wake up tomorrow and read that five people are dead in some kind of ritual murder-suicide and know for the rest of our lives that we could have done something about it?"

"I just want to wake up tomorrow, *period*."

Another flash.

"I've counted eleven shots so far," Alicia says. She takes a moment to catch her breath. "Whatever was supposed to happen in there has already happened. There's nothing we can do now. So we wait, then go in and check out the aftermath. Maybe there will be a clue."

"A *clue*?"

"Information. We gather it. It's our job."

"So, what, you get to decide our course of action now?"

"I feel like you're coming at me from a place of unconsidered anger."

He tries to focus on her face in the dark. It slips in and out of shadow. "And I feel like you forgot why we started doing this work in the first place."

"*Money*, Will. Because after you went away to find yourself—"

"See, you always bring up my walkabout thing, like—"

"Two years of your—of *our* lives is not *the walkabout thing*. You know, sometimes when I'm with you I feel like I'm regressing. I feel like a child, arguing with another child. It's really uncomfortable and depressing."

"Shh!" There's a new sound. A musical strain, a single drawn-out note in dissonant competition with the swell of crickets. Will slides along the wall. The hedges tug at his shirt. He stops alongside a window and leans over just enough to peek inside. It's a pitch-black void. The shrubbery rustles as Alicia follows him.

"I really don't like this," she says. A sour thought pops into his head: that his ex-wife just wants to get back to Carter the lawyer and his SoHo loft. Will knows about the SoHo loft because he has watched them enter it after leaving dinner at Eleven Madison. Carter must be a big shot at his stupid white-shoe firm because he has a driver who waits outside restaurants. He's in private equity, Will recalls. His grip tightens on the Sig. What would Carter do if Will pressed the cold barrel into the center of the man's forehead? Carter's a squeeze-the-eyes-shut-and-beg type, Will thinks.

On the other hand, Alicia could have stayed up on the embankment. Hell, she could have stayed in the city, greeted his request to partner up one more time with a hearty *no fucking way*. But she didn't. She came with him, all the way up to the Adirondacks, a hundred miles outside of bumblefuck. And just now she followed his ass down the hill.

A flash lights up the interior. He pulls his head away from the window.

"Oh shit." He blinks. The scene is burned into the back of his eyelids. A shiver ripples down his spine.

"What?"

He doesn't know where to begin. "They're not gunshots."

The man and the woman from the van are standing on either side of the vast, concrete floor. Their mouths open in unison and the bright light flares. Will has the terrible impression it's some kind of photosynthesis—light as nourishment. Something getting fed. The three acolytes are naked and entwined on the floor between the pair Will thinks of as the leaders. Their limbs, extended strangely, form a pattern. An articulated exoskeleton that moves with a buglike, jittering movement. This bizarre conglomerate is surrounded by objects on the floor. A ring of bulbous fruits the size of beefsteak tomatoes. Flashing light catches their fuzzy skins.

A queasy rush takes him. It's the insect drone, the noise coming from outside soundtracking what is happening inside. His mind connects the two, and now he can't experience them unlinked.

Necks of the acolytes contort, tongues lash, teeth gnaw. The fruits are reduced to slimy pits with wet, shiny pulp hanging in tatters.

Alicia moves to the other side of the window and looks in. "Nope." She turns away, back against the bricks, shakes her head. "No no no."

Will is unsure if he wants to see it again but he's compelled by some force to peer inside. He waits. All is dark.

Flash.

He can't figure out how it's possible that such radiance is coming from the mouths of the leaders. He keeps his eyes trained on the trio in the center of the floor, and the image imprints again as the warehouse goes dark. There are forelegs, bent at strange angles. Three faces contorted in pain or concentration. A skitter, a crawl.

Flash.

The acolytes are weaving. There is a tidal undulation. A rippling, rising action.

He can't look away. He wishes he were inside. Wishes he could freeze time to have all night to examine this madness.

"Will!" Alicia grabs his arm. He shakes her off.

Flash.

Red eyes. Big crimson globes. Will recalls the boxes the acolytes unloaded from the van. It seems like another time. A few minutes ago. A lifetime ago.

"We're leaving," Alicia says.

Will presses his forehead against the glass. "I have to see."

She exhorts him to get the fuck out of there. Her voice fades into distant obscurity. She is clawing at him, pulling hard. Rooted in place, he barely feels it. He wishes he could share this moment with Alicia, but he knows she is beyond appreciation. Her revulsion annoys him, because what is happening inside the warehouse holds a strange beauty. It has fully aligned now with the drone all around him. It buzzes from inside his head, tickling his eardrums and the back of his throat.

Flash.

The entwined acolytes have shifted to face the window. The woman at the head is staring at him with her big unblinking red eyes. At her back the bent limbs of the others rise and fall with jointed, right-angled grace. The skittering brings the trio—

Flash—

—closer to the window. Alicia is screaming from across some vast and lonely plain. Her nails rake the flesh of his arm. The leaders bend at the waist. They vomit light. The strobe effect is amplified. One flash per second. The trio arches its collective back and climbs the window and presses its flesh-woven undercarriage against the glass. A single pane separates Will's face from breasts and bellies and genitals, ever climbing. A word pops into his head: *abdomen*. He had expected to encounter ritual but had no idea it would be so glorious. So impossible. So *real*.

The drone comes from his throat now. He is joining the chorus. His body tingles with something like warmth. Or, perhaps, acceptance.

Finally, Alicia pulls him with such force that he has no choice but to let himself be wrenched away. He glances over his shoulder as he stumbles toward the fence. Backlit, the abdomen is darkly segmented against the window. The earsplitting drone spirals out into the night, everywhere and nowhere. Will and Alicia cross the access road toward the embankment. The blank sign of the empty restaurant is a pale blotch on the night sky.

5

Vicky eases her hybrid hatchback into the driveway and kills the lights. The radio plays softly. A mournful saxophone trails off and the resonant voice of the host welcomes her back to *Jazz from the Witching Hour*. The stench of the old lady's house clings to her clothes. She should have tossed the whole outfit—J. Crew blazer included—and changed into some sweats from her locker at the station.

Her hands clench the steering wheel as dawn breaks across Fort Halcott. Sadie's toys, scattered across the front lawn, emerge from the shadows. Power Wheels Jeep, tricycle, giant plastic ladybug (girlfriend of George). Lights come up in her neighbors' houses—ranches and Craftsmen and the odd Colonial. Inside her own modest split-level, Kim the absolute godsend of a babysitter sleeps in the guest room—a glorified closet—next to Sadie's room.

Vicky knows she too will have to sleep at some point. She will have to give in to the dreams. After two years in Major Crimes she has reached a place of acceptance. But the inciting incidents—the fuel for her nightmares—usually aren't this bad.

The fingertips have been a particular fixation on the drive

home. Shriveled nail beds. Precise extractions. Cuticles and hangnails cleaned and trimmed.

Knowing what she's in for doesn't make it any easier to lie down and close her eyes. She reaches into the glove box and finds her tin of Altoids, for something to do.

"All right," the radio says, the DJ's voice a soothing coo, "night hawks and night owls and all our friends out there in the nocturnal world, I've got one last cut before I fade into the morning."

Vicky pops the mint and settles back in the driver's seat.

"This is Miles live in '83. No more first great quintet, no more second great quintet. So much greatness in his rearview, but he wasn't done. Exhibit A. Berlin Jazzfest. 'Star on Cicely.' Until twilight brings us back together, I wish you nothing but love."

Vicky's eyelids are heavy. She refuses to close them.

Boxes under the table. Boxes full of hair, nails, and teeth.

And inside her lovely little house her daughter sleeps, oblivious to the world's inexplicable evil.

If a small city in the middle of nowhere like Fort Halcott can hold such things as the Winters boy pinned to a tree and an old lady desecrated on her own dining room table, what hope is there for the wider world?

The wider world Sadie will one day enter blindly into, no matter how much Vicky prepares her. Visions of watching grown Sadie turn her back and walk away, heading into college, bag slung over her shoulder, The World waiting in the wings like a predatory demon, biding its time. Autumn leaves falling slowly, settling on the manicured grass of whatever school she can afford ten years from now. New students milling about in a daze, thunderstruck by newfound and total freedom. Party invitations chalked on sidewalks.

Sadie's carrying a box of her things, special mementos for her dorm room. A box full of hair and nails and teeth...

Vicky's body jerks. She's been drifting. Muted trumpet winds into a never-ending spiral. Vicky turns off the radio and rubs her eyes. A new sound hangs in the air, only slightly muffled by the air-conditioning. Those darn crickets! Or, no, not crickets. Cricket-adjacent insects. Vicky smiles. *Cricket-adjacent.* Grimes would scoff at that one.

All around her, Reservoir Road is coming to life. Her next-door neighbor retrieves his newspaper in a bathrobe. The couple down the street who own the Cup 'N Saucer Café head to work together in their Jeep. The scene should be soundtracked with birds and barking dogs. But there is only the ceaseless drone.

Surely morning light should have silenced these not-crickets? What kind of nocturnal bug doesn't go quiet at daybreak? Vicky has lived her entire life in Fort Halcott. Some regional species of 24/7 chirping bug ought to be on her radar.

She opens the door and steps out beneath an eggshell-colored sky. She takes in the neutral smell, grateful after that oppressive stench for the blandness of it all. There's a hint of fresh blacktop from the neighbor on the other side, who just did a resurfacing yesterday, and nothing more. The insects' chorus clings to her like the humid air. The sound is both piercing and percussive, as if they're rubbing wings together violently in unison. A car goes by, another neighbor's black Camry. She catches a glimpse of a silver travel mug hoisted and then he is gone. *Oh,* she thinks, *to work normal hours.* To leave the house at first light and come home before dark. Regular meals. Consistent exercise regimens.

Restorative sleep.

"All-nighter again?" It's Sam, the neighbor in the bathrobe, yelling from his front porch. His voice strains to rise above the insects.

Vicky puts on a rueful smile. "Wasn't supposed to be. Got caught up."

"Everything okay?"

"Just fine." She tosses off a casual wave. "Have a good one."

He grins. "They're early, huh!" He waves the paper around over his head.

Vicky pretends she can't really make out what he's saying and points at the front door. "Babysitter's gonna kill me!" The smile is plastered to her face.

"The cicadas!" Sam calls out, positively screaming.

"Oh!" Vicky says. "Yeah!" Like she knew that all along. "Have a good one!"

Inside, she closes the door behind her, and the noise dies away. She lets her purse fall onto the end table. *Cicadas*. Sam's a font of esoteric knowledge. He's been on disability for eight months. From his wife Vicky knows that Sam's internet usage is robust. She has no reason to doubt him on this one. He's probably got eighteen cicada-related browser tabs open. The word brings to mind a hazy memory of an early high school summer when she worked at Puttin' Plus Mini Golf. The incessant drone, the infestation of flying roach-things that shut down holes eleven through fourteen. Sweeping up their empty husks with a push broom after closing.

"Flippin' cicadas," she says out loud. She places her keys in the little glass dish. Her face in the flower-shaped mirror is a portrait of gloom. Her hair is a tragedy. She tames it with a stray bobby pin from the dish, smoothing out The Spot—the cowlick with its own habits and whims. Then she takes off her shoes.

Underneath the end table is a cardboard box, and Vicky's moment of peace in a still-sleeping house is shattered. It's a collagen supplement delivery that Kim must have accepted and taken inside. Healthy hair.

Teeth.

Nails.

Shaking it off, she heads down the hall past the framed

headshots of Sadie, ages one through eight. There is space left for ten more years. After that, Vicky supposes, there will be something creepily obsessive about it, so the series will be discontinued. She suspects it may already be weird for Sadie when her friends come over.

The guest room door is ajar. Vicky peeks in. Kim's jet-black hair is splayed across the pillow, and the blanket rises and falls with her measured breathing. On the nightstand, the babysitter's plugged-in phone lights up with a text alert. There's a fat paperback, a can of seltzer, a plastic case for contacts. Light sneaks in through the cheery lemon-colored curtains. How many times has Vicky come home to this exact scene, everything in its right place, no matter how chaotic her night has been? Her tired heart swells with gratitude toward kind, reliable Kim.

Vicky pays a price for what she does, and the past twelve hours have exacted their toll. Now she revels in the tranquility. The familiar domestic scene. Perhaps this is what it felt like for Grimes to come home to his wife, back when he was married. Something familiar to cushion the psychic landing. She moves down the hall to Sadie's room, silent on stockinged feet.

She peeks in. Warmth spreads outward from her chest. Sadie's room is a glimpse into the little girl's wondrous brain. All her interests colliding. Big shark cutouts swim along the wall above her dresser, hammerheads and makos and a monstrous great white. Fantasy paperbacks crowd her bookshelf, stacked between bigheaded figurines. A white wicker chair hangs from the ceiling, piled with purple cushions and fuzzy blankets. A pair of stuffed owls lie in the exact center of a rug shaped like a lime slice. And in her bed, Sadie curls on her side, one arm thrown across George the ladybug.

Vicky goes into her room and undresses. In the shower, she cranks up the hot water. She imagines the steam eroding the layers of filth from the old lady's house. She still remembers her first shower after putting Silas Nedry down: wreathed in steam, body motionless but thoughts racing. Suddenly unspeakably weary, Vicky fights the urge to close her eyes right there in the shower, lest she find herself haunted by last night's events and Nedry too. She turns off the water. Silas Nedry had smiled as he raised his weapon. A toy, it turned out. The man who drove a railroad spike through the belly of a child had armed himself with a cap gun.

Vicky stands there dripping until the steam is gone.

In the kitchen, she makes herself a lemon ginger tea and cups her hands around the mug. Kim has the air-conditioning cranked. She sips slowly, standing at the sliding glass door to the backyard. The bright morning has chased away the vestiges of dawn. A red plastic bucket is overturned on the small square patio. She sips her tea and gazes outside, takes stock of her small yard and its weather-beaten fence.

The grass is dry and brown. Rain has been scarce. The lone tree, a stately oak, is an oddly hazy presence, as if it's wavering in the sunlight. Indistinct and unsure of itself. Vicky sets her mug down on the counter. She looks again and rubs her eyes. The tree is wreathed by a cloud of dirt like the one that clings to Pigpen from *Peanuts*. She shakes her head. *No, dummy. Not dirt: cicadas.* She remembers the infestation from Puttin' Plus, the way the little roachlike babies climbed the trees at the edge of the mini-golf course and emerged from their shells as fat winged adults. She folds her arms and watches, immersed in the gauzy memory.

Seventeen years old, the summer she worked at Puttin' Plus. Senior year rushing up to meet her. Free ice cream from the soft-serve caboose. Closing shifts with Jeremy Feinberg... She smiles. The only thing she knew back then was that she'd never, ever become a cop like her father. She eats a banana and watches the insects flit about the tree trunk.

Kim's phone alarm goes off at seven sharp, the sound of a UFO hovering just down the hall. Vicky preps the French press. A non-caffeine-user, she accommodates other people's habits with no judgment. Though it drives her nuts when Grimes makes them wait in the drive-thru line at the Dunkin' on Fairfax. The man's coffee and cigarette breaks alone account for half his overtime. Grimes is in his mid-forties and still does not seem to grasp how much less chaotic his life would be without constant hangovers, an alarming caffeine intake, and a pack of Camels a day. She imagines his personal physician gets hives when he slinks in for his yearly physical.

Kim glides into the kitchen as Vicky's pouring coffee. The babysitter tucks her shiny hair behind her ears. Tattoos curl around her forearms, complex line work, abstract patterns. Compared with the horribly misguided tattoos that Vicky comes across at work, they're gorgeous and tasteful, befitting an art school junior. Her eyes widen as Vicky hands her a steaming mug.

"Amazing, thank you." She takes a tentative sip. Vicky notes the hint of the fake British accent Kim's been affecting all summer, ever since her return from study abroad in London.

"You're a lifesaver, Kim. I am so sorry about this."

"It's all good, I don't have to be at the bowling alley till tonight. Did work go okay?"

"Fine. How about here?"

"Same. I told you about the almost-catastrophe with George, but we tracked him down before the emotional collapse could fully set in." Kim does her little smile-laugh where she sticks out the tip of her tongue. Then she goes to the fridge and retrieves the milk.

"Oh, darn it," Vicky says. "Light and sweet. I always forget."

Kim shakes her head in exaggerated mockery. "Maybe a cup of coffee would improve your memory."

"Never!" Vicky laughs.

Kim dunks a spoonful of sugar and stirs. She leans against the counter by the sink and glances out the window. Vicky watches her eyes settle on the massive oak.

"They're early," Vicky says, parroting Sam from next door.

Kim scratches her belly under her tank top. "Who?"

"The cicadas. That's them around the tree."

"Wow, we get cicadas in Fort Halcott?"

"Apparently. But you would have been about three the last time they were here."

"I don't remember."

"Right. You were three."

Kim looks at her. "I actually have what's called natal recall? Meaning I remember events from as early as two months. Actually, earlier. I have images of my birth. Like, visions."

Vicky blinks. As far as she can tell, Kim is serious. "Wow."

"It was a C-section," Kim says. "I was warm then I was cold."

"Anyway, they're supposed to show up every seventeen years." This is the one thing Vicky knows about cicadas. *Eat your heart out, Sam.* "But I guess they jumped the gun."

Kim considers this. "Cool. Why seventeen?"

"No idea."

"Kind of wild that bugs could have an internal clock like that."

"It is."

"So how early are they?"

"I was seventeen last time they showed up, and I'm thirty-three now. So they're one year ahead of schedule."

"You're *thirty-three*? I thought you were, like, twenty-five, tops."

Vicky laughs. "Did you think I had Sadie in high school?"

Kim shrugs.

"Trust me, there are no twenty-five-year-old detectives."
And thirty-three-year-old detectives are rare enough.

Kim goes to the sliding door, stands next to Vicky, and peers out. She smells like face cream. "They really love that big-ass tree. Is that what's making that noise?"

"Yeah. I thought they were just really loud crickets last night."

Kim sips her coffee with an eager slurp. "This is so great."

"Well, I'm glad you like it."

"The cicadas I mean. It's like, an *event*, you know? I think it'll inform my work in a really interesting way."

At the bowling alley? Vicky thinks but thankfully does not say. "I didn't realize you were working on anything."

Kim laughs. "I'm always working. Our studio intensive starts next semester, and I have to have a rationale in place by October first. There's this one guy in my program, Foglin?"

"Foglin?"

"He's from Montreal."

"Oh."

"So every incoming class has this one full-ride scholarship winner, somebody who did exceptional work in high school. It's like a predictor of success."

Vicky keeps an eye on the oak tree. She can't decide if the cicadas look upset, irritated, or just busy.

"And Foglin's that guy. Everybody loves him, and of course he's talented but also, like, *so nice* too. So if you resent him in any way it makes *you* the asshole, right? But he's also a big-time coke-head. Oh!" Kim catches herself. Her hand goes to her mouth. Her eyes go wide.

Vicky turns to Kim. "I'm not going to drive out to RISD and arrest Foglin, Kim. Rest easy."

Kim relaxes and tries to look sheepish. It's poorly done and theatrical. Vicky studies the girl as she once again turns her hazel eyes toward the yard. Kim's giving off odd energy, and even as tired as she is, Vicky picks up the hum of a new frequency. She's suddenly certain that what just went down was a clumsy attempt by Kim to get this Foglin character in trouble. She wonders at the wonky connections sparking in Kim's brain.

I know a cop.

Cops arrest people.

It would be nice if Foglin were out of the way.

Vicky goes to the kettle to top off her tea. This is a moment that always comes with suspects in the interview room, with colleagues, with the few women she's dated seriously. When the casual veneer falls away and the messy, impulsive animal at the core is revealed. Overdramatic, maybe, but the sentiment is real. Even after all Vicky has seen there's still this naive hope she clings to, that one day another person's wholesomeness will shine through unblemished by some shabby, illicit desire. It's childlike, this incessant hope. Unbefitting a woman of her profession. Yet she clings to it nevertheless.

Steaming mug in hand, she dismisses her impression of Kim. It's been a rough night, after all.

Out back, the cicadas move in frantic disarray, launching themselves from the tree, returning to cling to the bark.

"Like, the cyclical nature of time," Kim is saying. "How our cells change every seven years so we're literally a different person?" She drains her coffee and glances at the empty French press.

"I can make more," Vicky says.

"Mommy?"

She turns at the small voice. Pajama-clad Sadie stands at the threshold, George dangling loosely from her fingers.

"Hey!" Vicky calls out. She sets her mug down. "It's my favorite kid!"

Her sleepy smile is connected to a knot in Vicky's chest that loosens as Sadie crosses the linoleum.

"Monster hug!" Vicky says, wrapping the girl in her arms and lifting her up. "I love you I love you I love you!"

She sets the girl down. "How did you sleep?"

Sadie rubs her eyes. Vicky swipes the crusties from her face with a practiced hand. "I had a dream about a dinosaur shelf. Hi, Kim." Sadie waves.

Kim waves back. "Good morning, Sadie."

"Thank you for helping to find George," Sadie says.

The knot in Vicky's chest comes totally undone. Sadie is polite and thoughtful and warm. Other kids do things like march into the kitchen demanding breakfast.

Vicky glances at the clock. Quarter after seven. "We've got time for Connect Four before I have to take you to camp," Vicky says. "Best two out of three."

Sadie is recently obsessed with the game. Vicky has noticed she is enamored with the sound of the pieces falling into place.

Sadie turns to Kim. They share a coy, mischievous look.

Vicky puts her hands on her hips. "Anything you want to share with the class?"

"You never know what day it is, Mommy."

Vicky frowns. Kim mouths *Saturday.*

Right. The weekend. No summer camp today. "Okay, so we *really* have time for Connect Four. Best three out of five?" Sadie smiles. "Best nine out of eleven? Best seventy-seven out of ninety-four?"

Sadie laughs. "Best million out of a billion!"

"Million out of a billion it is. And since I have recently been informed that it's Saturday, we're having blueberry pancakes."

"Chocolate chip!" Sadie yells. Then, sheepish at her outburst: "Please?"

"One chocolate chip and one blueberry," Vicky says. She opens the cupboard and retrieves the box of batter mix.

Sadie sits at the table. "What's that noise?"

"Cicadas," Kim informs her.

"Bugs that come up out of the ground to find a mate." Vicky clatters around the lazy Susan until she finds the nonstick skillet. "It's very special because they only appear every seventeen years."

"Except they're early this time," Kim says.

"Oh," Sadie says, taking this in. She sets George on the table and moves an empty cup in front of him. "Do they bite?"

"No." Vicky plunks down a mixing bowl and locates the whisk in the dishwasher. "They're just loud."

Her phone vibrates on the counter. Kim rinses her empty mug. Outside, the cicadas drone on and on. Vicky glances at the screen: GRIMES.

A shadow moves across the kitchen. The night she'd just managed to leave behind, creeping out of the margins. A dank, sour corruption easing its way into the morning she's sharing with Kim and Sadie.

Cat piss.

Vicky picks up the phone and steps into the hall. Kim moves to the bowl and takes the whisk. Sadie gets up and goes to the sliding glass door.

"What's up, Kenny?"

Grimes's voice cracks with the smoke of his own all-nighter. "We got another one."

6

Will's room at the Mountain View Lodge is lined with cedar panels buffed to a semi-reflective sheen. He sits on the creaky bed and stares at his blurry form in the wall. Alicia paces at his back. Will looks over his shoulder. His ex-wife goes to the balcony door and gazes out at dawn breaking over thick pines. The furniture on the balcony is plastic. An ashtray overflows with butts from a previous guest. The trees block the view of the mountain.

The bugs' drone seeps in through the walls. Will imagines the sound like a rope, a lasso slowly squeezing the life out of this motel. The single-serve coffeemaker on the dented wooden bureau pops and shudders as it brews. A framed portrait of a nineteenth-century fur trapper hangs above the small TV. Alicia claims the motel has recently been reinvigorated, so its shabby aesthetic is actually shabby-chic. Will wonders if the dank air and stale smoke are piped in as part of the vibe. He watches Alicia tap a fingernail against the glass.

"Okay," she says. "So what did we really see? I mean, what do we *know* that we saw. A ritual. Some dumb cult shit. Creepy, yes. Fucked up, yes. But beyond that, I don't think we can be sure of anything."

Will turns back to face the wall. His shadow-reflection raises an arm. A long thin limb grows and bends at one joint. Then two. He blinks and the limb vanishes. The coffee machine emits a sharp *crack*.

Will rubs his eyes. "You looked away. I know what I saw."

Alicia whirls around. "I saw some Gen Z'ers playing a weird game."

"Sure, for half a second. I watched the whole thing. There was light coming out of those people's mouths."

"That could have been anything. The angle you were looking in from. Any kind of trick."

"Right." Will's eyes go slack. The room blurs. It's as if he's just downed a six-pack. A reckless sort of contentment washes over him. His shadow pulses in the wall.

In the wall?

He shakes his head. His vision sharpens. *On* the wall. Confirmed.

"Hey!" Alicia whacks his shoulder. "Space cadet Will, this is mission control, suck a dick."

Will turns to look his ex-wife in the eyes. "I think I'm going to get some sleep."

Her head darts forward like a snake. Her eyes bulge. It's her look of incredulity, when she just can't believe what she's hearing. "We have to talk to the client at eight."

"So wake me up at seven fifty-five."

She lifts the paper cup off the coffeemaker's plastic pedestal, takes a sip, winces. "This tastes like a gas station toilet."

He gets up and pulls back the sheets. "Maybe they forgot to reinvigorate it."

She goes to the bathroom. Will hears the coffee being dumped down the drain. "Don't get in that bed!" She comes back out. Will takes his shirt off. "Do not lie down right now. Please."

Will sighs. He pauses, then puts his shirt back on. "I'm not going to argue with you anymore. I'm too tired."

"I'm not arguing with you. It's a discussion. It's a *brainstorm*. No wrong answers in brainstorming."

"You've been telling me I was wrong since we got back to the motel."

"I did not say *wrong* even one time. Don't put words in my mouth."

"I think Carter's rubbing off on you. You're like a lawyer now."

"I'm going to let that go in the interests of a productive client conversation this morning. So. Let's go over it again."

Will closes his eyes. The buzzing drone washes over and then *through* him. An electric current surges from his teeth to his toes. Then comes a skittering behind his eyelids, the echo of the limbs of the three acolytes, the carapace formed of their bellies. Hairless, shrunken genitals.

He opens his eyes and looks at Alicia. Like, *really* looks at her. Her despairing face begs him to confirm that what they saw was an illusion. He knows he need only say a few words to placate her. Then he can crawl into bed.

"You saw what I saw," he says. The acolytes' connection as they moved up the window. The tautness of the belly. The shiny segments. "The three of them became something else."

Alicia laughs bitterly. She throws up her hands.

"No wrong answers in brainstorming," he reminds her. She stalks over to the balcony door. "The ritual wasn't just standard cult bullshit. It *led* to something. There was a result. I saw it."

Alicia is silent for a moment, gazing out at the ashtray and the patio furniture. She raises her eyes to the tall pines. "Do you remember our Hawaii trip?"

"I remember you drank eighty-five piña coladas. I remember

thinking, *Great, she can only stand to be on a trip with me if she's wasted every second.*"

She lets her head fall forward and rests her forehead against the glass. "It was our first real vacation together, after you came back."

"I'd been back for like a year at that point."

"But things were a whirlwind, remember? We hit the ground running with the business and didn't have time to breathe." She pauses. "I really was blown away by how committed you were to making it work." She pulls her head off the glass and turns to look at him. "I was kind of in awe of you back then, to be honest. I thought, *Hey, maybe he actually did find himself out there.*"

"I'm no better than anybody else."

"But then on the plane to Hawaii, I had this weird sinking feeling. Like we hadn't had a non-business conversation since you came home. It was all about repairing, and rebuilding, and moving forward at a dead sprint. Plus I was still pissed at myself for taking you back after you just freaked out and left."

Will can feel heat behind his eyes, in his sinuses. The all-nighter is tweaking his emotions. He turns away from Alicia, gets interested in the tiny microwave next to the dripping coffee machine.

In awe of you, she'd said. He swipes a finger under his eye and it comes away wet. The drone swells inside his head. Legs, antennae, wings rubbing together.

He snaps back to reality. Alicia has just finished saying something. "What?"

She makes a noise of exasperation. "You space out at the weirdest times, I swear. I was saying, you remember when we went out on the rocks at the resort to watch the manta rays?"

"You fell down and cut your knee."

"That's a reductive take on the whole thing, plus you're burying the lede."

"You just threw out two accusations in one sentence."

"Okay, but I fell down *after* we saw the Loch Ness monster."

"Its Hawaiian cousin, you mean."

"Yes. I do. But what I'm getting at is—"

"We both agreed we saw *something* under the water that was definitely not one of the manta rays because it was the size of a nuclear submarine."

"You maintained it was just a quote *underwater shadow*, whatever that is, and I was pretty insistent that it was some kind of living thing."

"*Then* you fell down. On account of the piña coladas."

"I feel like you're harping on that as a sort of dig. Can we go find a Starbucks, or its Podunk equivalent?"

"I don't want coffee. I want to sleep."

"Why are you snapping at me?"

"Because I'm fucking tired!" He knows what Dr. Capaldi would say about bottling things up until they explode. How jarring it is for their relationship. But they don't have a relationship anymore, right? He stalks over to the balcony door and slides it open. Sound waves spiral into his head, a helix of drawn-out, desperate chirps. Pressure swells in his forehead. He cries out, staggers back to the bed, presses his palms to his temples.

Alicia slides the door shut and the sound dies down. The ringing in his head subsides. He swallows. "Oh man."

He sits on the bed with his head in his hands. The warehouse window flashes in his mind. One of the red eyes fixed on him. Whatever the acolytes became *noticed* him, he's sure of it. "That noise is really getting to me. What kind of crickets do they have in this goddamn town?"

"Reason number four million not to leave the city."

Will goes into the bathroom and runs the cold water. The tap hiccups. He splashes his face. His eyes are so puffy, it looks like he's been in a bar fight. He takes a deep breath and tries to focus. When he comes back out, Alicia's typing on her phone.

"What's up?"

"Texting the client. Buying us a few hours. You need to sleep."

Will looks at his ex-wife in disbelief. *That's what I've been saying!* He stops himself from raising his voice. He waits a beat. "We both do."

She shakes her head. "I just took an Adderall. Remember after we saw the Hawaiian Loch-Ness-monster-slash-underwater-shadow?"

"We had to go to the front desk to get your knee bandaged."

"After that."

"Piña coladas on the terrace."

He strips down to his boxers, aware that Alicia averts her eyes. He imagines Carter the Private Equity Attorney's pricey, gym-toned abs. The health club membership paid for by his firm. Placing his wristwatch in a little velvet case before he works out. A locker room attendant handing him a towel, which he accepts wordlessly.

"We sat and drank and talked about what we thought we saw," she says, staring at her phone. "Eventually, there was this moment. I remember it like it was yesterday. Everything *flipped*. I was suddenly arguing that it wasn't anything at all, and you were adamant—like, leaning forward in your seat, waving your arms, *adamant*—that it was a previously undiscovered sea monster."

He crawls beneath the sheets and tries to fluff the flat and uninspiring pillow. The Hawaii trip percolates in his head. "So you're insinuating I'm wishy-washy on this stuff."

"You're always so quick to assume I'm *accusing* you of something!"

He closes his eyes. "We don't say *always*."

"Touché. But what I'm getting at is, what we see is totally different from one minute to the next depending on our moods."

"Fine," he says, turning onto his side and curling fetally. "I don't know what I saw. It was just some dumb ritual. My eyes were playing tricks on me. Let's just figure out our next move."

He braces himself for Alicia's response. *You're just placating me.* At the same time, he can feel himself starting to believe it was just some weirdos playing naked Twister. The flashing lights could have been anything.

Silence. He opens one eye to find her frowning at her phone. "What is it?"

"My texts to the client didn't go through. No service."

"Oh."

She looks at him. "There was service earlier."

"The Wi-Fi password's around here somewhere."

"There's no signal."

"Check with the desk. They're probably just resetting it."

THUNK.

Something hits the glass. Hard.

"Jesus!" Alicia whirls around.

Will sits up. "Was that a bird?"

THUNK.

This time he sees it: What looks like a cockroach comes down from the pines and careens over the balcony, buzzing erratically, and slams into the sliding door. Then it falls to the thin green Astroturf and crawls around. The three roach-things weave in a madcap route. Will throws back the covers and joins Alicia at the sliding door. He is conscious that he's in his boxers, and it would only take the slightest movement for her to brush up against the bare skin of his chest or his thighs.

"What are those," she says, "locusts?"

"I don't know. Is it locust season? Is that a thing?" He has the miserable impression that Carter would know. Carter would be rattling off locust factoids by the dozen right now. Latin names, regional obscurities. *I took a biology elective at Princeton on a lark.*

"I have no idea." She goes to the scuffed round Formica table and comes back with her camera. "Should we call the desk?"

"And ask if it's locust season?"

She raises the camera to her face, peers into the viewfinder, and adjusts the lens. "I meant ask about the Wi-Fi."

A fourth bug lands on the plastic table and drags itself through cigarette ash. It pauses long enough for Will to get a better look. Two inches long, he thinks. Dark, shiny head and midsection. Almost oily in its blue-black coloring. Wings are delicate and shot through with veins or connective tissue. Its twin antennae waver softly, deliberately. Will has the impression the insect is orienting itself to its new perch. He steps closer to the glass. The insect's eyes are bright-red globes. An exquisite shudder cascades down from his shoulders.

The eyes of the acolytes, searing crimson dots in the night, regarding him at the window, aware of his presence.

Will finds that his fingers are splayed, their tips pressed against the glass. A current runs through the balcony and into the door. A chittering drone sifts through the whorls of his fingerprints, an invisible ink staining the patterns of his skin. More bugs come spiraling off the evergreens. Alicia's voice rings dully in his head. She snaps photographs. The balcony's infestation grows. The drone runs in rivulets beneath his fingernails. He can feel it like a vibrating splinter sunk deep into his skin.

"—coming off the goddamn trees," Alicia is saying. "A million of them!"

Will stares outside. The trees shiver in a heat haze. Clouds of tiny dots are flung from their branches, curtains of swirling electrons suspended in midair. They are falling so thick on the balcony now that he can't see the floor, only this living carpet of locusts or flying roaches or—

"Cicadas," he says.

Alicia looks at him. "How do you know that?"

"The signal begins in the soil," he tells her. Words flow from him like a fluid exodus of insects emerging from the dirt. "The echoes of what came before toll the moment of the rising."

Alicia blinks. "*What?*"

The rightness of his words and the noise coursing through his body make him shiver with ecstasy. He looks at his ex-wife and smiles.

The cicadas hurl themselves against the glass.

7

Vicky closes her eyes. The phone is hot against her ear. *We found another one.*

"Either this guy works fast," she says, thinking out loud, "or the body you just found is in an advanced stage of decomp."

"I don't know, Vic." He sounds haunted. Diminished, somehow, by what he's seen.

Vicky feels her body lighten as dizziness comes and goes. She opens her eyes, watches Kim pour Sadie some apple juice, and lowers her voice. "What do you mean you don't know?"

She can hear the crackle of burning paper as he draws on an unfiltered Camel. "Scene looks like the same deal as the first one. Total absence of flies, maggots, anything that chows down on a corpse. Anything at *all*, for that matter."

"Meaning?" Her heart pounds. She already knows. The inkling had crossed her mind too.

"Like you said, no spiders either, right? No cockroaches. No insects, arachnids, millipedes. Nothing of the lower fucking order anywhere. All the creepy-crawlies *vamoosed*."

Kim places Sadie's empty glass in the sink. Sadie goes to the hutch in the corner and retrieves the Connect Four box, holds it up. Kim gives her a nod and gestures at the kitchen table. Vicky lingers on Sadie as she carefully removes the cover and places it next to the box. Not askew, in perfect parallel. This meticulous side of Sadie is frightening in its consistency. Chalk whittled down to equal lengths. Crayons sharpened to perfect points. Meals eaten without dropping a crumb. Not for the first time Vicky wonders what unconscious molding she has done to Sadie. This is parenting: the ever-present fear that some ingrained action on your part has triggered something deep down in your kid, planted the seed of a compulsion—or, worse, an addiction—they will never understand, bequeathed to them through some means Vicky herself doesn't understand either.

"You there?"

She tears herself away from Sadie and Kim and moves farther down the hall. Her eyes come to rest on a framed black-and-white of the Utah desert, a place she's never been. Fear surfaces that what she's doing *right now* is contributing to some form of trauma or another. She imagines Future Sadie in a late-night conversation with her college roommate: *My mom was obsessed with her job, she never slept, left me with babysitters all the time...*

"I'm here. What about the skin thing?"

"Yeah. And there's more. A lot more. You just have to see it."

Vicky loses herself in the arches of Moab. She can feel the pull of desolation. No phone signal. Just rocks, a backpack full of trail mix and water, sweaty bandannas, sore feet.

A long sigh escapes her. "What the heck is going on?"

"A whole pile of *heck* is what, Vic. A whole flippin' heck sandwich."

Vicky lets her eyes go slack. Moab blurs into a gray haze. The sound of the sliding door comes from the kitchen, Kim taking Sadie out back.

"Hey," she says. "You were right about the crickets not being crickets. They're cicadas."

"Uh-huh. Listen, I know you're supposed to be off, but Captain Barker's taking a heavy hand with this one. We can't keep it under wraps for long and there's gonna be questions."

Vicky turns away from the desert. Her eyes settle on a framed newspaper article. The *Fort Halcott Gazette*. FHPD SERGEANT BOWLS 300 GAME. A photo of her father holding a trophy shaped like a bowling pin and a mug of beer, grinning, the lanes at his back.

What would Sergeant—and later Captain—Paterson do now?

Vicky knows the answer, of course. It isn't *play Connect Four and get some much-needed shuteye.*

"Text me the address," she says, then hangs up and pockets the phone. Her father grins back at her from the grainy 1983 photo. Her mind revs up with a fresh checklist.

Eat some nonfat yogurt with a little granola. Have another cup of tea. Beg Kim to stay through the early afternoon. Pay her double. Line up someone else for the evening.

She heads back down the hall, her thoughts turning to the case. They need to talk to a scientist, somebody from the university, about the lack of maggots. They need to get the pathologist to drop everything else.

In the meantime, she needs to water this poor withered succulent in its clay pot. She needs to—

"Help!"

Kim's cry is piercing.

"We need help out here!"

Vicky is across the kitchen in three seconds. The Winters kid was abducted in broad daylight. She never lets Sadie out of her sight when she's playing outside, but Sadie's with Kim, and Vicky was just down the hall. She wrenches the glass door to one side with such force that it hits the end of its track and returns. Vicky's outside before it slams shut behind her.

The drone amplifies. A keening, whining *skreeee* backed up by a billion saltshakers.

Kim is kneeling down in the dry grass, hunched over, moving her arms as if paddling furiously. Cicadas darken the air around her. The bugs rise up from the ground in angry clouds. She swims against a current of them, enveloped by a surging, swirling nimbus. Sprinting across the lawn is like moving through a hailstorm.

The feeling of mindless bug-parts on flesh. The tiny scramblings of pointed limbs and antennae.

Then she's down on the ground beside Kim. It's like slipping into some foul jet stream, a strange current alive with feverish churning. Her ears ring with the noise. Kim is screaming.

On the ground before them, cicadas seethe over Sadie.

The sight whisks away Detective Paterson and all she knows about calm certitude under pressure, leaving in the detective's place Vicky, mother of Sadie.

And Vicky almost freezes up. It's more like half a second of slow motion, when time grinds to a halt and what lies before her is truly revealed.

A writhing, chaotic mass the deep-blue color of a late-winter dusk. Pops of translucency, flickers no more substantial than heat shimmers. The instant impression of great numbers of tiny things in some senseless collaboration with a single-minded goal. The sight brings to mind ants overtaking a fallen meat scrap from a grill.

A swarm.

Covering Sadie.

Blotting out her face, her body, her fingers and toes.

Encasing her completely.

With a strangled cry, Vicky pounces on her daughter and time clicks back into place. Her frantic paddling matches Kim's. The two of them, swiping away. Sadie's not making a sound. It's hard to tell if she's even moving beneath her shell of constant motion. Vicky shouts her daughter's name, feels her hands hitting cicadas, dozens of them, flinging them off Sadie only to have new ones crowd in to take their place. Patching the holes in the mass that shrouds her daughter. Each winged adult is the size of a huge cockroach, what her father called *waterbugs*. The noise of the swarm is deafening. A high-decibel drone that drills into her skull. Kim repeats something, over and over, that harmonizes queasily with the noise of the swarm. Vicky feels light-headed, floaty, like she's looking down at this from above.

Cicadas land on her, flit mindlessly into her face, her eyes. They alight upon her flailing arms. There are too many. Thousands. Millions. A fragmented thought flashes—they are trying to lift her only child up and spirit her away. They will form a living helicopter and there will be nothing she can do. Sadie will be taken up into the sky, beyond the trees, gone forever.

Vicky changes tactics. If they can ditch the bulk of the swarm, they will be better equipped to deal with the bugs already covering Sadie. She works her arms underneath what she hopes are her daughter's legs and upper back and lifts the whole mass up off the lawn. Wings like stiff tissue paper flutter against her face. The angry drone is everywhere and nowhere, rhythmic as a pulse pounding between her eyes. It dawns on Kim what Vicky's trying to do and the babysitter scrambles to her feet, sprints to the door, holds it open. Vicky lifts her daughter and runs toward the house. A comet's tail of cicadas follows, stretched out into the yard by the whisking-away of their target.

Vicky rushes Sadie through the open door. The swarm is exploring her arms, flitting about her face. Delicate legs tickle the back of her neck. Kim slams the door closed behind them. Vicky hears the latch click. The monstrous drone is muffled at her back and also prolonged, tinnily, inside the house.

Sadie's head, cloaked in insects, lolls senselessly back, dangling off the edge of Vicky's forearm.

"Counter!" she yells at Kim. She sweeps away the Connect Four game, clearing the surface. Little plastic disks clatter across the tiles. A glass shatters. Apple juice splashes the dishwasher. Gently as she can, Vicky lays her daughter down on the granite countertop. A cloth napkin hangs off the edge.

In here, away from its fellows, the swarm is stretched thin. It seems agitated as it struggles to patch the holes in itself. Sadie's sunflower pajamas peek through the gaps, cheerful little smiley-face flowers. A glimpse of a closed eye, long lashes gummed together, ratchets up Vicky's panic. A cicada flies into her face, smashing into the bridge of her nose with an irate *bzzz*. Vicky screams and half swats, half grabs it. Trapping it against her loosely cupped palm, she slaps her hand down on the granite. The insect splatters with a soft wet crunch.

She screams as she grinds her palm into the counter. She feels the chitinous bite of its legs, the brittle wreckage of its exoskeleton. The juice of its innards. Meanwhile Kim's clearing cicadas from Sadie with more success now that they're shielded from the main body of the swarm by a tempered-glass patio door. Her hands move along Sadie's forehead, the contours of her face, clearing bugs and tossing them violently away, swatting them when they attempt to return. And return they do, again and again. Their flight patterns are erratic. It's impossible to do more than bat them around the air. A few stragglers have dispersed to the edges of the kitchen to alight upon the cabinets, the toaster, the freezer door, the knife block. But there are still more, always more.

Vicky tries to wrap Sadie's head up in a tight embrace in the crook of an elbow, leaning in to box out the insects. "Come on, baby," she says. "Stay with me."

An idea pops into her head. She lets her daughter go, rushes to the pantry, and snatches the vacuum cleaner. She plugs it in and drags it back through the kitchen with grim determination.

Wrenching the hose with its wand attachment away from its hook, she flicks the switch. The motor joins the cacophony. She tries to suck a few cicadas out of the air, away from Kim and Sadie, and only ends up bashing them with the wand, sending them spinning away to regroup. She aims the wand at Sadie's prone form. Cicadas circle and poke tentatively and lift off, a madcap dance. A jolt of pain blossoms outward in Vicky's chest. To leave Sadie alone and vulnerable like this, to use her as bait, even for five seconds, is agony.

The diminished swarm descends. Vicky aims the wand directly at Sadie, coming at her sideways, like hoovering up the fallen pine needles that litter the tree skirt every Christmas.

The first of the cicadas thumps into the clear plastic filter. Still alive, it beats its wings, struggling against its newfound prison. *Thump.* Another vanishes down the tube. *Thump.* Vicky moves the wand across Sadie's face. *Thump thump thumpthump.* One closed eye appears, then two. Growing wise to this new attack, cicadas begin to scatter.

"Get off her!" Vicky screams. Kim grabs a metal spatula from the sink. She smashes bugs that make the poor decision to scuttle across the counter. Dark fluid splashes across her shirt. The vacuum's motor overtakes the irate droning of the indoor swarm and begins to drown it out. A sound like a low keening moan comes from Kim as she thwacks the countertop, again and again.

Sadie's mouth appears, half open in a heartbreaking stupor that nearly stops Vicky's heart. Blue lips, slightly swollen.

No no no no no.

The vacuum stutters and hiccups. Suction dies. Vicky glances down. The filter is crammed with cicadas, stuffed so tight they have been crushed against the clear plastic. With a final vicious slice with the wand, knocking a solo cicada out of the air, Vicky lets it fall to the floor.

"Come on, come on, come on," Kim says through gritted teeth. She drops the spatula and works her hands gently underneath Sadie's head and stares dumbly at her closed eyes. A few stunned cicadas crawl up her stomach. Others stalk the perimeter of the kitchen. Vicky ignores them.

"Oh God." Kim looks up at Vicky. "What do we do?"

"Go start my car."

"Shouldn't we call—"

"Start the car!"

Kim grabs the keys and runs off. It occurs to Vicky a moment later that she should have told her to *be careful*, that for all she knows the cicadas are swarming the front yard too. There's a red maple that hangs over the driveway. But it's too late for that. She places a hand against Sadie's forehead. *Like wax.* She tilts her head to place an ear just above Sadie's mouth. There's a faint trace of breath. Her heart leaps. At the same time she places two fingers just underneath Sadie's jaw. The soft skin of her neck feels almost nonexistent. A faint pulse throbs.

Vicky lets her training take over. Fingers interlocked, both palms down. Heel of her palm resting against the underside of Sadie's sternum. So small, so fragile. Like bird bones. Her mind screams at her to be gentle but she knows that's useless. She presses. Hard. One compression. Two. Out front, the car starts. Five compressions. Six. Seven. No cinematic cough from Sadie, no dramatic sputter and sudden snapping open of the eyes to break the tension. Just a little girl's body bouncing limply. Vicky goes on autopilot. She hits thirty compressions, pauses, and leans in to administer rescue breathing. Sadie's lips on hers make her spine tingle. Not cold and not warm. A peculiar tang moves from Sadie's mouth to Vicky's—earthy and musty and old, like a stack of forgotten magazines in a decrepit tree house. She tilts Sadie's chin and pinches her nose and, with their lips clamped tightly, begins to breathe. Sadie's chest rises and falls. One more and then she'll have to—

The lump passes so quickly from Sadie's mouth to her own, it's as if her throat is the vacuum hose. She recoils, lifting her head from Sadie, stepping back, clawing the inside of her mouth, hooking fingers along her gumline, jamming at her uvula, gagging.

The cicada she's just sucked up from Sadie's body is *alive*. It writhes and beats its wings in the back of her throat. Vicky convulses. It is the most revolting thing she's ever felt—frantic little legs clawing at her soft, wet esophagus. It feels simultaneously small enough to swallow and large enough to choke her. Vicky heaves. She makes a fist and pummels her stomach. Her eyes blur with tears. The cicada slides down her throat. The wrong way. Into her body. *Oh God Oh God Oh God.* She draws a deep, gurgling pressure from that netherworld where her sinuses meet her throat. The cicada holds still, the runaway car balanced on the cliff's edge—

And then, in a slick wet rush, it rises and is expelled from her mouth. It falls to the kitchen floor and scrambles madly in a broken circle, one ruined wing propelling it. A slug's trail of snot and saliva makes a mess of the tiles. With a fierce cry, Vicky smashes it with her foot. She rushes back to Sadie, flicks away a few cicadas that have landed to explore her exposed hands and face. Sadie is still prone, her breath a shallow ghost of a thing.

A shadow falls across the kitchen. She glances up at the door. The swarm is pressing against the glass in its lust to get inside. To get at Sadie. The primitive, squirmy undersides make Vicky sick.

A pair of cicadas zip across the kitchen to bash themselves against the glass, desperate to rejoin their brothers and sisters.

Vicky lifts her daughter—so light, so helpless—sets her gently over her shoulder, and carries her away.

The vacuum, clogged with both the living and the dead, grinds to a halt.

8

A hard slap turns Will's head. His hand goes to his cheek. A dull pain spreads to his lower jaw.

"Ow!" He glares at Alicia. "What the hell?"

Thunk. A cicada smacks the glass. The balcony is alive with insects, buzzing about in a wild cacophony. There is a rote anger to their erratic flight. Not so much purpose as compulsion. He steps back from the door. The ashtray vanishes under a living carpet of bugs. A vague sense of disgust builds inside him. He feels like he's trudging through an untidy, decrepit basement. That crawling sensation of tiny legs up and down his neck, sticky webs on his face, creatures left to flourish in the dark.

"Tell me again what you just said," Alicia demands.

"I said *what the hell* because you slapped me in the face," Will says.

"Before that."

Will pauses, thinking. "Before that we were talking about Hawaii, and then…" He trails off. There's a gray blotch in his memory, a cloudy zone of fragmented images. He tries to remember and is met with a jolt, an itch beneath his shoulder blades, down his spine, *inside* the small of his back.

"You said something about a signal," she prods.

He shrugs, disturbed. "I don't know."

She points at the seething balcony. "You told me those things are *cicadas*. You spoke with great authority."

"Cicadas," he says. The word is alien in his mouth. He doesn't know shit about cicadas. The gray blotch trembles behind his eyes. His vision hazes and sharpens. Bugs spiral down off the evergreens in endless droves. "Are they supposed to do this?"

Like their intolerable noise, Will can't imagine the people of Fort Halcott dealing with this kind of insect behavior. He imagines a yokel out in front of the general store, *Damn critters are at it again*.

Alicia eyes him warily. "You tell me, cicada man."

"I don't know what's going on. I don't know why I said that."

She glances at her useless phone. "Well, we can't google *normal cicada behavior*." Then she takes a moment to scrutinize Will's face. "Are you okay?"

"I mean..." He looks outside. "I guess?"

"Tell me right now: Are you fucking with me?"

"In what way would I be fucking with you?"

"When you said that thing, *The signal begins in the soil*, your voice was different. Like you were reciting scripture in church."

"I don't know," he says. The gray blotch in his mind is a maelstrom. His thoughts push against the cloud. Inside stick-thin limbs quiver and flash like heat lightning. Saliva floods his mouth, and he goes to the bathroom sink to spit. His face in the mirror is drawn.

When he comes back out, Alicia is packing her camera in its padded case. "We're leaving."

"I thought we were just gonna go ask somebody about this."

She scoops up a pile of dirty shirts and stuffs them into her open suitcase. "Nope. We've officially become the stupid city assholes who linger too long in a weird-ass upstate situation."

"We can't just leave, we're here to do a job."

"I'm officially handing in my resignation."

Alicia goes into the bathroom and comes out with her toiletry bag and hair dryer. He sidesteps to plant himself in front of her suitcase. "Is this about last night at the warehouse?"

She pushes past him. "It's about *right now*, Will." She drops the bag atop the pile rising from the suitcase. Then she turns to the glass door. "It's raining insects onto our balcony. There's no cell service and no Wi-Fi. This is biblically twisted."

"We've never just abandoned a client! Remember in Mexico City when—"

"Mexico City wasn't *infested*."

"It was infested with people trying to kill us."

"That, I can handle."

He takes her gently by the shoulders as she's stealing the Mountain View Lodge notepad and pens from the small desk shoved into the corner. The drone dopplers from one side of his mind to the other.

"Let's just go ask the guy at the desk what's going on. He'll probably be like, *Y'all are lucky to see the great cicada migration this year!*"

She flinches at his voice. "These people aren't southerners, Will. We're practically in Canada."

"Come on. We can ask about the Wi-Fi and find out what's going on." He reads the uncertainty in her eyes. Cicadas pour over the balcony wall. The evergreens beyond are alive with them, while clouds of bugs stretch across the sky. "Dr. Capaldi recommended I practice tempering my emotional responses, right? This is me being calm and normal and collected."

"Okay," Alicia says after a moment. "I respect that. But if Cletus at the desk says this is in any way out of the ordinary—"

"We'll be back in civilization before your Adderall wears off."

Will puts on his sneakers and heads out into the narrow corridor. He resists the urge to turn around to see if Alicia is behind him. A moment later, he hears the door shut, footsteps trailing him.

He has spent hours looking at Carter, the private equity attorney, on various websites. Will has pulled up photos from charity events and stared into the man's steely-gray eyes, trying to discover in them what he himself lacks.

So now he walks down the hall like a character in an action movie walking away from an explosion. At the same time he understands how pathetic this is, the notion that Alicia will be impressed by his rakish confidence in the weird-smelling hallway of the Mountain View Lodge. He pushes with great fervor through a door marked with a stairway symbol. The stairs are painted bright red. The walls are lined with black-and-white portraits of mushrooms. He does not hold the railing as he bounds down to the first floor and into the rustic lobby. It's a cross between a ski lodge and a bowling alley from the 1980s, all knotty-pine beams and neon signage. A newspaper sits folded on a leather armchair.

Will stops halfway across the patterned tile floor. The lobby is empty. There's no one behind the front desk. Alicia comes up next to him, stands on tiptoes to glance over the top of the walnut-colored counter as if an employee might be hiding back there. She slams her palm down on an old-fashioned bell. The chime rings, echoes, dies. Nobody appears.

"Maybe they're in the bathroom," Will says.

Alicia checks her phone. "Still nothing."

The door to the stairwell bursts open. A big, bald, goateed man in a checked flannel shirt barrels into the lobby. Two kids follow: a boy and a girl in the throes of gangly teenhood. The man's breathing hard as he stops short. His eyes dart around the lobby and settle on Will. He clears his throat, straightens his back, pulls himself together a little sheepishly. He gives a bro-nod toward the desk.

"Nobody around?" He catches his breath. "I swear this place is only staffed half the time. And there's no ice anywhere. Supposed to be an ice machine, right?" He turns to the kids. "Go sit, I gotta talk to these folks."

The kids shuffle over to the armchairs. The girl looks at her phone, makes a face, then picks up a magazine and begins methodically flipping. The boy turns in his chair to gaze up toward one of the small round windows that line the lobby like portholes on a ship.

The man moves in close. His jowly face is shaved and scrubbed nearly pink. "There's some kind of, uh, bug thing happening outside our room."

"Cicadas," Alicia says.

"No shit?" The man's small blue eyes move beyond her to the desk.

"We rang the bell just now," Will says.

"You guys getting any service?" He brandishes his phone.

"Negative," Will says.

The man pockets the phone and folds his meaty arms across his chest. Will notes the old-school digital watch on the man's wrist. He taps his foot on the carpet. A frown curls his mouth into a shape that runs parallel to his mustache. "This don't seem normal," he says.

"I agree," Alicia says. "It seems like a situation we should be getting far away from."

The man looks at her, lost in thought, nodding slowly. "I just feel a little bit weird, you know." He glances at his kids. "This is my weekend with them, and we took this trip, and now we're cutting it short because of some bugs." He shakes his head. "Carol's gonna have a field day with this one. Ah, shit. Sorry." He holds out a thick-fingered hand. His pinkie is gnarled, curled viciously into his palm, fused with a flap of skin. "Bing Keller."

Will takes his hand. The bent pinkie squishes between their palms. "Will Bennett. Good to meet you. This is my, uh—"

"Alicia," she says without offering her hand.

My Alicia, he thinks.

"I mean," Bing says, "we got big crickets and biting flies and the like where I'm from, but these things are like big flying roaches coming down off the trees. And they're never-ending. I just thought we should at least switch to a room without a balcony. And we're supposed to go zip-lining today. They got that big one here. But now, I don't know. It's in the woods. The zip line is."

"Dad," the boy at the window says.

"One second, Jeff," Bing says. He looks at Alicia, then at Will. His eyes are imploring. Searching. His body shifts with the discomfort of a man who must be decisive for his children's sake. Will is nearly overcome by the urge to reach out in sympathy.

"I think we just need to talk to somebody," Will says. He reads a flash of disappointment in Bing's eyes. Bing who was hoping for more from him. Bold leadership, or at least reassurance that this is nothing, this is seasonal, this is a funny local quirk.

"*Dad*," Jeff says. "There's a guy outside."

"Who cares?" the girl says without looking up from her magazine.

"He's, like, being crazy, *Kayleigh*," Jeff says.

Will turns to find that Alicia has already made her way over to one of the windows. "He's at the edge of the parking lot," she reports. "He's pointing at the trees and yelling like a total fucking maniac."

Jeff laughs at the profanity. "Yeah he is!"

"Don't stand on the chair," Bing tells his son. The boy presses his face against the glass. Indecipherable words in red drippy text parade across the back of his shirt.

"How can there be no phone signal and no Wi-Fi?" Bing says.

"The mountains," Will says vaguely.

Bing does a fish-face thing with his lips and narrows his eyes. Will cocks his head—the cicadas' drone, muted to a dull flatline by the lobby walls, surges with a pointed shrieking energy. *Mating call*, Will thinks. There's some kind of deep unnatural tingling around his waist and inner thighs. Meanwhile Bing puts his hands on his hips and watches his children with nervy disapproval. "All right," he says. He raises his voice. "Jeff, Kayleigh, let's go get packed. We're heading home."

"Goody," Kayleigh says with soft contempt. She flips a page.

"Shit," Alicia says. She leans forward on tiptoes and plants her palms against the wall to better peer outside. Then she darts away from the window and pulls the boy down from the chair.

"Yo, chill!" he says, jerking his shoulder forward to break her grip.

The *crack* of a gunshot sends Will hurtling toward Alicia and the boy.

"The guy's maybe twenty feet away," Alicia says as Jeff moves across the lobby toward his father, who intercepts him on his way to grab his daughter. "Shooting at the trees."

The girl, Kayleigh, holds the magazine open in her lap and stares off into the middle distance as her father pulls her up with one arm to clutch her tightly against his belly.

A second shot rings out. Closer, louder. Bing stoops reflexively, dragging his children down to the floor.

Will and Alicia take cover behind the front desk.

"My Sig's up in the room," Will says.

"Good," says Alicia. "You popping off too is the last thing we need. The guy's shooting at *bugs*, Will. He's a psycho."

"He's gonna hurt somebody."

"Not us." Staying low, she shuffle-runs to the front door and turns the deadbolt. She's back at Will's side a moment later.

Will raises himself up, peers over the top of the desk.

Outside, a warbling voice climbs up over the ceaseless drone, a dissonant strain in search of a harmony line that never comes together. The voice soars with righteous fury.

"The appearance of the locusts was like horses prepared for battle!"

A quick pause is punctuated by a gunshot.

"And on their heads appeared to be crowns like gold!"

Two more shots. Alicia's hand rests atop Will's, both of them lightly resting on his knee.

"And their faces . . . "

One shot. The voice is closer now. Hysterical. *"And their faces were the faces of MEN!"*

Six bullets gone, Will thinks. If he's got a revolver, that's it. Anything else, and there's probably—

BANG!

—more.

Glass shatters. Alicia squeezes his hand. Will peers around the side of the desk. Bing is using his big body to cover as much of his children as he can, splayed out in a wrestling move. His kids' skinny limbs jutting out all over, their bodies hidden. A few feet across the floor, glass shards twinkle in the overhead light. One window is spiderwebbed with cracks radiating from an off-center hole.

The door handle begins to rattle.

"Hey!" The man's voice comes through loud and clear. He's right outside.

Will and Alicia rise to their feet.

The man pounds a fist against the door. Dull thuds echo through the lobby. "HEY! OPEN UP!"

Bing pushes himself gently off his children and stands fully upright with surprising grace. His flannel is half untucked. Ex-athlete, Will thinks.

"There's gotta be a back way out of this place," Bing says,

dragging his kids beyond the desk, where silver coffee carafes sit on a rough-hewn wooden table. He opens a door, peers into a storage closet, slams it shut. His eyes scan the lobby. The only other door leads to the stairwell.

"MOTHERFUCKER!" The man outside throws himself against the door, again and again.

"We're safe in here," Will says, putting an arm out in a *stay calm* gesture to Bing. "We can all go back to my room and just wait it out. He'll go away."

"No," Alicia says. She looks at Bing. "You're right. We should try to make a run for our cars now, before it gets worse."

Jeff watches his father, wide-eyed, arms crossed, hugging himself. "Out *there?*"

The man outside pummels the door. Kayleigh turns and glances over the top of the desk, then reaches out and lifts a landline phone. Will frowns. None of them thought of that. She puts the receiver to her ear.

"Dead," she says, letting it drop.

A shift in the light captures Will's attention, a sudden shade like a cloud passing across the sun. The lobby windows have begun to darken with cicadas. At the same time, he jumps at a pair of gunshots, startlingly close. The doorknob falls and clatters against the floor. Alicia takes his arm. Bing unsnaps a small leather holster attached to his belt, revealing a utility knife.

With a yell, Will rushes the door as it swings open. His feet leave the ground, his shoulder connects, and the door slams shut. The proximity of the man with the gun makes his body tingle. There's nothing but a two-inch slab of wood between them.

Then Bing is there beside him, shoving one of the massive armchairs into place. Will throws his weight against it as Bing goes back for its twin. Alicia and the kids drag the coffee table across the floor. The man outside is screaming. Gloom falls across the lobby. Light comes through curtains of writhing cicadas in pencil-thin beams. Will lets the first chair go while Bing shoves the second one into place as a bulwark for the first. Bing flips the coffee table and yells at his kids to get back upstairs as he drives the table into the makeshift barricade. The man outside is gibbering. His nonsense crests to a shriek.

Alicia pulls Will back. Bing ushers his kids toward the stairwell. Will stops in the middle of the floor. The irregular rhythm of the cicadas beats in his heart, his ears, the back of his throat.

"Come on!" Alicia gets in his face. Will points at the broken window. A surge of elation courses through him. His breath catches. He tries to speak but finds that he cannot.

"Oh Jesus." Alicia's fingers dig into his forearm. "What the fuck."

Cicadas squeeze single-file through the bullet hole in the glass. They jet inside the lobby like water from a pressurized leak. Will turns to see Bing's kids vanish into the stairwell. Alicia pulls Will along. He hesitates, just slightly. The first contact of chitinous legs on the back of his neck sets his nerve endings on fire with a keen sensation.

Recognition.

9

Move move *move!*"

Vicky lays on the horn. The sound is tentative and polite. Everything about this hatchback is tentative and polite. She wishes for her cruiser. Lights, sirens, V-8 engine, five hundred pounds of torque. Shotgun in the trunk.

A minivan crawling through the intersection at the end of Reservoir Road slams on its brakes to let her through. The brick sign at the edge of her neighborhood—WOODLAND GLADE in rustic block lettering—comes and goes. Vicky pushes the gas pedal to the floor. The hatchback obliges politely. The cruiser would leap forward with wolfish hunger to eat up the pavement. The hatchback stutters, the gears engage, the car picks up speed.

"It's okay, baby girl," she says, laying her hand across Sadie's clammy forehead. Not cold and not warm, same as before. Some kind of limbo state. The girl's face is pallid. A sheen of sweat beads her upper lip and forehead. Sadie thrashes and flails. Her foot connects with the door.

"Hold her!" Vicky shouts.

"I'm trying!"

Kim, in the front seat, curls her body over Sadie to rein in her movements. Vicky presses her hand down on Sadie's forehead.

She has to believe that her touch is soothing, even if Sadie can't perceive it.

Vicky's mouth is dry. She swallows and nearly retches at the muscle memory of the cicada inside of her, swimming and clawing its way down toward her stomach. Tiny spiked legs scrabbling against soft tissue. That sandpaper dryness as it came rushing up. The earthy taste of ancient dirt.

The fact that it was a thousand times worse for Sadie breaks Vicky's heart. One second she's playing in the yard, exploring with her curious mind the strange new bugs around the backyard oak. And now she's in shock, lost somewhere inside her head.

Her lips are the color of the robin's-egg crayon she uses to draw the sky.

Vicky tries to keep her eyes on the road. She moves her hand down to Sadie's neck, feels her faint pulse.

The curves of Market Street come and go. The hybrid's low center of gravity—its one saving grace—bites down as she steers without braking. Trees blur past—stately old evergreens that hide the ramshackle houses of the original settlement, the gentleman farmers that founded Fort Halcott in the aftermath of the French and Indian War.

The hospital is halfway across town, a fifteen-minute drive at normal speed. Vicky runs a red light, scopes out oncoming traffic, then punches it through the intersection. The northern stretch of Market Street unspools, mom-and-pops from her father's time swept away by regional megastores, in turn swept away by consolidation. Parking lots where she made ceaseless arrests in her uniform days, addicts nodding off in cars with kids in the back, nickel-and-dime meth deals in the after-hours loading docks.

The Applebee's that once got robbed in broad daylight comes and goes. She runs another light. A Camaro blasts its horn. Tires squeal. She barely notices. The world narrows. What she could have done differently hammers inside her skull. Stopped Kim from letting Sadie go outside. Ignored the call from her partner. Played Connect Four and sipped herbal tea and watched the cicadas from inside and checked the news and waited for this freak infestation to pass.

The road weaves over Frenchman's Creek, the fast-moving ribbon of mountain runoff that splits Fort Halcott in two. There's the Rusty Waterwheel, the restaurant perched like some Venetian manse over a bend in the creek. She grips the wheel with both hands, ten and two, as tightly as she can. An old stone house with a historical marker flashes by, followed by a dilapidated barn with a caved-in roof, scattered farm equipment, a scarecrow in an overgrown field, the Big Sheep trailhead with the all-caps sign that says PICK UP YOUR TRASH NOBODY WORKS HERE.

"It's okay," she finds herself saying, over and over again. Vicky has never been one to dissociate in times of great stress. The whole point of disciplined living is to meet challenges with boldness and clarity of purpose. But her daughter in distress has rendered her panicky. Now Sadie's head moves slowly from side to side, a parody of a person falling asleep. "It's going to be okay."

Vicky races to tailgate a black SUV. She lays on the horn until the SUV pulls onto the narrow shoulder and she flies past. The driver gives her the finger. Some irregular rhythm comes from deep within Sadie. Her head seems to vibrate, hummingbird-quick.

The protected forest looms darkly on the left. A thin blade of the endless woodland acreage that surrounds the town, bisects the creek, and stretches like a bicycle spoke to Collins Park. And this forest is alive. The trees are trembling, disintegrating, vibrating like Sadie's body with billions of cicadas, cascading down from the Adirondack foothills to swarm the edges of town. Then the strip of forest is behind her and drab commerce once again looms. She runs a red at an intersection with a TGI Fridays whose owner was busted in a happy-ending massage parlor raid last April.

Cicadas dot the pruned shrubbery that hugs the road alongside the strip mall with the wax center and the health food mart. They flit about, seemingly at random. Yet there had been a vicious logic in their pursuit of Sadie.

Kim is saying something. Kim who is in the front seat, bent over Sadie, clamping her in place.

"She's trying to talk!" Kim says.

"Sadie, we're right here!" Vicky tells her daughter. "We're right here with you!"

She strains to listen. She moves her hand down to Sadie's chest, just below her clavicle. There are vibrations. Sadie's voice comes out in a low moan, hardly more than a breath. Outside, a Shell station comes up fast. Vicky scans a lot full of cars parked at strange angles.

The northbound side gains a second lane. Vicky nudges the hybrid into it and cruises past a line of cars exiting the eastern sports complex, site of summertime baseball tournaments. In the rearview she glimpses a pickup as it swerves free of traffic to bounce down a grassy embankment into the road—someone equally frantic.

Sadie screams. Vicky, startled, nearly jumps the center line.

"What is it?" Brittle and frightened, she doesn't recognize her own voice.

"I don't know!" Kim shouts back. "I can't tell what she's saying."

Vicky glances over. Sadie's lips are moving quickly like she's weaving a silent spell. She moves her hand to the girl's mouth, just to feel the softness of her breath. This, at least, is warm. She moves her hand back to Sadie's forehead, where irregular vibrations course through her.

The big box stores loom, their parking lots chaotic. A busy swarm inhabits the carefully pruned trees clustered by the Walmart sign.

She wriggles her phone from her pocket and calls St. Mary's Hospital, the direct line for the ER intake desk. She knows most of the duty nurses and admins. All she has to do is tell them she's bringing Sadie in, and they'll assemble a team to meet her in the drop-off lane.

But the phone does not connect. No dial tone. Nothing. Keeping her eyes on the road—the hatchback pushing a hundred—she hands the phone to Kim.

"I punched in the number for St. Mary's," Vicky says. "Keep trying."

Kim takes the phone, taps the screen, holds it to her ear. Vicky hangs a hard left, heading west toward the park. The commercial strip falls away. A red maple, dulled by summer, is at the center of a storm of insects.

"There's no signal," Kim says.

"Keep at it."

"No, I mean, it's not just the hospital. There's no signal at all. I can't call anybody."

Vicky processes this. She has made phone calls from every inch of Fort Halcott. Unless you're up in the mountains, there's decent service everywhere.

"Give me the phone."

She looks for herself. It's true: The upper left-hand corner of the screen reads NO SIGNAL. She tosses the phone in the hollow of the center console. While she stays focused on the moment, her detective brain is percolating: drawing a through-line, as mystical as a constellation, among the happenings of the past twenty-four hours.

The old woman on the dining room table, divested of hair, teeth, and nails.

The incessant buzzing that began last night as the cicadas appeared in the dark.

The second victim at a scene Grimes is attending right now.

The attack on Sadie.

The dead phone.

The dots connect across a vast and lonely sky in the back of her mind, glowing lines that form a simple carapace, a new constellation, *Cicadoidea Major*.

"Oh no," Kim says.

The hospital complex rises beyond neatly planted rows of maple trees buzzing with activity. There's the illusion of disintegration again, as if the bark itself is coming apart into tiny blue-flecked pieces.

She slows down just enough to tear through a hard right turn. Sadie mutters and flails. Kim holds her tight.

Vicky slams on the brakes. The hospital parking lot is clogged with cars and ambulances from the three private services that cover Fort Halcott. She cranks the wheel to steer around the vehicles stalled all the way up the long drive. A white CR-V with the same idea beats her to it. She bashes the horn with a fist. The CR-V grinds to a halt when another car boxes it in. An alarming fantasy comes and goes: pulling her service weapon, clearing a lane—except the Glock is back home in her gun safe.

"Hold on," Vicky says. She swings the car wide to outflank the CR-V. They bump down an embankment and bounce through a runoff ditch. The car noses up the other side, wheels spinning helplessly in the dewy muck before catching and flinging the car up over the top. The frame rattles and the engine protests with a mechanical clatter. The car fishtails as Vicky aims it across the field that stretches from St. Mary's to the road. She steers into the skid and straightens the car out, cruising past vivid perennials and benches etched with donors' names, threading a pair of stately elms.

"Look out!" Kim yells.

A figure staggers out from behind a tree. It's as if he's walked through a dark sheet pinned to a clothesline and kept moving, tearing the sheet away and wearing it like a billowing shroud. Insects are thickly clustered around his face and torso. He reminds Vicky of a man she once saw running from a burning house, the top half of his body wreathed in flame. This man turns on his heel with eerie elegance, hopelessly swatting. Vicky tries to steer around him but his movements are erratic. There's a *thud* as the passenger-side mirror clips him. Kim cries out. Sadie kicks the door. The man goes down, spinning out of sight. Vicky does not stop. The car skids along the grass as she swings around a miniature garden. An American flag rises from a circle of shrubs to whip against the brilliant sky.

She notes a pair of black drones rising from the tree line beyond the hospital, toward the community college.

The parking lot slides back into view. From this angle the chaos is evident. Ambulances parked everywhere. Cars abandoned, doors left open. EMTs race stretchers toward the hospital. The horseshoe intake zone, sheltered by a concrete overpass, is swamped with people carrying limp figures in a procession of dangling arms and legs. Vicky gets as close as she can, hitting the brakes at the edge of the lot, where grass meets concrete.

"Oh my God," Kim says, taking in the hundreds of people trying to deliver loved ones to the ER. Movement across the lot brings to mind some mindless stampede. "What's happening?"

Vicky throws the car into park and unbuckles. "Give her to me."

Kim slides Sadie into Vicky's lap. She opens the door, plants her feet in the grass, then lifts Sadie out of the car. The frenzied insect-buzz is suddenly amplified. Sadie is feather-light, skin and bones, so pale and helpless. Her blue lips form shapes. Not long ago they were setting up their Connect Four game, having a Saturday morning together. Now this.

Billy Winters was riding his bike, same as he did every day, when Silas Nedry pulled him into his rust-pocked LeBaron.

Vicky leaves the door open, keys in the ignition, and takes off running. Kim hollers something after her.

She's a hundred yards from the intake zone. Sadie weighs nothing. The weariness of her all-nighter is gone. Adrenaline spikes can be useful but there will be a price. She thinks she should have brought George the ladybug. EMTs cut in front of her wheeling an old man on a stretcher. An oxygen mask covers half his face. His eyes are glassy and vacant. Then the medics are gone, clattering ahead with their patient.

Despair rises. There will be no special treatment for Sadie. Vicky's status as a respected Major Crimes detective means nothing in the throes of this apparent epidemic. Vicky turns sideways to squeeze between cars. She glimpses the interior of a Camry. A woman is slumped in the front seat. Something hard strikes Vicky's shoulder and she's spun halfway around. A burly man barrels past, elbowing people out of the way with one arm. His other arm clutches at his throat. A cicada perches on the doglike scruff of his bunched-up scalp.

Vicky hits the intake zone. The world dims as she races beneath the overhang. Just ahead, dozens of people converge at the big glass sliding doors. Kids are carried. Adults are wheeled on stretchers or simply dragged. A teenage boy sprawls in a child's red wagon. His head moves from side to side. A sudden metallic crash echoes across the lot. A car, coming in too fast, smashing into traffic. The man ahead of her is moving slowly, limping along. Vicky pushes ahead of him into the bright corridor. She's been here dozens of times. Typically there's a nod from the duty nurse, a doctor coming up to take charge. Today there's only the crowd seething into the hospital like the cicadas that sent them here. Vicky lifts Sadie higher, so that she can be seen by someone who will take her to a bed. Except triage has collapsed. There is only desperation. All Vicky can do is join the chorus.

"Help we—"

"—need help over here—"

"—my sister, please—"

"—*inside* him!"

An ER doctor she knows attends a patient on a stretcher. Vicky cranes her neck. "Dr. Ghoshal!" she calls to the woman. "Vishi!"

Vishi and Vicky. They shared a late-night laugh about that back in the day. But the doctor is harried from all sides and Vicky's voice is drowned out. A man charges through the doors and into the corridor holding a girl younger than Sadie. The girl slips from his hands, slams into a woman's back, then hits the floor before anyone can catch her. The man skids to his knees and claws at his throat. Someone shouts behind her. Screams, contagious, cascade up the hallway. Vicky turns. The man on his knees has brought cicadas in with him. A thin fluttering line of them, trailing back through the doors. She watches people drop loved ones to swat away bugs. She hunches over Sadie, shielding the girl with her body.

"SHUT THE DOORS!"

A piercing scream.

"MOVE BACK!"

The automatic doors require clearance to close and people are jammed in too tight. There is a push from behind, a ground-swell of movement. Vicky's feet leave the ground and momentum carries her forward.

"No!" A pair of nurses hold out their hands as if to stop the flood of all this pained humanity. Sadie thrashes in Vicky's arms as she's wrenched sideways by the inexorable current of the crowd. They move like a Ouija board planchette, the force of the mob swaying this way and that. Sadie's leg catches on a fallen woman. Vicky tries to free the girl but she is too gentle, too halting. Sadie is slowly ripped away from her grasp. If she does not let go she risks snapping a brittle limb. Vicky cries out, a single voice buried in the fog of desperation. Heat rises along with an odd stench: fear and body odor and the clammy skin of the afflicted. Sadie is borne aloft as Vicky tightens her grip on her daughter's hand. There are no individuals here, only a mass of poking elbows and knees. Stuck fast in this web, Vicky's grip is wrenched open and Sadie is carried away into the teeming throng. Someone up front goes down and the disruption ripples back. Vicky twists in midair and the scuffed linoleum comes up fast to meet her.

10

Will surveys the second floor of the motel. A dozen or so guests are gathered in the hallway. Three of them wear Mountain View Lodge bathrobes. Half the guest room doors are open. Faces peer out. The white noise of a TV tuned to static mingles with the insects' song. Other people mill about, listening as Bing gestures wildly, his voice booming down the corridor.

"We blocked the front door so the psycho with the gun—" He pauses to catch his breath. "—can't get in. But there's a hole in the window."

"*Gun?*" a woman says.

One of the bathrobe guys holds up his phone. "I got no service."

"None of us do," Kayleigh says. "And the landline's down."

A peering face draws back and a guest room door slams shut. Will can read the stark choice in the faces of the others: Wait out whatever this is in their rooms, or try to escape. Another door closes, then another. That leaves one bathrobe lady, two young men with a toddler, a trio of hipsters (Will wonders if the term *throuple* applies), and an elderly man dressed for a safari with binoculars around his neck. He meets Will's eyes.

"I'm here for the migration," he explains.

Alicia practically pounces on him. He steps back, blinking behind thick glasses, as she stalks over. "You came here for this *on purpose*? You *knew* this was going to happen?"

He puts up his hands. "No, the rock finches, the rock finches!" His back hits the wall. The electric sconce behind him flickers. Alicia doesn't move. "Mountain birds!" he clarifies, pointing in what might be the direction of the mountains. "They come across the Great Lakes in June to roost in the Adirondacks. They're native to the region. They've actually been added to the vulnerable list in the last decade, it's really a remarkable—"

"Okay!" Alicia says. "So you don't know anything about cicadas."

The man bristles. "I know *some* things."

"Has this ever happened before?" Will chimes in.

The man frowns. "Every seventeen years, I should guess."

"Jesus Christ." Alicia brushes past him through the open door to his room, where the curtains are closed. "Did you get dressed in the dark?"

"I have light sensitivity upon waking, it's better if I acclimate slowly by—"

Alicia pulls the blackout curtain aside.

"Oh my," he says. Cicadas crowd the balcony door. Even from out in the hall, Will can sense their crawly plump undersides. A flash of exquisite pain jolts his head and he presses his palms against his temples. The memory of what he saw in the warehouse throbs like a heartbeat inside his head. A blood-rush of sense memories: the entwined acolytes climbing the window as one connected entity, a shared abdomen and thorax of woven flesh, its underside wet looking and segmented. The leaders behind them, vomiting light.

This ecstatic vision is a carnival ride. His sleepless brain drags him through the vertigo of images connecting, overlapping. The cultic ritual and the bug-covered sliding door. Cause and effect rattle in the back of his mind, the satisfaction of two points plotted on a graph. Will knows he's in thrall to what he saw in the warehouse—how could he not be aware of it? The memory draws him in. But if he is to be used by it, then he can also put it to use.

"This is beyond any of us," he finds himself saying. "It's beyond time itself."

Bing frowns at him. "What's that, buddy?"

Will stares into space. He can see—no, *feel*—the little stubbly hairs of Bing's salt-and-pepper goatee quaver as Bing's lips move. "You okay, Will?" The man's voice echoes down the hallway, swimming into his ears.

"Hey." Alicia's soft hand is on his arm. He blinks. She has exited the bird-watcher's room to stand before him.

"Hey," he says.

"Stay with me."

He nods. The guests of the Mountain View Lodge look to him, as if he's poised to speak the words that will give them purpose and direction.

"This is ludicrous," the bird-watcher says, coming out of his room and shutting the door. His binoculars sway on their strap, smacking softly against his sunken chest. Just below the lenses, his belly curves out in a little bowling-ball shape. "Even if it's an infestation, or something of that sort, cicadas are harmless to humans. Really nothing more than a nuisance. A *temporary* one." He presses his khaki hat down on his head. "Good day to you all." He brushes past Will and heads toward the stairwell.

"Hey, man," Bing calls after the bird-watcher, "we blocked the front door!"

"There's a guy with a gun out there, ranting and raving," Will reminds him.

The bird-watcher pauses with his hand on the door to the stairs. Then he sighs, reaches into his fanny pack, and pulls out a tiny derringer pistol, the weapon of a scorned lover in a folk song. "The rock finches' mating window is vanishingly short. I will not miss it."

"Damn," Bing says. "All right, then."

The bird-watcher leaves. Will studies Alicia as she watches him go. The look on her face is inscrutable. An intrusive thought floats by: *She respects him more than she respects me.*

"So are we gonna take a vote?" Bing's son, Jeff, says.

Will looks at the teenager. "On what?"

Jeff shrugs. "I don't know, like, what we should do? In movies they take a vote."

"In movies they also just do whatever they want," Kayleigh points out.

"People who just do whatever they want *die*, dumbass," Jeff says.

"Hey!" Bing says. "No one's going to die."

The scream comes from below. Instantly, the men with the toddler rush back inside their room and slam the door behind them. Will doesn't wait to see what the other guests do. In five seconds he's in and out of his own room, pistol in hand.

"Jesus, Will," Alicia says. He ignores her and heads down the stairs.

When their separation began last March, Will's most vivid fantasies came in the dreary predawn hours when he'd wake slowly at first, then abruptly. He would cling to whatever dream tumbled him through his rough night, refusing to let in the merest notion of yet another day without her. The fantasies that leaked into his numb reality would range far beyond sexual. There would be epic incidents, a framework of missions and jobs and stress and danger. Plain old adventures for the two of them. Nonsensical plots, yes—but the spirit of their partnership remained intact. Will and Alicia, together forever, fighting the chaotic-good fight. Or at least a neutral one. He would lie there, curled fetally, eyes clamped shut against the onrushing day, urging the story along, even cheating a little, coaxing his subconscious into expanding the season into multiple arcs.

Will and Alicia in some Mad Max apocalypse, scavenging in stylish tatters.

Will and Alicia in a hostage situation, communicating wordlessly, mounting a brave resistance.

Will and Alicia, alone together at the end of the world.

The situations grew increasingly elaborate. He would find himself moving numbly through his days hell-bent on earlier bedtimes like a kid on Christmas Eve, forcing himself to sleep to make the morning come faster. For months he lived for these scenarios. Disasters piled on disasters. Hollywood catastrophes. Collateral damage, populations decimated—none of it mattered as long as he was together with Alicia, forging a new alliance in the face of despair and hopelessness.

Well, asshole, he thinks, hand on the door to the lobby, *you got your wish.*

The shriek hits him as he opens the door. A shrill cry that pierces the droning buzz like a solo violin soaring over a low thrum of cellos.

Will stops in his tracks. The barricade of tables and chairs still holds at the front door. The psycho with the gun hasn't breached the lobby.

The psycho with the gun is not the issue.

The bird-watcher's safari hat sits upside down on the floor. It's now a bucket teeming with insects. The hat's owner is down on his knees. A veneer of cicadas covers him, loops around his body like some poured sentient liquid. Will's heart flutters. He is horrified and disgusted and spellbound. The cicadas coalesce in patterns that shimmer wetly like oil on concrete. There are hints of translucent rainbow hues.

The bird-watcher claws at his throat. His head turns toward

Will and he flails, beckons, gurgles. Cicadas skitter across his eyes, down his cheeks, and up his neck. They slip like long lozenges between his lips. Will notes the silver glint of the derringer pistol flung halfway across the lobby. The bullet hole in the porthole window has widened slightly. Cicadas pour inside. Will's mind picks out separate jet streams of insects, winding inward like helixes, DNA strands of cicadas bearing down on the bird-watcher.

"Hey!" Will shouts, waving his arms like he's facing down a bear in the woods. "Hey, get away from him!"

The swarm does not flinch. There is no acknowledgment, only progression. The bird-watcher collapses. The insects fall upon the man like a settling cloak.

"GET THE FUCK OFF HIM!" Will rushes the prone form. Cicadas thump against his body. It's like running through a hailstorm. Translucent wings swish drily in his ears. Insects pelt his face. He keeps his mouth shut. Pointy legs prod his lips. He swipes them away.

Down on one knee he punches through a blue-black morass and finds the bird-watcher's bony chest beneath. He sets the gun aside and swipes away cicadas. It's like trailing his hands through water. He can carve a path, but the space will be filled a moment later as the cicadas crest over the bird-watcher in fresh waves. Will gets to his feet. Bugs circle his head, and he swats them away. There will be no helping the man here—not while the swarm can replenish itself from the broken window.

He will have to drag the bird-watcher upstairs.

A hand on his shoulder spins him around. Alicia. Will's heart soars.

"Leave him!" she shouts, grabbing his wrist, pulling him away. "We gotta cover that broken window!

Together they move through the outer dregs of the insect cloud, lone bugs in madcap flight. Will rummages behind the desk, fending off the erratic advances of stray cicadas. The bird-watcher has stopped moving. Will tries not to look. He tucks the pistol into his belt and reaches for a framed print on the wall: a panorama of the Adirondack landscape in autumn, mountain peaks dotted with blotches of orange, red, yellow. Rock finches hiding in there somewhere, maybe. He rips it off the wall, brandishes the print like a shield, and moves through a cicada cloud until he can slam the print against the window. Vibrations of invading insects course up his arms. He imagines them gathering in the little space between the window and the back of the frame. Hundreds of writhing bugs, crammed in. And the second he takes his hands away they will explode outward into the lobby.

"I need something to hold this in place!" he calls out.

Alicia bolts for the storage closet they discovered earlier. Outside, a shot rings out.

Will knows he should be terrified. He is exposed, his back to a room thick with swirling insects. For all he knows they will tire of the bird-watcher and come for him next. Yet a strange calmness has veiled his fear, a massage of pressure points in the back of his skull. The mating call has split into stereophonic sounds, Dolby surround in a theater. He understands all at once—as strobe-light sense memories flash behind his eyelids—that the drone is not a monolithic utterance. It's not some mindless cry but a complex and beautiful symphony. His own voice echoes in his mind, and at last, he remembers the words he spoke earlier:

It's beyond time itself.

His own voice buffeted on the strange carnal winds of hungry insects.

Flash.

The acolytes skittering up the window.

Flash.

A vast plain of desolation teeming with monstrous tunnels of flesh...

"Will!"

He turns to glance over his shoulder, expecting Alicia to be running toward him with a hammer and nails, or a tube of crazy glue.

Instead she's swatting bugs. A long skein of cicadas, broken off the mass enveloping the bird-watcher, hunting Alicia. Will lets the framed print fall to the floor. Trapped cicadas spill down the wall like ecstatic roaches in filth. He nearly knocks Alicia off her feet as he reaches her at full speed and manages to wrap his arms around her. Like this, they make for the nearest safe place: the storage closet. Will pulls the door open, shoves her inside, slips in behind her, and slams the door. There's a split second of darkness as he finds the light switch. A handful of cicadas cling to Alicia. Several more buzz about. Together they swat them. There are few enough to keep them at bay. More of a nuisance than a swarm.

Will recalls the bugs he witnessed slipping into the bird-watcher's mouth. He points to his own mouth and makes the universal sign for zipped lips. Alicia nods, wide-eyed. The drone is muted in here, but Will can still feel its complex melody in his guts, in his throat, between his ears. Separate strains of communication, parallel inquiries, an expansive suite of call and response. *Beyond time.*

Will and Alicia poke around the cramped closet. Cheap modular shelves are crammed with Windex, bleach, paper towels in bulk. A mop handle juts from a bucket. Tissue boxes are stacked like bricks. Will's heart sinks. It has been a spur-of-the-moment solution, hiding in here. They are safe from the swarm invading the lobby, but there's nowhere to go. Meanwhile the bugs have free rein to pour in through the broken window.

His vision swims. He braces himself against a shelf. Word-lessly, Alicia comes to him, puts her arms around him. His body is soaked in adrenaline that ebbs and flows without warn-ing. Some deep wellspring of emotion breaks. The fussy little bird-watcher, in town for his rock finches. An odd little man celebrating his niche hobby. Earlier the man had woken in the dark, excited for the day ahead. Now he's lying on the lobby floor, covered in cicadas.

What on earth are they doing to him?

SMACK. Alicia destroys a single bug against the shelf. Alone they are no threat. She wipes her hand on a paper towel. Will snaps out of it, takes a breath. He moves to the back of the closet. A rickety metal shelf pushed against the wall holds folded towels, washcloths, stacks of toilet paper, rubber gloves. A single cicada alights on the shelf, its red eyes staring back at him. Will takes a step toward it, hand raised to strike—and nearly loses his balance. His feet tilt forward, inexplicably, into empty space.

He beckons Alicia closer. They kneel down and examine the interruption in the floorboards. The shelf seems to straddle a dark hole in the ground. Together they slide it away from the wall. A narrow staircase appears, wooden steps leading down into darkness. Alicia lights the way with her phone. There is no discussion, no wordless debate. They have no choice but to see where it leads. Together they descend. With each step Will internalizes a strain of the cicadas' harmonic intensity as if he's pulling threads of melody from the lobby down with him, trail-ing musical phrases that loop and repeat. Meanwhile each step brings him back to the window of the warehouse, back to a majestic denial of reality.

At the bottom of the stairs his feet come down onto some-thing soft and a little bit slippery. Will turns slowly, in a cir-cle, illuminating the motel basement. Somewhere above, the symphony crests: the drone from the lobby, split into choral lines that overlap in gorgeous dissonance.

The light from his phone slides along the wall. There are grainy black-and-white photographs tacked up everywhere. Will struggles to make out the images. Close-ups of insects, diagrams of head, thorax, abdomen. Circled irregularities. Cross sections.

"Oh God," Alicia says. Will trains the light on her as she kneels down and lifts something from the floor. Long wispy strands dangle from her fist.

She looks at Will. "It's hair. It's human fucking hair."

Will shifts his flashlight to his feet to find piles of hair, like a swept barbershop after hours. Shades of blond, brown, red. Long braided clumps. Pubic hairs, coarse and twinkling. "Jesus."

They move forward slowly. Will's light moves along the floor. He pauses to examine a pile of clothes. Dress shoes, dark slacks, a forest-green polo with a name tag attached: DENNY.

Will vaguely recalls the affable kid from the front desk who checked them in. The one who'd apparently abandoned his post.

"What the fuck," Alicia says.

Will lifts his light from the floor. At the far end of the surprisingly long chamber, a corridor winds away into the darkness. "Maybe it's a way out."

Alicia considers this. "We don't have a choice anyway. We can't go back to the lobby now."

Will thinks of Bing and his kids up on the second floor. Jeff and Kayleigh bickering about what to do while Bing tries to come up with some fatherly command to set everyone on the safest path. The barrier between them now makes him despair, a little.

"Those people up there..." Will trails off.

"You don't owe them anything," Alicia says.

Five years ago, before his walkabout, before this strange career, before the divorce—a different life!—he would have agreed. Today the notion clings to him that he is in a perpetual state of owing. But there is nothing he can do about that now. The symphonic drone has died away, lost somewhere above, muted by concrete. Yet the energy of this place buzzes and pops behind his eyes. He is in thrall to a feeling he can't identify.

As they move toward the corridor, he aims his light at one of the enlarged images tacked to the wall. Something from the earlier part of the century, lightly sepia-toned and washed out in its enlargement. It is most definitely a cicada, shot from above. The translucent wings folded back, the bent and mantis-like forelegs, the fat abdomen and tapered thorax. But there's something off about it. The perspective, perhaps. Or the size itself.

"It's fucking huge," Alicia says. "Look." She points to what Will assumed was some washed-out negative space beyond the insect. "It's sitting on a desk." She moves her hand up to a metal device that seems to crouch above the cicada. "And that's one of those lamps like the dentist has, that you can move around."

Now Will sees it: the size of the bug relative to the lamp. Unless it's a tiny dollhouse lamp, the cicada is at least six inches long and plump as hell. He studies the photograph, searching its margins for some other clue.

A sudden harsh gurgling noise floats through the basement. Will swings his light away from the photograph, toward the source of the sound. His hand finds Alicia's. The gurgle trails off into a keening moan. Will hands the phone light to Alicia and pulls the pistol from his waistband. His shoe crunches what feels like scattered bits of gravel. Alicia lowers the beam to the floor, and her breath catches in her throat.

Teeth. Scattered underfoot. Human teeth trailing bloody roots. They press up into Will's soles like tiny pebbles.

Her hand squeezes tighter. They step together into the hallway at the end of the basement room. The walls are bare cement. Will feels the crossing of this new threshold like a blast of moist, swampy air. The moaning rises into a wail of pain.

Will swallows. Clears his throat. "There's four of us!" he calls out. "And we're armed!"

The voice descends into a gasping, breathless panting, like a dog gulping down air on a hot day. They round a corner. Will's shoe comes down on another tooth. They pass a closed door. The corridor straightens. The panting grows raspy and desperate. The sound of a man psyching himself up, Will thinks. Anticipation.

Then a howl of pain. They round another bend and emerge into a second basement room. The air is foul and laden with dust. Alicia's light plays upon a cement floor smeared with dark streaks. A single white sheet is tacked up on the wall, adorned with a spiral painted in bold crimson. Two almond-shaped wings jut from the spiral, filigreed with tiny precise lines like bloodshot eyes.

The kid comes out of nowhere. He's nude but for a pair of striped boxer briefs—a skinny, hollow-eyed waif. Will recognizes Denny from the front desk.

"Stay back!" Will shouts. He steps in front of Alicia and levels the pistol, aiming for center mass. Not that there's much mass in the birdlike contours of the pale kid's chest. Will recalls the boy had a thick head of wavy brown hair. Now he's bald except for patches of stubble. His mouth is a slurry of blood, clown makeup smeared by a violent hand. Strands of pinkish saliva dangle from his chin. A pair of pliers juts from his fist. Bloody bits are scattered at his feet: teeth, yes, but also other things. Nails, perhaps. Ripped from fingers and toes.

The boy does what Will says. He drops the pliers and puts up his hands. For a moment, Will is surprised at Denny's restraint.

He had expected a gibbering madman to rush at him, to force him to shoot. Instead Denny backs up against the wall.

"on't urt ee!" he spits out.

"What are you doing?" Alicia steps out from behind Will, riding a wave of disgust and hysteria and fear. "What is this place?"

Denny makes a mewling noise, then spits out a mouthful of blood. He speaks slowly and manages to articulate.

"The Order of Hemiptera," he says. He pauses to wipe his mouth. "The true bug."

A shiver courses through Will's body. For a split second he's back at the warehouse window, in thrall to the flashing lights, the crawling trio.

"The signal begins in the soil," he hears himself say.

Denny's eyes go wide. His ruined mouth breaks into a bloody grin. "Brother!"

The buzzing drone slithers into Will's mind. He rides its comforting peaks and valleys. Then he shakes his head, snaps himself out of it. Alicia's light wavers as she looks from Will to Denny.

"Is there a way out of here?" she demands.

Denny holds up a finger. He lowers his arms and turns, bends down, comes up with a small zippered pouch, like a clutch purse. He moves to open it.

Will levels the weapon. "Slow!" he commands.

Denny smiles the crinkled grin of the righteous. His wraith's body curls over the pouch. Then he extracts a single cicada. Its legs pedal empty air. He whispers something to it and the bug stops moving. He pinches the insect between his fingers and slips it into his mouth. His throat convulses as he swallows. He closes his eyes, savoring. Then he lifts his arms. His mush-mouthed, bloody words are difficult to make out. Will thinks he hears, "We mark the moment of the rising."

The kid opens his eyes and dips into the pouch and holds out a cicada toward Will.

Will tells himself he is revolted. Yet he eyes the insect with a certain reverence. He is six years old again, and his mother is showing him the communion wafer. In his young mind, the body of Christ and this odd circle of bread struggle to align. The wafer is stamped with a cross, a little off center, clearly a factory job that renders the whole mass production of the Body of Christ a little false, even to a six-year-old. Now, faced with the disgusting prospect held forth by a maniac, Will is for the first time appreciative of the majesty of transubstantiation.

"Violet Carmichael," Alicia says. "She's one of you. Do you know her?"

Will snaps out of his fugue. He's in awe of Alicia's presence of mind. At the same time he is ashamed at his own wandering thoughts.

He reaches for the cicada. Alicia slaps his hand away. Denny shrugs and consumes the bug himself. Will notes that he does not chew. As far as he can tell the insect slides down his throat intact and alive. He situates himself in this bizarre moment. His mind does a quick calculation, a ranking of their worst jobs: Is this one better or worse than Mexico City? Worse, he thinks, but still better than Budapest. He'd rather be here, in this basement, facing down a hairless, toothless kid eating cicadas, than in the 8th district running from those Nazis...

"Violet is our sister," Denny says, swiping the back of his hand across his mouth.

Will forces himself back to the matter at hand. The symphony fades. "So you're all in this cult, the Order of Hemiptera."

"The true bug," Denny says again, flecking the air red. He has the wide-eyed earnestness of the missionary at your doorstep. All pain seems to have deserted him. "It is our time," he enunciates carefully.

"Where can we find Violet?" Alicia asks.

Denny looks puzzled. He holds out his arms. "We are everywhere."

"Violet Carmichael, specifically, though."

He shrugs.

Alicia lets out an exasperated sound. "Why did you do that to yourself?"

Denny doesn't seem to understand. His eyes slide from Will to Alicia.

"Is there a way out of here?" Will asks.

Without another word, Denny turns and pulls the painted sheet to one side. A staircase comes into view.

Will gestures with his pistol. "Over there. Face the wall."

Denny obeys. Will watches as the kid lets his upper body lean forward until his forehead is resting against the cinder blocks. Denny mutters something Will can't make out. He thinks it might be *Yes, brother.*

Alicia shines her light up the stairs to a set of metal doors laid flat. Will goes up first. He ducks his head and places a palm against the cool underside of the door. The drone slips in, works its way into the back of his mind.

During his solo travels he read a book about an American platoon in Vietnam whose job it was to take a hill where the North Vietnamese were entrenched. They spend the first third of the book taking the hill, the middle third trying in vain to hold it, and the final third getting pushed off by the enemy. The book ends with their commanders ordering their depleted, exhausted force to retake the hill.

Time, in cahoots with land, conspiring to chew people up. Will is struck by his own motion, the cycle up from the lobby to the second floor, back down to the lobby, and then this descent into some homemade lair for the Order of Hemiptera. And now he is poised at the moment of another rising. The cycle

of the cicada (the true bug) transposed onto his futile movements. What is he now but an insect set on its path, obeying the
signal to rise? The symphony swells. He pushes the door back
on its hinges. As if he's been waiting for years underground, in
accordance with the countdown of a molecular clock outside the
bounds of known science, the light is blinding.

11

A stampede is an elsewhere thing. A tragedy that happens to other people in distant places. Part of her has always thought: Surely it can't be *that* difficult to avoid being trampled. It's not metal walls closing in, it's just a bunch of soft bodies. And there's enough oxygen to go around.

But now, in the crush of the ER intake, Vicky gets it. It's one of those medieval tortures, being tied to two horses that drag you apart. Her left leg is wrenched one way and her right arm another, and Sadie is gone. Her forehead is pressed against the floor. A black streak where a stretcher's wheel skidded is all she can see. Her body is an inferno, and she is slick with sweat. The crowd pressing in around her stinks of fear.

An elbow slams into the back of her neck. The arm attached to it holds her down. Her ribs are squeezed by a great weight. At the same time she manages to kick a leg free. She works her knees underneath her body. Now she has some leverage, but her arm is still pinned. To force herself upright would be to dislocate a shoulder. The air is so hot in her lungs. How absurd it would be to die like this in a gosh darn *hospital*.

She screams. Her voice joins the chorus. She lies there huddled as people fall around her, her cries unheeded. There is blinding pain in her right arm as it hyperextends. Vicky panics. There is nothing she can do. Just before the pressure becomes unbearable—snap of bone imminent—the crowd shifts to the right. The big man pinning her arm is tossed aside. She pulls the limb in tight, beneath the shell of her arched back.

Like the sun breaking free of a cloud, Vicky senses a shift in the air around her. She uses the little window of time to push herself up to her feet. A wave of dizziness takes hold. She shakes it off, snaps herself into action. A sea of faces swirls: none of them Sadie's. There is room to breathe now—the crowd straggles farther down the hall. She reaches down to help the big man up. He's lying on his back, shirt bunched up to reveal a hairy tattooed belly. His face is pale and sweaty, lips the color of dead fish. His eyelids flutter. His lips murmur. Vicky retracts her hand. The man is suffering in the same way Sadie is. There is nothing she can do. Her breath comes back to her in great heaving gulps. How precious it is, to be able to breathe.

She bends down to lift a little girl. *Not Sadie not Sadie not Sadie.* The girl is deadweight in her arms. Her skin is clammy. *Sadie can't be far.* She lays the girl back down. All around her now, people move with the creaky hesitation of survivors after a battle, tending to their wounded. Vicky lays her fingers aside waxy necks, takes pulses. Helen from the flower shop kneels over her husband. Pat from the hardware store carries his son over his shoulder.

"Sadie!" she calls out. Bodies litter the corridor. Prone forms, barely breathing, exuding pure stasis, trapped in a between-state. She pictures the man popping out from behind the tree, covered in bugs, trailing them like smoke. How many people in Fort Halcott have been overcome?

She recalls the parking lots on Market Street, the gas stations and big box stores. Cars were pulling in with nowhere else to go, seeking concrete as refuge while insects billowed out from manicured lawns.

"Sadie!" She works her way down the hall past bodies on stretchers. Fallen IV drip stands and plastic chairs lie across the floor. A computer monitor, smashed by a rubber-tipped cane, hangs by its plug.

"Vicky!"

A familiar voice calls her name. There's Hassan, waving his arm above his head even though he's only a few feet away. His short-sleeved uniform top with its American flag patch and silver badge is half untucked. A stethoscope is draped across his neck. Vitiligo patches are like pale continents against a sea of dark skin.

"Hassan," she says as he rushes toward her. "I lost Sadie." She finds that those three words steal her breath. She's panting.

"What do you mean you lost her?" His hands are on the sides of her arms, pulling her close. "Where is she?"

She shrugs him off. Right now she wants space. Suddenly there is not enough air. Panic swells. Hassan's face retracts telescopically. "There's something wrong. She got attacked by the bugs, she's catatonic."

Hassan lets out a breath. A pungent, boozy warmth hits her: vodka fumes stinging her nostrils. No wonder he's so calm. She hasn't checked in with him in several months. He could be mid-bender for all she knows. The uniform is no indication: He's always functional until the law of attrition that governs all functional addicts imposes too much chaos on daily life and the facade cracks.

Someone rushes past, bashes her shoulder, spins her sideways. Hassan holds her up. "I haven't slept," she tells him, for some reason. Her thoughts become irregular. Her head lolls back. The fluorescent lights line the ceiling in radiant parallel. She feels herself drifting.

"We have to get you checked out," Hassan is saying from someplace far away. "You're hurt." He produces a cloth from somewhere and dabs lightly at her forehead. It comes away smeared with blood.

Hurt.

She wants desperately to close her eyes and then wake up in a soft bed, gauzy light streaming through half-parted curtains, Sadie curled up in a chair in the corner, clutching George the ladybug to her chest...

Hurt.

Shame rips her back to reality. Her discipline has lapsed. She is giving in to weakness. She rights herself and steps back from Hassan. The fluorescent lights paint the corridor in a too-bright sheen, unreal soap-opera lighting. His bloodshot eyes are full of worry, his lids at half-mast.

"I'm fine," she says. A nurse rushes past to attend to a collapsed old man. "Comparatively." She takes a breath. "Help me find her."

Hassan turns toward the ER entrance and scans the crowd. Vicky's gaze follows. Hospital staff wade among the residual carnage like knights picking through the mountains of dead after the battle. Victims of the stampede, mostly elderly, are being helped into chairs or escorted away from the bodies that litter the floor. These are the insect victims: the ones who share Sadie's affliction. Clammy, lukewarm skin. Lips like the frozen sea, muttering whispered gibberish. Erratic flailing and halting, slow writhing.

The front doors are still closed. Vicky can see the dark flickering curtain across them. Cicadas, pressing themselves against the glass. Forming and dispersing like murmurations in the sky. Patterns come and go as the bugs, in thrall to some insatiable hunger, are desperate to get in.

"Come on," Hassan says, leading her down the bustling hall. "We dragged away the people up front to clear the bottleneck.

The kids got moved along first. Docs are trying to set up some kind of triage on the fly. If she's out cold, they'll get her a bed."

Vicky detects the strained formality in his speech. The over-enunciation she recognizes from the relative midpoint of his most drawn-out benders. This is when he's overcompensating to keep up appearances, so afraid of slurring that he course-corrects to an almost theatrical stuffiness. In another day or two there will be no more compensation. He will be too far gone for that. The chaotic energy of his oblivion seeking will have grown too big to fail. There will be boisterousness teetering on the edge of the maudlin and the self-pitying. Too-big grins and twenty-dollar bills sunk into dive-bar jukeboxes for songs that'll play long after Hassan's stumbled out the door. Regrettable texts and rambling calls (though Vicky's long past being on the receiving end of those—she just assumes someone else has taken up the mantle).

"What the hell is going on?" he says. As far as she can tell, it's a serious question. As if she knows. As if she's privy to some insider information regarding this brood's motivations.

"The cicadas came early," she says, recalling her neighbor in his bathrobe. "Jumped the gun by a year."

"And started *attacking* people?"

"Yes."

What more can she say? They move past numbered surgery rooms with big doors to accommodate stretchers and equipment. Green cloth partitions hang from metal frames on wheels, carving out space in the corridor. Vicky pokes her head into every makeshift treatment nook. She absorbs snatches of conversation, stray words that can be grafted onto her own horrible morning.

Backyard

Trees

Happened so fast

All over him

Couldn't breathe

"What the hell is going on?" Hassan says again. Inside an open operating room, she glimpses a nurse leaning into chest compressions. The patient is flopped, senseless, on the bed.

"Just look for her."

"Sadie!" he calls out. A pitchy edge to his voice. It's absurd, she knows, to call Sadie's name as if she's capable of answering in her state. But she understands the impulse. It's impossible not to.

Vicky steps into the past: two years ago, in this very hallway. Sadie had fallen off the seesaw at recess and was mildly concussed. Hassan had staggered in, far too late, meeting them on the way out, bloodshot and reeking. Upon seeing Sadie in her head wrap he'd burst into tears—a more or less appropriate reaction from a father in the abstract. But Vicky knew the tenor of Hassan's heaving melodrama. The tears had been for himself—the plunge into *what a waste I am*, and a litany of apologies spiraling down into a black pit where he'd flagellate himself for a few days before climbing out and turning over the same well-worn, crumbling leaf.

He pulls a pair of white round pills from his breast pocket. "You want one?" he asks without telling her what it is.

"No," she says.

"Desperate times."

"No."

He pops them both. She figures it's Vyvanse or one of the other uppers he uses to get him through work.

"I'm on graveyards again," he says. He flags down an attending nurse Vicky doesn't recognize, a short, plump redhead.

"Hey Debra!" he calls out. "You seen my little girl?"

Vicky winces. The usage of *my* grates on her. Plus how does this woman know Sadie? She imagines Hassan showing her photos on his phone as if he's a proud, active, involved father. She brushes irritation aside. There's no time for that now.

"Might be up on two," Debra says, pointing at the ceiling. "They're taking people right into intensive." Then Debra is gone.

Vicky heads for the elevator bank. Hassan is lagging. A pair of white-coated doctors move past and turn the corner. Hassan bumps one of them. He moves at half speed, staring off into the middle distance. When his roving eyes alight on Vicky his face scrunches. His upper body jerks as he begins to sob.

"No flippin' way," Vicky says. She takes him by the arm. "Hey! Don't do this now." She pulls him toward the stairs. He shakes his head viciously, letting his jowls hang loose and flap like a dog's. He makes a weird motorboat noise. He rubs his eyes.

"Sorry," he says. "I'm okay. It passed. Let's find Sadie."

"How drunk are you?"

"Zero point zero."

Vicky doesn't bother to dignify this, just runs up the stairs.

On a normal day the intensive care unit of St. Mary's is like a calmer, sleeker version of the ER: large patient rooms with glass doors, stocked with CPAPs, bedside monitors, tubes for various -otomy procedures, kidney machines, lines and drips hanging from metal frames. Today the influx from below is choking the atmosphere. Vicky takes one look at the patients crowding beds shoved in hallways and her heart ratchets up.

"They got 'em on ventilators," Hassan says as if Vicky doesn't know what a ventilator looks like. He stops and stares, perfectly still. There is none of the hangdog looseness that typifies the drunk person's motor skills. She figures the uppers are taking hold. Having never self-medicated with drugs of any kind, Vicky can only imagine what the movies tell her: the pupils sucking out to saucer-wide portals, the teeth-grinding intensity of a million thoughts a minute. She moves down the hall, taking in the scene.

Kids, teenagers, adults, elderly men and women—a dozen

incapacitated human beings on this floor with plastic masks strapped to their faces like fighter pilots, trailing thick blue tubes connected to bedside monitors. Doctors and nurses and PAs shout at each other. A patient's arm topples a bedside table.

A disorienting sense of time dilation takes over. Vicky retraces her steps. Running Sadie inside the ER intake, the staff killing the automatic doors to blunt the force of the cicadas following people inside. The panic. Sadie being spirited away in a forest of limbs. The floor tiles coming up fast—

The blood on her face that Hassan wiped away.

Vicky presses a hand to her forehead and winces at the stab of stinging pain. Definitely an open wound. How long was she out? How much time slipped by? She wishes she'd gotten a few hours' sleep. The overhead lights are too bright. The windowless ICU is a radiant place.

"Sadie!" Her voice sounds like it's trying to escape a plastic container. Hassan stops to talk to a fellow EMT. The woman has a swollen, puffy eye. The speaker microphone clipped to her shoulder crackles. Vicky follows the snaking cord down to the boxy radio in its holster at her hip. Something simmers in the back of her mind. She stays focused. Off to the left, behind a sliding door, a handful of personnel are gathered around a bed. A nurse moves to attach a ventilator to the blanketed patient. Suddenly the nurse jolts backward in shock. Vicky watches as a single cicada rises up from the bed and begins carving a frantic pattern into the air. It bumps into a framed watercolor painting of a farm and changes course. The doctor bends away from it as it buzzes her head.

"Jesus," Hassan says, watching the single cicada scare the shit out of five grown adults.

Vicky moves on down the corridor. A slender woman in a white coat backs out of an open doorway. Her lapel is spattered in insect guts.

"Vishi!" she calls out. "Dr. Ghoshal!" She rushes up, Hassan on her heels. The doctor turns. Vicky reads amped-up shock in her eyes. "I can't find Sadie. I lost her." How many minutes ago? Vicky has no idea. "I can't find Sadie!" she says again. Dr. Ghoshal's head jerks back. Vicky realizes she's been shouting.

Dr. Ghoshal places both hands on Vicky's shoulders. "We've got her."

"I had her and then—"

"Vicky." The doctor gives her a light yet insistent shake.

"I couldn't—"

"Vicky! She's just up the hall. Room sixteen." Dr. Ghoshal pauses. "She's as stable as anyone else right now."

"Thank you!" Vicky yells over her shoulder as she runs. Hassan's heavy boots thud after her.

Room sixteen is glass-walled on the hallway side and Vicky catches a glimpse of the child-size ventilator before she can make out her daughter. Inside the room, a nurse in blue scrubs attends to Sadie's bedside monitor. He turns, startled, as Vicky comes to a stop at the edge of the bed.

"Baby girl," she says. "I'm here. I'm here now."

"Me too," Hassan says. "Your dad." He seems uncomfortable with the word and shakes his head. "Your father."

Sadie's condition appears unchanged—clammy skin and bloodless lips. Behind the mask her mouth moves in odd shapes. Her eyelids flutter. Every few seconds, her left arm rises with fingers splayed before sinking back down to the bed. Vicky has perched at her daughter's bedside many times, especially in the early days of single motherhood, when she felt compelled to helicopter-parent lest flu symptoms turn deadly overnight. Now she feels like she's failed Sadie in some new and irreversible way.

Vicky has always slotted Hassan himself into the category of her small failures. Lately even their professional overlaps have been few, far between, and brief. What must Sadie think of this man, this biological father who isn't exactly a pariah, but is steadfast and unwavering in his own personal catastrophes?

Vicky has often wondered if Sadie will someday be enough for Hassan to pull himself out of his endless, meandering spiral. So far, no dice.

Now Sadie's little hands clutch at nothing. Vicky wishes she had George the ladybug. The thought of Kim hits her out of nowhere. Kim, back there in the parking lot. Did she even make it inside?

"Her vitals are wacky," the nurse says quickly, watching Vicky and Hassan gaze silently at their kid.

Vicky looks up. She'd nearly forgotten the man was still there.

"Her breathing's so shallow," Vicky says. "And her skin..."

"It's the same with everyone," the nurse says. He indicates the monitor, as if Vicky's supposed to know how to read the display.

"Her body temp is *fluctuating*?" Hassan says, narrowing his eyes at the screen.

"Pulse rate," the nurse says, "BP—they're all unstable. It's the weirdest thing I've ever seen." He pauses. "Well, except for everything else that's going on." He looks at Hassan and Vicky in turn. "I don't know what's happening," he says. "All I know is, I'm staying inside."

Kim, Vicky thinks. *Grimes*.

She reaches out to lay a hand on Sadie's sweaty head. When she makes contact, Sadie's left arm goes up. Her fingers extend. They wiggle a bit. The arm stays up, motionless in the air. A low sucking *whoosh* escapes the ventilator, a rhythm of false breath.

"So now what?" Vicky says.

The nurse looks at her. "No idea," he says. Then he's gone.

"Vic," Hassan says. "That time she fell off the seesaw, being here with you now, it's hard not to think of it—"

"Jesus, Hassan," Vicky says. She makes the sign of the cross. A reflex, a penance. She's long since lapsed but still doesn't like taking the Lord's name in vain. "It doesn't matter now."

"It *does* matter," Hassan says. "All of it matters."

Vicky doesn't ask what he means by this. He sounds decisive now, the self-assurance no doubt derived from the pills. She notes that he doesn't lay a hand on Sadie or even approach her bed. The ventilator churns, the monitor beeps softly. She lets her eyes go slack while Hassan speaks. Then she refocuses on Sadie. *This is really happening*, she tells herself. *Sadie is really in this hospital bed, vital signs defying logic. Outside, the cicadas are swarming.*

"I'm going to get us through this," Hassan says, winding up his speech that Vicky didn't listen to.

"You don't have to do anything," Vicky says. "I told you eight years ago, none of this is on you. You're not expected to be there for her, or me, in any way. That hasn't changed." She is swamped in weariness. She makes herself look him in the eyes. "You are who you are, Hassan." She doesn't mean for this to sound cutting—she's aiming for a sort of hazy benevolence, maybe even understanding—but she can tell by the way he winces that she's struck a nerve. She is so tired.

"You don't have any idea who I am," he says. "Did you know I got really into jazz, like *super* into it, a year and a half ago? On the same day we had that solar eclipse? I'm talking beyond just Miles and Coltrane and the stuff everybody knows. I'm talking deep dives. Obscure shit. I own a record player, did you know that? A vintage one."

"I did not know any of that, Hassan. Did you know that Sadie's favorite game is Connect Four?"

He opens his mouth, then closes it again.

"I'm sorry," she says. "Forget I said that. Of course we don't know things about each other. We barely speak. It is what it is."

"It is what it is," he parrots back at her. "You are who you are."

She sighs. "Listen, let's just—"

His radio crackles. A voice comes through, first-responder jargon, mild hysteria. Absently, he switches the shoulder mic off.

"Wait," Vicky says. The half-formed thought from earlier completes itself. "Let me see that."

Hassan unclips the shoulder mic. The cord stretches to the radio at his waist. "The whole thing, please," Vicky says.

Hassan unholsters the boxy device and hands it over. Vicky cycles through channels. The police radios that the FHPD uses are dinosaurs, left over from her father's era. Captain Barker's got a long list of upgrades, and the whole department is at the mercy of the city's budgetary woes.

Vicky used to curse the ancient system. It's untrunked, which means there's no encryption and anybody can listen in. Other departments in other cities are walking around with mobile phone tech for radios. But here, with these ancient child's toys, Vicky can jump from the emergency services channels right to the Major Crimes airwaves.

Not that any of the veteran detectives have much use for their radios anymore—it's more of a uniform thing. But homicide has its own personal channel. And Grimes is smart.

There are more than twelve hundred channels allotted for first responder traffic. She clicks over to 1138, some random netherworld of the frequency that Major Crimes calls its own.

"Grimes, this is Paterson. You out there? Over."

She waits a moment. Nothing but dead air. Hassan turns to Sadie and folds his arms, studying his daughter with an inscrutable expression.

She tries again. "Kenny, come in. Come in, Kenny."

A moment later, a reply crackles. "Still waiting on that banana."

"Kenny." The name exhaled with relief. "Sadie's been hurt. We're at the hospital."

"Ah, Jesus, Vic."

"She's stable." The ventilator makes a sucking sound. Vicky closes her eyes, squeezes them tight, opens them again. "More or less. Or at least no worse off than anybody else who got hit." Hassan looks expectantly at her. She wonders if he's waiting for her to say something like *I'm here with Hassan.* "Are you all right?"

"I'm in my car. I'm still outside our second crime scene. I couldn't..." He trails off. "I didn't want to wait this out in the house. With the whole scene like it is, you know? I had to come out here."

Vicky's mind rolls back to Grimes texting her the location of their second victim. *We got another one.*

"The place is way out east," he says, "by the skate park. Past Mott. I'm riding it out for now. Barker's been on the horn. Everybody's mobilizing. He's getting as much insecticide as he can from public works."

"Okay," Vicky says. It feels strange to shift gears into public service. But of course that is what she will have to do. Her brain fog clears a little. There is simplicity to the pursuit of helping others. A linear, uncomplicated forward motion that she often craves.

But then she will have to leave Sadie's side. What if—

"You have to see this, Vic," Grimes says. There's a hushed sort of awe in his voice. The cynical husk that coats his words has fallen away. His tone gives her chills.

"I don't think the best use of my time right now is driving all the way to the east side." *Far from Sadie,* she thinks.

"I *need* you to see this." He pauses. "I think we might be the only ones with a line on what's really going on here."

She picks up his insinuation right away. "You think the cicadas are connected to our two victims. Our killer."

Hassan looks up from Sadie, frowning at Vicky with an odd look on his face.

"Oh yeah," Grimes says. "I'm sure of it."

Her body tingles. "Why?"

"This victim's even further along, if you catch my drift. The, uh. The skin. And there's more." Grimes sounds haunted. "It's just beyond anything."

Vicky pictures the tanned-hide hardness of the old woman's torso, a tautness that made a clacking sound if you rapped your knuckles against it. Flesh and exoskeleton in some kind of discourse, twined at a molecular level. She eyes Sadie and shudders.

The dismal outcomes she sees nearly every day at work can be so easily grafted onto your own child's fate. All it takes is a single intrusive thought and your brain is off to the races. Sadie in a car crash, Sadie in a school shooting, Sadie on a date with the wrong person.

Sadie in a hospital bed, infected by some creeping malady that twists her into something awful.

Vicky's resolve grows. If she and Grimes have hit upon clues to the heart of this catastrophe, then she has no choice but to follow them. For Sadie. For everyone in Fort Halcott.

"So can you get over here?"

The last text Vicky received before the signal went dead had been the address of the second crime scene. She performs a quick mental calculation. Back across the river, merge onto Mott and head east toward the skate park—

Blink. There's a few seconds of missing time, a video stuck buffering.

Vicky finds that she has collapsed into a chair in the corner of the room. Hassan is standing over her, holding the radio. "She needs to rest," he says into the mic.

"Put her back on," Grimes says.

Vicky reaches out to snatch the radio. Hassan pulls it out of reach. "You need to sleep," he tells her. "I'll find a cot. You can crash in here. You don't have to go anywhere."

"I'll be there as soon as I can!" she yells at the radio. Hassan clicks it off.

"I was talking to my partner," she says.

"You were passing out on your feet! How long have you been awake?"

She stands up to prove that she's fine and forces herself to stay on her feet. The ventilator churns. The monitor beeps softly. Shouts come from another part of the ICU. Footsteps pound down the corridor. "I worked last night," she says. "But you heard Kenny. The things we saw yesterday—I think he's right, Hassan. I think we're onto something here."

"No," he says, shaking his head. "No. We should all be staying here, as a family."

We're not a family, she practically blurts out. *We never were.*

Hassan reads it in her eyes. He changes tactics. "This place is safe, Vicky. There are no windows in the ICU." He nods at the door to Sadie's room. "We can always barricade ourselves in here if worse comes to worst. We're surrounded by doctors. Medical equipment."

"So what, we stay here and ride it out while other people have to deal with whatever's going on?"

"Yes," he says. "That is exactly what we do." He points at the bed. "For Sadie's sake. So when she wakes up, she still has a mom and a dad."

Her thoughts grind against themselves. The chair beckons. It's surprisingly soft for cheap polyester. She could just grab a quick snooze. Then, when she wakes up, it will be easier to sort things out in her head. Maybe, by then, Sadie will be awake too. Maybe this will all be behind them, and the nurses will be jubilant, the sun will be shining, the hospital doors will be open wide, and everyone will dance across the husks of cicadas on their way to hug their loved ones. *We made it!*

No one would blame her for staying here with Sadie. No one would really even know, in all the chaos. There will be heroes and cowards when this is all sorted out, the usual litany of characters who emerge in the aftermath. And then there will be the thousands of people who trod the middle ground, surviving, taking care of their own, keeping their heads down.

Hassan's eyes shine with booze and pills. He radiates nervy energy. *That could be us*, he seems to say.

"Look, I know this is corny," he begins, "but when's the last time the three of us were even in the same room? This is the part of the movie that teaches me what's really important, except I already know what's really important, and I always have, I just have trouble, you know, expressing it, and also living up to your expectations." He shakes his head. "Not *expectations*, that's not what I mean, so before you say *I have no expectations for you*, I'm sorry I misspoke. I just mean, I know what's right. The right thing is the big shining beacon on the hill, right? And I'm on the path toward it. Like, perpetually. You would think it would be easy. There's an obvious beautiful bright part and then there's a dark muddy swamp full of creatures with weird beaks that smell like rotten eggs. And so normal people have no problem walking along the nicely lit path toward the peaceful good things. But people like me, for whatever reason—and I want you to know I'm not downplaying my own agency, I'm just saying—"

"Hassan."

"—not that I've totally changed and I'm moving one hundred percent toward the peace and the light, but maybe a part of me—"

"Hassan!" She reaches out and grabs his wrists out of the air as his arms animate his speech. She looks him in the eyes. "This isn't about you right now."

In the early days his late-night calls would be full of justifications centered on his personal journey. There's a certain brand of sadness to the repetition, all these years later.

"I know," he says, indignant. "It's not about me at all. That's why I said *us*. Our family."

"Okay," she says, letting it go. "Well, I have to meet Grimes."

His blinks, uncomprehending. "What?"

She lets go of his arms and goes to Sadie, places her hand on the girl's forehead. The icy lukewarm clamminess—like swimming in a lake and suddenly coming upon a vein of frigid water up from some deep wellspring—freaks her out all over again. She watches her daughter exhale into the ventilator mask, a million miles away.

So Vicky will leave now and her heart will pound with adrenaline and she will throw herself into ending this terrible new reality. Her heart leaps at the prospect—not of leaving Sadie alone, God no, but of being hurtled forward into an investigation, an uncovering of truth, a saving of lives. It's a craving. And in this, perhaps, she's not so different from Hassan.

She catches a glimpse of herself in the reflection of a polished steel cabinet: a pale blur of motion, no features to speak of.

She says a quick silent goodbye to Sadie. *I'll be back as soon as I can.*

I love you.

"What am I supposed to do?" Hassan says.

"Stay with Sadie," she says. "Get me on the radio if anything changes."

He takes a deep breath and straightens his spine.

Vicky hesitates. "If things go south in here, you protect her, Hassan. You keep our girl safe."

His eyes are wet. He nods. Then he holds up a finger. He produces the bottle of pills and holds it out toward her. "Before you pass out again," he says.

"No."

He gives the bottle a little shake. A sound like maracas.

"No, Hassan."

He grabs her hand, shakes a pill into her palm, and closes her fist around it. Vicky shoves it in her pocket, grabs a tissue from a box on the bedside table, and wipes blood from her forehead. She tosses the wet clump of paper into the wastebasket and leaves the room. Striding down the hall, she turns her thoughts to the cicadas covering the doors and wonders how the heck she's going to get out of here.

12

The car keys are back in the motel room. Everything is back in the room except for the clothes on Will's back, his useless phone, and his gun. When he ran down the stairs of the Mountain View Lodge at the sound of the bird-watcher's scream, Will hadn't been thinking about leaving for good. He hadn't been thinking about anything at all except helping a man in need.

And, perhaps, being bold and action-oriented in front of Alicia.

Now they're running through the parking lot. Will's leading Alicia toward their RAV4, though he has no idea what he'll do when they arrive at the vehicle. They stay low, as if their proximity to the ground will fluster the cicadas. Maybe it will. Who knows.

The drone, the resonant stream of chatter, hangs heavy over the blacktop. Bugs jet in great swooping ribbons through the air, skimming the tops of parked cars. The insects seem to treat the lack of foliage as a minor inconvenience, an irritating borderland. The mountains that rise up at the western edge of town loom green and impassive in the summer heat. Will imagines he can see them shiver with trillions of bugs, tiny pixelated visions. He fights off the impression that this infestation—this new rendering of reality—is the most beautiful thing he's ever seen. Denny's mush-mouthed voice loops through his head: *We mark the moment of the rising.*

Alicia, at his side, keeps her mouth shut and her eyes on the sky. Will glances back at the entrance to the motel. No sign of the gun-toting madman. To the right of the door is the broken window. Cicadas coat the glass, oozing inside according to some organizing principle that hammers at the back of his skull. He understands it even if he cannot articulate it: the logic of the ur-swarm breaking off into little chunks of consciousness to serve its billion little tendrils. He shakes his head, pushes this knowledge away. He does not want it. Not now.

They reach the door of their car. Alicia looks at him expectantly. An elongated swirl of bugs swishes drily across the roof of a nearby van. Will mimes putting a key in the lock, then looks at her and shrugs. He holds up his empty palms. She stares back for a moment. He defends himself from her silent interrogation.

Why did you take us to the car if you don't have the keys?

I have a plan, don't worry.

Will glances around at the cars in the vicinity of their vehicle. It takes him three seconds to spot the oldest, shittiest one: a beige Chevy Caprice, mid-1990s vintage. The ultimate old-person sedan, first cousin to the Buick LeSabre.

The cicadas moving overhead swirl into patterns that some deep part of him can actually parse. *Brother,* Denny had called him. He glances up to behold them fully, seeing them as millions of individuals and as one throbbing, pulsing formation at the same time. He once read that Daredevil can taste every ingredient in his food. It's a little like that, he thinks.

He beckons for Alicia to follow him to the front of the Caprice. Without a moment's hesitation he pulls the gun from his waistband, flips it so the grip juts out from his fist, and smashes the driver's-side window. The blow bends the glass

inward but doesn't shatter it. Two more strikes and the glass falls
to pieces. He reaches in and unlocks the door. With the side of
the pistol, he sweeps glass off the seat as best he can and climbs
inside. He reaches across and unlocks the passenger door. Alicia
hustles around and slides in next to him. The car smells like stale
smoke. A sun-faded air freshener dangles from the mirror. The
seats are worn leather.

Will finds the telltale groove in the steering column, the
seam running up the side. Ideally he would have a kit with him:
flathead screwdriver to break the locking pins in the ignition,
pliers to strip wires.

"Check the glove compartment," he says.

Alicia glances outside. She's still reluctant to open her
mouth. It's reasonable: They might be in the car, but there's also
a big hole where one of the windows used to be. She opens the
compartment and Will takes a look. Assorted pens and pencils,
yellowed fast-food napkins, a Happy Meal toy forgotten by some
grandkid, a lurid carrot-topped Muppet he doesn't recognize.

"Never mind," he says. Then he bashes relentlessly at the
steering column until the lower panel falls away. A trio of wires
drops down. He finds the battery and starter bundle—red and
yellow wires. Without pliers with which to strip them, Will
improvises. He picks up the biggest shard of glass from the floor.
Carefully, with aching slowness, he braces the wires against the
column and slices away small chunks of insulation. When he
twists them together, the dashboard panel lights up. The radio
blasts static.

Cicadas flatten themselves against the windshield. Alicia kills
the radio, but Will knows it's not the noise that attracted them.
They smell our pheromones, Will thinks—yet he also knows it isn't
smell, not really. He basks in the impressions of raw humanity, the
senses that stir an insatiable hunger. At the same time he grasps
the dangling starter wire. This one is live. He has to concentrate.

Even with a good pair of pliers this is dangerous. Alicia reaches over and slams down the lever jutting from the steering column. The wiper blades go straight to high gear, sweeping insects off the windshield. Will shudders. He felt it, being abruptly and brutally swept away like trash.

Like Alicia had flicked him away last spring, leaving him to twist in the wind…

A cicada zips in and brushes against the side of his face. He flicks it off and tries to focus. A second cicada buzzes around the inside of the car. Alicia swats it. Will presses the corner of the glass shard to the insulation. A cicada's legs tickle his ear canal. Alicia's hand slams one down on the dashboard. He pauses. Then he works at the hard rubber until the copper threads are exposed. Next to him, Alicia is squirming in her seat. One hand covers her mouth. The other swipes the air. A single lilting strain of the drone fills the car as more insects join in harmony.

Will touches the exposed starter wire to the twined ignition and battery wires. The old engine turns over, sounding morose and put-upon. Poor car craves an oil change stat. Will hits the gas. The engine revs. He ditches the starter wire, lets it fall away beneath the column. When he shifts into drive the sedan lurches forward. The gun bounces where he set it on the center console. Alicia snatches it up and tosses it in the glove compartment. The Mountain View Lodge diminishes in the rearview. Will's eyes scan the second floor. Up there somewhere, Bing and his kids are wondering what to do. Maybe even waiting for him to come back. Meanwhile in the basement, Denny is mutilating himself to mark the moment of the rising.

Will hits the edge of the lot and takes a sharp turn onto an empty road. Route 42, he recalls from their GPS-mapped drive into town last week. The same route the bird-watcher would have taken up into the mountains to observe the rock finches.

Alicia rolls down her window and swats away the handful of cicadas. They slip outside and are sucked into the wind. She turns in her seat, examines the back of the car. Satisfied, she opens her mouth.

"You need to turn around."

Will looks at her. She's staring out at the road. "You want to go *back*?" He thinks for a moment. "It's just a camera!"

"I mean you need to be going the other way on 42. We need to be going southeast, so we loop around the town and pick up that road that gets us back to 87."

Route 87, he thinks. The thruway. The outlets at Woodbury Commons. The bridge formerly known as the Tappan Zee. The Major Deegan. The city. Great landscapes of concrete. A hostile place for insects seeking greenery. Home.

"Also," she says, "nice job hot-wiring this fine-ass Chevy Caprice."

"Still got it," he says, pulling a U-turn. Roadside foliage slides past the windshield, trees full of cicadas. A million little flight patterns burn trails into the backs of his eyes. As he straightens out to head southeast, the patterns trace themselves across his vision. Ancient glyphs. Cave letters. Runes he can't decipher. He reaches over and takes Alicia's hand. She doesn't resist.

"You okay?" he says. The inadequacy of this question hangs in the air between them.

"Let's just get the hell out of here."

She takes out her phone. Her hand is remarkably steady. Will wonders if she's in shock. He's seen this before in Alicia: hiding from those neo-Nazis in Budapest, threats of torture and death hanging over their heads, Alicia transcending peak stress to a level that seemed, to Will, nearly inhuman in its emotionless control. It was only afterward, post-adrenaline, that her body language betrayed any kind of fragility. He recalls the spasms, the odd half smile tugging on her lips...

She jabs angrily at the screen. "Still nothing. How is that possible?"

"Maybe the cicadas swarmed the cell towers? That's all I got."

"Maybe," she says, unconvinced. "But the Wi-Fi went out too."

Will has no answer for this. "They could have...chewed through...I don't know."

The Caprice's engine rattles like it's trying to expel a clump of gravel.

He can feel her looking at him. "Are *you* okay, Will?"

"Totally fine," he says. "Unscathed." She slides her hand up his forearm, gives his biceps a squeeze, keeps going, digs a finger into his upper back, right between his shoulder blades. Then she runs that finger gently up the back of his head, the way she used to do, to feel his close-cropped hair against her skin. He reaches up and kills the staticky radio. The air coming in through the broken window has a peculiar smell to it. Oily and scorched.

"The Order of...Hemothra?" she blurts out. "Hemotomia?"

"Hemiptera," Will says.

"I'd google it, but, you know."

"The true bug," he says.

"I don't know what that means."

"I don't either," he says. It's not a lie—he's no more famil-iar with the cult they were sent here to save Violet Carmichael from than Alicia is. But it's also not the whole truth. Just saying the name out loud—*Hemiptera*—stirs something inside him. The painting of the winged spiral is etched in the back of his mind. He gives voice to something he's known, on some level, since the cicadas surfaced.

"There are no other bugs here," he says. He understands that word of the new brood's majestic rising has sizzled down the insect airways like a warning: Make way, make way.

There's a moment of silence before Alicia speaks. "Okay, *what* is happening to you? You're coming out with these cryptic pronouncements now and it's beyond freaky. I swear, it's like everything's gone sideways and I'm the only sane one left."

Will hangs a left to stay on Route 42. The Caprice's big old engine crackles. A soft-serve ice cream shop housed inside an old train caboose comes and goes. "No spiders," he says. "No ladybugs, no beetles, no grasshoppers. No flies, even. How do you not see a single fly? Nothing but cicadas. It's not the kind of thing you notice while it's happening, but now..."

"We need a bulletin board," she says. "Some red string and index cards. A stack of photos."

"We've got a stolen Chevy Caprice and a couple of useless phones."

"The way we did it in Budapest."

"Bratislava. Budapest was Nazis."

"Still beats Mexico City." She gives the back of his neck a light squeeze and takes her hand away. "Seriously, Will. I need you to talk to me, because everything's so crazy I feel like I'm losing my mind. And you're all I've got."

Warmth blossoms out from the center of his chest.

"So I need you to tell me what's going on with you," she continues. Her eyes burn into the side of his face. "It's like you're tapped into all this in a way I can't really understand, or feel. That poor kid in the basement back there—he called you *brother*. And not in the 'white kid trying to be down' kind of way. His eyes lit up when he realized you were on his wavelength. And if you *are* on his wavelength, I think I have a right to know. Especially if you're bringing something back with you to the city. Some aspect of what we saw here. If it infected you in some way."

"I'm not going to rip out my teeth, if that's what you're worried about."

Alicia's quiet for a moment. "Yeah," she says, as if realizing it herself for the first time. "I *am* worried about that. I'm worried about *you*. I don't..." She trails off. "I don't want to lose you."

Will's forced to slow down as they round a curve and traffic comes fully into view. It takes him a moment to parse her words. *I don't want to lose you.*

Light-headed, he hits the brakes. The white minivan in front of them is piled high with suitcases and backpacks. A stick-figure family of six waves from the back windshield. A single cicada floats lazily into the car. Will raises a hand to smash it against the dashboard but changes his mind at the last second and nudges it back out the window instead.

"Lose me how?" he says after a moment.

"Just, in general."

"So, what, you still want to hang out, grab a drink now and then, maybe team up for the occasional job like old times?"

"What if I do want that?"

Will is floored to find that he never really thought about their shared future that way—as something that would actually happen. When he'd asked her to partner up for this job it had been a Hail Mary pass, a half-drunk text he'd instantly regretted. He'd assumed her immediate one-word response (*sure*) had been a joke until she showed up at his place, suitcase in hand, camera bag slung over her shoulder. This whole time he's been riding it out, minute by minute, like an alcoholic white-knuckling the first few days of sobriety. Floating on the pink cloud, knowing it's only a matter of time before it dissipates and leaves him cartoonishly suspended in midair.

A voice in his head warns him: It's a terrible idea to accept having her in his life this way. He can see the future unfold—her inevitable wedding to Carter, watching from afar as the rising attorney becomes managing partner and Alicia starts some kind of fancy Manhattan PI firm and the two of them raise their adorable kids in a Brooklyn Heights town house that Will skulks tipsily outside of like the unwashed, lonely freak he will no doubt become.

"I mean, that would be cool," he says. The minivan up ahead crawls along. Traffic's backed up at the entrance to a long curving highway on-ramp that vanishes behind a half-abandoned strip mall. Trees are mercifully sparse here. The drone is nearly drowned out by the coughing engine, a distant song played on a half-buried radio. Someone lays on their car horn, igniting copycat honking.

"Jesus Christ," Alicia says. She pulls her legs up to her chest and laces her fingers together to lock them in place.

Will broaches a subject he's been curious about since she showed up at his place last week, ready to hit the road. It's seemed like such a potential minefield, he's been avoiding it entirely. He lowers his voice. It sounds almost meek, the way it comes out.

"So, Carter doesn't mind if we hang out? Or go on jobs, or whatever?"

A woman leans out the minivan's window. She tries to see what's going on up ahead. But there's nothing to see. The road curves. The strip mall blocks the view.

Alicia's quiet for a moment. "I broke up with Carter," she says.

Sparks pop behind his eyes for a dizzy, weightless second. Two seconds. Three. *Beyond time.* All manner of perilous and borderline-insane situations have been navigated, leading up to this moment. Will transcends the dismal ponderings of that lonely future. The timeline shifts, the universe course-corrects. At the same time, fresh anxieties rise. The woman's head draws back into the minivan. She lays on her horn. Someone shouts.

"Oh," he says.

"Yeah."

"Okay. Wow." He pauses. "I'm sorry."

She bursts out laughing. Her forehead rests against her knee. Will sits silently with his hands tight on the wheel of the idling Caprice. Outside, the oily mechanical smells grow more pungent. The pounding dreamlike terror of the past two days asserts itself now—the burnt ashes of a sleepless night sifting through his brain. *The moment of the rising.* Suddenly it seems silly and childish, this notion that all they have to do to set things right is get out of town.

"I was curious why you never asked me about it," Alicia says. "Did you really think this guy I'm in a monogamous relationship with would be cool with me going on a trip of indefinite length with my ex-husband?"

"I don't know," Will says. "I didn't want to ask. I don't know the guy."

She laughs again, clipped and bitter. "As in, maybe this is some weird sex game Carter and I are playing? Maybe it's a fetish of his?"

"*No!*" The word *sex* at all associated with Carter is odious. All this time he's conceived of Carter as this uptight, sexless WASP incarnate. The fact that Alicia even jokes about this indicates that there might have been actual sex games between them. "I just meant, it's your business. The two of you. I was just happy you were here." He looks over at her. She peeks out from behind a knee. "Seriously."

"I was happy too," she says after a moment. "Until, you know."

As if on cue a stray cicada floats into the idling car. It lands on the dash, antennae twitching. It's about two inches long and somewhat plump in the abdomen. Red globes bore into Will's eyes. It moves, jerkily, to look at Alicia. She clamps her mouth shut. He flashes to Denny in the basement of the motel, plucking cicadas lovingly between his fingers and sliding them down his throat. His foul grin as he consumed them, one after another. What madness gripped him? Will squirms in his seat. *Brother.*

Alicia lifts a hand to smash the bug. He halts her. *Wait.* She eyes him warily as he focuses all his attention on its curled forelegs, the flat triangle of its non-face. Something's buried within this creature, the key to unlocking the altered perceptions he's been experiencing since—*flash*—the trio of acolytes climbed the wall and—*flash*—exposed their shiny segmented underbelly and—*flash*—commanded his attention so that part of him still lingers at that warehouse window, awed at the twisted majesty. He places his hand, palm up, before the insect. The bug skitters forward, then bends to his flesh. It's the motion of a dog sniffing out a new person, a rite of impending companionship. Then, seemingly satisfied, the cicada flies away.

"Anyway," Alicia says. The single word speaks volumes. She clearly has so much she wants to address with him. Like, for example, the quasi-romantic moment he just had gazing longingly at a bug.

Will, agitated, clenches his fist and joins the chorus of blaring horns.

"What's that gonna do?" Alicia says.

Will lays off. He pokes his head out the window, like the lady in the minivan. It's impossible to see what's going on. At the same time, a black Jeep comes cruising past in the opposite direction. The driver slows down and calls out as he passes by.

"They're not letting anybody out!"

The Jeep moves on.

"*They?*" Will says.

"What the fuck," Alicia says. "You gotta be kidding me."

The dam breaks. The minivan surges hard to the left. Another car comes the opposite way. Both drivers hit the brakes and lean on their horns. Will cranks the wheel and goes for the shoulder on the right. A Range Rover has the same idea. So do a few vehicles. All they succeed in doing is creating a new traffic jam ten feet to the right of the old one. Now there's a mess of cars at conflicting angles. A little red Fiat tries to pull a U-turn and smashes into the side of a white SUV. Will glances over his shoulder. Behind him, a blue sedan is stalled perpendicular to the road, parked across both lanes.

"Stay here," he says, reaching for the glove compartment.

"No." She unbuckles. He grabs the gun. It's no use arguing.

"Okay, then keep your mouth shut."

She zips her lips, throws away the key.

Will gets out and tucks the gun in his waistband, pulling his shirt down over it. The air's getting hot and sticky, with an oppressive sun in a cloudless sky. The smell of chrome and oil is stronger out here. With Alicia at his side, he jogs along the shoulder, close to the guardrail. The on-ramp bends around the strip mall. A few other would-be escapees mill about on the roadside. At the point where the ramp ought to feed out onto the highway is a roadblock in the form of official-looking vehicles: a row of black Escalades and a pair of camo Hummers.

Above this barrier, black birdlike asterisks hover against the sky—a row of drones, evenly spaced. Will counts four of them across the highway, and more stretching away into the distance, hugging the perimeter of the town.

Back on the ground, beyond the vehicles, a fence of icy bluish-white chain link has been stretched across the road. The fence is alive with an unlikely shimmer that seems to refresh itself periodically. And there's a wet look to the metal, a sort of digital moisture. He's never seen anything like it.

The handful of figures guarding this strange barricade are dressed in tactical gear: body armor, automatic weapons, head coverings like bike helmets of pounded steel with flat planes that reflect the sun in rippling waves. Their faces are hidden. They bear no insignia. The smell is more potent here, the superheated copper tang of the rippling metals.

Will reaches out and takes Alicia's hand. They both halt. He can't see much beyond the tree line on either side of the highway ramp, but he imagines the barricade snaking through the underbrush, circling the entirety of Fort Halcott, cutting off the river. Alicia meets his eyes, holds up her useless phone, nods at the drones.

Yes, he thinks. She's right.

The cicadas haven't chewed through some fiber optic cables or swarmed cell towers. This perimeter functions as some kind of EMP for cell and Wi-Fi signals. A kill switch for communication. He stares at the fence, lost in the gentle rippling of concentric waves radiating out as if from a rock landing in water. The seriousness of this operation creeps across his mind like a black cloud. The cicadas might be some unprecedented natural event, but they are attended to by his fellow human beings: the kid from the front desk, Violet Carmichael, the acolytes in the warehouse window. Ritual and madness. Thrall and celebration. And now this: some mercenary force showing astonishing speed and organization, turning Fort Halcott into an inescapable petri dish.

"It's impossible," he says. At the same time he can swear one of the helmeted mercenaries is staring directly at him. Sunlight flashes in the mirrored visor. "It isn't the nineteenth century, you can't just cut off an entire American city, even if it's in bumblefuck. News is going to spread, fast. It's gotta be all over social media already."

Alicia glances around. Then she pulls up the notes app on her phone and types.

Maybe they're just buying time.

"For what?"

She shrugs.

"And who's *they?*"

She types: *3 letter agency.*

He takes a long look at the personnel manning the perimeter. No flags, no insignias, no badges. "I don't know. Maybe."

Twentieth-century history is rife with examples of bureaucratic machinery creaking into place in the wake of pandemics, hurricanes, terrorist attacks. But this feels different. It's like these border guards sprang up from the ground as a fully formed perimeter enforcement team. Like they knew it was coming. Like contingencies were already in place, operations rehearsed. Elements of this disaster arrange themselves in his mind: the Order of Hemiptera, the rise of the swarm, the closing of the exits. A full quarantine, Beijing-style. They even managed to take out the *landlines.*

Alicia takes his arm and commands his attention, pointing at the segment of the fence that stretches along the highway ramp. Will watches as a silver Jetta interrupts the steady stream of vehicles turning around and slinking back the other way. The Jetta pulls out of line, threads the procession of cars, and points itself at the fence. There's a moment of Wild West stillness as it idles, facing down the impassive team manning the barricade. The Jetta's windows are tinted. The unseen driver hits the gas hard. Tires bite pavement.

"Don't do it," Will mutters. But it's too late. The Jetta surges toward the barrier. A guard raises his weapon. The warning is implicit in his stance.

The cicadas' song surges through Will's mind. They flit about a cluster of evergreens that crowds the shoulder of the road. Meanwhile the Jetta is halfway to the fence. Will is aware of a rising tension in the swarm as the cicadas respond to the attempted breach. Their agitation courses through him, but it's not blind and unfeeling. The cicadas are not so far from us that we cannot understand them. There is pain in the patterns they weave. They mourn a loss. No, Will thinks: not a loss. An *opportunity*. He's trying to parse this distinction when the *crack* splits the undercurrent of their song.

A single shot punches through the Jetta's windshield. The mercenary lowers his weapon and jogs to the side of the ramp. The Jetta falters. Will imagines its driver's hands falling, dead, from the wheel. The car cuts a shallow angle but it's already aimed toward the fence. The cicadas' current splits into parallel dissonance. Alicia turns away. Will, enthralled, watches as the fence's rippling shimmer absorbs the car without a sound. No shrieking metal or collapsing steel. The fence bends concave, like the ropes of a boxing ring stretching to catch a fighter on his heels. The drones hovering above do not move. The car is brought to a stop. The fence reconstitutes. Its pixelation infects the Jetta. Glimmers of ice-blue tendrils unfurl along its silver body. Slowly, evenly, with a measured push, the car slides backward as the barrier goes flat, sucking itself in, forming its steady line.

For Will, seeing firsthand the cold inscrutable logic of this perimeter has opened up a vast chasm between what he knows and what he thought he understood about the world. This is the implacable steel gate slamming down in the portcullis, the frigid calculation of some AI buried deep in a nuke-proof bunker, apocalyptic outcome #4593 according to some ruthless algorithm.

The invisible hand, surfacing, revealing itself.

He reaches for Alicia just to feel softness and heat. She leans into his chest. They watch, along with the other stunned onlookers scattered up and down the shoulder of the road. The guards make no fresh moves. No weapons come up to target them. The Jetta sits where it was expelled by the fence. Will scans the tree line, his gaze delving into the woods beyond the ramp. He knows Alicia is doing the same thing. How likely is it that these people have managed to secure every inch of the perimeter? Compared with the city, sure, Fort Halcott is sleepy. But it's got a sprawl of its own, out here in the Adirondack wilds.

Will and Alicia make for the guardrail. Over the side is a runoff ditch. He scans the sky. Drones curve away into the distance. The fence glimmers in pieces, broken up by the idling cars. Will is surprised there isn't more of a frantic exodus. Then he realizes what's going on: a pair of identically armored mercenaries, planar helmets glinting, are pulling the driver from the Jetta. It's a kid, no more than eighteen or nineteen. Deadweight in their arms.

"Come on," he says softly, as if the perimeter team can hear, which maybe they can. He lifts a leg to step over the rail. Alicia tightens her grip, pulls in a breath. He looks toward the fence. They have to *move*. It's only a matter of time before all these cars vacate the scene. They have to be out of sight by then. Into the woods.

Alicia points. He puts both feet back on the ground. Of course.

The trees beyond the ditch are coated in a hazy sheen of insects. A living, swirling cloak of cicadas. Will loses himself, for a moment, in their crystalline passages through jet streams carved in time. All the while they weave the song, the glorious symphony of the rising.

PART TWO

SYMPHONY

13

Anton Hajek tosses a pair of twelve-sided dice against a small velvet backstop and rolls 4 and 11. He turns to the two decks of Thaumaturgy: World's End cards arranged before him on his desk. Discarding the top three cards from the first deck, he flips up the fourth.

"The Pit Colossus," he says out loud, studying the illustration on the card. A clear rip-off of Ben "The Thing" Grimm, with scaly rocklike flesh and enormous fists punching up from a gash in the earth. This card is from the game's first edition, long before it had come into its own. He reaches for the second deck and turns the eleventh card face up.

"The Insatiable Gnaw." A spidery apparition, half obscured by chimney smoke, is depicted skittering across the rooftops of a pastoral village.

Anton sits in his high-backed chair and contemplates this draw. It's a system of his own devising, a Tarot-adjacent game that ostensibly provides guidance but more accurately gives him a momentary diversion when he wants nothing more than to leap howling from his skin.

The Pit Colossus is a simple creature of legend, a symbol of the myths of ancient times in the expansive universe of Thaumaturgy. It's a creature summoned with earth magic, a basic building block of a decent deck. Considering the Pit Colossus alone, Anton would take the portent to mean something like *Stay the course. Remain steadfast and immobile in the face of overwhelming doubt.*

The second card, the Insatiable Gnaw, complicates this interpretation. That's precisely the point of the system: Each card has a tempering influence over the other. Drawing a single card and acting according to its theme would be laughably prescriptive. It's all about the way the two cards interact.

The Insatiable Gnaw is a haint born on a windswept cliff where villagers gather to send the burnt remains of their dead into the sea. Alas, some of the ashes and bits of bone cling to the moss on the face of the cliff. There's a bit of magical hand waving here, a blank spot in the footnoted legend in the Thaumaturgy creature compendium, third edition. But anyway, one night an eerie presence crawls up from the rocks.

The Gnaw is an enigmatic being, not exactly an evil presence but certainly an unsettling one.

Anton melds the spirits of these two characters in his mind. *Be an immovable ancient force and also a wispy ghoul.* He imagines a twenty-ton boulder dressed like Robert Smith from the Cure. A more useful distillation of the pair might be *Steadfast yet stealthy.*

At the same time, he knows on a deeper level that he is using the dice for tactile comfort and the cards for a quick nostalgia hit. It's all distraction, or dissociation in moments of great stress. Whatever you want to call it, he's both ashamed of himself and as helpless as an addict before his drug of choice.

He ignores the bank of eight monitors rising above his desk, as large and commanding as a departures/arrivals screen in an airport. The monitors are engineered to curve dramatically together as one. The effect, upon walking into his private office, is of a man sitting within the embrace of a screen. It looks like endless streams of data are one final contortion away from wrapping themselves entirely around Anton. He knows because employees have mentioned this with some trepidation, finding him in here at all hours, flipping cards and tossing dice and interacting with the fundamentals of his system, his company, his life's work. His assistant, Kevin, calls it *the womb*.

Steadfast, he thinks. *Stealthy.*

He tilts his neck from side to side, feels the *pop*, and rises from his chair. Lacuna headquarters is housed in floors eighty-one through eighty-four of a slender skyscraper that punches up through the stratosphere of Midtown East. His office's single window is a massive rectangle that affords Anton a panoramic view. It's a fine, clear morning in New York. Cloud shadows darken splotches of the East River. A barge slides underneath the Queensboro Bridge. Anton's eyes trace the span of the bridge to its thick stanchions on Roosevelt Island and beyond, his gaze sweeping east through Queens to hazy Long Island beyond the border of the city, interrupted only by the single office tower and the residential high-rises of Long Island City that loom over the water.

Basking in the warm distraction of turning back the clock, he traces 21st Street up to northern Astoria, where his parents raised him after immigrating from then-Czechoslovakia in the waning days of the Soviet bloc. The row house itself is too far away to pick out, though he can locate himself right in the heart of his old neighborhood, just south of the smokestacks that rise from the generating station.

Odd movement catches his eye. Astoria Park, that long green rectangle laid out along the water between the Hell Gate and RFK Bridges, seems to be pixelated. He rubs his eyes and gives it a hard stare. The park almost looks like it's shedding its skin, moving little pieces of itself around, grass and trees and leaves and dirt switching places in quick little movements. The lively image never coheres into the park he's looked at a thousand times. He figures it's a trick of the distance, some misty morning smog unfurling along the river, blurring his line of sight. He shifts his gaze to the row houses that stretch on and on, east of the park. He breathes deep and can almost smell his mother's smazeny cyr and the garlicky, lemony fish from the Greek restaurants on every other corner.

There is another timeline for Anton, a different flip of the cards. Perhaps like so many other first-generation immigrant children in his neighborhood, he continues to live at home through his twenties, taking summer trips to Prague to stay with aunts and uncles, ride the tram out to Prirodni Park to look over the city of his parents' birth, like he's doing right now over his own—

The knock on the door pulls him away from the window. He gathers himself, strides across the office, and opens it.

It's Kevin, his assistant, with a vaguely fried countenance and neat ponytail, looking like he just got back on the red-eye from Burning Man and has only halfway cleaned up for work. He gives Anton a nod.

"They're ready for you, sir."

"Thanks," Anton says. "I'll be right in."

Kevin gives a double nod, lingers for a moment, then retreats to his nook a few feet down the corridor. Anton shuts the door and goes to his walk-in closet. It's full of spare hoodies and shirts—some long-sleeved, some short. Some button-downs with collars, some with faded band logos. Immediately upon filing papers to establish Lacuna six years earlier, he'd dismissed the idea of a Steve Jobs–like sartorial affectation. Wearing the same thing every day is, frankly, weird as hell. Ever since the company's early days, when he started getting press and attracting VCs, he'd been self-conscious of being ranked among performatively quirky start-up founders. His solution is to never lean too heavily on one style. Some days he's sporting buttoned-up business casual like any other Midtown office worker, other days he's in cutoffs and a death-metal long-sleeve.

He squares up to the mirror. Today he's rocking a salmon-colored polo shirt, retro acid-washed jeans, and white high-top sneakers. It's an off-putting look, perfect for someone who just drew the Pit Colossus and the Insatiable Gnaw. With his shaved head and high cheekbones, he looks like one of those skinny Slavic dudes who work construction under the table and exude an air of vague menace. Another perspective might be that he looks like a dumb nerd. Well. It's not important. The outcome of this meeting is going to be the same no matter how he looks.

Anton shuts the closet door and squeezes in one final dose of distraction before he heads down the hall to the conference room. He ducks back inside the womb and checks his dashboard. Diagnostics run perpetually for Lacuna's thirty-seven beta-test sites, from mega-cities such as Shanghai and New Delhi to remote spits of land such as his proprietary R&D algorithm's last-minute addition: Bava Atoll in the middle of the Pacific.

He scans the screen, trying not to lose his shit thirty seconds before he goes to meet with the board. The Lacuna network is inconsistent, with full prolonged outages reported in twenty-three of the sites. Bava Atoll is spotty at best, verging on terrible connectivity.

The board members will be staring at this real-time data on their laptops when he enters the conference room. He shakes his head and turns to another screen: news from around the world, aggregated from social, mainstream, and independent media sources.

He frowns. An unfolding story's jumping to the top of the feed, trending hard. Some kind of disturbance in upstate New

York. Images cycle across the screen, organized by relevance. Mobilization of some three-letter agency or another. Humvees and weirder vehicles, DARPA shit everywhere.

There's another knock on the door. He exits the womb and opens it. Kevin again.

"They're getting antsy," his assistant says. "Willamina's threatening an early lunch."

"Sorry," Anton says. "I'm heading there now."

Kevin shoots him a lopsided grin. "Hey, man. I think it's a good look. You're a busy guy."

Anton steps out into the corridor and shuts the office door behind him. "I'm really just dicking around."

The conference room is named Jacob, after Jacob Esterly, the creator of Thaumaturgy: World's End. It boasts the opposite view from Anton's private office—a vista stretching across the Hudson to the North Jersey wastelands, all the way to MetLife Stadium. This view holds no nostalgic sway over Anton. He doesn't give it a second look as he pushes open the frosted-glass door and enters a realm bathed in the rich scent of espressos and pastries from Lacuna's boulangerie on the eighty-second floor. The company runs lean except for employee snacks, which are free and bountiful.

The table, a basic polymer slab, is laden with sparkling water in blue glass pitchers, carafes of coffee, trays of pain au chocolat and Greek yogurt. Lacuna's four other board members—Anton himself makes five—sit with laptops open and plates empty.

A woman in her late forties—Willamina Friedrich—rises and leans forward slightly with her fingertips tented on the table. Before joining Lacuna's board she'd been the US ambassador to Germany. She regards Anton with the imperious scrutiny of an old-money matriarch eyeing a wayward child just returned from shaming the family in some foreign port.

"Good morning, everybody," Anton says.

"It's practically lunchtime," Willamina says.

"That depends on what time you eat lunch," Anton points out.

A squat, bullet-headed man with a lotus flower tattoo snaking up his neck spins his laptop around so Anton can see the Lacuna dashboard on his screen. Twenty-three beta-test sites are flashing red. "The numbers continue to be shit. Connectivity levels like the fucking heyday of dial-up. What Lacuna represents, at this moment in time, is *regression* across the board. If you were an alien sent here to sabotage human progress from within, you might design something like your network."

Anton regards Brian Karcher as placidly as possible. Under the table, his leg bounces. Karcher's a fellow founder who's been through the IPO circus four times with his companies. He lives on a mountain in the wilds of western Canada, which he bought when everybody else was buying private islands. Anton has known him for a long time. In recent years his Ivy League libertarianism has darkened to a shade of sovereign citizen cosplay.

"Six years pissing away money on R and D," Karcher says. "And this is what we have to show for it. Fucking dial-up modem in Mom's basement shit."

"I don't have to tell you that we're in an *extremely* fortunate position." The soft-spoken man opposite Anton at the end of the table is Raj Goswami, former chairman of the law firm Benson Goswami Klinger. "The fact that Tencent's keeping their acquisition offer on the table after their due-diligence phase is nothing short of remarkable."

"This coffee tastes like compost," Willamina says, sitting back down. "Germans make a shockingly good cuppa." She looks at Karcher as if he'd asked about German coffee. "Especially in

Munich." Then she looks at Goswami. "Yes. Agreed. It's borderline reckless of them."

A smartly dressed woman to Karcher's left dabs at the corner
of her mouth with a napkin. Deandra Palantino, former executive vice president of the biotechnology conglomerate EnTech.
"Frankly, it's a concern. What do they see in these numbers that
we don't?"

It's Anton's turn to speak. *Pit Colossus and Insatiable Gnaw,* he
thinks. "Maybe," he begins, "they're not as numbers-obsessed
as we think they are. Maybe they see something inherent in the
tech. In the system itself."

"There's been the same potential since day one," Karcher says.
"It has no more *inherent* value now than it did six years ago. It's still
just an idea. We might as well be selling a scribble on a bar napkin.
I could take my nutsack public with a better valuation."

"We're not going public," Palantino says. "And now we'll
never have to. Thankfully."

"He knows that," Willamina says, pouring herself another
cup of compost coffee. "We all do." She looks at Anton. "Don't
we, Anton." It isn't a question.

Anton doesn't know what to do with his body. He is hyper-
conscious of the way he's sitting in his chair, and the way the
muscles in his face are tightening up. He feels like his whole
body is clenched like a fist. He longs to be back in the womb,
the amniotic sac of data and news feeds, his Thaumaturgy decks
arrayed in front of him.

"I think it's good we're all here," he says after a moment.
"We definitely have some things to talk about."

He scans the faces of the board members in the wake of such
noncommittal diplomacy. Willamina puts on an air of vague disgust. Goswami purses his lips. Palantino types something on her
laptop.

Karcher coughs into his napkin.

Anton once read a story about Mark Zuckerberg, in the early days of Facebook, being offered a billion dollars by Yahoo! to acquire the social network. He strolled into the board meeting and said something along the lines of, "This'll be a quick meeting, we're obviously not going to sell."

Anton wonders what Zuckerberg's stake in the company was at that point, if he held sway over the board by virtue of his votes. If this had been a mere three months ago, Anton would have been able to outvote the whole board with his 51 percent equity stake in Lacuna: essentially, six votes to their four. But with Lacuna's Series C round came an injection of a hundred million from Karcher himself. Anton had been in no position to turn down the cash, but it came with a price: increased equity for Karcher, downgrading Anton's position to 49 percent. He could no longer act unilaterally. The board, antagonized and incentivized by Karcher, can now essentially hold him hostage to get what they want.

And what they want, more than anything, is to sell Lacuna to the Chinese before they change their minds. Even Karcher's performative xenophobia is no match for an $850 million offer for thus-far-unproven and dicey tech.

Suddenly, it all makes sense: Pit Colossus and Insatiable Gnaw. He needs to barrel ahead with Zuckerberg's cocky, slightly robotic swagger, but at the same time he needs to send waves of eldritch finesse in Karcher's general direction. With the billionaire mountain dweller on his side, Anton can out-vote the rest of the board. The click in his mind, the slotting into place of these seemingly at-odds behaviors, happens with such satisfaction that he wonders if the cards had been somehow supplied by the proprietary algorithm. The same titanic computing power that selected Bava Atoll and the other beta-test sites. But that would mean it somehow gamed the dice roll itself, which is impossible.

"I think, fundamentally"—*shitty beginning*, he chides himself, switching to a less smug-asshole tone immediately—"that we're not quite on the same page about this deal." Mouths open. Goswami's head cocks. Karcher's lip curls. Anton jumps back in. "And that's okay! It's okay. If we were in lockstep all the time, that would defeat the purpose of this board entirely, right?" He steamrolls over his own words to indicate that any questions are for rhetorical purposes only. "So what I'm hoping to do today is to zoom out a little bit. Well, a lot. Because I think this all might just be a matter of perspective. I want to do a little thought experiment with you."

"Jesus Christ, he's trying to *A Time to Kill* us," Palantino says.

Anton blinks. He's ready to deal with interruptions, but this one trips him up. "Um," he says. "What?"

Palantino narrows her eyes. "*A Time to Kill.* The Grisham novel they turned into a movie in 1996."

"You know the *exact year* off the top of your head?" Karcher says.

"Oh yeah," Anton says, though he has no idea what she's talking about. Legal thrillers from the 1990s are so far off his radar as to not exist. Besides, he was four years old.

"Right," Goswami says. "There's the part at the end where Matthew McConaughey tells the jury to close their eyes, and he takes them through the whole terrible crime, and his oration is so powerful that some of them begin to weep."

"I'm going to weep if we don't adjourn for lunch," Willamina says.

"I can get Kevin to get you something from downstairs," Anton offers.

Willamina lifts up a croissant and lets it fall back down to the tray. "I'm talking about a proper *Mittagessen*."

"And I'm talking about fresh salmon, new potatoes, and

farm-to-table root vegetables from the biosphere," Anton says. *The biosphere* is his employees' nickname for the Lacuna-sponsored atrium, which is a veritable forest transported from Westchester County and replanted in thirty tons of topsoil, all of it encased in a gigantic glass enclosure that balloons out from the mezzanine level. Anton shoots a quick text to his assistant, asking for a couple of to-go containers full of the freshest stuff from the biosphere kitchen.

He imagines Kevin springing forth from his nook at the exact moment the text is received, stoked to ride the high-speed elevator down to his favorite place: the deciduous forest in the atrium. They even have wildlife, though nothing larger than rabbits.

"We appreciate the rhetorical journey you're about to take us on, Anton," Palantino says, "but the hard truth is staring us all in the face. And it's this: The Lacuna networks we've deployed have performed abysmally. The tech just isn't there. Our Series C round dries up in a matter of weeks. Maybe we squeeze out another month or two if we go scorched earth on staff, office space, et cetera. Despite all that, for some reason we can't *begin* to fathom, Tencent's bid is still on the table, when anyone else would be biding their time and raiding our corpse for spare organs."

"What I was saying before," Anton says, "about Tencent seeing something inherent in the system—that was clumsily expressed. I didn't mean to imply that you don't have the same foresight. But what I do think is, you've let yourselves become distracted by how everyone else does things. You're seasoned. I get it. Every one of you has way more experience than I do. You say things like *not my first rodeo* all the time."

"I do not say that," Goswami says. "Ever."

"Nor I," Willamina says. Palantino stares at her laptop screen.

Anton ignores them. He looks straight at Karcher. He's going to appeal to the man's fiercely independent streak—or at least the notion that he wants to be perceived as a maverick. "Everyone wants a product that works," Anton says. "I get that. Obviously I want that too. But what I mean by *how everybody else does things* is, there's all these other start-ups in our space, they go public with monster valuations or they don't, they get bought or they don't, they pivot to something safe or they crash and burn. There's a framework in place for all of that. You've all risen to various challenges, and conquered them, within that framework, right?"

"You speak of us like we're hamsters on a money wheel," Willamina says.

"Exactly!" Anton says with vehemence that surprises him. He tones it down. "Exactly. We all are. Every one of us that plays this game is a hamster on a wheel. We're all fortunate that we've managed to make that wheel work to our advantage, no matter where we come from." Now he looks pointedly at Karcher again—his alcoholic mother died when he was a kid and his father was in and out of prison.

"And so what you are getting at is, Lacuna, which I want to emphasize I do very much believe in, Anton," Goswami says softly, "will transcend this shabby late-capitalist...allegory of the cave, maybe?" He frowns like he doesn't quite know if the metaphor works, then shrugs like it doesn't really matter anyway.

"Not transcend, exactly, no," Anton says. He cedes some control back to the board every time he engages with one interjection or another, but the off-the-cuff rhythm has a spikiness to it that he likes. "I don't want to get too founder-y with my words here, guys," he says. "So let's simplify. Lacuna's not a product, not really. It's better. It's a proprietary technology. We're not just iterating on something else. We *are* the something else. We're unreplicatable. And that's more valuable than any product. Right? *We have no competition.*"

"The whole goddamn global networking system as we know it is our competition!" Karcher says. "And iterating on something that already exists is exactly what we're doing! There's no shame in it, Anton, but you gotta know when to fold 'em."

"Wrong!" Anton says. "Brian, I'm sorry, but you're just not seeing it. I don't mean competition on the"—he looks at Goswami—"shabby late-capitalist playing field. I'm talking about a monopoly on the future."

Karcher scowls. "The future of what?"

"Everything!" Anton is practically shouting now. "Amazon sold books, right? Because books were easy to ship. But that was never the endgame."

"Anton," Palantino says, settling back in her chair, crossing her legs. "This isn't 1996."

"*A Time to Kill* isn't coming to a theater near you," Karcher says.

She ignores him. "The Lacuna network moves data instantly without the need for cables, or satellites, or hardware of any sort. It's incredible. We've all been aligned on that since day one. But this simply isn't an Amazon situation."

"I understand what Lacuna means to you," Goswami says. *No you don't*, Anton thinks. "I know it's difficult to let go. But I agree with my esteemed colleague. It does not scale in the same way. Moving data is what it does, and, to be frank, right now it does not do it very well."

"I'll bite," Willamina asks, eyeing the door for Kevin with the biosphere lunch. "Let's say it *is* a monopoly on the future. What kind of a future is it? What's Lacuna's endgame?"

"It's far beyond a new network," Anton says, voicing this fever dream for the first time, ever, to the board. "Moving data, even eventual neural-net data, is the absolute beginning of the story." He closes his eyes. "I'm talking about a totally new organizing principle for the way we interact with everything, whether it's living or sentient or AI or just a regular old object. I'm talking about a new system of the world, with the old barriers smashed for good. I'm talking about building a web of the deepest connections since—"

"Holy shit!"

He opens his eyes and realizes instantly that it was weird to say all that stuff with his eyes closed. Palantino picks up a remote control and aims it at the massive flatscreen television on the wall behind Anton. He turns. The screen comes to life. A moment later, she casts her laptop to the TV. A local NY1 broadcast from Columbus Circle is on. The camera's pointed at the southwest corner of Central Park.

The trees just beyond the monument to Columbus are enveloped in clouds of insects. The camera sweeps across the edge of the park. A blur of motion turns all of the lush summer foliage into atomized snow. Meanwhile the trees are linked via clouds of small flitting dots that disintegrate, re-form, and stretch across empty space. Then the camera zooms. Bystanders cry out. A woman bursts through the miasma, rushing from the park, swatting madly at the air around her, spinning into a full pirouette before falling to the ground.

A cloud of bugs trails her from inside the park, extending like pulled taffy up one of the hundred paths that Anton has walked, mulling over some problem, oblivious to the city around him like so many other preoccupied Midtowners. Like a comet, the cloud grows in size to encircle the fallen woman's head. Onlookers rush to drag her away. The bugs scatter and come back together. People who ran in to help begin to swat the air. Anton is surprised by the crispness of the insects' organization, the thrust of their intent.

"Jesus fucking Christ," Karcher says.

"Is this something we should be concerned about?" Goswami says. "We're very close to the park."

"This is *Manhattan*," Willamina says. "We don't have to worry about locusts."

"Queens has them too," Anton says, connecting the events on TV to his earlier view across the river from his office window. The strange appearance of Astoria Park, as if the grass and trees were scrambled, out of focus. His parents still live in the house on 37th, which Anton bought for them a few years ago after they refused to live anywhere else because they have friends in the neighborhood.

He takes a deep breath and reels in his panic. "Is this an emergency?" he says, thinking out loud. "What even is this?"

There's no alarm going off, no building security storming in to oversee various protocols. Anton doesn't even know what those protocols would be. On the screen, the broadcast cuts to a different section of the park, shot from the Fifth Avenue side, somewhere in the east 70s. Just over the low wall that lines the cobblestone path at the edge of the trees, dense masses of insects seethe across trunks and branches. Suddenly the screen goes dark. The autofocus goes wild. It takes Anton a moment to realize that the camera lens is covered in bugs. Everyone in the conference room leans forward. Karcher is up out of his chair. The bugs vacate the lens, and a single insect hovers in the middle ground between the camera and the park. Autofocus pins the bug in place. It seems to hang in the air, vibrating with a soft energy. Big wings the color of a cockroach, wide head flanked by two red eye-globes.

It stares directly into the camera.

"Cicada," Willamina announces. Anton looks at her. "I grew up in Iowa," she says. "We had them one summer when I was a child."

"They appear every seventeen years, correct?" Goswami says.

"I lived in New York seventeen years ago," Anton says. "There were no cicadas then."

"Either way, cicadas are harmless." Karcher sits back down. "Just a nuisance for a few days is all. Nothing to freak out about." Karcher's defiant nonchalance grates on Anton. "But you watch, another lockdown's coming." He turns to Anton. "You were saying? Something about a new system of the world?"

"Um," Anton says. He thinks of his parents, taking one of their morning coffee strolls, venturing to the grocer's down by the Bohemian Beer Hall to get a day-old copy of *Mlada fronta DNES* and *iSport*. How often do they decide to keep going all the way to the park to stake out a bench and enjoy a nice, peaceful morning with the news from home? Anton has no idea. He's been so busy, they haven't caught up in weeks, and now they could be casualties of this abrupt infestation. An awful vision flashes of his mother lying face down on one of the paths that wind beneath the span of the Hell Gate Bridge while red-eyed unblinking insects crown her head...

"We're going to have to pick this back up another time," Anton says, rising from his seat.

Karcher scoffs. "Tencent's not gonna wait around forever while we sit here with our dicks in our hands."

"Your genital obsessions are somewhat intrusive," Goswami says. "And inappropriate for this environment. I should have told you that years ago."

"We don't have to do the brutal-honesty-before-the-plane-goes-down thing from *Almost Famous*," Palantino says. "Nobody's dying."

"*They* might be!" Willamina says, pointing at the screen.

"None of *us* are dying," Palantino clarifies. "And besides, Brian's right—cicadas are totally harmless. So probably nobody out there is dying either." She casts an internet search to the TV—basic info about cicadas. Anton scans the words on the screen. "They don't bite, they don't sting." Palantino says. "They just kind of hang out, and then go away for seventeen more years."

"Can you go back to the news feed?" Anton says. Palantino navigates. A second later Central Park from a different vantage point fills the screen: Harlem, looking south. An unbroken row of trees, the brick-and cobblestone path, a vintage gas lamp nodding to the neighborhood's history, a row of parked cars. And weaving through all of it, amoebic shapes of flitting insects, flattening into curtains, half opaque like muslin, then stretching into ribbons from tree to tree. Anton turns up the volume.

A drone and a shriek harmonize, high and low tones settling into a mid-range frequency. Gooseflesh breaks out across Anton's body. Their collective noise ought to be an insular communication, indifferent to everything else. But right now he shivers with the recognition of a singular purpose in its ceaseless emittance.

He's heard echoes of this before. Or more accurately, *seen* echoes in Lacuna's network.

"Jesus!" Karcher shouts over the din.

Anton turns down the volume and tosses the remote on the table. He picks up his phone and dials his father. The call goes straight to voicemail. He tries his mother. Same thing. "I have to go see about my parents."

"You can't go out there," Willamina cautions.

"I agree," Goswami says. "There's no point in going anywhere. There will be traffic jams and subway delays, if the trains are running at all. We're better off where we are. We can monitor the situation from up here."

Karcher snorts. "*Situation.* There's being cautious, and then there's just being *soft*. We're talking about *cicadas* here." He stands up. "Call me when you people live with mountain lions."

"You don't live *with* mountain lions," Palantino says, "you live in a walled fortress *on* a mountain where mountain lions *used* to live until your team hunted them all down."

Karcher shoots her a sharp look. "I shot them myself. Some of them."

"From a helicopter," Goswami points out.

Willamina looks at Anton. "Does this building have a helipad?"

Anton shakes his head. "It does not."

He glances at the faces around the table. A shudder of unreality nearly forces him back down into his chair. The four Lacuna board members, people whose fates are intimately woven with his own, but whom he has no special fondness for or relationship with outside of this one context. He wonders if this is how people felt on 9/11, watching the towers come down with classmates and colleagues, people they wouldn't ordinarily seek out in a crisis.

Except, he tells himself, this is hardly 9/11. The city isn't under *attack*, it's just hosting a sudden infestation. A very bizarre one, involving bugs that don't belong in dense urban spaces—yet here they are, millions of them.

Swarming people on sight.

He watches as Goswami and Palantino huddle, speaking urgently in hushed tones. Willamina goes to the window and looks out across the city.

"Well," Karcher says, "that's it for me."

He pops his laptop into a shoulder bag with a sigil of what Anton assumes to be some esoteric anarcho-capitalist society. He heads for the door, then stops to regard Anton. Something like sympathy softens his face.

"Look, man," he says. "I get it. I've been there before, with MicroShare. It was my baby, and I wanted to coddle it and let it suckle my teats forever. But you know what? Once I let it go I realized that it wasn't just slurping up my milk, it was draining my lifeblood right along with it. As soon as it sold—I'm talking the very second—I felt like I'd taken a great big monster shit.

Just dropped a fat nasty. You know?" He lays a heavy hand on Anton's shoulder. "It's noble, what you're doing. You got some real Viking cojones. I respect it, I really do. But it's over, my friend. You don't have the votes. What you *will* have, very soon, is forty-nine percent of a whole assload of shekels. So keep your head up for a few more days and you'll be drowning in pussy." He looks Anton up and down. "Or dick. Whatever. I'm out."

Karcher puts out a hand to stiff-arm the conference room door, then pulls back, startled, as the door swings open from the hallway side.

"Kevin," Anton says, moving to take from his assistant a pair of oversize brown bags clutched against his scrawny chest, hiding most of his face. The rich, earthy scent of cooked carrots and garlic wafts into the room. Willamina turns and rubs her hands together, mantis-like.

"Did you see what's going on out there while you were downstairs?"

Anton tries to wrap his arms around one of the bags. Kevin just stands there silently. A vintage button pinned to the strap of his backpack says I LIKE IKE, the words emblazoned above a grinning, black-and-white Eisenhower.

"Kevin?"

Anton peers at his assistant's glazed and distant eyes.

"You okay?"

Kevin lets out a low moan. Then he collapses. Anton abandons the bags to try to catch his assistant. Compostable containers spill biosphere vegetables in savory sauces out across the conference room floor. Willamina cries out.

Kevin and Anton are locked in an embrace. Anton struggles for a moment, then lays his assistant gently down on the floor. Kevin's backpack, still slung over one shoulder, rests on its side. The clammy funk coming off the body makes Anton's head swim. Kevin tries to speak. A thin, hoarse cry is all that comes out. Anton marvels at the fact that Kevin was able to get all the way back up here with the food in this condition.

"What happened to you, buddy?" Anton says, down on one knee. He's never called Kevin *buddy* in his life. He struggles to stay in the moment. Everything is happening too fast. He feels like he's still giving his big rousing speech, one turn of phrase stuck like a splinter in his mind. *A new system of the world.* He shakes it off, locates himself in the here and now.

Kevin's lips move with alarming quickness. Weird murmurs escape. His eyeballs slide back and forth. Strands of his long, straw-colored hair fray his neat ponytail. An almost milky sourness comes off him.

Karcher lowers himself down and nudges Anton out of the way. He interlaces his fingers and slams his palm down on Kevin's sternum. His sleeves slide up his forearms, revealing tattoos like peeling flesh, a Terminator-esque steel endoskeleton inked beneath.

"I don't think you're doing it right," Anton says.

"Nobody else was doing shit," Karcher says, pressing down and releasing. Kevin's back arches. His mouth emits a halting, staccato gasp. Next to him, some kind of plum-colored sauce soaks into the carpet.

"Wait!" Anton's hand darts out and halts Karcher's chest compressions. "He's trying to say something."

Kevin's mouth curls into what looks like the barest hint of a smile, stifled laughter at some private joke.

"We're right here," Anton says loudly, like he's trying to reach a coma patient. The absurdity of the *we* hits him right away: like Kevin gives a shit about being surrounded by Lacuna's board members. Anton wonders who among Lacuna's staff Kevin counts as friends. He wishes he knew. "What are you trying to say?"

Anton leans in. Kevin's mouth opens and his body retches with a guttural expulsion. Spittle hits Anton's ear. Something brushes against the side of his face. At the same time, Karcher jumps to his feet with a shrill yelp. Commotion sweeps through the room at Anton's back. He swats at his cheek, hitting nothing but stubbly skin. Then it catches his eye: an object in flight, weaving a lazy pattern through the room. Several things dawn on him in quick succession.

It's not an object, it's a bug.

A cicada.

And it just came flying out of Kevin's mouth.

Willamina ducks as the cicada zips toward the window, bashes into the glass, then turns around. The bug performs a complex looping dive and skims along the tabletop, bumping into the conference call phone-speaker that nobody ever knows how to use.

THWACK.

Goswami's molded plastic laptop case comes down hard. He waits a moment, grinding it down into the table. Cautiously, he lifts it up. The cicada is stuck to the bottom of the case, a ragged mess of limbs and goop.

"I'm calling nine one one," Palantino announces. She puts her phone to her ear and retreats to the corner of the room.

"Okay," Anton says. "Good." He stands up. Kevin's condition is unchanged. Eyes closed, clammy pallor, lips moving in some uncanny whisper. He looks around the room at a tableau of fear and hesitation. Goswami inspecting the smashed bug with interest, Palantino making demands of the emergency operator, Willamina huddled beneath the window, and Karcher standing with his hands folded atop his head, looking stunned.

Anton tries to imagine what happened, eighty-four floors below. He pictures Kevin exiting the elevator at the mezzanine, descending the stairs by the indoor waterfall, touching down in the grassland studded with chicken coops and rabbit hutches. Then he hustles across the atrium biosphere, shouldering his boxy Swedish backpack, waving to scurrying assistants from various other companies. He picks up the lunch order from the open kitchen that's a cross section of a barn. Then, on the way back up to the elevator bank, he's suddenly beset by a cloud of flying insects.

Oh well, Kevin thinks, *no big deal, there's new species introduced to the atrium every month or so.* He swats them away—persistent fuckers!—when one of them flies *directly into his mouth.* It's gross, a bunch of scuttling legs halfway down his throat. He gets to the elevator, hacking up a lung. Surely this goddamn thing'll come up any minute. Surely it can't actively be trying to *stay in his mouth.* The elevator whisks him back up to eighty-four. He's past the point of choking now, but the bug is definitely still lodged in his throat. His vision gets hazy. He makes it to the conference room door, still holding the food bags...

"They're in the building," Anton announces. "The cicadas." In the corner, Palantino lowers her phone.

Karcher shakes his head. "He must've gone outside." He looks at Anton hopefully. "For the food."

"No," Anton says. "That's from our little farm downstairs."

"Fucking stupid fake-woke bullshit," Karcher says. "Trying to stick a goddamn farm in the middle of a Manhattan office building so the good little part-time socialists still mooching off Daddy for their apartments can pretend they're not in this game to make a pile of money like the rest of us." He takes a breath. "Oh shit. Oh *shit.* Of course. That's actually hilarious. They *want* people to eat bugs! It's been their plan for years." He laughs like he can't believe the audacity. "They're shoving it right in our fucking faces. *You'll own nothing and be happy.* Fucking world monetary fund..." He shakes his head. "It's the whole goddamn reason I live on a mountain—to be fully, epically removed from their control. And now the *one time* I'm in New York, they pull the trigger on their whole sick plan. Unbelievable."

"Yes, Brian," Palantino says, "this whole thing was orchestrated to ruin *your* day, specifically."

Karcher turns back to Anton. "You know what? Fuck the Chinese Communist Party. We're not selling. Congratulations, kid. You got the votes. It's still your baby to suckle."

"*Wean*," Goswami says.

Anton swallows. "I have to talk to my people."

There are hundreds of engineers, IT teams, developers, system architects, UX designers, spread across floors eighty-one through eighty-four. Someone from Leadership needs to take a firm, reassuring hand. Speaking of Leadership, the other C-suite offices are up here on eighty-four—the COO is on the West Coast for the week, but the CFO, Karen Chen, should be in her office, just down the hall. And a couple of VPs should be kicking around too. He needs to leave the board members to their own devices, assemble his people, see to the well-being of his staff. History will judge him for how he behaves. The thought makes him want to curl up in his childhood bed and pore over his Thaumaturgy cards under the blanket with a flashlight, letting their illustrations take him far away from everything.

Anton thinks of his parents across the river. All the other old people on his block, the Veselys next door with their three-legged dog, the frightful ex-secret-policeman who haunts the bodega.

Astoria Park, swarming with cicadas.

As if they all suddenly clocked the intensity of the moment, all four board members make phone calls. Cars are ordered, drivers commandeered.

"Hey!" Anton glances at Kevin on the floor, then turns to Palantino. "What did nine one one say?"

She holds up a finger and yells at someone on the other end of her call.

Thunk.

An unfamiliar sound bounces around the conference room. *Thunk. Thunkthunkthunkthunk.* A series of low, percussive taps, every few seconds at first, then with the increased urgency of popcorn in the microwave.

Karcher lowers the phone from his ear. "What the hell is that?"

Anton looks at the window. Nothing but blank sky. He looks at the table. Pastries and cold coffee and a single flattened cicada on the back of a laptop case. He glances up at the square A/C vent, neatly hidden among the grid of teak ceiling tiles. He goes over and stands beneath it. The building's climate control is whisper-quiet at all times. The noises are definitely coming from the vent.

Thunk. Thunk. Thunkthunkthunk.

A pitter-patter like tiny feet on a rooftop.

The duct is filling up with cicadas. There must be thousands of them rising from the soil of the atrium, flying up through the guts of the massive HVAC system. An infection in the building's veins.

The drone comes on all at once: a monotonous whine leaking into the room, a reprise of the horrible sound on the news broadcast. Suddenly it's all around them.

Anton lowers his eyes to the board members. "We have to get out of here. Now."

"Fuck yes we do," Karcher says. He pockets his phone, opens the door, and heads out into the hall without another word.

Anton kneels down, slips one arm under Kevin's upper back and the other behind his knees, and straightens up slowly.

Willamina screams. Anton's eyes flick to the ceiling vent. Cicadas begin to poke through. A gathering of small red eyes emerges from between the slats. Forelegs waver. Translucent wings follow.

Kevin is a wisp of a person, but Anton still struggles to lift him up. He has memberships at every gym in the city and has never been to any of them. Cicadas seem to dangle from the vent as if on a rope made of themselves. The rope whips to the side, propelling lone cicadas across the table. Goswami lifts his laptop case and swings it wildly at the advancing insects. Palantino covers her face. Willamina curls into a ball on the floor.

Fuck fuck fuck fuck.

"Come on!" Anton turns with Kevin in his arms, hip-checks the conference room door, and staggers out into the hall. He doesn't wait to see if anyone follows him. Kevin's limp frame and backpack hang from his arms. Brian Karcher is nowhere to be seen. This corridor houses warrens of assistants, conference rooms, a yoga studio, breastfeeding space, a row of nap pods. The art on the walls bends toward abstraction. Some doors are open, others closed. A few employees are gathered in groups of two or three, looking at phone screens. It's all oddly hushed. The drone, a ceaseless hum, throbs at the edge of his perception. A woman Anton recognizes as his COO's assistant, Carrie, spots Anton and Kevin and comes rushing over.

"Everybody evacuate!" Anton calls down the corridor. "This isn't a joke!"

Carrie changes course and begins speed-walking toward the elevator bank at the opposite end of the hall, gathering fellow employees along the way. Some of them look back at Anton. Some of them do not.

Palantino appears at Anton's side. Goswami rushes past, jostling Kevin's leg. Willamina takes off her high heels and runs by on tiptoes. Palantino trains her eyes on Kevin, then turns to Anton.

"Maybe we should stay here," she says in a low voice, like she's come up with a secret survival plan she doesn't want the others to hear.

"You think it's better in here than out there?"

"It's chaos either way. In here I think we'll have more control."

"But we'll be trapped in confined spaces."

She lowers her voice even more. "So we barricade ourselves in your office. Seal the vents. Wait it out."

"I have to talk to my people." But he makes no attempt to move. Perhaps the biotech EVP is right. He follows her gaze back up the hall to the conference room door.

Cicadas darken the glass in rippling waves of color and movement. It's like someone upended a rug to bash it against the door. The drone intensifies, settling at the base of his skull. The back of his head feels warm.

His shoulders and upper arms are beginning to go numb. He doesn't know how much longer he can lift Kevin on his own.

There's a pair of security guards around somewhere, mainly to usher people out of the office the moment they quit or get fired. They're nowhere to be seen at the moment.

Cicadas find the seam between the conference room door and the wall. There's a quarter-inch gap to allow the glass pane to swing open both ways. A steady stream of bugs floats out into the corridor.

"Shit." Anton and Palantino move toward the elevators, where the gaggle of assistants waits while Carrie mashes the DOWN button.

"Stairs!" someone calls out.

"We're on the eighty-fourth floor!" someone replies.

Two things happen at once. The building alarm goes off, a shrill klaxon Anton recognizes from the twice-yearly fire drills. At the same time, a door halfway down the hall swings open. Lacuna CFO Karen Chen pops out like a pinball, caroms off the opposite wall, and trips over her feet. A dark mass of cicadas trails her, then orbits her head with ferocious energy. They move in concert, a braided symphony that's almost beautiful in its careful execution. Anton can't tell if this pattern is being woven by instinct or by an elevated consciousness.

He sets Kevin down and rushes toward the CFO as she curls up, shielding her face with her hands, shrieking.

"Oh, fuck this!" Palantino says, and she's gone, past the elevators, around the corner.

Anton hits the floor with a cry of frustration as he swipes at the storm of bugs. They displace, careen away, re-form. Karen Chen's small body writhes. The back of her hand lashes out and catches Anton in the mouth. He tastes blood. Cicadas split off from the main group to wreathe his head. The noise, this close, makes his inner ears tingle. Another door bursts open and a big older man—Jerry from IT, Anton thinks—spins slowly out into the hallway, waving his arms at a dreamy half speed like a burning man already fading from smoke inhalation. He crumples to the floor, clutching his throat, brought low by a crown of insects. Anton protects his own head from the onslaught. Next to him on the floor, Karen Chen's cries turn to gurgles. Anton meets her bulging eyes and reads astonishment and mortal terror. He can only watch, stunned, as cicadas slip gently, one after another, past her parted lips and down her throat. Just last week they had shared a rare drink together at Malfi's, down the block from the office. Karen had opened up to him about her IVF treatments, her journey to becoming a single mother by choice at age forty-six.

Fire alarms, set high up in the walls, pop like flashbulbs. The cicadas press their relentless attack upon his own body and face. He keeps his mouth shut tight, lips clamped together. He tries to ignore the dreadful sensation of tiny jointed legs skittering across his flesh. There's nothing more he can do for Karen Chen. She's almost completely covered, blanketed in a living sheet of bugs. He scrapes and claws at his face as he scrambles to his feet. Hysterical screams come from every direction. The klaxons blare. At the other end of the corridor the elevator finally dings.

Anton fights the urge to scream as a cicada scrapes against his left eyeball. His vision blurs. He captures the bug in his fist and squeezes until wet innards sluice between his fingers. *Elevators*, he thinks. He has to get out of the building. The fleeting notion that he would be capable of captaining this ship, of selflessly herding his people to safety in total disregard for his own life, evaporates when the elevator doors slide open.

One of the blue-uniformed security guards flies from the elevator as if shoved from behind and falls to his knees. A deluge of cicadas at his back pours over him like water from a broken dam, obscuring him completely, engulfing Carrie and the rest of the employees waiting to board the elevators. Anton watches the insects race up the corridor. Something like despair roots him in place. Is this how it will end? In this complete and utter absurdity?

He wonders at all the others who have met their ends in catastrophes so sudden and unexpected as to rip sanity from its moorings. There is a Thaumaturgy card for this, of course: the Continuum Trident, a wrench in the gears of existence.

How strange that everything he's built will soon become meaningless! A final morning spent digging in his heels, hoping for a miracle that would allow him to continue to evolve his grand vision. And for what?

He might as well have stayed forever a boy, flashlight and deck of cards beneath the sheets, parents snoring in the next room.

He clamps a hand over his mouth. He believes the bugs clinging to his face are using their forelegs to *pry open his lips*. His entire body feels poisoned by its own nerve endings. Disgust nearly stops his heart.

Some lizard-brain survival instinct forces him back down the hall toward the conference room. It's like fighting his way through one of those nor'easters that blow through the city from time to time. Cicadas pelt him like hailstones. His eyes burn. Palantino's idea of taking refuge in his private office surfaces like a beacon. The suite is just at the end of the hall, beyond the conference room.

As he fights his way past his assistant, still stretched out on the floor, he reaches down, grips Kevin's wrists, and drags him along, backpack sliding after him. Cicadas hang off Kevin's body and swish along the floor like the train of a wedding dress. A cicada breaches his mouth, struggles past his lips. His office door is ten feet away. How good it would feel to close his eyes and clench his fists and scream. He parts his teeth—just slightly—and bites down. The crunch nearly makes him vomit. Then he spits out two halves of a dead cicada. A curious taste lingers in his mouth.

At the door to his office, he lets one of Kevin's arms drop to punch in the code on the keypad: 2113. Bugs slam against the door, right in front of his eyes. There will be no getting inside his office without letting some of the insects in with him. He swipes away as many as he can. A pair of cicadas squirm up into his nostrils. He pinches their heads inside his nose and their corpses fall away, leaving brittle chitins behind, tickling his nose hairs. He pulls open the door and with a final surge of manic energy yanks Kevin inside. A cloud of cicadas clings to him. He slams the door and the locks engage.

First, he rushes over to his desk. The womb's curved screens have dimmed in his absence. The cards lie face up: the Pit Colossus and the Insatiable Gnaw. He opens a drawer and grabs an old roll of packing tape. He pulls his desk chair across the floor and positions it beneath the office's A/C vent. Working quickly, he climbs up and seals the vent as best he can.

It will hold until he figures out what to do next. From this vantage point on the chair, he surveys the room. He estimates roughly two dozen cicadas followed him inside. Their drone is thin and ragged.

He's going to have to kill them one by one.

14

FLUKER'S BLUFF, LOUISIANA

Corpses litter the woodlands and the low rolling hills, bodies contorted in the abrupt manner of the dead. The open grave spans thirty-seven acres of unspoiled countryside that dips eastward to the banks of a stagnant marsh where purple loosestrife grows unchecked. A damp thickness seems strung between the cypress trees, dangling like invisible strands of kudzu, laying humid air down across the bodies. Odors of decay rise and mingle like swamp gas.

Dr. Rebecca Perez leads half a dozen masked summer-program students down a winding path, slick with churned-up muck the consistency of the organic almond butter she spreads on her toast. The silent kids—they're always silent on their first visit to the Body Farm—troop past the old-growth tupelos to the southern edge of the marsh proper. A boy walking just behind her lets out a gasp. There's a body lying face down across the path, half wrapped in a blue tarp that covers most of its bloated midsection.

Rebecca's stomach rumbles—she skipped lunch to get the class out here before the storm hits. She pulls a chocolate and

pretzel protein bar from her pocket and pauses to unwrap it, taking a step back so no crumbs drop on the body's exposed femur,
which juts from a wet-looking thigh the color of a rotten apple
with dark mushy spots. Spurts of vegetation grow tentatively up
through the exposed bone.

She turns to the students, brandishing her snack. "I realize
I'm playing into the cliché of the pathologist eating during a
situation that normal people find particularly revolting. The difference is, I'm not a pathologist, I'm a forensic entomologist, and
I would venture to say that none of you are normal people, or
at the very least your time among the normal is waning." She
takes a bite, chews, swallows. "But self-parody is self-parody,
and I suppose I'm not exempt. Does anybody have something to
drink?"

One of the students raises her hand. "I have a diet vitamin
water."

"Erin Jacoby. Lifesaver."

The student hesitates. Her eyes flick to the corpse. "Like,
now? Or..."

"Yes please." Rebecca scarfs down the rest of the protein
bar, folds the wrapper into a tiny rectangle, and slides it into the
watch pocket of her jeans.

Erin digs in her slender backpack then hands over a plastic
bottle. "It's half drunk."

"Dragon fruit. My third favorite. Thank you." Rebecca
accepts the drink it and gulps it down. "I'm going to need to
finish this," she tells Erin. "For science."

"Oh. Okay."

A moment later, she returns the empty bottle to Erin.

"This guy's been dead awhile," another student says, his
shoulder-length dreadlocks tied neatly back. He crouches down
next to the body, rests his elbows on his thighs like a catcher, and
eyes the corpse. There's always one or two students compelled

from day one to demonstrate how comfortable they are with the harsh and unsightly realities of death.

Rebecca figures this boy has a not-insignificant chance of being the first student to puke. The Body Farm is a stunningly quick route to curing people of their need to show off for their peers.

"Before this semester ends," she says, pivoting off the boy's comment, "all of you will be able to tell me just how long *awhile* is for this subject with a high degree of probability. There will be a transformation in your mind, during which you will come to see decaying corpses first and foremost as *clocks*, insofar as anything that changes with time can be considered one. But for now, Jason"—she looks pointedly at the student who is forcing himself to stare at the graying flesh that clings to the upper femur, where gristly cartilage hugs the knee—"this guy is not our guy."

Jason stands up, somewhat gratefully, and moves away from the body.

"I don't know if I'll ever be able to see a human being as a *clock*," mutters a third student, a boy of gentle mannerisms and a winning smile. Rebecca marks him as one of the summer-program Empaths. Not so much grossed out by the nuances of decay itself, but queasy at the unshakable notion that this was recently a person. It's essentially dorm room philosophy: *This rotten pile of flesh and bone once had hopes and dreams and thoughts and memories no more or less valid than mine.* To keep from alienating the Empath Faction, Rebecca finds it helpful to recall her earliest days on the Farm, when she was an anxious grad student.

She meets the boy's big, searching eyes. "That's okay," she says. "There's no rush to change your perceptions about anything at all. From an academic standpoint we're really just here to see what the bugs do, and you can place as much or as little weight upon other aspects of this experience as you're comfortable with." She sweeps her gaze across the small group, then raises her eyes to the sky. "There's a storm coming, and it looks like it's going to be bigger than our daily afternoon shower down here in the basin. So I'll dispense with the going-into-battle speech and just assume you're already so highly motivated that your burgeoning obsession with maggots is having adverse effects on your personal life and relationships." She makes a show of looking around. "Anybody? Not yet? Okay. Just a sneak preview of what you're in for in this line of work, then. Onward."

She turns and leads them up a narrow path through the neck-high loosestrife, stalks exploding with flowering stems like bright-violet cattails. Beautiful and invasive. Her face prickles with sweat. It's a triple threat out here—Louisiana air in June, in a literal swamp, just before a rainstorm. Mud sucks at the soles of her navy waders. A cloud of mosquitoes hazes the air above the brackish water. Despite downing half of Erin's vitamin water, Rebecca's parched.

Dare you to drink swamp water!

The voice chimes, lilting and hollow, across the back of her skull, from one ear to the other, and vanishes like a whisper on the wind.

'Not now,' she answers silently. 'I'm with a class.'

The voice giggles. *Diarrhea city.*

'It only looks stagnant down here. It's actually fed by the river. You'd have a fifty–fifty shot.'

Remember that time we—

'Mari, I'm busy. Talk later.'

The voice goes silent. There is petulance in its retreat. A chorus of slaps come from the students as they swat the backs of their necks and foreheads.

"We're almost there," she assures them without turning around. As if *there* is an air-conditioned suite and not more mosquito-infested swampland. A low metal cage of tightly woven chain link comes into view, just beyond the path, in the shadow of a stately cypress. Inside the cage is the body of a middle-aged white woman, skin the color of spoiled haddock, unclothed and minus a tarp. She's lying on her back, professionally placed, as if on a slab in a morgue. No attempt has been made to mimic the splayed legs and flung-out arms of the others. The cage has protected the corpse from larger predators and scavengers. Anyway, Rebecca knows this one's the freshest body on the Farm. She personally supervised its intake and placement.

Opiate overdose from somewhere in St. Tammany Parish. No visible wounds. Some professors prefer the trial-by-fire of a gaping shotgun blast or a lacerated torso. Dr. Halbert once launched his summer students straight into a sepsis case, infested with hundreds of third-stage larvae—so many maggots excreting into the massive wound that the air reeked of ammonia.

Rebecca believes that a quieter, more balanced start is best. You can always escalate to more complex cases, but you can't wipe your students' minds, make them unsee their first up-close-and-personal examination of the dead. She's not trying to weed people out on the first day of fieldwork. There will be natural attrition over time. She finds her colleagues who favor that sink-or-swim approach a bit sadistic.

"All right," she says, turning to face her students, who shuffle around and gather in a loose semicircle a few feet from the caged body. The faintest whisper of laughter brushes against the back of her mind. Mari's making an odd sound today—a kind of clicking, droning ululation at odds with her usual girlish lilt. Rebecca ignores it. As she begins to speak, her attention flows smoothly from Erin, to Jason, to the Empath, to the others. She is inclusive and egalitarian. Even as the summer program advances and favorites naturally emerge among her class, she will keep her body language and intonation in check so as not to clue anyone in on her preferences. There are intangibles to teaching that, counterintuitively, can't be taught.

"Consider this the preamble to the start of today's fieldwork, a sort of commentary on the lesson itself. I'm letting you in on the framework here because I don't want there to be any surprises. First and foremost, I want to stress that any reaction you may have is a valid one and nothing to be ashamed of. Physiological reactions are dependent upon so many personal factors that they don't mean anything in terms of evaluating your ability to do this work long-term. We all start somewhere. I'm not scrutinizing your behavior out here. I won't be hard on you about anything, unless I find out you're being too hard on yourselves for something you can't control. It's like a gag reflex." She pauses and searches their faces, waiting an extra beat for the more gutter-minded to suppress a guilty little grin. "However, since the first rule of crime scene etiquette is to remember that other scientists will have to conduct their own exams, so *do not destroy evidence*, I will ask that if you do have to vomit, kindly step away. The closer to the water, the better." Another beat. The steeling of resolve settles across their faces. Arms folded, weight shifted. "The first thing I'm going to do is lift the cage and set it to the side. Once our subject is exposed, we have officially arrived at our crime scene and it will be treated as such until the cage comes back down. Understood?"

Everyone nods.

"I'm going to perform as I would if I were the forensic entomologist called in to the scene. It will be more formal and painstaking than the work we've done so far this semester with our experimental animal carcasses." The Empath winces at some memory of the decomposing possum in the fenced-off area behind the lab. "It may even seem borderline theatrical. This is so we can use our time back in the lab to break down the methodology I'm going to display out here. If I am overly pedantic, it's not because I doubt your ability to understand; it's because the more you see the general shape of this process in action, the more ingrained it will be, and the more solidified your basis for discovery. I know you've heard me say this a million times in class, but in forensic entomology, it's what you *don't* expect to find that is often the most revealing."

While her students continue to nod in sober agreement, their eyes flick back and forth from her face to the corpse.

She bends to lace her fingers into the chain link atop the cage—

—and there's Mari's weird little noise again, stuck fast between her ears.

There's something familiar about it, but she can't place it. Even in life her sister was a mimic artist, punctuating their little spats with imitations of the whippoorwills that haunted the grounds of the compound where they grew up.

'Mari, stop.'

No reply. The droning buzz lingers for a moment, then goes quiet. Rebecca lifts the cage and leans it against the trunk of the overhanging cypress.

"We're already masked up, but you don't want to enter a crime scene without these." She pulls on a pair of blue rubber gloves. "This is one of the overly pedantic parts."

A few chuckles from the students.

"Chances are good that if you've been called to the scene, the pathologist is the one who did the calling, because they identified some way to apply insect biology to the investigation. So you want to ask them before you do anything: *Is there anything here at the scene you don't want me to touch?* Cops'll trample all over everything, and there's not much we can do about it after the fact. But there's an understanding among forensic scientists—or at least, we should do our best to cultivate one. Like so."

She turns her attention to Erin, her hydration savior.

"Dr. Jacoby, is there anything here at the crime scene that you don't want me to handle?"

"Oh," Erin says, standing up very straight. "Um, no, Dr. Perez. You can do whatever."

Rebecca smiles so that her mask crinkles and the smile is conveyed. "In that case, I'll begin."

She unslings the black satchel from over her shoulder and sets it on the ground. Then she produces a device the size of a small remote control that curves and narrows to a rubber nib at one end.

"First we need to establish the temperature of our body. Ideally, this is taken rectally. However, since this body is lying on its back, and we don't want to disturb it at this stage, we're off the hook for that little operation." She holds up the device. "This is our tympanic thermometer. Which goes?"

"In the ear," say most of the students. She suspects that Jason and the Empath simply moved their mouths, like the men sheepishly pretending to sing hymns in her father's church.

"It's going to be eighty-four degrees," says a voice from the edge of the class's semicircle. Rebecca looks up. The student, Ji-un, keeps her eyes on her phone. She clearly meant to say it quietly to Jason at her side. She shuffles her feet.

"Is that the ambient air temperature currently?" Rebecca asks.

"Yes," Ji-un says, hurriedly pocketing the phone. "Seventy-nine percent humidity."

Rebecca kneels down and places her hand gently on the corpse's forehead. Even through her glove she can feel that peculiar combination of rigor and swampy weather working its alchemy on the skin. Unreal to the touch—inhuman and, yes, *waxy*, that old chestnut—without the meat-locker chill of the indoor dead. Rebecca notes the first-stage eggs at the corners of the mouth and eyes. A few clusters clinging to the rims of the nostrils. Tiny off-white pellets that always remind her of the gel bits in some hellish boba drink. She inserts the nib of the thermometer into the corpse's ear canal and waits for the beep.

Bzzz!

Mari zaps her brain with that goddamn sound. Extra keyed up today, irritated at the lack of attention.

'Stop,' she says firmly and silently.

Mari heaves a sigh, which basks Rebecca's mind in a warm wind. *That's not me, dummy.*

The thermometer beeps. She removes the nib and checks the LED readout.

"Eighty-four degrees," she says. "Body temperature aligned with ambient temperature. I understand why that seemed obvious out here, in the infernal heat, but when you arrive at a crime scene, you have to be an empty vessel. You're not trying to impress anybody with what you can glean at first glance, you're gathering data to draw conclusions from. What if this body had been dumped from elsewhere a short time ago? Or kept in a freezer for a week?"

She glances at Ji-un—pointedly but without reproach. "Leave the snap judgments and assumptions to the cops. Trust me, you'll hear enough of them."

Rebecca replaces the thermometer in her satchel and removes a collapsible plastic container. She sets it down and slides a panel forward. The container fans out into a series of connected trays. She indicates a set of evidence collection tools.

"Forceps, plastic spoons, tiny brushes. There are degrees of gentleness required, depending on your specimens."

A thunderclap punctuates her remarks. She glances up at the sky. A boiling mass of lint-colored clouds pushes humidity down like hot water in a French press. The edges of her mask are damp.

She looks at her students and beckons them closer. "Don't be shy."

They shuffle toward the body and lean in as close as they can. Jason kneels down next to it. She doesn't encourage the others to do the same. They're close enough to see her select the tiny paintbrush from the set of tools. She uses the dry bristles as a pointer to indicate the eggs clustered around the corpse's cracked lips.

"After we've established temperature, it's time for the main event—specimen collection. Our female flies have detected this corpse, which they can do from a great distance thanks to their attraction to the smell of decomposition, and determined that it's a worthy place to lay their eggs. Now, since we know our girls are quite discriminating, they won't lay their eggs in any old place on the body. They'll seek out the charm and comfort of *wounds*, first and foremost. But since, as far as we can tell from our initial examination of the scene, this body is unscathed in that regard, we're going to take a good hard look at the natural orifices, the eyes, nose, ears"—she uses the tip of the brush to part the lips slightly—"and mouth."

"Looks like rice," Erin says, leaning in.

Rebecca pauses so her students can shuffle past one another to examine the eggs. No one else comments. *Rice* is the most common point of comparison for bluebottle eggs, the undisputed champion of forensic entomology, which is what they will certainly discover these to be. She has also heard *orzo* and *pine nuts* from a few out-of-the-box thinkers in classes past.

"Because the eggs are so delicate, the tool of collection here will be our brush."

She retrieves a sealed jar of clear liquid from her kit, sets it down on the expanded tray, and unscrews the cap. "Plain water," she announces. She holds up a plastic tube. "Collection vial." She slots it into a holder at the edge of her tray. Then she dips the tip of the tiny brush into the water and begins to swipe at the bluebottle eggs clustered around the mouth. After a few careful passes, half a dozen eggs are clinging to the bristles. Her students watch with rapt attention as she inserts them into the collection vial and replaces the cap. Forcing herself to work at half speed, she demonstrates the labeling system for the vial's plain white tag.

Thunder cracks across the basin. Loosestrife bends like wheat. Dangling strands of kudzu sway in a warm breeze. The echo of the thunder snaps a different sound into place: that goddamn nagging drone again. This time Rebecca sets the brush down, closes her eyes, and listens. To her students it probably looks as though she's just decided to meditate. She doesn't care what it looks like—the sound is driving her to distraction and she has to identify it before she can move forward with her lesson.

She determines that Mari is correct and floats her sister a silent apology: The sound is definitely external, sweeping in from somewhere across the Body Farm. It's stuck in her mind like a catchy song she can't quite identify or a Latin word on the tip of her tongue, a half-remembered genus or species. It's most certainly a mating call. She racks her brain to come up with a species that would be producing that very particular sound at this time of day. At this time of *year*. Unless…she shakes her head. That doesn't make any sense.

She opens her eyes to find her students studying her intently. Assuming her sudden reverie is part of the methodology, some kind of new-age processing of the crime scene. The Empath's eyes are wet and shiny.

A single raindrop splashes the skin below the corpse's sternum. Rebecca takes a small plastic spoon from her instrument tray.

"I know the temptation is always to use the forceps, but when we're dealing with larvae, the classic low-tech plastic spoon is a good way to keep the specimens intact."

A second raindrop strikes the corpse's thigh. A third hits the left knee. They have reached the tipping point: At any moment the Louisiana skies will open up and the deluge will begin. After a few minutes, the clouds will roll away like they're being chased across the heavens and the storm will end, leaving a steaming earth in its wake. Rebecca decides to pack it in as soon as she bottles up some larvae, so they at least have something to work with back at the lab. It's been more than a full day since the body was placed here, so there should be plenty of hatched first-stage maggots to capture.

"Remember," she says, placing a gloved thumb and forefinger on the upper and lower lips, "natural orifices are the name of the game."

She parts the lips. A small crew of curled, segmented maggots writhe and squirm on the corpse's tongue.

"Oh," Erin says. Rebecca can sense a sudden shift in the students' attitudes. A sense of the reality of this pursuit, its blasé embrace of what still feels forbidden.

The larvae are the color of bleached Cheetos.

"Carefully," Rebecca says as she uses the spoon to scoop a single maggot. She drops it into a collection vial and screws on the cap. Then she regards her students. "I'll get one for each of you, don't worry. Though I would suggest refraining from giving them names. It's best not to get too close."

The raindrops' cadence picks up. It's still a mercifully slow start, but they all know what's coming.

"I'm going to abandon all pretenses of actually teaching you something," Rebecca announces, "and collect these at double speed so we can get back before it gets biblical out here."

One by one, she scoops up maggots like a fussy kid picking the marshmallows out of a bowl of Lucky Charms. Three vials filled. Four. She slides the spoon past the parted lips for number five when the wormy cohort on the corpse's tongue displays an abrupt and unlikely agitation.

Rebecca pauses. Rain pelts the top of her head. Erin lifts her backpack to use as an umbrella. Ji-un squeezes under its too-small canopy. "Huh."

"What's happening?" Jason says, leaning in.

Rebecca stares into the open mouth. For a moment, she's at a loss for words. Maggots aren't very complex organisms. They pretty much just hatch, feed on tissue, pupate, and become flies. So what the hell are they doing?

"Oh God!" Jason says, scrambling to his feet.

That's the nastiest thing I've ever seen, Mari chimes in.

Maggots are predictable. Maggots aren't supposed to—*swarm*.

Rebecca lifts her hands away from the orifice as a few dozen maggots spew up from the corpse's throat, boiling out of its mouth to fall across its cheeks and chin. They hit the dirt and *keep going* in a mass exodus away from the body. This shouldn't be happening for another few days, when they've molted into third-stage larvae and exited the corpse to seek cozy burrows in the dirt where they can pupate. Anyway, it shouldn't be happening at this speed, almost as if they're frantic. Maggots don't get frantic. Maggots don't *get* anything at all, not even when their mortal enemies the hister beetles come to prey on them.

Rebecca, Mari says, *just go.*

Rebecca peers at the unlikely maggot commute in pure, distilled scientific fascination. She grabs her phone and begins filming, barely aware that her students have formed a new perimeter several feet away from the corpse, and that she's alone beneath the cypress, getting rained on, while maggots flee their orifice. It's as if they're responding to some kind of signal. A command on some incredibly simple wavelength that is nonetheless inaccessible to humans. Her mind spins out as the maggots fill the dirt next to the corpse and begin to seethe around her bent knees and her instrument trays. There must be hundreds of them overtaken by this sudden madness. She thinks, absurdly, of

St. Vitus's dance, of that old Lemmings computer game that
Mari used to love, of footage of the starting line at the Bos-
ton Marathon. Rain pelts the corpse, the trees, the students.
Her mask is plastered to her face. The class is calling for her,
uncertain and scared. *Dr. Perez? Is this supposed to happen? Should
we go?* Meanwhile Rebecca speaks thoughts aloud so her phone
records them, as if she's attending at an autopsy.

"What in the physiology of the larvae could possibly receive
and process a signal?"

Her body thrums with the possibilities of the unknown. Science is full of rare firsts, and *somebody* has to experience them.
Why not her?

Rebecca, Mari exclaims, so loud it makes Rebecca wince. *I
know what's making that sound! Remember that summer in the woods
behind the church?*

'That's impossible,' she replies, but she knows Mari is right.
It's a sound that's plagued humans for centuries—from the
Native Americans to the settlers of Plymouth who remarked
on their "constant yelling noise" to the eighteenth-century folk
who believed they were portents of war. She studied them in
undergrad, of course, but they haven't cropped up in any professional capacity for one very compelling reason:

Cicadas are not corpse-feeding insects.

Not impossible, Mari says. Her sister, who knows what she
knows.

Rebecca concedes this is true as the maggot exodus begins
to wane. It's not impossible for cicadas to emerge off-cycle. In
previous historical instances, this signaled the arrival of a new
brood. She considers this as the rain picks up, soaking the maggots that surround her, giving the corpse a shiny pallor. Rather
than dampen the noise, it seems to have amplified the cicadas'
mating call, as if they're determined not to be drowned out by
the rain. Her drenched students have started up the path without

her, though Erin and Ji-un have stayed behind, calling out for her to come with them.

Rebecca is just about to put away her phone when a huge, corpulent maggot peeks out of the dead body's mouth. Rebecca revises this impression instantly with a whispered "holy shit." Her hands tremble. She forces herself to hold the phone camera steady with two hands to ensure this gets recorded. It's not a fat bluebottle larva, not even close. There are antennae, and glowing red eyes, and forelegs that latch onto the corpse's lips to lift it out of the mouth. Folded-back, wet-looking wings follow.

A cicada. She tries to stay calm. Her thoughts fragment. The rain pounds down.

It's not supposed to be corpse-feeding. So what the hell is it doing deep inside a dead body? It doesn't make any sense. She knows on some primal level that this is the creature that spooked those maggots, chased them from their coveted protein source. Ji-un and Erin vanish around a bend in the trail, leaving Rebecca alone with this inexplicable happening. As soon as the bug has climbed fully out of the mouth to perch itself warily upon the upper lip, Rebecca pockets her phone. Without bothering to select forceps, she plucks the cicada from the corpse and deposits it into a collection vial. Then she slaps her instrument trays shut, stows them away in her satchel, and replaces the chain-link cage atop the body.

As she hurries up the trail to rejoin her students, a prayer comes to her unbidden. After a moment, Mari joins in, and Rebecca finds herself silently mouthing along. As if in answer, or in a prayer of their own, the cicadas shout from all around them. Louder now, then louder still. Words from an undergrad textbook come back to her, the governor of Plymouth Colony struggling to make sense of this new and deafening scourge:

The Indians told us that sickness would follow, and so it did.

The Buddy Roemer Agricultural Center at LSU's Fluker's Bluff Campus is built like a Brutalist spearhead plunged into the wetlands. The bottom level is a massive cylinder beset with cement stanchions that rise and angle outward to support five floors of labs and classrooms. Each floor is larger than the one below, with the fifth floor extending so far out above the building's base that it hangs above the wetlands like a canopy. Walls of glass curve around the structure and end abruptly in sharp-angled corners. If a giant were to lift the building, he would cut his hand.

The design of the Ag Center is widely reviled. Most kids call it the UFO. Rebecca loves it. Even after five years as an adjunct and four as a tenured professor, the sight of it still gives her a mild thrill. She pities her colleagues in other departments who work out of generic, utilitarian buildings. When she steps into the liberal arts building, for example, she feels her thirst for knowledge shrivel like a deprived flytrap. Sad floors, windowless lecture halls, teachers holding office hours in cubbyholes like crated dogs. It seems self-evident to Rebecca that staid old academic aesthetics aren't ideal for fostering wonder and engagement. If she had her way, every building would lean toward the fantastical.

Chill, Mari says. *You've been here ten thousand times and you're still so cringe about it.*

Rebecca ignores her sister's voice and ushers her summer students single-file through the revolving doors, across the lobby to a warren of corridors that lead to staircases placed at non-intuitive intervals. The interior of the Ag Center evokes the setting of a movie involving top-secret research bordering on the absurd. A place where serious discoveries are made with a slight edge of whimsy.

Oh my God, shut up, Mari says. *Bigger fish to fry today, sis. Strange things afoot.*

Rebecca ignores her again. She hates this fuzzy delineation between her inner monologue and her sister's dialogue with it. Rebecca believes there should be some boundaries in place—even though Mari, in death, seems to be privy to everything Rebecca thinks and feels, it seems like common courtesy to refrain from commenting on stray thoughts. Even the illusion of privacy would make the whole situation less maddening.

On the second floor she nods to a long-bearded colleague leaning against the wall beside a bulletin board, stuffing a sandwich into his mouth. Every bulletin board she passes on campus gives Rebecca a twinge of nostalgia for her own undergraduate days. The sheer mishmash of offerings, advertisements, and general oddities is like a portal back to a time when options were exponential. Join a band, cat-sit for a professor, snag a used bicycle, crash a party, get paid to drive somebody's car across the country.

You never did any of that shit, Mari reminds her. *You just studied like the queen of the dorks.*

'I was scared of winding up back home. You know this. Obviously.'

Rebecca turns a corner. Track lighting illuminates a series of black-and-white photographs. Lately there has been some cross-pollination between the Ag Center and the tiny studio art MFA program. Like uneasy sister cities, the two have been making overtures toward collaboration. The small framed photos that line this corridor represent one of these attempts: artsy, enhanced images of bugs under electron microscopes. Skin-crawling close-ups of beetles and houseflies, sharply rendered alien limbs given unsettling new poses via digital manipulation. Thick fur like bear pelts, vaguely human eyes.

Abominations, Rebecca thinks. She loves them.

Your heart is pounding, Mari says.

The first thing Rebecca notices when she enters her lab is the view from the glass wall across from the door. Dark clouds lie heavily across the protected wetlands and the rolling hills of the Body Farm. Treetops meet clouds with no sky between. Rain pours down the glass. The students file in, and she turns on the lights.

Three long tables run down the center of the room, each holding microscopes, containers for the laboratory-rearing of insects, various breeding nests, trays for specimen jars, pin blocks, inoculation chambers, and monitors. Here and there large hard drives rise from the polished black tabletops.

A silver counter runs along the room's perimeter, on which sit several clear plastic boxes with netting over circular entry points. Colonies of blowflies and bluebottles cavort inside. Next to them, aquariums house the lab's magnificent collection of live beetles: carrion, rove, hister, and the flesh-eating dermestid. Opposite the specimen containers, autoclaves and refrigerators line the wall.

Rebecca walks past the high-speed centrifuges on her way to the room's big statement piece: the scanning electron microscope. It looks like it's been transported to the lab from the bridge of a nuclear submarine, a weighty periscope rising from a shielded specimen staging area. Next to the microscope proper is the bank of monitors that display incredibly high-resolution images of the tiniest segments of arthropods.

"This is Ellie," Rebecca says as the class gathers. She looks at the faces of her students. They don't react to the introduction of a hundred-thousand-dollar microscope named Ellie. Some, like the Empath, look positively shell-shocked. Rebecca reminds herself that what these kids just witnessed was likely both surreal and disgusting.

"Normally you'd get to meet Ellie in a few weeks, after

we hammer on the fundamentals for a while—beginning with an examination of the maggots we just collected from our corpse—but special circumstances dictate that I introduce you to Ellie today."

It's supposed to be a big moment later in the summer term, this unveiling of Ellie's power. But the interests of science have superseded her curriculum. How could she, in good conscience, talk to her class about the proper labeling of specimen jars when they'd all just witnessed a mind-blowing phenomenon?

There's a cicada book on the shelf in the back, Mari reminds her. *You're gonna want a refresher.*

This is a good point. Given her nonexistent professional exposure to cicadas, she probably knows only slightly more than the average person about the periodical insects.

She places a hand on the periscope segment of the machine. She notes with satisfaction that it gleams.

"This is the electron gun. It generates the electrons that pass down through condenser lenses, which focus and tighten the beam. An accelerated voltage moves the beam"—she slides her hand down the side of the tube—"through filaments of tungsten and uranium. Yes, there is a small amount of uranium in here. Normal scanning electron microscopes have very low penetrating power." She pauses to wait for an inevitable snicker or two. None come. These kids must be really traumatized by those fleeing maggots. "But Ellie here—Ellie's a special girl. The radioactive material cranks up the beam so it can cover the entire surface area of a specimen. In other words, Ellie eliminates the need for us to slice the specimen into impossibly thin samples. We can just pop the whole insect onto the stage and receive an unbelievably detailed image in return." She removes the collection vial from her satchel and places it on the desk. Then she boots up Ellie's monitors. "Now. You were all cruising up the path after our little maggot evacuation, and I don't blame you. Right after you left, this fine little specimen crawled out of the corpse's mouth." She stands aside to let the class take a closer look at the cicada. It moves sluggishly inside its vial, limbs struggling to find purchase on the smooth glass. "Can anybody tell me what it is?"

"Locust," Erin says. "We have 'em back in Beaumont."

"Close," Rebecca says. "This is a cicada." She pauses for effect. "It's very strange to find one crawling out of the mouth of a dead body. Can anyone tell me why?" She looks from student to student. Finally, Jason speaks up.

"They don't eat people."

Some nervous laughter breaks out. "That's essentially correct," Rebecca says. "Unlike various flies and beetles, which we will study in-depth this summer because carrion feeders are the stars of forensic entomology, cicadas don't use decomposing remains for protein. Or reproduction. Or anything at all. They are not a necrophagous species."

"Could it just have been lost?" Ji-un says.

More nervous laughter. Rebecca smiles. "It's certainly possible. This one seems to be off-cycle, meaning it's jumped the gun by a whole year on the local cicada emergence. That could signify the arrival of a new brood..." She trails off.

Very interesting, Doctor, Mari says, reading her thought before it can fully form in her mind.

"Which means it really *could* be lost, in a sense." She looks at her reflection in the off-white metal of the electron gun. "It could be at the mercy of some new behavioral imperative, some kind of tweaked instinct. It's theoretically possible for a new brood to exhibit characteristics that seem downright bizarre."

You're freaking them out with alien bug talk, Mari says.

Rebecca turns to her students and brightens. "Anyway!" She smiles. "Precisely because they're not necrophagous, I am not an expert on cicadas. However!" She strides over to a bookshelf in the corner and scans the seldom-used tomes on the bottom shelf. She retrieves a comparatively thin reference book and holds it up for the class to see. "These people certainly are."

The book is the monumental, comprehensive *Bugs of History: Periodical Cicadas from the Ancient World to Today* by Karen Picarski and Alan West.

"Picarski and West were the leading cicada scholars back in the 1960s," she explains. "And nobody's really challenged them since." She pauses. "Maybe one of you will, someday, if you choose to broaden your area of interest to entomology as a whole instead of specializing in forensics."

Probably a good idea for that one kid to broaden his horizons to the cuddlier bugs, Mari says. *He might not be cut out for maggot studies. By the way, his name is Javier.*

Rebecca glances at the Empath. His eyes are wet. He looks morbidly fascinated, if a little nauseated. She's about to go back to Ellie when the atmosphere of the room changes. It's a subtle shift on the edge of her awareness, but enough to give her pause.

The beetles are stirring. She heads over to the plastic boxes and aquariums and peers at the histers—the maggot feeders, a sort of meta-necrophage, dining on the eaters of the dead. Normally clumsy, reluctant fliers, the beetles are taking flight en masse. Rebecca leans in. The small black bugs zip around their container in frantic orbits.

Those are some pissed-off beetles, Mari says. Rebecca doesn't quite agree. She reads something else in their flight patterns.

Fear. Panic. The instinct to flee versus the reality of being trapped.

The other beetles are just as agitated. Shiny carapaces glinting with a thousand tiny pinpricks of light, jointed legs dangling as they swoop and dive and weave. Dermestids, with their dusky speckled backsides, in a sudden tizzy.

"Whoa," Jason says. The students, drawn in by her sudden attention, are staring at the containers.

"Are they supposed to do that?" Ji-un says.

Rebecca flashes to the corpse. Maggots boiling up out of its mouth, falling to the earth, wriggling away as if fleeing a fiery death. She knows, academically, that insects—not to mention their larval stages—are incapable of "fear" as we humans define it. They don't behave according to free-floating paranoia and anxiety, at least not in a way that we understand. But she's certain—in the same way you might be certain of something in a dream, however off kilter its presentation—that these beetles and flies in her lab are suddenly and inexplicably *afraid*.

She tries to tamp down her rising excitement. When she woke up this morning, it had been a normal day. There had been an alarm, shower, coffee from the drive-thru, commute with a podcast. She drove her students out to the Body Farm in a world where the scientific principles to which she's devoted her life were intact and unassailable. Now she's returned to a world infected by some new strain, corrupted by some weird energy. Reality's being cracked open before her eyes, begging her to step inside the fissure, investigate, draw conclusions, pioneer a new way of seeing.

"You're bearing witness to some very idiosyncratic insect behavior today—to say the least!" she says with a too-big smile.

You should dismiss the class and get out of here, Mari says.

'I would've killed for a day like this as an undergrad.'

I've got a bad feeling is all.

'You are one perpetual bad feeling, Mari.'

She feels her sister's abrupt silence like a hollow itch in the back of her mind. Sometimes she forgets that Mari can be sensitive about her situation. She's full of wiseass bravado but doesn't always like to be reminded that she's a constant imposition. Who would?

'That was harsh. I'm sorry.'

Silence.

Rebecca goes back to Ellie, sets *Bugs of History* down on the desk, and faces her students. "I don't have anything more to teach you today," she says. "But I think we're all going to learn some amazing things together."

She pauses, waits for Mari to say *barf*, but nothing happens. The hollow itch persists. Well. They've had a million little spats. Mari will be back shortly.

Rebecca boots up Ellie. The microscope hums like an air conditioner as its internal cooling system revs up. The monitors on the desk come to life. She picks up the specimen vial and studies the cicada. There's something off about its shape. She can't put her finger on it. She thinks it might be larger than normal, but she can't be sure. She has nothing to compare it to in the lab. Its head and thorax are dark blue, almost oily black, and its wings are the color of Honey Nut Cheerios. (Is that a distant echo of Mari's snort-laugh?)

Rebecca transfers the vial to a small, boxy machine on the desk next to Ellie. The vial clicks into place like a coffee pod into a Keurig. There's a hissing sound. A moment later, the cicada stops moving.

"What's that?" the Empath says.

"The gas chamber," Jason guesses. Rebecca doesn't bother to extrapolate. He's essentially correct: a quick, lethal spritz of cyanide gas and the insect is now deceased, its carapace and internal organs completely intact.

Killing jars have come a long way since she was a student.

With a pair of long tweezers, she extracts the dead cicada from its vial and places it inside Ellie's staging area. Then she opens *Bugs of History* to a section on cicada morphology. She scans the text—the phrase *sucking mouthparts* leaps out—then turns the page to find a diagram.

"Wow," Erin says. Rebecca looks up to find that images from the scan are popping up on the monitor: an eerie grayscale 3-D bug, captured from different angles, floating in a black void as if caught at some great ocean depth. Its eyes are totally vacant, the filigrees of its wings gossamer strands, impossibly thin. Its forelegs are bent mantis-like, and the shrunken hunch of the pose strikes Rebecca as sad and vaguely human.

She looks from the diagrams in the book to the images on the monitors. She's not sure what she's looking for, exactly— perhaps some kind of structural anomaly that might account for the cicada's presence inside the woman's corpse.

At the same time, she can't resist drawing her students in with Ellie's power. "Ready for this?" she says. She highlights the cicada's forelegs and keys in a command for an extreme close-up. Instantly, any semblance of a recognizable limb vanishes. In its place is a forest of narrow spines. From a close enough vantage point, every single thing on earth, living or dead, is a fantastical landscape that bears no resemblance to its actual self.

"The fossorial legs are primarily for digging," she explains. But teaching a class, at this point, is cursory. She's in a world of her own, referencing the textbook, then flicking her eyes to the monitors, shifting the view.

"Unreal," Jason says.

"We're looking at a female," Rebecca says.

"How do you know?" Ji-un asks.

Rebecca rotates an image of the cicada to focus on an area halfway down its side. "The abdomen contains all the organs of digestion and reproduction, and if this were a male, there would also be these white convex structures on the first segment. Ribbed." She pauses. No snickers. She wonders if kids even wear condoms these days. "They're called tymbals, and they emit the cicada's mating call you heard out in the Body Farm earlier."

"So the females don't sing?" Erin asks.

"The males don't either, technically," Rebecca says. "They just vibrate their tymbals to produce the sound."

She points out a few other interesting aspects of the cicada's anatomy. The ocelli, three small eye-like bumps on the front of the head, between the actual eyes, are used to detect light and darkness. The scutellum is a large triangular plate between the wings.

"And finally, unique to our female, the ovipositor." She pulls up an image of the cicada's underside. The cursorial legs are folded underneath the thorax as if in prayer. "Where the male's abdomen ends in a blunt nub, our girl's ends in a point, which houses her egg delivery system."

She blinks. There's the ovipositor, up on the screen. Or at least, the place where the ovipositor is supposed to be.

You're still a bitch, Mari says, rushing back, filling the hollow of her absence. *But holy shit. What is THAT.*

Rebecca flips through the morphology section in *Bugs of History*. Every illustration and photograph indicates that female cicadas' abdomens end in a point that gives the body a teardrop shape. It's not a spike, or a barbed tip, or a needle. There's nothing particularly fearsome about it. You could almost describe it as *subtle*.

In contrast, the ovipositor of the specimen she collected from the corpse is an extra appendage. A proboscis, thicker than the forelegs, extending from the base of the abdomen, culminating in a triplicate branch, as if it were trying to hold up three fingers. Each "finger" narrows to a sharp tip. The whole appendage evokes cat-o'-nine-tails, some whiplike medieval device, long enough to extend just beyond the span of the swept-back wings.

Her students crowd in closer to get a better view of the monitors. In her peripheral vision she catches Ji-un standing off to the side, frowning down at her phone.

"That's weird, right?" Jason asks.

"Yes," Rebecca says. She increases magnification. "That is most definitely weird."

"It looks like a deep-sea thing," Erin says. "A part of one of those crazy fish you only see a million miles below the surface of the ocean."

"I hate it," Javier says in a low voice.

"Something's happening," Ji-un says. Rebecca barely registers the girl's voice. She pilots Ellie, sweeping across the proboscis on the screen, close enough to render it as some kind of lunar surface, but not enough to dive completely into abstraction.

Stop! Mari says. *Go back.*

Rebecca reels the image back slowly, scanning toward the base of the abdomen. It's like mapping a ridged landscape, all craters and berms.

There!

A perfect spiral is imprinted in the final segment, where the abdomen narrows to the base of the ovipositor.

"You guys," Ji-un says, her voice edged with hysteria. "Seriously, you have to check the news."

Rebecca senses other students at her back retrieving phones from pockets and handbags. All she cares about is what's on the monitors. She snaps high-res screenshots.

Only Jason is still dialed in, focused on what Ellie has revealed. He's right next to Rebecca, staring at the screen alongside her. The murmur of the other students rises to chatter.

"It looks like somebody carved it into the cicada," Jason says. He's right, Rebecca thinks: It's as if someone took a minuscule knife, or some kind of sculpting tool, and etched a spiral directly into the insect. She has seen countless examples of unusual markings on bugs: the cartoonish eyespots of the sphinx moth caterpillar, the neon horns of the oak treehopper, the liquid crimson on the backs of predatory stink bugs.

But this is so perfect, and so tiny, it's like the cicada has been branded by some microscopic iron.

"That can't be, though, right?" Jason says.

"No," Rebecca says. "That can't be."

She thinks of a little plastic toy, a doll, marked with a tiny insignia of the toy company or the trademark symbol. Mari's voice is rising in volume and urgency. It rattles around in her skull. Pressure rises in the front of her forehead and forms a knot between her eyes.

'Hush, Mari! I need to think.'

I'm thinking for you. Something is terribly wrong and we need to get far away from here. We should have just gone home after we heard the cicadas out at the Farm. We should have—

'Quiet!'

Rebecca's lost in the images on the monitors. The corrupted ovipositor, that elongated, hellish instrument. The imprinted spiral. The excitement of discovery is tempered by a growing uneasiness, something she hasn't felt since she and Mari were kids—young enough to be enthralled by their father's magnetism, yet old enough to realize his church was not at all like the churches their friends belonged to. There was ritual, yes, and pomp—but they were strange versions of what she'd heard about and seen on TV.

The spiral etching sends remarkably similar shivers down her spine. A deep wrongness, wrapped in uncertainty.

All around her, the students' alarm grows. They begin to look to her, their teacher, for guidance. Finally, Jason shows her the screen of his phone and pulls her attention away from the magnified cicada.

It's a news clip that appears to be from New York City. A mass of brown flecks like confetti swirls out of a park and onto the sidewalk. Rebecca can't believe it. More cicadas! Thousands of them in the midst of a concrete metropolis.

What the hell is going on?

She watches, enraptured, horrified, as the bugs stretch out into ribbons, then whip together like a hundred elastic bands, snapping to enfold a pedestrian. He goes down to his knees, swatting and bashing his hands against his own head. A nimbus of bugs forms around his skull. He collapses flat to the sidewalk.

"They've quarantined a city in upstate New York," Ji-un announces, scrolling madly.

"Well, it looks like they got out!" Erin says, nearly hysterical.

Jason cycles through social media—shaky dispatches from Charlotte, Atlanta, Cleveland. Swarms of cicadas, moving in concert, jetting off into separate clouds, splitting into distinct formations only to come whirling back together.

He flips to a post from New Orleans: a blanket of cicadas rippling across a street in the Garden District, obscuring wrought-iron gates. A woman with a stroller flees down the street. Insects pour from a fenced-in yard like some oily liquid, elegant in flight. The woman stops in her tracks. She loses control of the stroller. She jams a hand down her throat, eyes bugging out.

Rebecca imagines the triplicate spikes of that alien ovipositor scraping her esophagus. "Cicadas don't do this," she says. "Nothing does this."

That video was taken eighty miles from Fluker's Bluff.

But Rebecca knows the distance doesn't matter, because based on the escalating drone she heard out at the Body Farm—

"They're here!" Javier cries out. He's over at the massive window that looks out upon the wetlands. Her students rush to join him, but Rebecca stays put. She can see what's happening. Millions of insects, rising as one to choke the foliage beneath a cloud-smeared sky. The sheer impossible scope of it is magnificent and terrible.

Mari begs her to run, but Rebecca doesn't see the point of delivering herself straight into an army of mutated cicadas.

The beetles and flies make frenzied attempts at flight inside their habitats, emitting frightened buzzes and hums of their own, sounds Rebecca never thought them capable of before. Their fear is contagious. The cicadas' song descends over the lab. No. A *symphony* of mating calls, intertwining, within and without.

One of the plastic containers actually *trembles* with the violence of the blowflies' agitation.

Rebecca closes her eyes, takes a deep breath, tries to locate herself amid the chaos. Instead she finds Mari and clings to her sister's voice.

—just fucking run to the car and—

'Mari, I need to think. I need you to help me.'

I'm telling you what to do!

'That's no good. I'm responsible for these kids.'

They're not kids, they're little adults who can make their own decisions.

'I need to tell somebody about the mutation.'

Okay but first—

'The CDC, or something. I don't know.'

She takes out her phone and stares blankly at the screen. The first step isn't calling the CDC, it's going down the hall to check on her colleagues. There are a dozen brilliant minds in the Ag Center alone—surely they can put their heads together and figure out the best course of action.

"Dr. Perez!" a girl shouts from the window. There's a dull *thunk*, then another, and another, until the percussive sounds are coming in rapid succession. Cicadas are bashing into the glass, flinging themselves against the window—hundreds of them at first, then thousands, blotting out the wetlands.

It's only a matter of time until they find their way in.

'Even if they do, they're just cicadas.'

You and I both know that's not true.

Rebecca looks at the automated killing-jar apparatus. There are canisters of cyanide stored inside. The machine is designed to expel the gas in puffs so small as to be harmless for humans in case of accidental exposure. But what if she modified the canisters to expel a greater quantity of gas?

It's a suicide mission.

She turns to her students. All of them have backed away from the window as it steadily fills with cicadas. "Follow me," she says, heading for the door.

Javier doesn't budge. "Where are we going?"

"To find some gas masks."

PART THREE

BORDERS

15

FORT HALCOTT

I can't let you go out there, Detective Paterson."

The hospital security guard is named Travis. He's got the fair skin and freckly face of a doll Sadie used to play with, some kind of floppy redhead moppet. He stands with his arms crossed in front of a haphazard barricade: plastic folding chairs, portable metal shelves, gurneys turned sideways, someone's office couch. Through gaps in the barricade, Vicky can see the parking lot and the lawn beyond. The air outside is still thick with cicadas, but they seem to have backed off the glass. Their drone is low and dispersed.

"Travis," Vicky says, "you know me. I can take care of myself."

Travis shifts uncomfortably. Before she made detective, Vicky had picked him up on a broad-daylight B&E over in the Highland Trailer Park. Back then he'd been a gaunt wraith on his sixth day awake, tearing up a neighbor's place for couch cushion change, a few old DVDs, and a busted stereo—the desultory spiral of meth psychosis.

Now, clean and sober, he glances over his shoulder at the

barricade, then turns back to shake his head at Vicky. "I mean I can't let you open the door. We got it under control in here for now. If nobody goes out, then nothing gets in."

"All right," Vicky says. It's reasonable. Hospital staff has managed to seal the building. Who's to say fifty thousand cicadas won't swarm inside the second someone opens a window and pokes their head out? "For how long, though?"

Travis shrugs. "We got plenty of food. Medicine. Doctors. Everything we need." He pauses. "We're *lucky* to be in here."

"Right," Vicky says, "but what about everyone who's not so lucky?" She tilts her head toward the barricade. "The people stuck outside?"

Noises bounce down the corridor at her back: unbridled weeping, gurney wheels on tile floors, shouting back and forth, the chaos of ER overflow. There is, at least, a measure of control to it now. The feeling that the hospital is going to become a war zone has simmered away.

Travis shrugs. He looks to be in incredible discomfort, like Vicky is driving a needle into his ear canal with her inquisition. His thought process is the epitome of gears visibly turning.

"Have you been able to get hold of your aunt?" she asks, recalling that Travis's aunt Sarah is the one who let him stay with her during his work-release—the one person, so far as Vicky knows, who ever gave him a fair shot. Vicky's mind is a Rolodex of these relationships, the web that ties together the margins of Fort Halcott society.

Hassan's in there somewhere, weaving his own crazy strand.

Travis shakes his head. "Nah. Everything's down."

"Right. Everything's down." Vicky hates the patronizing tone she's fallen into, but as Grimes would say: Travis is fried, extra crispy, and she's trying not to jump out of her skin with the urgency of all this. If she creates a scene by trying to dismantle the barricade, she's just going to find herself dragged away by more security. She has to slip out without attracting attention.

"So here's the thing, Travis. You're thinking short-term survival. And that's valid. That makes complete sense. But I'm working toward a long-term solution."

Travis frowns.

"We can't stay in here forever," she tells him. Behind her, one of the doctors rattles off a string of medical patter. Sneakers squeak down the hall. A door slams. Vicky feels exposed. The hospital is existing in a weird stasis right now, where no one seems to be in charge but people are working together as best they can. A makeshift society propped up by unspoken agreements. She has to violate it quietly, without attracting attention to herself. She imagines it will only take one spark to send the temporary calm veering off, once again, into catastrophe. So she tamps down the urge to punch Travis in the face.

"My partner has a lead that might be the key to stopping all this," she embellishes. "And I need to get out there to work with him. So your aunt will be safe. And everyone else who's not lucky enough to be in here with us."

Travis looks beyond her at the people clustered around the intake desk, walking dazed into the branching hallways beyond. "All right," he says, lowering his voice. "I can't leave my post. But there's a loading dock, where the Sysco trucks bring in the cafeteria food. You gotta go down one level to the basement then up a ramp that takes you out to the far side of the parking lot." He flicks his eyes toward the hallway that cuts along the intake desk toward the overflow waiting room. "That way, then down the stairs."

"Thank you, Travis." Vicky looks him in the eyes. She tells him what she sometimes tells Hassan, when he's at his most empty and despondent. "You're a good man." There is something about the addict-brain that never seems to believe this, so

Vicky finds it an easy salve to deliver, even if *she* doesn't entirely believe it.

"Good luck to you, Detective Paterson."

"You too."

She makes her way down the hall past signs for FINANCIAL ASSISTANCE and REGISTRATION, hits the waiting room, and stops. At least a dozen bodies are draped across the chairs. A clammy heat sours the air. Some of the insensate thrash and moan, others simply turn their heads and mutter nonsense at no one. She remembers Hassan's astonishment at Sadie's condition: *Her body temp is fluctuating?!*

Thoughts of Sadie crowd her mind. The sides of her head feel like they're going to detach and float away from her skull.

She considers the pill in her pocket, then dismisses the notion.

The only way out is through. For Sadie, and for everyone else in Fort Halcott.

The sound of wheels and metal breaks her reverie. A pair of nurses rolls a gurney into the room, scoops up a young woman, and takes her away. They pay Vicky no mind. She keeps moving while all around her the murmurs and whispers build to maddening gibberish. She feels like she's wading through a swamp of nonsense syllables.

Beyond the waiting room, the corridor branches twice. She passes a cart piled high with folded towels. Spray bottles poke up from a plastic bin that hangs off the side. A half-open closet door reveals buckets and mops and shelves full of paper towels and liter bottles of cleaning solution that looks like blue Gatorade.

"Come on, you motherfucker!" a desperate, imploring voice comes out of nowhere. Vicky glances around, then peeks into a small, cluttered office. A man in cargo shorts and a golf shirt is lying face up on the floor. A teenage boy is kneeling beside him.

Keep moving, Vicky thinks. Then she does the opposite. She can't help herself. Before she knows it, she's trying to pull the boy away from the body. He struggles, throws an elbow. Vicky lets him go.

"It's *inside him!*" the boy screams. He is ramming his hand into the man's mouth. The lips are split at the corners. Blood wells up from his throat.

"Stop!" Vicky yells. She wrenches the boy's arm up and back. He fights.

"I have to get it out!"

Vicky gathers her strength and gives the boy's arm a vicious tug. It pops free of the man's throat, fingers slick with blood and mucus. The man sputters. His hands curl into fists and he pounds the floor. His eyes stare straight up at the ceiling.

Now the boy folds himself into Vicky's arms, body going limp as he's racked with sobs. "He's going to die," he says.

"He's not," Vicky tells him. "He's going to be okay."

The boy gives Vicky a shove that catches her off guard. He scrambles up to glare down at her. "How is this okay?" His hysteria verges on madness. "How is this fucking okay?"

"Just take a deep breath," Vicky says. "We'll find you a doctor."

"There's nobody," he says. "I have to do it myself."

"No!" Vicky dives forward, but it's too late. The boy drops to the floor and plunges his bloody hand with great force into the man's mouth. His fingers disappear. He wriggles his thumb past the lips. The man gurgles.

She tries to grip the boy's arm, but it's slippery with blood. He grits his teeth and presses down, down, down, driving his shoulder toward the floor. The man's feet kick.

"I think I can feel it!" the boy cries out, triumphant.

Vicky fights her cop-instincts demanding she Do Something and lets him go. There's no use fighting this kid. The damage is done, Grimes is waiting across town, and whatever he's found takes precedence. She forces herself to turn her back on the boy.

"Motherfucker!" He starts to laugh as Vicky turns a corner.

Her exhausted mind serves up a dreadful vision of Hassan, wasted and left to his own devices, reaching past Sadie's parted lips to perform his own extraction...

She shakes it off and arrives at a large metal compartment marked FREIGHT ELEVATOR. Next to the elevator bank is a door. She pushes it open and descends a staircase. A moment later, she's moving through a dim cavern with the ambience of an abandoned parking garage. The smell of diesel wafts from the oil-slicked cement. Ahead there's space for trucks to unload via three garage doors positioned about five feet off the ground, all of them closed. Portable orange ramps with rubberized surfaces slope up from the floor to facilitate carts and dollies.

Vicky hustles up the center ramp. A pair of rectangular windows, speckled with grime, let in daylight just above her head. She steadies herself at the edge of the ramp and jumps straight up. The loading dock appears through the plexiglass: white lines on pavement, clouds of cicadas hovering. She comes down and her feet hit the ramp.

Okay: At least the insects aren't swarming the doors. She closes her eyes and pictures the layout of the hospital grounds. If she sprints across the dock and up a short access road, the parking lot should be right there. She figures it's about a quarter mile to where she left the car. One lap on a high school track.

A track swarming with cicadas bent on invading her body.

To the right of the garage door is a metal box flecked with old yellow paint. Protruding from the box are two large round buttons: UP and DOWN. She takes a breath. *For Sadie.*

Her palm hovers over the UP button. She hesitates. Once the door opens and she rushes outside, what's to stop a million cicadas from buzzing into the hospital through the truck-size opening? It's not like she can close it remotely. She'll be leaving a gaping hole in the side of a tenuously locked-down building.

Vicky braces herself against the door as a wave of dizziness comes on. Once again she considers the pill in her pocket. Once again she dismisses the idea. You justify it *just once* to get through a high-stress situation, and then you've opened the floodgates. Before you know it, every situation is stressful, and taking the edge off becomes a craving all its own. She's seen it again and again, out on the streets, in her family, among her colleagues. The slow erosion of discipline that in turn eats away at your humanity—just look at Hassan. He was going to be a neurosurgeon, once upon a time.

A new sound echoes through the loading dock. Laughter? No. Weeping. She whirls around. Moving slowly across the cement is the boy she left behind. He's a hollow-cheeked kid, a beanpole in a baggy tie-dyed T-shirt. He walks under an overhead light and the design on his shirt resolves into blood spatters. One hand is closed into a loose fist. Dark fluid drips from his fingers.

The other hand holds a surgery tool, a stainless-steel bone saw.

"I did it," he says, smiling through his tears. He takes one step up the ramp and holds out his fist as if to present his prize to Vicky. "I got it out."

"Oh no," she says softly. *I'm sorry I left you alone I'm sorry I'm sorry I'm—*

The boy stops. He looks at the bone saw, then raises his eyes to Vicky. "He asked me to get it out. He begged me to."

"Who is he?"

Was. Who was he.

The boy cries as he ascends the ramp. Vicky tenses. The bone saw, stained with blood, glints in the light from the small windows.

"My dad." The boy pauses. "He plays guitar in church." He holds out his hand, insistent. "Saint Mary of the Snow."

He's close enough now that Vicky can see what he's presenting to her. A cicada, motionless, swaddled in blood and mucus. Despite the fact that this boy is brandishing a razor-sharp surgical tool, Vicky can't help but lean in to look at the bug. She is certainly no insect expert, but it strikes her as *off* somehow. It's engorged, for one: midsection swollen, carapace cracking open in long thin slits as if it can no longer contain its innards. It makes her think of a fat clown in a tiny vest.

"He begged me," the boy says again.

Reality shifts. It hits her all at once, how ignorant she is. There are millions of "lesser" organisms squirming through the hidden places of the world. And now this one has risen to the surface and demanded to be seen and heard. A tail of sorts extends from what she assumes to be its rear end. The tail splits into three segments, and at the end of each segment is—no.

Vicky takes a deep breath and fights the urge to look away. There are clumps of meat skewered on the sharp points at the ends of the triplicate hindparts.

Guts, she thinks. *Stomach lining or intestines.*

This insect had been anchored inside the boy's father, its tendrils buried in his organs.

She meets the boy's eyes. At the same time her mind blanks except for a single thought: One of these things is inside Sadie right now, growing and feeding and *suckling*, and God knows what else.

The boy locks eyes with Vicky and begins to come back to himself. He glances down at his hands and screams. He tosses the insect and the bone saw off the edge of the ramp. Then he gives out a keening moan and falls to his knees. He wriggles, rubbing his limbs against the worn rubber surface of the ramp, as if trying to scrape himself clean.

Vicky goes to him now, this broken child. Only twenty-four hours ago, if she had come upon this boy covered in blood, clutching a surgical tool, with the body of his father down the hall, she would be cuffing him. But now the laws that she's dedicated her life to enforcing have been twisted by circumstance into a new, more malleable framework of punishment. She lowers herself and lets the boy crawl into her arms. His body jerks. The reek of blood and sweat hits her hard. She asks his name.

"Franco," he says. "After Franco Harris. My dad's from Pittsburgh."

"I'm sorry, Franco."

He stops trembling, then begins again. "Oh Jesus," he says. "What's happening?"

"Franco," she says, slipping into gentle authority. "I'm going to find out. And I'm going to do something about it. I promise. Okay? But I need your help."

After a moment, he nods.

"You see those buttons up there?"

She waits for him to figure out what she's pointing at.

"You're going to hit UP," she says. Then she mimes diving for the base of the garage door. "And I'm going to roll underneath." She waits for him to nod.

"Then—as soon as I'm out of sight—you're going to hit the DOWN button. This is the most important part. You can't let the door come up all the way. Just keep hitting DOWN so it stops after I'm through and then comes back to the floor. So it's only open for the second it takes me to scoot outside." She pauses. Franco's expression is dazed. "You got that?"

Franco gets to his feet and walks over to the switch and nods at her to prove that he's in the zone.

"One last thing," she says. "If any of those bugs get in here, you don't let them get up those stairs and into the hospital. Keep your mouth shut and kill them all before you go back in."

He takes a deep breath, glances back across the cement, then nods again.

"Okay," Vicky says. She lets her arms go loose and floppy, like she's about to do some pull-ups. She exhales, shifts her weight from side to side, and tries not to think about a cloud of insects swooping down on her as soon as she rolls out onto the pavement. She looks at Franco, who's fixated upon the door itself. "Hey! Franco! You with me?"

"Yeah," he says. His tone is vacant, almost sleepy. A far cry from the weeping mess of a boy that presented her with the cicada torn from his father's body.

Vicky mentally rehearses her low roll into a dead sprint through the parking lot. A quarter mile. One lap.

"Hit it!"

Franco's palm strikes the button. Gears grind. For a moment, nothing happens. Then the garage door lifts. Vicky hits the floor as daylight washes in. A split second later she's outside, up on her feet, three strides into her run.

Her first impression is that the cicadas are in some kind of eerie stasis—a holding pattern while they buzz about almost lazily. She indulges in wishful thinking. *Maybe they don't notice me, maybe they're tired, maybe they're not interested.* The sun is in her eyes, the heat dancing off the blacktop. Cicadas hover in loose collectives, their drone lethargic. She's pumping her arms, feet smacking pavement, halfway across the loading dock. The adrenaline spike cranks her heart rate.

Just ahead is a neat little garden of pruned shrubbery and maple trees. A path lined with benches cuts through, veers right, and connects to the parking lot. She risks a glance over her shoulder to make sure Franco shut the door.

At first she can't believe what she sees. Her feet stop short and momentum nearly topples her as she turns to face the way she came.

She opens her mouth and risks a scream. "No!" The rush of her pulse jackhammers inside her head. "Go back!"

Franco has followed her out of the garage, his gangly limbs cycling up and down. Behind him is a square, truck-size opening because he failed to perform his one task. It's a breach in the hospital's defenses large enough to admit a thousand bugs a second.

She waves at him, urging him back with her arms. "Shut the door!"

He bears down silently. She thinks he might be closing his eyes as he runs. The bloodstains on his shirt look shiny and black in the sunlight.

The drone ticks up all at once from background noise to an immense wall of sound. The air is flecked with movement, updrafts of bugs colliding and swirling into one another.

"Franco!"

Her head jerks back. There's a sudden pressure in the back of her throat. Dry, papery wings flutter against her sinus passage. She stays on her feet, gagging, trying to force the muscles of her esophagus to contract. Tears come to her eyes.

The insects sense a foothold. The swarm is all around her in an instant, the drone hammering her eardrums. Smells hit her: freshly turned earth and decay. She keeps one hand around her throat, desperately milking upward, trying to force the bug out. The other hand swats to no avail. There are too many of them. They blot out the sun. A bug stops up a nostril and with a *smack* she smears it across her face. She catches one more glimpse of Franco, down on his knees, buried under a cresting wave of cicadas.

All Vicky cares about is the open door. This is a catastrophic mistake. Even through her primal terror, she is ashamed. She has to get back inside and hit the button. The unsealed hospital is as vulnerable as an exposed underbelly. She takes a step.

The trapped cicada slips down a notch. She stops moving. Forward progress is impossible if she's to maintain the constriction in her throat. It's either one or the other. The cicada's limbs are scrabbling against the soft, pliable flesh behind her tongue. As she swats bugs from her face she flashes to the cicada Franco brought her.

The grotesque appendage, those sharp tips penetrating her tender organs. The body of the insect growing thick as it roots itself to her guts.

The sheer disgust is too much and she doubles over, coughing fiercely. *No no no no*—the violent retching could push the bug down her throat. She chokes herself while wings beat against her face. Red eyes glimmer and blur like berries on a shaken tree. Franco stops moving as the bugs blanket every inch of his body. Vicky looks past him to the open door. Dizziness nearly brings her down but she fights to stay upright. Her vision swims as her oxygen-starved body rebels. She doesn't dare let up her grip on her throat.

All she can do is watch, helpless, as the swarm lifts off Franco and curls like water down a drain through the open door. *No no no no.* More bugs follow. Soon enough they will reach critical mass and any hope of containment from inside the hospital will be shattered. She digs her fingers into her throat until the dull pain turns to agony. She focuses on clearing her sinuses, imagines pulling forth a massive clump of phlegm as if on a rope that hangs from her mouth. The cicada changes tactics. A searing pain shoots through her throat. She knows this pain will cease if she just lets go and gives the cicada what it wants.

Perhaps, as the cicada pulls her into its world, she will meet Sadie there, in some half-conscious between-place where they can be together again. Her grip begins to loosen. There will only be a tiny sliver of pain, and then sweet relief. It's as if the swarm is reassuring her of this. Urging her to simply let go.

To lay down her struggle would be bliss. All she has to do is let go and someone else can do the fighting. There must be thousands of bugs inside the garage by now. Anyway, the whole town's been overrun. Grimes could be dead by the time she gets to him. And there's nothing she can do for Sadie. Better to simply join the others. No more shame at her failures and mistakes.

The pain in her mouth turns from hot to a free-floating chill, like the first creeping seconds of the dentist's Novocain. She has the dreadful notion that the cicada's appendage is injecting her with a toxin. The drone flattens to a dull sound, both within and without, and her mind stretches with it to the edges of perception. She travels now, unbound from the prison of her body, sailing in her mind's eye over vast landscapes of turrets made of mud and earth. Ziggurats rise from blasted plains, giant towers of layered muck stretching upward from the ruins of cities and towns.

(Is this where Sadie is now, deep inside herself, roaming this lonely metropolis?)

In this place, Vicky is overcome by the scope and the vision. There is ambition in its structures, calculation in its patterns. It evokes within her an inhuman solitude so profound as to be more despairing than the sealed-off hospital, more tragic than Franco's evisceration of his own father.

To drift into it will not be bliss. It will be capitulation to something far worse than she can comprehend.

Her resolve strengthens and she comes back to herself. The drone amplifies, the sun breaks through the infernal vision. She's back in the loading dock behind the hospital. The cicada squirms at the root of her tongue. Her revulsion has deepened. The insects are not simply obeying some twisted biological imperative. They are *malicious*. This dovetails with something she's learned as a detective: Intent is the engine of morality.

She lets go of her bruised throat and sticks her middle finger in her mouth and jams it as hard as she can into her uvula. At the same time she bends at the waist and heaves. The cicada spews out in a torrent of vomit.

Instantly, she clenches her teeth, trapping sour bile. Her throat burns. Cicadas gather at her mouth, their forelegs prying at her lips.

She takes one last look at the open garage door and turns the other way. It's too late now: The hospital will have to fend for itself. She has to get to Grimes. Cicadas swirl like thick smoke. With newfound purpose she puts the loading dock behind her, sprinting with her mouth clamped shut. Bugs pelt her chest and *stick*. They quickly become a weighty hindrance. She marvels at the sensation. How many insects does it take to physically drag an adult human to the ground? Is it even possible? Tiny legs scratch at her eyes. Mashed and mangled bugs hang from strands of her hair.

The parking lot appears beyond the trees. It's worse than when she arrived, choked with cars and bodies. The path meets the lot and she stumbles. Her senses are overloaded with the prodding of thousands of tiny legs, the flutter of a million paper-thin wings. Their relentless onslaught is sapping her energy. One knee hits the ground. Again the notion of giving up and letting them take her crosses her mind.

She flashes to the turrets, the corrupted ruins of cities. Then she rolls around on the blacktop like she's on fire. Cicadas crunch beneath her body. Others scatter in self-preservation. She pushes herself up and scans the lot for her hybrid hatchback. No sign of the car.

Her hip slams against the open door of an SUV and sends her reeling. A child's body, still buckled, dangles off the seat, dark hair hanging to the running board. She catches a quick glimpse of herself in tinted windows, a pale specter trailing ragged columns of insects.

Vicky is lost in a sea of vehicles. A shirtless old man in Rollerblades gazes sightlessly up, straight into the sun.

Her head swivels at erratic bursts of a familiar sound: the hatchback's feeble horn. Halfway across the lot, toward the community college, a single car is moving.

Vicky waves her arms above her head, scattering insects, driven by pure relief.

Kim had the good sense to hole up inside the car, and now she's heading for Vicky, laying on the horn.

Vicky flanks around the side of an empty ambulance and intercepts Kim near an island of mulch and perennials. She meets Kim's eyes through the windshield. The girl looks terrified. Vicky knows she can't open the car door yet. She holds up a finger and runs back the other way. Then, flailing wildly, she turns around and rushes toward the car. She makes the most of this twenty-yard dash, burning through the last of her adrenaline, shedding cicadas.

At the last second Kim flings open the passenger door and Vicky dives inside, pulling the door closed behind her.

At least a dozen cicadas follow her into the car. Together with Kim, Vicky massacres them in a rage. A few days ago she would have balked at squeezing two-inch bugs in her fist. Now she relishes the chance, smearing their innards everywhere. When the last one is pulped, Vicky dares to open her mouth to let out a long-held scream.

A cry for Sadie, for Hassan, for everyone in the hospital. A cry for her own stupid scheme to enlist a traumatized kid to close the door behind her. A cry for Franco himself and a cry for his father. Kim leans across the center console and wraps Vicky up in a hug. Cicadas bash themselves against the windows.

"Sadie?" Kim asks, wiping her hand on the side of the seat, leaving a blue-black smear.

Vicky catches her breath. "Inside. On a ventilator." She pauses.

Inside, where they were safe for a little while. Until I single-handedly breached their perimeter. "Hassan's in there with her."

Perhaps, by now, Hassan is in that comatose between-place with her too. Perhaps they all are: Dr. Ghoshal, Travis the security guard, those stampeding citizens who almost crushed her to death.

"I screwed up," Vicky says.

Kim just nods. Vicky squeezes her hand. Utterly spent, she sinks down in her seat while Kim eases the car through the congestion. The lot's an eerie place now, mayhem frozen in time. Vicky gives Kim the address Grimes texted. Then she shuts her eyes and lets a miserable half sleep claim her.

16

FORT HALCOTT

It's going to be okay," Will says.

Alicia's eyes dart to the tree line where cicadas crowd every leaf and branch, singing their epic song, weaving their timeless stories. Will feels blessed to receive the beauty of their symphony—judging by Alicia's reaction, all she hears is bug noise.

She types in her notes app and holds the phone so he can see.

Why are you opening your mouth to talk? You told me to keep mine closed but you've been talking out loud since we left the hotel.

Will has no answer for this, at least not one that will satisfy Alicia. Intellectually, he's afraid of this invasion because it's unprecedented and inherently terrifying. He's as scared as anyone else of the implications. Yet he simply can't muster up the proper fear response.

When he thinks back to the warehouse now, he doesn't see the flashing lights, the openmouthed leaders, the impossible joining of the acolytes in some kind of ritual. He *feels* it all as if from the inside, no longer an observer but a participant. He knows—again, intellectually—that cults prey on the lonely by offering them familial bonds and a sense of belonging. But the kind of belonging he saw—no, *felt*—back in that warehouse ran much deeper than some charismatic charlatan and his goggle-eyed followers.

"I don't know," Will says. "But we have to get going."

He can tell by the look in her eyes that she considers his answer a complete cop-out. The only saving grace is that he's right—they *do* have to get going. He's on one side of the guardrail, Alicia on the other. The soldiers, or mercenaries, or whatever they are, have dragged the dead kid from the Jetta somewhere out of sight. Now they're reestablishing order, taking their positions in front of the barrier that runs perpendicular to the on-ramp. Sunlight glints off planar helmets. Nobody else dares to try for that shimmering perimeter fence. Quiet desperation hangs over the dispersing traffic.

Will holds out his hand. Alicia's eyes again flick to the cicadas roosting in the trees on the other side of the runoff ditch.

"I got you," Will says. She hesitates for another second or two, then steps over the guardrail to take his hand. "Stay close."

It's not like he can prove that he's somehow immune to attack—and to think that he's been *accepted* by the cicadas in some way is absolute lunacy. Yet that's how he feels.

Either way, Alicia's here with him—and getting her out of this place is all that matters.

He wonders if she was going to tell him that she broke up with Carter if this hadn't all gone to hell.

They skid down the damp grass of the ditch and climb up other side. Will is certain the guards at the border fence see them. He imagines optical feeds whirring digitally inside those mirrored helmets, smoothly zooming in on them while facial recognition splashes across the viewing lens. He figures that as long as they look like they're fleeing the scene, the guards won't mess with them. His hand brushes the grip of the Sig Sauer tucked in his belt, hidden beneath his shirt.

Across the ditch there's a narrow strip of weeds and tangled vegetation. Will aims to plunge through it straight into the woods, but Alicia stops short, tugging on his arm. He reads the fear in her eyes.

Just ahead, the cicadas are massing around a stately oak. This tree has been a meeting point for past broods, he's sure of it. There is recognition in the way the insects gather, a halting remembrance of some half-glimpsed history. It's not like he can suddenly see through their eyes. It's more like a taste of a sense memory. Yet these vague impressions contain multitudes: Centuries of broods rising every seventeen years to find nothing but unspoiled wilderness. Then, seemingly all at once: less wilderness than there once was. Great gouges of dirt in the landscape traveled by humans—newcomers to this world. Forest paths turned to gravel roads turned to highways.

The echoes of what came before toll the moment of the rising.

Will blinks and the impressions vanish. He's left with a deep sense of melancholy, the sweet hurt of the bare trees on a visit to Prospect Park the night before he jumped on a plane out of his life, walking hand in hand with a silent Alicia around the botanic garden.

Does the hive-mind store up sensitivities to change, reactions to seasonal anomalies?

He looks at Alicia. If only he could communicate to her the richness of what these insects have brought to the world!

"Through there is how we get out," he says. "This town is surrounded by woods and there's no way they can patrol it all." He casts a wary eye on the fence. They're far enough away now that the guards blend into the digital noise of the perimeter. Once they slip past the trees, they'll be out of sight for good.

Alicia doesn't budge.

Will takes both her hands. "Look," he says. "We've been through worse shit together. Right?"

She frowns, then jabs at her notes app. Will glances at her phone. *FUCK NO.*

Her fingers fly over the keypad.

I don't want to die here.

"You won't," Will says. He's never heard Alicia express fear like this before, not even on the Mexico City job.

As if to underscore the weakness of his claim, a hysterical shriek comes across the ditch. Someone he can't see, freaking out, in great pain.

"I got you," he says.

She shakes her head. Her eyes blaze with an anger he knows well. He's not being honest, he's giving her some kind of emotional half measure. Alicia hates platitudes and a false sense of security. He takes a deep breath. Dr. Capaldi has urged him to practice being wholly honest with Alicia, even if it leads to conflict.

"Ever since we saw the weird shit go down through the window of the warehouse," he says, "I've been feeling out of sorts. Like something I saw there changed me. I don't know why it's affecting me this way and not you. Maybe because you turned away after a second and I kept watching. But I feel *closer* to these things, somehow." He gestures at the cicadas. "Their song is, I don't know, some classical music piece. Everything about them is complex." He pauses. "And beautiful. And yeah, we might walk into the woods and they might eat us both alive, because I've gone completely fucking nuts and none of what I just said is actually happening to me like I think it is. So you're just going to have to trust that, *one*, I'm not insane, and *two*—my number one priority on earth is getting you out of this alive. And if you do die here, in Fort Halcott, New York, you won't be alone, because I'm dying here too, right by your side, where I fucking belong, Alicia. Okay?"

Will and Alicia, alone together at the end of the world.

He's suddenly out of breath. He wishes he could dive into her eyes and swim around in her irises. He brushes his fingertips against her cheek. The drone settles around him with great tenderness.

"Also fuck that Carter guy, I'm glad you two broke up. Now let's go."

Alicia cups her hand around the back of his head and pulls him in and presses her lips against his. Their tongues touch. She places her hand against his chest. For a moment, they stand very still, locked together. His whole body comes alive. Then she pushes him gently away and nods toward the trees. Together they make their way through the undergrowth. Will's heart pounds and a woozy sort of ecstasy spurs him on. Even the notion that he might be leading them both to their deaths can't dampen it. Cicadas stretch from the trees in small orbiting spheres of insects. They hover close to Will and Alicia. *Sentries*, he thinks.

Alicia shrinks away from their advances, turns her head, covers her mouth.

"It's okay," he tells her, squeezing her hand. *I've been marked,* he thinks, without knowing exactly what it means.

He feels her body tense as she steels her resolve. At the tree line, cicadas hang like the bead curtain they used to have in their apartment separating the living room from a storage nook. Will loved everything about that apartment, their crotchety landlady, the steel wool shoved into the gaps behind the radiator to keep out the mice.

The way Alicia would wordlessly turn over in the mornings so they could fuck on their sides, half asleep, while dawn broke across the city.

A million red eyes regard him with muted interest. Will steps through the curtain. Cicadas alight upon his face. He'd encountered them back at the hotel, back when his new perceptions first began to appear. Then, they were a threat, despite his under-standing of their rare beauty—he'd battered them away from the fallen bird-watcher as best he could. Here, forming the gateway to the forest preserve that surrounds Fort Halcott, the insects treat him with a curiosity that's almost puppyish in its guileless exploration of his scent. He is only "afraid" in the sense of this being an entirely new experience, without precedent. Next to him, Alicia radiates terror. He turns to her and her eyes widen.

His face is almost entirely covered in insects. It feels like someone is rubbing a cheap scratchy towel across his skin.

"Don't worry," he says to her. Cicadas explore the edges of his mouth but don't invade. "Just don't let go of my hand. And stay close."

She averts her eyes and sticks right by his side, weaving her arm into the crook of his elbow, pressing herself against him. A low moan escapes her as the bugs circle around them, darting in to trouble Alicia's forehead and ears. Will notices with relief that they don't attempt to overwhelm her, at least not while she's with him.

They move into the overgrown preserve. Massive oaks with dozens of branches prop up fallen, hollow trunks. It's so wild here, Will thinks. So different from the city's attempts at "nature," with greenery allotted to certain geometric spaces between concrete and brick. He keeps up a steady patter of reas-surance. The heat of Alicia's body brings to mind other jobs they've been on, the smell of her sweat after a long day in the field.

"One foot in front of the other," he tells her. "You got this, baby."

The drone slithers into the center of his brain. Leaves burst with color, photosynthesis lighting up their razor-thin pathways, all of it exploding around him in a riot of light. He wonders if this is how those tiny red globe-eyes see the world all the time.

Being given even a fraction of this insight is a tremendous gift. He doesn't know what he's done to deserve it, is the troubling part.

He steers Alicia over a fallen log teeming with cicadas, hovering with their wings half open. She whimpers as they envelop her legs.

"Look, it's working so far, right? You're doing great. Almost there."

Will has no idea if that last part is true. On the map the big splotch of green in the middle of the state seems to encompass hundreds of miles. But surely, eventually, they will come to a road.

"Stop right there!"

The command is inhuman, a scratchy voice filtered through a speaker. One of the guards steps out from behind a tree. He's twenty or so feet off to the right, aiming his weapon at them: a long gun Will doesn't recognize.

Will and Alicia halt. What else can they do? The guard got the drop on them. His concealed handgun digs into his belly. It's tempting—but reaching under his shirt will likely get him drilled by a high-caliber round before he can even draw the gun.

"Lemme see some hands!"

Careful to keep Alicia's fingers intertwined with his, Will shows his palms.

The mercenary takes five steps toward them. The barrel of the gun stays fixed on their position.

"Turn around and go back," he commands. "Now." The speaker crackles. His voice comes from somewhere along the helmet's smooth planes.

Will and Alicia don't move. It's not the first time they've had a gun pointed at them.

Will waits for Alicia to say something to simultaneously put the man at ease and keep him off balance—her specialty. In

Bratislava, she told a bunch of neo-Nazis that she thought Hitler was sexy, that he deserved better than Eva Braun. That had given them pause.

Then Will remembers that she can't open her mouth at the moment.

"You could just let us pass," Will says. He makes a show of looking around. "There's nobody else here. No one will ever know."

The mercenary takes another step closer and gestures with the gun barrel. "Turn around," he says slowly. "And go back the way you came. Or I'll kill you both."

The symphony swells. Will feels the song in his bones; the electricity of it pops behind his eyes. There is nothing to fear. Alicia elbows him. She holds up her phone so he can see it and types: *show him that they don't affect you.*

"Hey!" the man yells. "I'll count to ten."

"Look at me," Will says in reply. He opens his mouth wide. "Do you see how I can live among them?"

"One. Two. Three."

"Look! They don't attack me, okay? I'm immune."

Alicia elbows him again. The look in her eyes says, *More!*

"Four. Five. Six."

"I'm important!" Will shouts. "You can see it with your own eyes. Don't you think it's weird how they don't bother me? What if I'm the key to all this? My blood, or whatever. Isn't that your job? To figure out a way to end this?"

"My job is containment," he says. "Seven. Eight."

"The Order of Hemiptera!" Will says, playing his last card. "The true bug!"

The mercenary pauses his count. "Shit," he says. Then he races forward, elbow up, weapon leveled like he's going to put the barrel right through Will's head. *"Get the fuck down on the ground! Both of you! Now!"*

Even through his body armor, the mercenary's apprehension is obvious. Will and Alicia kneel down in the loam.

"Hands on your heads!"

Will hesitates. "I have to keep touching her."

"I said hands on your motherfucking heads!"

The man radios for backup, barks out a few coded numbers. He moves around Will and Alicia carefully, keeping the gun barrel aimed at their heads. The cicadas seem indifferent to what's going on. Will feels disappointed, like they've abandoned him in his time of need. He has an idea that if he just stretches his consciousness toward them, they will understand the danger he's in.

He tries to reach out.

The man is behind them now. "I need you to listen to me here," Will says. "The cicadas won't hurt me, but I need to keep her close so they don't hurt *her*. I don't know what will happen if I let her go. Do you understand?"

"Shut up," the man says. But he doesn't repeat the order. The Sig Sauer is an awkward lump pressing up into Will's rib cage as he kneels on the ground. One arm is hooked around Alicia's, but the other is free. Maybe now he could work a hand up under his shirt—

"Don't fucking move," the man says. Cold metal digs into the back of his skull. Will freezes. The insects whip around them in sudden agitation. Alicia trembles as half a dozen land on her body. One crawls up the side of her cheek.

"It's okay," Will says. She takes a deep breath, holds it, lets it out. The cicada rests just below her left eye. Its wings flicker as if casting off dirt.

At the same time, something crashes through the underbrush. Will doesn't dare turn his head to look. A moment later, there's a new presence at his back: a woman. The two mercenaries speak in low voices. Will can't make out what they're saying, but then the gun barrel prods him between the shoulder blades.

"Stand up," the man says. "Slowly. Hands where I can see 'em."

Will and Alicia get to their feet. The second mercenary moves around to face them. She's roughly the same size as the man, and the body armor and mirrored helmet makes it impossible to tell them apart. Her long gun is secured across her chest.

Will tries to pick out an insignia on her all-black uniform, but there's nothing. She gives him a quick expert frisk, removes the Sig Sauer from his waistband without surprise or comment, and hands it to her colleague.

Then she steps back and regards them, her hand resting on the stock of her weapon. Will catches his warped reflection in her visor.

"Open your mouth," she says at last. He does as he's told. The murmurations of cicadas swell and fade all around them. A thin cloud of insects descends and wreathes his head. Alicia clings to his arm, her hip pressed against his. Not one of the insects moves past his lips. The woman watches silently. Will can feel the man skulking at his back.

"So it's true," she says. Will closes his mouth. "How do you do it?" she demands. "Is this what your rituals are for? Immunity?"

Will thinks quickly. He imagines what Alicia would do if she could speak: She'd take advantage of what they're saying. Use their preconceived notions as a springboard.

He lets out a quick laugh, aiming for smug superiority. "It's so much more than that." He shakes his head. "You think what we do is some kind of magic, but that's ridiculous. It's all about forging a connection."

She considers this. "Your Order got what you wanted. Why are you leaving town?"

"My work here is done," he says.

The mercenary turns her head so that her visor reflects Alicia, distorted and concave. "What about her?"

"Her initiation wasn't completed before the rising," Will improvises.

The woman nods. She gestures with her weapon, indicating they should head back the way they came. "Move."

Will hesitates. "Where are you taking us?"

The mercenary doesn't say a word as she joins her colleague behind them. Will meets Alicia's eyes. She shrugs. Not like they have a choice. A gun barrel prods him in the spine. He starts walking, Alicia at his side. They retrace their steps through the low tangles of ferns and what Will assumes to be a metric ton of poison ivy. The cicada clouds stretch to a uniform thinness that dims the light coming down through the trees.

Will tries again to put himself in a trance, to meld his thoughts with the insects' song, to beg them for help. But nothing happens. He feels ridiculous. He flashes forward to some future banter with Alicia, adding this moment to their tally of "times we were held at gunpoint and taken somewhere."

When they emerge from the forest, their captors steer them up through the ditch and over the guardrail. The on-ramp is mostly clear now, except for a few abandoned cars—Will and Alicia's stolen Chevy Caprice among them. The Jetta that tried to run the blockade is nowhere in sight. A pair of mercenaries tosses a woman's body onto the back of a truck. Will doesn't know if she's a victim of a cicada or a bullet.

They move up the asphalt toward the perimeter fence. Will is enthralled by its design. Up close, the fence hums with energy that contrasts sharply with the organic, overlapping symphony of the cicadas. The fence gives off a metallic crackle that tickles his skin, even thirty feet away, like TV static projected outward. The structure itself is solid yet pliable as elastic.

On the shoulder of the road is a prefab Quonset hut, as black as the mercenaries' uniforms. Sunlight swims in its shiny arched ribbing. While her colleague keeps his gun trained on Will and Alicia, the woman goes to the front of the hut, kneels down, produces a small cylinder, and holds it to the place where the siding meets the pavement. There's a loud *hiss*. Thin seams appear: the outlines of a door. She pushes it open. The man ushers Will and Alicia inside.

They enter a dim anteroom the size of a small closet. The woman shines a penlight in every corner of the cramped space. *Checking for cicadas*, Will thinks. When she's satisfied that none of the insects have followed them into the Quonset hut, she bends over to place the cylindrical tool against an inner wall. Another *hiss*, another door comes into being. *Air lock*, Will thinks. An extra layer of protection against, say, a giant cloud of angry cicadas.

The woman ushers them inside and seals the door behind them. They step into the hut's main room, and Will clocks it right away as an operations center. A huge screen on wheels like a whiteboard displays an overhead topographical map of Fort Halcott. Will picks out the foothills at the northern edge of town, where the unfortunate bird-watcher's rock finches are making their rare appearance. A few plastic chairs are huddled around the screen. In the center of the room, a large folding desk holds a pair of monitors. Each one is divided into a grid, like a grocery store's security feed. Inside each square is what Will guesses to be a different section of Fort Halcott's perimeter. His heart sinks as he scans the extent of this mercenary army's incursion. He spies border walls around the warehouses, the highway exits, the two-lane roads that wind up into the forest preserve.

A slight, balding man with wire-rimmed glasses sits behind the desk, skimming a finger along a tablet computer in a thick tactical case. He wears a black polo shirt unbuttoned so that his hairless chest looks almost pink in the weird light. Their escort stands against the wall, hand on her weapon, finger pointed straight out with typical military-style trigger discipline.

Alicia laughs. Will is startled for a moment—but of course the whole point of this place, with its double-sealed exterior, is to ensure safety from cicadas. She's finally free to vent.

"You stupid motherfuckers think you can cut off a whole goddamn *city*? You think this is the 1950s? A hundred thousand people on TikTok knew you were rolling in before you started sealing off your first street. Cutting off communications *inside* Fort Halcott doesn't do shit when everybody *outside* Fort Halcott can just roll up and broadcast from the other side. You do realize that, right?" She looks from the man at the desk to the soldier across the room. The man puts down his tablet and laces his fingers together atop the desk. The woman stands impassively. She does not remove her helmet. Alicia stalks over to the map screen, studies it for a moment, then turns around and throws up her hands.

"Hello! Your little operation is probably national—no, *inter*-national news by now. Al Jazeera affiliates in stone villages in the middle of the Sahara are doing breaking-news segments on it as we speak. So my questions for you are: One, who are you, and two, why are you so fucking stupid?"

Alicia tries to stand in one place, glaring at the unassuming man behind the desk, but she's spent the entire day in a state of fearful silence. She vibrates with pent-up emotion. Will lays a hand on her shoulder and she shrugs him off.

The man holds up a bowl of candy. "Mini Snickers?" he says. Then he tries to hand her a bottle of water. She ignores it, grips the edge of the desk, leans forward, and gets in the man's face.

"You can't keep sixty thousand people in here to die," she says.

The man puts down the candy and the water. "Suit yourself. You'd be surprised how many more people would survive high-pressure situations if they just remembered to eat and stay hydrated."

"What are you," Will says, "some kind of rapid response team? FBI? FEMA?"

The man smiles by moving his thin lips to one side then letting them relax. "Something like that."

"So this is supposed to be containment," Will says. At the same time, the cicadas' wondrous song gallops through his head, the strains of melody separating and coming back together like a double helix.

"In a manner of speaking," the man says.

Will takes a breath. Words flash in his mind: *The signal begins in the soil.* A truth he understands without having learned. *The echoes of what came before toll the moment of the rising.*

He is almost offended at the notion that this brood's rising could be contained by such shabby, earthbound measures. "And you think you can keep billions of cicadas under control with some fences and guns?"

"Of course not," the man says. "The brood has already been awakened—globally. The proverbial cat has been let out of the bag. Many thousands of bags for many thousands of cats."

Alicia straightens up. She looks at Will, processing this revelation.

Globally.

Cicadas rising around the world. Blanketing the English countryside, the rain forest, the Russian steppe. Invading New York, Seoul, Jakarta.

The scope of the event makes him woozy. He doesn't have the imagination for it. His mind churns against itself, struggling to multiply everything he's seen by a factor of billions. It simply isn't possible. He can superimpose cicada swarms over places he knows, cheap cinematic flashes of his parents' brownstone, the cobbled street outside of Carter's place, his cousin Leon's block up in Inwood—all the quick-hit locations of his life, overrun by flying insects.

He chases the visions away. "So what's the point of all this, then?" Will says. "What are you after?"

The man smiles once again. "You."

17

FORT HALCOTT

The house is an old Victorian on a hill surrounded by a wrought-iron fence. A cupola rises from the roof. Verandas abound. The whole place has gone to seed now, the lemon-and-navy accents all but faded away. The neighborhood is full of houses like this, once-grand whimsy gone stale with age and neglect. A historical marker out front proclaims this house as a meeting place for Tammany Hall–aligned politicians in the nineteenth century. The overgrown yard hosts a low convergence of cicadas. They hang in thick, fluid globs across the tall weeds and pokeberries.

Vicky rubs her eyes. She'd woken periodically on the long slow journey across town and looked out into an unfolding nightmare. Traffic snarls had clogged the routes out of town, with cars backed up so far that getting to the actual city limits of Fort Halcott would have been impossible, had they been attempting to flee. Route 74 had been an obstacle course of abandoned vehicles and exposed bodies out on the pavement. At the last second Kim had been forced to swerve around a pile of children clinging together along the center line, like they'd held one another for comfort as the cicadas descended upon them. A few feet from the children, a pair of police officers had been lying face up, their bodies trembling. As Kim eased the hatchback past them, one of the cops' heads turned to stare blankly at the car as it passed. Vicky caught his vacant eyes, and then was behind them.

She thinks of the bloody cicada in Franco's cupped hands, with its pointed triplicate appendage. That single bug's evolutionary tweak—replicated millions of times—has anchored itself in the guts of half the citizens of this town. *Her* town. The place where she grew up, the place she's sworn to protect and serve.

She wonders if she's doing either one now, or if it even matters. There's still no internet, no phone service. No way to tell how far this cicada brood has spread.

Kim parks by a crooked gate that hangs askew from the fence on one functional hinge. Next to them, Grimes's beige sedan sits empty. A pine tree air freshener hangs from its rearview mirror. Manila folders and crumpled Camel soft packs crowd the dash. Vicky's tired eyes go slack, and the cicadas in the yard haze into a smear of motion. There are just so many of them. Their ceaseless dissonant racket is maddening. Bugs skitter across the windshield. Kim turns on the wipers, and the insects fly away.

"I should have grabbed some surgical masks from the hospital," Vicky says. She catches a whiff of her own body odor. There's a spare deodorant in the glove compartment. She doesn't bother.

"You had enough to worry about," Kim says. Vicky looks at the babysitter, really looks, for the first time since she saved Vicky's butt in the hospital parking lot. Strands of her sleek, shiny hair stick to her face. The car's parked, but she sits with both hands on the steering wheel, ten and two, staring straight ahead like she's taking a road test.

"Thanks, Kim. For being there for me."

Kim licks a finger and smooths an eyebrow. "It was just dumb luck," she says. "I was too scared to do anything but sit in the car. I kept telling myself, *Drive away*, but I didn't know where to go. I thought, *What if the bugs, like, figure out how to run me off the road?* Then I also thought, *What if I'm just sitting here and they figure out how to fly up through the exhaust pipe, or through the air vents, into the car?* But there was nothing I could do about that. I wasn't going to actually get *out* of the car, that would have been the stupidest thing. So when you showed up, I was just *there.*"

Vicky thinks of Franco. "No, you weren't just there. You kept your head in a beyond-crazy situation. That counts for a lot, Kim."

Kim takes her hands from the steering wheel and wipes her palms on her denim shorts. "You know, whenever I get stressed at school, like super bugged out, like not sleeping, grinding my teeth, hearing auditory hallucinations, sometimes I lie there in my bed and think how amazing it would be if some kind of majorly fucked-up catastrophe took place during the night, like a nuclear attack, so I wouldn't have to go to class in the morning and present my work. Or sometimes if I'm like vaguely bored and fed up with life or whatever, I just want a big change to come. Once I thought, if an earthquake destroyed the eastern seaboard then whatever—at least it's a fresh start, you know?" She looks at Vicky, then winces. "Oh my God, I am so sorry. This must sound like I'm a total sociopath, especially after what you're going through with Sadie. I mean you know I love Sadie. But anyway what I was getting at is, now that it's happening, it's not some cool break from reality, it just really sucks." She pauses. "I'm sorry. I'll shut up."

"It's okay," Vicky says. She understands on some level where Kim is coming from—it's just that Vicky has never fantasized about some great tragedy coming to wash away her obligations and responsibilities. She sweeps her eyes across the lawn. The open gate is much too small to drive through. They'll have to exit the car and make their way up the stone path to the front door. Vicky estimates she could run the length of the path in five seconds. Is that enough time for the cicadas in the yard to swarm her?

"I think I can make it," she says out loud.

Kim starts. "I forgot we have to actually get out of the car."

"You don't," Vicky says. "You can stay right here."

Kim picks at the frayed hem of her shorts. "Sometimes I want your life, you know. I hope that doesn't freak you out."

Vicky is taken aback. What is it about college kids these days that makes them want to confess any twisted little desire that floats through their mind?

"My life's nothing special," Vicky says, which goes against her long-held belief that her life *is* special, because she's been granted the incredible gift of Sadie.

"I know," Kim says, hitting the wipers to chase away a few insects. "People at RISD all talk about how they would rather sever their own genitalia with a butter knife than live the way you do, with the house in the suburbs, and the kid, and the steady job, because we're all supposed to want this life of feverish creation and being hot degenerates, but I think that what you've got is kind of soothing."

At this, Vicky laughs. "You've been up close and personal with my household for a while now. Anything about it strike you as particularly *soothing*?"

Acute sadness washes over her. Her household revolves around Sadie.

Sadie who's all the way across town, hooked up to a ventilator, with one of those *things* inside of her.

"I'm sorry," Kim says, "I know I sound like the absolute worst. I think I just hate making art, you know? Like, everything about it. The process, the other kids, the teachers, the work itself. The end result. I suck."

"Kim. You do not."

"I do. It's gross. Art's gross and dumb. Look at this"— she gestures toward the Victorian's front yard, teeming with cicadas—"like, my whole life is pointless. I just sit around all day worrying my potential installation concepts aren't going to be conceptual enough, and everyone's going to laugh at me. And I seriously can't draw for shit. I can paint, sort of, but I have no idea how I got into RISD if I'm being honest. Now *this* is happening and nothing I've ever done means anything at all. There's only this."

Not for the first time, Vicky marvels that someone so vocally self-absorbed can be such a caring and empathetic babysitter.

Her eyes flick to the house. Grimes is waiting for her inside. A dark vision comes to her: Grimes in a heap on the knotted hardwood floor, body crawling with cicadas...

She shifts in her seat. It's past time she left this car, but something about sitting here with Kim compels her to stay a minute longer. Right now the car is a bubble in which she's not required to make impossible decisions.

Scattered cicadas hit the windows. One leaves a dark smear. "Listen, Kim. I think what you're feeling is normal. I also think a lot of people are in the same boat. Everyone's lives have been derailed for this." She pauses. "You're a good person. Sadie loves you. You'll figure it out someday. Or you won't, and that's okay too. Now stay put. If I'm not out in thirty minutes, my car is yours. Get the heck out of here."

Kim's eyes widen. "And go where?"

"Well, I'm sure your dad is worried sick."

"He's in Boca Raton. And the one person I give a shit about from high school is dancing on a Disney cruise all summer." She picks a scab on her knee. "I'm going in there with you."

"No," Vicky says automatically. Franco's doomed escape from the hospital is etched in her mind. "I don't know what I'm walking into. And there's no reason for both of us to risk getting out of the car."

"I don't want to just sit here by myself and think. I want to stay with you."

Bugs pelt the car in soft little percussive *smacks*. One of the insects crawls up the passenger-side window and pauses. Its abdomen is a rounded-off nub. No extra appendage. She files this fact away: Some cicadas have the extra appendage, and some of them don't. Perhaps it's a male/female thing.

She looks at Kim. Who's to say it's any safer out here in the car? Kim's fear of cicadas crawling up the exhaust pipe sounds excessively paranoid, but it's not like Vicky has any idea what these insects are capable of. Perhaps it's better Kim stays by her side, where she can keep an eye on her.

"All right," Vicky says. "But you follow my lead exactly. On three, we're going to open the car doors, shut them behind us quickly, and sprint to the house."

"Got it."

"Remember: mouth closed. The whole time."

"For sure."

"And no stopping for any reason." She takes Kim's hand and squeezes it. "I'm grateful for everything you've done for Sadie and me." She tries to crack a smile. "And George the ladybug."

Kim nods. "Sadie's gonna be okay. I know she is."

Vicky takes a breath. "Okay. On three."

Kim grips the door handle and pulls the lever.

"One."

Vicky does the same.

"Two."

They look at each other, then out at the lawn.

"Three!"

Vicky shoves the door open. Her feet hit gravel. She slams the door behind her and takes off. Cicadas carom off her body like hailstones. She's half a dozen strides from the car when she hears the scream. Her heart sinks.

Don't open your gosh darn mouth, Kim!

She risks a look over her shoulder as she bounds across the worn stones of the path to the front porch. Kim's just inside the front gate, hunched over, clawing at her eyes. Vicky glimpses blood in a vivid-red splash. The music of the cicadas swells as they zero in on Vicky. She wears them like a crown in motion. Slapping at her face and head, flicking them from her shoulders and chest, she reverses course. A burst of nearly blinding anger takes hold. This *will not* happen again.

The next thing she knows, she's dragging Kim along the stone path, fighting off insects with one open hand. A shock of pain surges and her vision blurs. She smacks a cicada flat against her left eye. The crust of its body lingers. They hit the porch. She reaches out for the doorknob and fear swells. *What if it's locked, what if Grimes is dead, what if—*

The door opens and an arm shoots out. A hand closes around her wrist and yanks her and Kim inside. The door slams behind them. Vicky falls to her knees and Kim collapses. She is aware that Grimes is hovering over them both. She rubs her left eye. The pain is fiery. She blinks through tears and goop. At the same time she's trying to examine Kim, who won't relinquish her hold over her own face. Vicky has to pry her hand away.

Kim's eye is a red mess. The sight of it alone lessens Vicky's pain—her eye is not nearly as bad as Kim's. There's something off about it, like it's been shifted out of joint, not exactly swollen but pressed forward out of its socket. The cornea is flaming red. Blood rims the lid and trickles from the corner.

Kim looks at the palm of her hand, smeared with blood. Vicky turns to Grimes. Her partner pulls a tissue pack from the pocket of his suit jacket. Vicky snatches it away, rips out a clump of tissues, and presses them gently to the side of Kim's eye. Instantly, the tissues go red and soggy.

"They went for my *fucking eye!*" Kim shrieks. Vicky drops the tissues and holds out her hand, beckoning Grimes for more. Her vision begins to clear up. The pain dulls. The cicada must have only inflicted a glancing blow.

"It hurts," Kim says. "Oh God, it hurts it hurts it—"

She emits a guttural sound, then trails off into raspy nonsense. Her hands go to her throat. Behind them, Grimes is in motion. Vicky turns to see him brandishing a sneaker. He slaps it against the face of a grandfather clock. The baritone chime rings out. A dead cicada falls to the floor. She is aware of them all, suddenly—the handful of insects that darted inside before Grimes could shut them out. He goes after them one by one, a lit cigarette clenched in his mouth. The sound of rubber on wood echoes through the foyer.

Vicky turns back to Kim. Her one good eye stares into the middle distance. Her hands fall away from her throat.

No.

Vicky lays her down and begins chest compressions. Maybe she can force the bug up that way.

Come on come on.

She grits her teeth and drives the heel of her hand down into Kim's sternum. The girl's body bounces. Her arms flop, elbows slamming against the floor. The damaged left eye protrudes like some grotesque cartoon.

Kim mutters something incomprehensible. *No.* Vicky drives harder. Kim's eye leaks blood and mucus. Whispers escape her mouth.

Hands grip Vicky's upper arms and pull her to her feet.

"You're going to crack her ribs," Grimes says. Vicky lets him steer her away from Kim's body. "There's nothing more you can do."

Vicky looks around. The hardwood floor is littered with dead bugs. She turns to regard Kim, lying there, invaded. "We were *so close!*" she cries out.

"I know," Grimes says. He doesn't look any worse than usual, with his mussed hair and rumpled suit. He doesn't run his mouth. "I'm sorry," is all he says.

Vicky lets out a breath. She forces herself to look at Kim. *Meet it all head-on.*

Kim who's having an artistic crisis. Kim who doesn't know what she wants out of life. Kim who was supposed to have time to figure it out, like every other kid her age.

Kim who saved Vicky's life in the hospital parking lot.

It feels so wrong to simply move on with Kim lying there, afflicted. But Grimes is right: There's nothing more to do in this moment. What she *can* do is try to find something that will save Kim, and Sadie, and everyone else in Fort Halcott.

She takes in the foyer. A chandelier hangs from a golden cord. Rectangles of wainscoting frame intricate carvings. Dusty portraits line the walls—hunting dogs, racehorses, old people from another century. Two arched corridors lead away from the small anteroom. It takes her a moment to realize what's missing.

"There's no hoard at this scene," she says.

"There's not even *stuff*, not really," Grimes says. "There's furniture, but nothing in the kitchen. Cupboards are bare. Shelves too, mostly. So cross *hoarder* off your victimology bingo card. I'd wager that was incidental with the last one."

"How'd you find this one?"

"Barker had it on the board for Navarro but I grabbed it. Gut feeling. Seems the lady that called it in is the daughter of the family that owns the place. Her mom kicked it last year, she hasn't decided what to do with the house yet. For now it's just sitting here. Except the last couple weeks there's been activity reported. Nighttime creepy-crawlies. She figures it's kids, goes to take a look. Finds the, uh..." Grimes makes a face like his ulcer is acting up. "You just have to see it."

He turns and leads her down a hallway past a massive steam radiator that rises to her chest. Cobwebs link the heater and the wall. Not a spider in sight. "No insects?" Vicky asks.

"Not so much as a housefly. That's consistent."

They move through a living room with a circular red velvet sofa for a centerpiece. A glass-fronted credenza sits empty against one wall. A streaky, gilt-framed mirror hangs above it. Their reflections are mush in the low light.

"Have you been here alone all this time?" she asks.

"There were some uniforms. I sent them away when the cicadas starting violating norms of polite society. Figured they could do a lot more to help out there than in here."

She pauses next to an end table with an empty vase, a green wooden box, and a yellow-shaded lamp with a crystal body. "*You* sent them away. What's going on with chain of command? I haven't had access to a radio except for the two seconds I called you."

He shrugs. "All you gotta do is step outside and there's a million people who need help. Only the mouth-breathers need *orders* in a time like this."

Vicky bites her tongue. It's a reflex for a lack of discipline, a breakdown in command structures, to irk her. But all she has to do is look at how she's behaved in the wake of the cicadas' appearance. She didn't report to the precinct. She didn't even take a second to try to check in. Her sole priority was Sadie. And when she finally had Hassan's radio, she didn't reach out for Captain Barker, or her sergeant, or anybody who might need her help implementing a relief plan for the city.

There are two hundred officers and other personnel on the FHPD. Multiply her own devotion to her kid by every one of them, trying to save their own families. It's easy to see how even the definition of *duty* might be malleable in a catastrophe with no precedent.

She flashes to those cops lying in the street next to the pile of kids. "I wonder how many we've got left," she says.

"We got you and me," Grimes says, tucking a cigarette between his lips. He flips his Zippo lighter open and holds the flame to the tip of the Camel. He moves his cheeks. Smoke billows. "You eaten anything?"

"Not really, no."

"Fridge here is empty."

He pushes open a door halfway down a tiled hallway to the kitchen. Wooden steps lead down into darkness. He flicks a switch and the basement staircase lights up. He turns to her. "We should plan on the power going out at some point. Honestly, I'm surprised it's still on when they cut the phones and internet right away."

Vicky frowns. "Are you saying the *cicadas* made a concerted effort to take down our communications? And that they can do the same to the power grid?"

Grimes pinches the cigarette between his thumb and forefinger and takes a long drag like he's gulping down precious life-giving air. "I'm saying there's another wrinkle. Some of the guys on the radio are talking about some kind of outfit sealing off the city. Establishing a perimeter." He shakes his head before she can ask. "It's not us. Not even Feds, from what I hear. Paramilitary, maybe. I don't know."

Vicky considers this. "It makes sense to quarantine the city. I'm just amazed they were able to do it so fast."

"That's how I know it's not FEMA. Which begs the question. Who else?"

Possibilities swirl beyond her grasp. There's so much ground-level mayhem to deal with, she can't elevate her thinking to whiteboard-style RICO cases. Adrenaline from her sprint to the house and its aftermath is almost fully dried up. Weariness descends yet again. How much of this can she take before she simply collapses?

"No idea."

"There's other chatter too." Grimes blows smoke. Vicky waves a hand to clear it. "Talk of an assault on the perimeter. Some of our guys, a few of the local psychos. Militia types and weekend warriors, staging a breakout. I figure Carl McTeague's leading the charge on some kind of Mad Max school bus with a cowcatcher welded on. Guys in iron masks chained to the roof."

"Carl's in jail," Vicky says. "That Airstream behind his house turned out to be a meth lab."

"Never would've guessed."

Grimes leads her down the stairs. The ceiling is low, the walls stone and mortar, the floor packed earth. Light comes from a single bare bulb. Empty wine racks are everywhere. The room is unexpectedly long, the far end fading away into smudges of negative space.

"What's that smell?"

Grimes doesn't answer. Vicky wrinkles her nose. It's an odd scent, damp and a little spicy, like moldy cloves. She notes her partner's lack of crime scene protocol. He hasn't bothered with shoe covers or gloves. Ash falls from his cigarette.

For some reason, this terrifies her.

They move toward the rear of the basement. There are no more wine racks, just bare earth and stone. There's a shape in the dark, a presence Vicky senses more than sees. It's as if the floor has been lifted and warped over time by a surfacing root system. Nodules and frozen rivulets of twisted dirt, wrapped in shadow.

Grimes halts. "You ready?"

Vicky stops moving. "Yes."

He turns on a flashlight.

Vicky's mind shrieks. A ghastly inner howl splits her head in two. What the light illuminates belongs to her most feverish dreams born of too many dreadful crime scenes and gruesome aftermaths. She has so rarely lost her grip in her waking life that the grinding of her thoughts feels like a precursor to death.

Limbs, not roots, disturb the basement floor. Two legs and two arms, hardened and grown over with black-speckled leather, like some poorly tanned hide. Stretched and desiccated, the limbs plunge into the ground, rise, intertwine, submerge, and vanish. It is a nest of frozen lashings, corrupted flesh whipped into what Vicky thinks might be a rough spiral. Yet all this chaos resolves aboveground into the torso and head of a young woman. Her body is made up of the same tough, fibrous skin that crossed their first victim's stomach underneath her housecoat. But where that desecration seemed unfinished, half formed, what has been done to this young woman is the resolution of the incomplete act.

Vicky loses track of time. The sheer refusal to accept what's before her begins to abate. Her mind claws itself back to awareness. For once she's thankful for Grimes's terrible health habits. The smoke from his Camel, acrid beneath the low basement ceiling, helps reframe her perception around this fresh horror. She can cope with this. She will not break.

A minute or an hour later, she takes one step forward. Then another. She comes to the place where the legs enter the earth in parallel. Kneeling, she beckons for Grimes's flashlight. He hands it over and she trains the light on the legs' entry point. There is no violence to their plunge. If they had punched down into the dirt with great force, Vicky thinks there would be more of a disturbance in the way the basement floor was flung aside.

"It looks like they *grew* down here over time. You see what I mean?" She wiggles the flashlight around the entry point. "It's relatively smooth, not ragged and torn up."

"That's what I thought too," Grimes says. "It's worse that way, somehow."

"How so?"

"Check out the head."

Vicky moves the flashlight along the nest of limbs. Up close, the torso appears to be fully encased in its new flesh, all ripples of a fused, once-malleable carapace. The shape is still more or less recognizable as a young woman of average size and weight. Light moves across the nacreous slopes of dehydrated breast-lumps, then up a mottled neck. When she comes to the head, her body feels almost fizzy in its lightness. At the same time, a profound sadness descends on her like a dropped veil.

"Oh God."

The skin of the cheeks and forehead is mostly intact, with the pale-pink sheen of a person taking a nap on a hot summer day. The head is tilted back, rictus holding it aloft. The woman's mouth is frozen open in a rough oval. Vicky moves to the side of the nest, past the torso, and shines the light in her mouth. She knows what she's going to find—or not find.

"No chompers," Grimes says.

Vicky can't see the hands or feet—if they still exist—but she assumes that they are devoid of fingernails and toenails. Like their first victim, this woman's scalp has been roughly buzzed. Dirty-blond stubble grows in wisps and clumps.

"She was alive the whole time," Vicky says. There's no scientific proof, of course. But by the way the woman's skull is still bound in human skin, Vicky imagines the infernal transformation began with her limbs and worked its way up her body.

The sadness deepens. What had her existence been like down here in this terrible place, what horrors visited upon her?

She lets out a shaky breath and examines the scene holistically. Her light picks three boxes out of the darkness.

"Hair, teeth, and nails," Grimes says, stubbing out his cigarette on a rafter just above his head. "The three musketeers."

Vicky sweeps the light across the back wall. Her breath catches in her throat.

Grimes laughs softly. "The graffiti's a nice touch, right?"

Each large stone embedded in the wall is decorated with red paint in the shape of a spiral.

"What are the other parts supposed to be, do you think?" Vicky asks. Two red blobs protrude from each spiral.

"Wings," Grimes says. "Best I can figure anyway."

Winged spirals. Hundreds of them. Vicky chooses a large one and runs a finger lightly over the paint, tracing the design. She wishes she could time-warp herself back to the crime scene in the hoarder house. She's certain she would find more of these augmented spirals there, carved on the underside of the table or into the baseboards. They open up new pathways in this investigation.

"I don't know if we can even classify this as a murder," Vicky says.

"Right," Grimes says. "Suicide. I was thinking that too. Nice clean way to go."

"I just mean that given what we know—"

"I understand, Victoria. That's why I needed you to see it. It strikes me as ritualistic, like the kind of shit a bunch of horny goth kids reading from a spell book might try to pull off. Except *this* little ritual actually did something. Something big."

Grimes sounds almost uncomfortable airing these thoughts, like he's afraid Vicky will accuse him of being silly. "You think *this*, specifically, ushered in the cicadas."

"A couple days ago I'd force a loony-bin hold on *myself* for saying this, but yeah. I do. Or at least played a part in it.

Otherwise we're dealing with some pretty fucking out-there coincidences."

Vicky walks around the narrow space between the anchored monstrosity and the wall, moving the flashlight's beam through its flesh-bent crevices. Despair wells inside her. She'd staked everything on coming here. Somewhere along the line, like a game of telephone played only with herself, she'd convinced herself that this crime scene would hold the key to reversing Sadie's condition. This knowledge had burned inside of her, stoking the fire that kept her going. And the risks she's taken to get here—she can barely think about her escape from the hospital without wishing she could take it all back. If only she'd stayed at Sadie's bedside with Hassan. Because this? This is another door to nowhere. There is no key here.

The spirals, she thinks, are apt. She's lost in one now.

It's crazy that she thought she could put things right with some good old-fashioned shoe leather and hard-nosed detective skills. Kim's right, she thinks: You can look at your life and rack up all the good and all the bad side by side, but when you're faced with catastrophe it ceases to matter. Grimes ruins his body and mind with alcohol and cigarettes, you preserve yours with discipline and abstention. But right now, who gives a crap? You are another faceless domino in the millions of tilted rows that make up the human race. *Ashes, ashes, we all fall down.*

Sadie, Kim, Franco. Everybody.

"I'm sorry, Kim," she says quietly, suddenly conscious of the girl upstairs in the foyer as if her weight is pressing down on the basement ceiling.

Grimes sets an awkward hand on her shoulder. "It's not your fault. None of this is."

"I know," Vicky says, shaking off the mounting guilt. Even now she's not one to self-flagellate. It's an odious trait, one she's careful to stamp out in herself. "It's just—what do we even do with this?" She gestures at what's left of this young woman. Or, more accurately, what she's become. She breathes in the odors of the basement: cigarette smoke and turned soil. A whiff of clove-scented decay.

"There's gotta be something here," Grimes says.

She works her way around to the corner of the room and kneels down. Shifting her viewpoint delivers waves of anxiety, like aftershocks from the mind-altering force of seeing it for the first time. Down here, behind the woman's shaved head, the flashlight illuminates the space underneath her torso.

She feels sick. "Grimes. Take a look."

A pair of nodules protruding from just below the shoulder blades lift the torso off the floor. Growths branch into a curved fibrous frame. *Spirals with wings.* A third nodule grows from the lower back and stabs directly into the ground. Vicky shakes her flashlight to indicate it to her partner.

"Back at the hospital I saw a cicada up close," she says. "A teenage boy had just cut it out of his father's stomach."

"Judas fucking Priest," Grimes says.

"It had a long growth, like this, from its lower abdomen."

Grimes is silent for a moment. "So this *thing* here is mimicking cicada anatomy."

"The tip of the growth split into three small spikes. It hooked onto the man's insides that way." She swallows, thinking of Sadie and Kim. "Dug itself right into his internal organs."

Grimes exhales. He stands up, knees popping, and rubs his forehead. "All right. So what do we got? Possible occult bug ritual sparks a mutant cicada uprising. Comm networks go down. Unknown force cordons off the entire city. What does that add up to?"

Vicky's head feels stuffed with cotton. She plays the flashlight around the tight space underneath the woman's body. She passes over yet another leathery lump, then pauses and swings the light back.

"Holy crap," she says. "Check this out. I almost missed it."

Grimes is halfway to lighting a cigarette. "You want me to get back down there?"

"Just do it, Kenny."

Grumbling, he lowers himself down and peers into the rat's nest of limbs and upturned earth.

"There," Vicky says.

"Holy fucking shit," Grimes says.

"Her purse."

Vicky holds her breath. To snag the purse, she has to move her upper body beneath the torso and stretch out an arm. Her hand brushes one of the growths and she grits her teeth. It feels like birch bark—solid but also brittle. Maybe a little moist. There's a rank, humid feel to the air trapped beneath the body. Her fingers close around the purse strap and she yanks it out.

Vicky scrambles to her feet and moves away from the body's weird miasma. Grimes joins her by the wine racks. There, she overturns the purse. Wallet, keys, tampons, phone, pepper spray, lipstick, compact, hair ties, four Hershey's Kisses. She opens the wallet, flips through a stack of credit cards, and comes up with a driver's license.

"Violet Carmichael," she says. "Twenty-four years old. New York City address."

"Organ donor," Grimes says. "Good for her."

Vicky picks up the phone and clicks the power button. Nothing happens. "Obviously."

"There's a charger in the kitchen," Grimes says. "I saw it earlier."

Half a minute later, they're standing at the kitchen counter, plugging in the phone. The air up here is noticeably cooler. Cicadas buzz against the big casement window above the sink.

Their muted song hangs about the room, lying dully across the knife-scarred butcher block, the great wooden slab of a table. Vicky and Grimes wait together silently, lost in thought. She fights the urge to sit in one of the chairs pushed under the table. She might never get back up.

The phone screen comes to life. Vicky studies the wallpaper photo. A young woman—Violet Carmichael, she guesses—grins out at her, captured in a moment of casual, unforced joy. She's the picture of carefree youth, with ruler-straight bangs, smiling green eyes, and a tote slung across her body. Her arms are over the shoulders of two other twenty-somethings, a boy and a girl, all of them beaming. Behind them, a drab, low-slung building sits beneath a gray winter sky.

"Look at this," Vicky says.

Grimes is peering inside an empty cabinet above a teal Chambers stove. He turns. "You unlocked it?"

"No. We need our tech guys for that. But check out the home screen."

Grimes frowns at the phone. "Happy days."

Vicky lays a finger on the building behind the trio in the photo. "Recognize this?"

"Generic warehouse number four two three," Grimes says.

"It's the one just off the turnpike. Up by the old hot dog place on the hill, where they roller-skated out to you."

"The Sock Hop," he says wistfully. "Best chili dogs this side of the Great Lakes."

Vicky indulges a memory of taking Sadie there when she was five or six, before the place closed. They'd split a strawberry milkshake for a special treat. Vicky remembers being torn about the whole experience, wondering if she was setting a bad precedent by taking her daughter to eat junk.

"I used to be so uptight," she mutters out loud without really meaning to.

"You've really chilled out," Grimes says.

Vicky can't stop staring at the phone. "That warehouse used to be the linen supplier."

"Yeah. Restaurant uniforms."

"They went out of business too. So why are Violet Carmichael and her friends taking a photo in the empty parking lot of an abandoned warehouse?"

"The atmosphere? Kids like this thing called *ruin porn*, I saw it on *Sixty Minutes*."

She sets the phone down on the counter. "We have to go there."

Grimes studies her face. "All right. I don't disagree. It's the only real lead we got. But first you need to sleep."

Vicky scoffs. "We can't go all the way home, then back out. Who knows what we'll run into out there. No." She shakes her head. "We stick together, and we go now."

"I am with you to the end, Vic. Scout's honor. But you are wilting where you stand. I'm afraid you're gonna collapse. If we're going to survive this, and actually do something that counts, for Sadie and for everybody else, we need to be sharp." He pauses. "Just a few hours."

Her partner fishes a cigarette from his soft pack. Vicky can't believe Ken Grimes is advocating for a healthy choice, but she knows he's right. Once the adrenaline fumes left over from bearing witness to the horror in the basement evaporate, she'll be a dull-witted husk of a person. If she recharges now and through the evening, she can get going again in the early predawn hours with a clear mind.

"You mean we should stay here," she says.

"There are five bedrooms upstairs," he says. "They all have mattresses." He pauses. "One's got a weird stain. So let's say four bedrooms."

She stares at her partner. *Stay here*, where Kim is lying

insensible in the foyer. *Stay here*, where the corrupted remains of Violet Carmichael haunt the basement. She can't imagine closing her eyes and going to sleep in the same house as that *thing*.

"It's either that or a tent in the yard." Grimes gestures to the window. Cicadas beat softly against the glass. "Seriously, Vic, go pass out. I'll keep watch."

"All right," Vicky says. "Wake me up in a bit and we'll switch so you can get some sleep."

He opens a cabinet door, shuts it, opens another one. "Oh, fuck me." He pulls out a half-full bottle of gin. "Dinner."

Vicky sighs. "Don't get too messed up."

"Good point." He opens the bottle and takes a sniff. "If there's one thing the end of the world demands of us, it's sobriety."

"That reminds me." She reaches into her pocket and pulls out the pill. "Hassan gave me this. I think it's an amphetamine. You want it?"

Grimes blows smoke and coughs out a laugh. "Why don't you hold on to it."

"For what?"

He raises the bottle. "For when shit gets worse."

18

FORT HALCOTT

We knew this day would come," the man behind the desk says. The woman who escorted Will and Alicia here remains at attention against one wall of the fortified Quonset hut. The man reaches into his desk drawer and pulls out a granola bar. He starts to unwrap it, then sets it back down. "We *knew* it. We've had eyes on you people for decades. And yet we're still one step behind, fighting a goddamn rear-guard action." He laces his fingers atop the bald crown of his head and leans back in his chair, elbows out. "I gotta hand it to you—you caught us by surprise. I told the chief—I said, the Order of Hemiptera is non-hierarchical now. This isn't the '90s, we can't just take out the head of the snake and watch you scatter. You already *are* scattered, and that's the whole goddamn problem."

He lowers his arms and scoots his chair back from the desk. The monitors behind him flash to various points on the Fort Halcott perimeter. It looks like the mercenaries are setting up more structures around town—Quonset huts and windowless modular boxes. The fence shimmers from different angles in the grid of the screen.

"It was a masterstroke to wait as long as you did to spring it," he says. "Hiding in plain sight, passing down knowledge to new generations since, what, the 1940s? Incredible." Will shoots Alicia a glance. Wordlessly, they both agree to keep as quiet as possible, to let this man air his thoughts. Will figures the second he confesses to not actually being a member of the Order of Hemiptera, this meeting will be over.

The man finishes unwrapping the granola bar and sets it on a plate. Then he produces a steak knife and a fork and begins slicing the granola bar into neat bite-size pieces.

"What the hell," Alicia says. "Who eats a granola bar like that?"

"Please," the man says, taking a bite off the tip of his knife, "call me Gerald." He waves at his subordinate. Will catches his murky reflection in her visor. The mercenary shifts her weight. There's a soft metallic click as her rifle moves along with her. "She knows me as Colonel Cassidy, but I'd prefer to be on a first-name basis with you two." He spears another piece of granola bar. "It'll make our conversation that much easier."

Gerald chews like he's savoring a fine cut of filet mignon, then washes it down with a swig from his water bottle. "So what do I call you?"

"I'm Will. This is Alicia."

"Will and Alicia. And you're friends?" He looks for affirmation. "Friends with benefits? Lovers? Cousins?"

"We used to be married," Alicia says.

Gerald smiles. "I commend you. My ex-wife hates my guts. She certainly wouldn't be caught dead traipsing around the woods with me." He thinks for a moment. "I wonder how she's faring, during all this." He pauses. "You know what? I don't give a shit. I hope she's choking on a mouthful of cicadas."

"I'm sure she feels the same about you," Alicia says.

"Yes, yes, I'm sure you're right. You two have kids?"

"No," Will says. He looks at Alicia. His walkabout had put a damper on any family planning. And afterward, riding the wave of job after job, traveling to far-flung places on business, it never seemed like the right time to pick that conversation back up.

"Me either," Gerald says. "I mean, given what we both knew about what was coming, that was the only responsible choice. Again, I commend you. You seem like solid citizens." He stabs a chunk of granola bar and eats it. "That's what's so unbelievable to me. Still, after all the shit I've seen. After all the institutional knowledge we've gained about you people. It still boggles my mind how much you all *blend in*. It's not that I don't get the compartmentalization. Plenty of serial killers and their ilk have managed to do that successfully, to pull off marriages and kids and jobs without a slip-up. It's the *why* of it that bakes my god-damn noodle. The Order's spent, what, eighty-some-odd years working toward the rising. You bought the ticket, you're clearly down to take the ride. So why bother with the shit all the rest of us schmucks have to plod through like assholes every day of our lives? I mean, some of you are *actuaries*, for fuck's sake. Why bother doing the most boring job in existence if you believe that your secret society is going to bring about the end of the world? I mean, what do *you* do, Will?"

He still hasn't found a good, pithy way to answer that question. He tried using "fixer" as a job title for a while, but it made him feel like a network TV character. "I help people get out of bad situations."

Gerald freezes with the last bite of granola bar halfway to his mouth. "You're fucking kidding me." He glances at his subordinate and laughs. "You hear this shit?" She nods. Gerald spreads his arms wide. "Well, here we are, motherfucker—the baddest situation in human history. *I* would sure like a way out of it. Are you going to help *me*?" He shakes his head. "No. Because why? Because you *catalyzed the whole thing to begin with*."

Gerald stands up and rises to his full height, which Will estimates to be roughly five foot four. He's small-framed but wiry, with ropy little strands of muscle winding up his arms. The knife remains in his hand, and with its tip he taps out an off-kilter rhythm on the desk. He nods at the mercenary. "Get Duvall in here."

"All right, look, *Gerald*," Alicia says, "there's no need for Duvall. Tell Duvall he can keep on doing what he's doing. This has gone way too far. We don't have anything to do with the Order of whatever. We don't live in this backwater shithole. We're just two people trying to get the hell out. I can't speak for Will, but even before the cicadas I hated this fucking place."

"I didn't love it," Will admits.

"And that's it," Alicia says. "That's our whole deal. There's nothing else. We really have no idea what you're talking about, but it clearly doesn't concern us. We're just wasting each other's time."

Gerald looks from Alicia to Will. Then he turns to his subordinate. "This man demonstrated immunity, correct?"

"Yes, sir," she says. "This man opened his mouth out there in the woods, surrounded by cicadas. Fearlessly. When we apprehended him, he invoked the Order, and—see for yourself."

She jabs the screen of a small device attached to her forearm. A moment later, the huge map display is replaced with footage from the forest preserve.

Body cam, Will thinks. His heart sinks as he watches himself inhabit a cultish persona. He remembers Denny, the hotel desk clerk who'd ripped out his own teeth and swallowed cicadas right before their eyes. His own performance is more measured, but its believability startles him. He thinks back to that moment in the woods, and a snatch of the insects' glorious symphony reverberates inside him. Had it really been a performance at all?

He watches himself speak with the gentle fanaticism of the

proselytizer hoping to win recruits: *You think what we do is some kind of magic, but that's ridiculous. It's all about forging a connection.*

He's so absorbed in reliving the moment, it isn't until the footage ends and the map returns to the screen that Will realizes how damning it all is.

The mercenary stands at attention. Will detects a note of pity in the way Gerald regards them.

"Look," he says, "you've already unleashed your masterpiece on the world. Your purpose has been fulfilled. You've *won*. What would it hurt to answer a few simple questions for me now?"

"I just said that bullshit back in the woods so your people wouldn't kill us," Will says.

Gerald tilts his head. "Your bullshit was remarkably specific and well informed, don't you agree?"

"I'm a good bullshitter. It's part of the job."

Gerald wipes the knife blade against his thigh. Bits of granola fall to the floor. "It doesn't matter what you *said*, Will. The fact remains: You opened your mouth. You spoke without hesitation. Yet the insects did not attack. Any one of us would have been invaded in a matter of seconds." He nods toward Alicia. "Including you, I presume, which is why you clammed up. But *you*"—he turns back to Will—"are a man without fear, and rightfully so! Why should you fear your own foul creation?"

"Oh Jesus Christ," Alicia says, *"Will didn't make this happen! How would that even be possible?"*

Gerald's eyes go cold. The knuckles of his hand are white as he gestures with the knife. "Look around you. The restrictions on what's possible are significantly looser than most people think. But you and your kind have known that since 1943."

Will's about to protest, yet again, when Gerald jabs the knife toward a battered old metal lockbox sitting on the corner of his desk. It's the kind of fireproof container in which Will's parents kept the deed to the brownstone, their wills, and other vital keepsakes. Gerald flicks open the lid, sets the knife down, and removes a photograph, black-and-white turned sepia with age. He sets it on the desk so that Will and Alicia can see it. There's two men from another time wearing short-sleeved collared shirts tucked into belted khaki shorts. One is a rail-thin white man in wire-rimmed glasses, the other a stocky Latino. They're grinning, holding up champagne flutes, caught in a private moment of celebration. Palm trees flourish at their backs. A slice of the ocean is visible between the trees.

Gerald glances up with an expectant lift to his bushy sea-captain eyebrows.

"Looks like a fun vacation," Alicia says.

"You think we haven't been to Bava Atoll?" Gerald says. "We combed through every mousehole on that godforsaken place." He looks from Alicia to Will. A granola crumb clings to the corner of his mouth. "Every inch of your fucked-up holy land."

"Mousehole?" Will says.

Gerald removes a second photo from the metal box and places it next to the first one. It's a more candid shot of the same two men in lab coats and ties, huddled around a workbench, poring over what appear to be blueprints. People in the background attend to large microscopes and other more esoteric equipment. The setting has the gleaming patina of a very expensive laboratory.

Gerald taps the face of the white man. "I've looked at him a thousand times," he says, "trying to find something in his eyes that might give it away. But it's always the same, and I never see anything at all. I mean, how many people, throughout history, have thought about the eradication of our species? And how many delusional maniacs have actively worked to bring it about? I don't know. Because they were bush-league also-rans compared with your boy here." He studies the photo for half a minute. Somewhere, a hard-drive coolant fan whirs. Then he looks up at Will. "And with you, it's the same thing. You'd think there'd be some kind of, I don't know, *mania* in you. The street preacher kind. Because what else would make you discover an ideology of eradication and think, *Lemme hitch my wagon to this.* Or am I thinking about it all wrong? Is my framing of what you people are all about simply misguided? Tell me. Please."

"I lost track of what I'm supposed to be telling you," Will says.

Gerald removes a battered manila envelope from the lock-box. It bears a faded, off-center stamp: PROJECT HEMIPTERA. He bends the edges to make it into a tube and tilts it downward until an object slides out and lands on the plate, displacing crumbs.

"Jesus," Alicia says.

"Far from it," Gerald says, "I assure you."

Will stares at the thing on the plate. It's the dried-out husk of a dead bug—the shell of some nearly foot-long monster insect, brittle wings folded back along its body. There's something prehistoric about it, the armored segmentation and foreleg pincers harking back to the insects that clung to the undersides of giant leathery herbivores with long skinny necks. He can feel himself drifting into the thrall of this impossible specimen, the corners of his mind twittering with fecund impressions of what this creature had been like, how it moved, the plump segmentation of its abdomen and thorax, the weird skittering grace of its legs...

The door sealant hisses and brings him back to reality. A second mercenary enters, carrying a black, hard-shell briefcase. He takes off his helmet and hangs it on a hook. Then he nods at his counterpart and gives Gerald a crisp salute. "Sir."

"Sergeant Duvall. How are things looking out there?"

"Hairy, sir." He turns to Will and Alicia. This man is thick-necked and lightly pockmarked. A slightly unkempt mustache hides his upper lip. His face curdles with disgust when he meets Will's eyes. "This him?"

"It is indeed, Sergeant." Gerald retrieves a folding chair from the corner of the hut and sets it up in front of his desk.

Will's heart pounds. They've been in tight spots before, but he's never felt so trapped. Both their standard avenues of escape have been denied. There will be no talking their way out—the body cam footage has seen to that. And fighting is a non-starter. They've scrapped before, Will and Alicia, even once back-to-back like in the movies, but not when the odds were so lopsided. Even if it weren't three to two, both the woman and Sergeant Duvall are heavily armed. If it were only Gerald and his stupid granola knife, they might have a chance...

Without acknowledging the desiccated insect, Duvall sets the briefcase down on the desk, snaps the locks, and lifts the lid. Will can't see what's inside. More giant exoskeletons? Gerald sets up a second folding chair facing the first.

"Why don't you both have a seat," he suggests. Will doesn't move. Neither does Alicia. The helmeted mercenary trains her weapon on Will. Duvall removes a device from the case. It resembles a metal spider with a body the size of a hockey puck. Jointed legs dangle. He sets it on the desk.

Will's mouth goes dry. He thinks of the odd, shimmering fence capable of repelling a car. Esoteric weapons, door sealants, tactical equipment beamed in from elsewhere. He does not like the look of Duvall's little item. He thinks he knows what it's for. He puts up his hands.

"Okay, okay." All at once he knows what he has to do. There's so much lingering shit between him and Alicia, so much unsaid despite their anguished sessions with Dr. Capaldi. And this trip upstate has left him in tangles. It would almost be easier if she were still fucking the lawyer—at least wallowing in self-pity had been a predictable state of being. Love and the possibility of letting it in is so much more complicated. Maybe that's why Alicia reads his indecision as a pronounced, spiteful act against her. Well. There is no place for that here. Not now, not anymore.

"Let her go," Will says. Alicia shakes her head in alarm, mouths *no* at him. "Let her go and I'll tell you everything about the Order of Hemiptera. I'll give you the secret to immunity. I swear. Just let her go."

Gerald sighs. "William. You *just said* you didn't have anything to do with the Order. Your credibility is plummeting, my friend."

"Let her go and we'll talk."

"I'm sorry," he says. "We're way past that now." He nods at the helmeted merc. She steps forward and shoves Alicia down into the chair.

"I am going to fuck you up when I get out of here, FYI," Alicia says. The merc pulls Alicia's arms together behind her back and zip-ties her wrists together. Then she kneels and fastens Alicia's ankles to the legs of the chair. "You think I've never been tied up before?" Alicia says. "I rescued a kid from the Russian mob *in Russia*." She laughs. "Well, Belarus. Same thing." Will recognizes her false-bravado voice, as much for her own benefit as their captors. "Those tattooed fuckers are about a thousand times scarier than you, by the way. Like haunt-your-dreams-for-the-rest-of-your-life scary. And I'm still here."

Will knows what Alicia's about to do before she does it. *No,* he implores her silently as her head goes back and darts forward like a snake's. A wad of phlegm spatters the merc's visor. She pauses for a moment. Duvall hands her a paper towel. Wordlessly, she wipes her visor clean. Then she raises her rifle and with a quick piston-like movement slams the butt into the side of Alicia's head. Will lunges forward. Alicia's body is wrenched to one side. The chair legs lift off the floor. The merc flips the rifle in a split second and levels the barrel at Will before he can take a step. At the same time, he feels the tip of Gerald's knife pressing into the back of his neck, just above the highest vertebra.

He freezes and puts up his hands. Alicia's chair rights itself. Her limp body swings the other way then slumps. Duvall doesn't look up from the device he's assembling on the desk.

Will's rage is a molten ball in his chest. He draws a searing breath and stretches his mind once again, through the walls of the Quonset hut, out into the trees alongside the highway ramp, where the cicadas caper and sing, carving oneiric patterns into the air. He knows he can't tap into their hive-mind and command them to come to his aid—but he latches onto their harmonic caterwauling and it calms him. The hut's interior fades. Gerald is pushing Will down into the second folding chair. The man is speaking, but Will cannot hear over the echoing din of the cicadas in his mind.

His thoughts pierce the symphony with remarkable clarity. The path that he walks, alongside Alicia or all by himself, is its own harmonic strain that fades in and out of the cicadas' music. There is a greater part for him to play yet. Late at night, during his walkabout, lying sleepless on the thin mattresses of cheap hostels in Eastern Europe, North Africa, Vietnam, Will's mind expanded to contemplate in new and unfamiliar ways the system of the world. Then, as now, it had been a vast and ponderous conundrum. He pictured it as a cloud that occupied whatever space it wished—air or water or the solid matter of the earth. And this cloud was capable of holding great data—the knowledge of entire civilizations come and gone. It was also capable of making itself devoid of information so that it could accept whatever came into its wispy embrace. According to one of the weirder philosophy books he got his hands on at a bazaar in Marrakesh, Will's late-night overtures toward understanding the threads that weave the world put him on a collision course with *hyperobjects*—phenomena so massive and complex as to defy human comprehension. He had accepted this as a given at the time. Of course there were events and happenings beyond his grasp and the grasp of every human being. But now, as he's shoved roughly into a folding chair by Gerald, he thinks he may have been too hasty to chalk the system of the world up to an ungovernable hyperobject. Because as the man cuffs his wrists and binds his legs to the chair, Will is elsewhere, riding the currents of the cicadas' symphony, backing far enough out of the frame to grant himself a panoramic view of the insects' ministrations upon this world. And there it is, scrawled across the backdrop of the rising: Whatever happens to him in this room, it will not be the end.

He comes back to himself. Across the floor, Alicia is still out cold. He burns for her. Gerald gets in his face.

"Where is the origin point?"

Will stares back silently. Gerald's face puckers in frustration. Duvall steps out from behind the desk, metallic spider dangling from his fist. He glances at Gerald, who nods once in return. Duvall works his way around behind the chair. Will's body tingles in dreadful anticipation. Then: pressure against the place where his neck meets his head and tendon slips underneath bone. There's an almost magnetic pull from inside his skull as the "body" of the spider is adhered to the back of his head. The sensation grows increasingly uncomfortable.

Gerald speaks slowly. "Tell me where the origin point is."

A smooth whir tickles Will's eardrums. The device's metallic limbs close around his head. They dig into the flesh of his face in eight places, from above his eyes to beneath his jawbone. The pressure increases. With the device in place, Duvall steps out from behind Will, walks over to Alicia, and opens a vial under her nose. A moment later, she revives, moaning. Duvall grips her chin and steers her face so that she's looking straight at Will. Her eyes widen.

"It's okay," Will says.

"The origin point," Gerald says again.

Will shifts his eyes to meet Gerald's. "Did you check your asshole?"

The colonel sighs. He nods at Duvall. "Watch," he says softly to Alicia. Still holding Alicia's head, he jabs at his forearm device.

Will braces himself for pain—but instead, the pressure on his skull suddenly subsides. Confusion reigns. He had steeled himself for torment, and now, finding none, his body is tensed with coiled anticipation. The metal fingers undulate up and down his face. It takes him a moment to realize what is being stirred up inside him. The pressure hasn't subsided, he realizes. It's simply shifted.

Hopelessness. His feelings of pathetic impotence are magnified, but he is only aware of the magnification for a moment before it simply becomes his reality.

He is a truly useless piece of human shit.

Across from him, Duvall pulls a trench knife from a sheath on his belt. Will's eyes flood with tears. Gripping Alicia's head, Duvall makes a shallow cut in her forehead. She screams. A curtain of blood drips down her face.

Will knows he is the reason that Alicia is in pain. He squirms against his bonds. He can't protect her. Duvall taps his forearm. Will's mind throbs. The margins of his sight flutter. A bottomless pit of despair opens up inside of him. It is the anxiety of a terrible hangover mixed with the deep understanding that his life has been a waste. He strains against his bonds. He wishes he could puke out every defining characteristic of Will Bennett. Anything that makes him *him*, he wants to excise.

Across from him, Duvall holds the knife against the top of Alicia's right ear.

"Just tell me where the origin point is, and this will end," Gerald says.

"I don't know!" Will shouts.

Gerald turns to Duvall.

"No!" Will screams. Duvall nicks Alicia's ear with the blade. She shuts her eyes and grits her teeth. Duvall taps his forearm. The spider legs tap out Morse code on Will's face. The pressure in his head clicks into a fresh sensation, the most acute self-loathing he's ever known. It's evident that he's rotten to the core. The demons that visit him before he falls asleep and force him to remember the awful things he's said and done appear before him now, shrieking venom. The cicadas' song is muted. White noise fills his head. Its frequency rises in pitch as, across from him, Alicia's face distorts.

His own rotten soul is corrupting her flesh. There was once a marriage between them, and his vows, written and rewritten and worried over for weeks, had been so laughably insipid. He knows that now. Their life together has led them both to this repulsive moment. These people will cut her to pieces, slowly, while he comes apart.

His eyes dart around the room. If only his hands were free! He could at least try to grab a knife—not to free himself, fight back, save Alicia; he's too much of a coward for that. What he will do is plunge the blade into his own neck. Death will be his only salvation. Alicia's face begins to melt, flesh like hot wax dripping off her chin. Her howling mouth elongates. Oh God, he's so sorry he was ever born. If he could peel off his own skin he would. His body trembles with a sudden violence that nearly tips him over. The man whose name Will can no longer remember holds him in place. At the same time, the man shouts to be heard above the cacophony inside his head.

"Where is the origin point?"

Will bites his tongue and tastes blood. The flavor makes a screaming sound. Alicia's tender flesh hangs from her filthy bones.

"Tell me and this will end!"

He tries to speak. *Please*—he will tell this man anything. But all he can do is weep.

19

NEW YORK CITY

The evening sky is a dull watercolor wash on the security camera footage. Union Square is surrounded. Regular NYPD cruisers and a phalanx of Emergency Service Unit armored vehicles, some with tanklike treads, fan out from a mobile command post on 14th Street. The only people on the street are officers dressed in bulky tactical gear, weapons secured with straps across their chests and pointing at the ground. Their helmets, already equipped with visors, have been modified to seal their heads in an airtight rubber ring that hugs their neck.

Cicadas rise from the park in great spirals and helixes. They roost on the statue of Washington on his horse and cover Lincoln in their shuddering masses. The Marquis de Lafayette's pedestal is completely veiled by insects, piles of them, bubbling up and overflowing like water in a fountain.

The mayor's office is acting with admirable intent to contain the swarm's spread. It's the execution that's being slowed, inevitably, by the unbelievable nature of what is happening.

Barricaded in his private office on the eighty-fourth floor, Anton has watched the evolution of the city's response.

He switches views and accesses a camera from the 17th Street
Barnes & Noble, looking south. ESU officers patrol warily past
neat rows of New Yorkers lined up in the streets and on the
sidewalks surrounding the park. They look dead from the somewhat grainy perspective this camera provides, but Anton figures
they're in the same weird between-state as his assistant, Kevin,
who lies on Anton's sofa. He's mostly still, but racked with epi-
sodes where his low murmuring boils over and he thrashes and
utters clipped bits of nonsense.

Anton toggles through various feeds surrounding the
park. Containment has been an abject failure. When they first
emerged, the cicadas seemed to favor areas with grass and trees—
like the biosphere in the lobby of the Lacuna building. But
within an hour of their emergence, the insects had begun venturing far beyond the confines of city parks and green spaces
to flood the streets, subway tunnels, bridges, and buildings. An
incredible preponderance of bugs, seemingly self-generated,
manifesting in the way alchemists of old theorized that dead
bodies actually *birthed* maggots, or that fruit flies sprang fully
formed from some transubstantiation taking place at the core of
rotting apples and pears.

At the same time, news aggregators fill the remaining
womb screens. GLOBAL CICADA INVASION BAFFLES SCIENTISTS.
Wide-eyed and sleepless, broadcasters in a dozen languages
deliver unbelievable stories from a place beyond horror. Shanghai, Dublin, Buenos Aires: vivid dispatches from the unfolding
catastrophe, cities of millions overrun by a never-ending stream
of cicadas flooding parks and streets and waterfronts.

The invasions follow a predictable pattern: Cicadas swarm
in. People are overcome, their bodies littering the streets and
sidewalks. Traffic snarls with people trying to escape. Emergency vehicles can't proceed. Mass transit stalls. Civilians and
cops and military personnel are forced to travel on foot. They, in

turn, are overcome by more swarming insects. The power goes out. Face coverings don't work—cicadas find a way in. Motorcycle helmets are the best solution, but only a small percentage of the population has them. It doesn't take long before congested urban areas around the world are hurricanes of mayhem.

Images of the French countryside fill a screen, a photo series that begins with crisp, composed shots of cicadas fanning out in curtains from neat rows of trees. Anton imagines the photographer as a man with a vintage bicycle, out enjoying a summer day in *la campagne* outside of Cassel. First he hears the noise as he crests a hill. Then he sees the clouds of insects billowing out from the foliage. How strange. He dismounts and snaps a few photos.

Then the insects rise, darkening the sky. The photos become blurry as the hapless man whose day just took an impossible turn wrestles with the urge to document the unthinkable as he flees.

"They're learning," Anton mutters to himself, and possibly to Kevin. It seems that when they first appeared, the cicadas mostly kept to the small towns and suburbs where foliage was more plentiful. But with astonishing speed, they figured out how to move in and infest the urban centers. Which should be impossible.

As if there was any doubt, Moscow's Red Square pops up, blanketed in waves of insects, littered with bodies crawling with bugs. Russian army vehicles—including tanks—crowd the square's edges.

He turns his attention back to his own city. These security feeds are silent, but Anton knows exactly what sound is smothering the five boroughs, lying thickly across the skyline and threading the glass and steel canyons. He can hear it just beyond his bulletproof office door, almost entirely muffled by the cold-rolled steel. Only a thin and distant buzzing finds its way in, one tiny line of melody from the choral arrangement resounding in the corridors.

Just as there are bodies strewn in the streets, Anton knows there are probably thousands of workers rendered immobile and half dead throughout the building. And if these bugs are smart enough to travel through the ventilation system of a skyscraper, then surely no building in the city is entirely safe from attack.

Anton wonders if *attack* is even the correct term. But what are the chances of this being some kind of freak natural occurrence? Zero, he figures. It's got all the earmarks of a bioweapon, either some DARPA fuckup or a state-sponsored act of war. Honestly, the origin doesn't really matter to him. Not when he can't leave his office or get ahold of his parents in Astoria. The cell networks are impossibly snarled. The Earthbound Internet—what Lacuna die-hards call, derisively, the global system of cables and hardware that connects every device—is still up, at least for now. But his parents haven't responded to any of his frantic texts or emails. He picks up his phone and scrolls their family chain to the last message his mother sent him this morning, before the meeting with the board.

Be true to yourself today. We love you!

He stares at the simple words inside the little gray box on the screen of his text app. He imagines his mother typing it out slowly, sitting at the little round table on the landing of their front stoop while Sasha, the elderly Pomeranian, smiles up at her and his father opens the gate with the Czech paper folded under his arm.

Anton shakes off the scene before it can fully imprint itself in his mind. He's been down this road already today: thoughts of his parents darkening to dread at their fate, despair at his inability to help them, and shame at the fact that he survived the initial attack while so much of the city did not. He might as well be one of the billionaire assholes with panic rooms in their penthouses. He's always considered himself a different species of capitalist than the Brian Karchers of the world, but that's really just a convenient salve for his own self-consciousness about being a fucking "founder" in the "tech space."

Anton leans back in his mesh Vingegaard chair and takes a holistic view of the screens curving around him in the womb. The nerve center for his backend view of Lacuna's operating systems has become a nonstop security feed, with hacked imagery from cameras throughout the city cycling across his monitors. He stares at the cicada victims around Union Square, which the ESU cops have taken to lining up like bodies from a plane crash in a gymnasium, waiting to be identified by loved ones.

He taps into a system of cameras surveying Astor Place, a few blocks south. The big black cube sculpture is crawling with insects. A flat mass of bugs seethes down into the subway station while another cloud envelops a coffee cart. Here, just a few blocks from Union Square, there is no perimeter, no presence of ESU or national guard or even regular NYPD. It might as well be a different world. Bodies lie at haphazard angles in the streets. Anton spots a minivan coming down Broadway, veering into a miraculously unclogged lane before jumping the curb to the sidewalk, where it runs over a pair of bodies, spitting them out in its wake. The bodies flip like rag dolls and land in a torn heap. Then the feed blinks out and the screens go black.

Kevin lets out a warbling moan.

The city's power grid, already a patchwork, is showing signs of catastrophic failure. Anton figures the insects have invaded some of the natural gas plants in the city proper and some of the hydroelectric plants upstate. When those invasions reach a critical mass and personnel either flee or are afflicted, the entire grid will shut down. Lacuna HQ has backup generators, of course—but these will only last a few days.

Anton goes to the couch and wets his assistant's dead-fish lips with a cloth dipped in water from the sink in his office bathroom. There's a lukewarm halo souring the air around Kevin, like he's fallen asleep in a bath and let it go almost cold. Actually, the whole office is taking on an unpleasant humidity. He glances up at the air ducts, which he's sealed as best he can with every inch of packing tape he could scrounge up. Corpses of cicadas litter the floor where they fell as he smashed them, one by one, between a pair of gym shoes. He squeezes the cloth and wrings out a few more drops into Kevin's partially open mouth. His assistant's wet lips close. He imagines a squirming cicada somewhere deep in Kevin's esophagus, soaking up a little drink...

On the floor next to the couch lies Kevin's backpack, the one he was wearing when he returned from his ill-fated lunch errand to the building lobby. (Anton thinks now of Willamina, so desperate for her midday meal.) His own stomach is cramped, the biological necessity of food twisted up in a knot of dread. Suddenly enamored with the notion of distraction, however brief, Anton sits cross-legged on the floor and unzips the backpack. Expecting a laptop, hand sanitizer, and a vape, what he finds instead is vegetables from Lacuna's lobby farm. He removes a fistful of neatly bunched leeks, thick asparagus stalks, and several small red peppers. Then his hand closes around what feels like a massive, furry kiwi. Or maybe a monstrous peach? He pulls it from the bag to find himself holding a bulbous fruit the size of an heirloom tomato from the farmers market in Union Square. It smells, vaguely, of laundry steam issuing from a vent. He presses on it with a finger and pierces the skin with his nail. Juice the consistency of olive oil leaks out. The scent intensifies.

Now Anton can't help himself. He sticks his finger in his mouth. The juice tastes milder than it smells. Pleasant but not overpowering, a bit like starfruit. The backpack contains two more of these curious fruits. Leaving the vegetables behind, he takes the fruits over to his desk and places them in a row behind his keyboard.

Back in the womb, Anton toggles up the West Side Highway as seen from various buildings on Twelfth Avenue and Riverside Drive. A line of stalled traffic stretches from the Upper West Side all the way down to Battery Park at the southern tip of the island. Thousands of cars and trucks, their drivers and passengers only safe for as long as they can hold out in their vehicles with the windows up—in the middle of summer in New York.

The swarm stretches thinly across the highway, but Anton knows that when people begin to emerge from their vehicles, the insects will work themselves up into a blood frenzy. A prickly feeling starts in his gut and moves into his arms and legs. To be trapped on a jam-packed highway, knowing it's only a matter of time before you have to choose between baking in a hot, airless car or choking on an invasive cicada. Watching your children or parents suffer the same fate. Thousands of people pissing and shitting in their cars for fear of opening a door. Back on the couch Kevin moans and thrashes.

Half the West Side Highway cameras go dark at once. The outage is spreading. He zips across town to the cameras that line Fifth Avenue's Museum Mile. A security feed just outside the Metropolitan Museum of Art shows pathways snaking through the east side of Central Park. Aerial rivers of cicadas wind around one another, tributaries flowing in all directions. Anton zeroes in on a different kind of movement. A man, running headlong through the crush of cicadas, whipping his arms over his head, swatting bugs and turning in circles. Anton flips to a camera high up on the exterior wall outside the sculpture court, that airy high-ceilinged indoor piazza where he once met with the head of Tencent's acquisitions team.

How strange that the looming acquisition had seemed like the most important event in his life. He'd been prepared for the outcome of the board meeting to define Lacuna's—and by extension, his—future.

This angle provides a better view of the lone figure in the park. The man is dressed in the layered rags of the long-term homeless population, sweatpants and denim that have been molded together by time and decay. His long hair swings from side to side as he shakes his head. Anton wonders where the man's been holed up to have escaped the fate of so many others. He wills the man to go back from where he came and *hide*, but of course it's too late. The cicadas cling to him like a shroud. Hundreds, thousands of them, until there's nothing but a vaguely humanoid figure moving up the path trailing a ragged tail of bugs. The man runs into a water fountain and collapses. The insects swarm over him. There's nothing left to see, but Anton sits staring with his elbows on his desk until the Museum Mile feeds go dark.

His own lofty words from the meeting come back to him as if in mockery. *I'm talking about a totally new organizing principle for the way we interact with everything, whether it's living or sentient or AI or just a regular old object. I'm talking about a new system of the world, with the old barriers smashed for good.*

The old barriers are certainly being smashed much sooner than he'd anticipated.

The womb's screens cycle through an East Village brunch spot overrun by cicadas, the infield at Yankee Stadium, the parking lot of a Home Depot in Queens where bodies lie across the blacktop as if shaken and tossed by a giant hand.

Kevin's soft murmurs lift into a droning warble. The back of his head slams against the couch. The distant chatter of the cicadas outside the office harmonizes with what Kevin is emitting. The drone, intertwined, is almost unbearable. Anton covers his ears and watches Kevin until he calms down and goes back to whispering.

On the womb's screens, Anton is granted quick glimpses of disparate corners of New York, from the desolate Rockaways to a disturbingly unlit Times Square to the body-strewn sidewalks of Inwood. Suddenly every screen goes black. Half a minute later, the womb goes dark except for the Lacuna admin dashboard.

The power grid is dead.

Anton takes a deep breath. Shame is palpable now, a pressure in his chest. He couldn't warn his employees in time. His parents are MIA. He's trapped in his office. The moment he opens the door, he'll meet Kevin's fate.

A new system of the world.

He stares at his dim reflection in one of the black screens, and something stirs in the back of his mind. He swivels in his chair and tosses a pair of twelve-sided dice. Six and eleven. He flips the sixth card in the first Thaumaturgy deck. The Sleepless Walker, a faceless ghoul with an inexorable drive toward oblivion but not as a death wish—as a gesture of hope for a better world on the other side. There's an endless-journey feel to this card, an atmosphere of ceaseless forward motion.

He takes the eleventh card from the second deck. Undying Lore. An interesting card, one he's never drawn before. A sort of mystical library, a repository for the world's knowledge in the form of a pinkish, many-tentacled monstrosity attended by an army of tiny creatures who labor day and night to protect the lore-brain and safeguard its historical memory.

Anton looks from one card to the other. Stubborn advancement toward the void. The cumulative knowledge of an entire species. He begs the game for guidance as a devout worshipper might beseech his God. It never used to be this difficult to slot the meaning of these paired draws into his daily life. Now he wishes for something prescriptive, an invisible hand to nudge him toward... what, exactly?

Kevin shouts nonsense.

Anton stares at the cards, feeling more helpless and stupid with each passing second. Life as he knew it is no more. He could go to the door and open it and let the swarm take him, give in to the endless river of cicadas. Perhaps what Kevin is experiencing is a form of bliss. Perhaps he's been warped to some bright shining heaven. What if all he has to do is step outside and open his mouth and he'll be reunited with his parents in some other place?

A place where a new purpose might even be forged.

He looks at the images on the cards. The shrouded wraith in its endless sojourn across the veiled lands. The squishy tentacled brain tended to by an army of crablike servants.

Here it is, he thinks. *My true system of the world. A card game ruled by random chance.*

Something inside him boils over, and with an open hand he sweeps the cards onto the floor. They land interspersed with dead cicadas on the plush carpet. He gets up and places a gentle hand on Kevin's clammy forehead. He tells himself that it won't be so bad. His assistant doesn't seem like he's in pain.

Anton goes to the window and looks out across the river. Astoria Park shifts and sways like some speckled and discontented beast, millions of cicadas flitting across its lawns and pathways. He puts his forehead to the glass and looks straight down at Third Avenue. Cars and trucks line the streets as far as he can see in either direction. The city of his birth is choking to death before his eyes. He takes his shoes off and walks slowly across his office, savoring the way his feet sink into the carpet. He does slow circles around his private sanctum, delaying the inevitable. Pausing at his vintage toy shelf, he picks up the 1979 prototype of a rocket-firing Boba Fett, one of only a handful in existence. He holds the molded plastic in the palm of his hand, trying to give it meaning, to imbue with spiritual weight a goodbye to an inanimate object he paid a quarter of a million dollars for. But he doesn't feel anything at all. Perhaps that's actually a good sign. Perhaps that signifies a stoic acceptance. He puts the toy back on the shelf and walks back over to the womb. The Lacuna dashboard presents its bland and unsurprising data. Power outages notwithstanding, shitty connections abound, as usual. Shanghai, Delhi, Jakarta, San Diego: jackshit. Bava Atoll: touch and go.

Anton tries to fortify himself against this final dose of regret: the system he dedicated his life to never really worked properly. It's almost hilarious that Tencent was willing to pony up $850 million for its spare parts and intellectual property.

He looks at a half-empty Diet Dr Pepper, his beverage of choice. There are a few more in the fridge—he could drink one now, for old times' sake.

No.

He will just keep finding new delay tactics if he doesn't act now. And then he'll be no better off than the people trapped in their cars while the cicadas hum around them, biding their time.

He tears himself away from the womb.

At the door of his office, he presses his ear against the shiplap that hides several inches of bulletproof steel. Even through this practically soundproof barrier, Anton can hear the unceasing buzz of the insects in the corridor. The moment he pulls it open, they will swarm him. He vows to open his mouth wide and make it quick. Taking half a step back, he places a hand on the doorknob and turns.

BWAAAMP.

He freezes. The sound is coming from the womb: a deep French horn blast, all the rage in early-2010s movie trailers. Anton applied it as an alert in the Lacuna dashboard for one very specific set of circumstances. He lets go of the doorknob and races back over to his desk.

BWAAAMP. A second alert sounds. He scans the backend data.

Beta-test sites in Delhi and São Paulo are suddenly running at full capacity, with 100 percent connectivity. Before his eyes, more sites switch from red or yellow to green: Prague, Jakarta, the home test site in New York City. The French horn blasts overlap.

Even Bava Atoll comes online.

Anton blinks. The fact that he'd been seconds away from delivering himself to the swarm outside is forgotten. He meets this new data with total bewilderment. This level of simultaneous connectivity has never happened before. Today is by far the best day in the history of Lacuna—which is impossible. In all the years the world had been functioning more or less normally, the Lacuna system had never been more than 50 percent operational. Some sites would report successes for a few days while others faltered. Then they would flip-flop.

BWAAAMP.

The Lagos site comes online. Then Houston. Then Vancouver.

"Holy shit," Anton says. He sits down at his keyboard and begins navigating. The dashboard vanishes. All eight womb screens light up with data as he dives in.

The existing global network is dead. And Anton doesn't know how, or why, but Lacuna is risen.

20

The cicadas are inside the Ag Center.

Rebecca doesn't know how they got in, but now it's a moot point. What matters is that her plan to turn her lab into a massive room-size killing jar has taken on a new sense of urgency. They've done active shooter prep, and Rebecca had been operating as if this were an extension of those drills. Doors locked, heads down, wait for the all-clear in the form of text alerts from the administration. But now those tactics seem as laughable as the nuclear attack drills must have during the height of the Cold War: Hey kids, just duck beneath your cheap wooden desks to save yourself from the fifty-megaton blast.

She surveys her students, all of them holding gas masks scrounged from a storage locker in the basement. When Rebecca thinks of gas masks she pictures the haunting alien-faced masks from World War I, with their long snout tubes and featureless rubber. But the ones in the Ag Center are modern, top of the line, designed for special forces and first responders. The only time they'd ever been used was at last year's holiday party, when an eggnog-drunk Dr. Halbert had insisted his colleagues wear them for a photo. Now she watches the Empath—Javier—try his mask on and adjust the straps around the back of his head.

"It's hard to breathe in this thing," he says.

"There will be a small amount of breathing resistance," Rebecca says, "due to the filter." Her mind is reaching in several different directions as she moves around the room, checking all potential points of entry. The massive window that looks out upon the Body Farm is covered in cicadas. Rebecca finds them mesmerizing. Now that she knows what to look for, it's easy to pick out the triplicate proboscises of the females as they crawl across the glass. And if she presses her face right up against the window, she can even see the tiny spiral brand on some of the insects. At the same time, the males emit their never-ending song, rising and falling in pitch according to some unseen conductor.

Meanwhile, the beetles and flies that reside in the lab are in the throes of an extended freakout. Their plastic boxes and aquariums are actually *moving*, making slight shifts and jumps as the bugs inside agitate. This peculiar chaos is not helping the anxiety levels of Rebecca's students. They pace around the room, talking quietly among themselves, gas masks dangling from tight fists, shooting awed and terrified glances at the infestation crawling across the window.

Rebecca is most worried about Erin Jacoby, who sits on a stool in the corner farthest from the window, arms folded across her chest, hugging herself, rocking back and forth. Heading over to comfort the girl, Rebecca stops at the door to check the lab's sole exit. Together with Jason, she has sealed the gap at the bottom of the door with a rolled-up towel, then pushed filing cabinets in place to form a barricade that hopefully blocks any other unseen gaps around the hinges or doorknobs.

She pauses next to the filing cabinets, which cover the door's small square window. She can't see the hallway, but she knows they're out there. For a moment, she feels completely unmoored from reality. It doesn't make any sense that cicadas would invade a building. Simply put, there is nothing here for them. No tree branches or shrubs in which to lay their eggs, no dirt for their nymphs to populate after they emerge.

Welcome to the bizarro world order, Mari says. *I told you to run.*

'Run where? There are millions more cicadas outside than in here. This is still the best possible place to be.'

That's only true by default, because you didn't get out when you had the chance.

Rebecca comes to Erin, places a gentle hand on her shoulder. "How you holding up?"

She's great, Mari says. Rebecca ignores her sister.

Erin looks up at Rebecca as if trying to remember who she is. She speaks like she's pulling words from a deep well. Her voice is soft. "I don't want to die."

"Nobody's going to die."

Or else everyone is. One or the other.

"My dad died last summer," Erin says. "He had lymphoma."

"I'm really sorry to hear that."

"He didn't even try chemo." She looks off into the middle distance. "He didn't fight at all. He just left us."

"Hey." Rebecca moves so she's in Erin's line of sight. "Listen to me. These cicadas—they're acting contrary to their biological imperatives, and that is certainly strange. But there's no reason to think this will last very long. Cicadas don't spend much time aboveground. They're here, and then they're gone."

"But they're killing people!" she wails. Students' heads swivel.

"*Shhhh*, we don't know that for sure."

Rebecca has seen the same news and social media clips as her students: human beings all over the world swarmed by masses of cicadas, taken down to the ground, overcome. But until she's looking at incontrovertible evidence that this brood of cicadas is *actually murderous*, acting in opposition to every cicada brood throughout recorded history, then she refuses to let her students give in to hysteria.

There's a shriek out in the hall, followed by babbling cries. Erin perches her feet on the edge of the stool and buries her head between her knees. Her entire body trembles. Rebecca leans in to give her an awkward hug, then goes over to the long table that holds Ellie, the electron microscope, and the killing apparatus that resembles a large Keurig coffeemaker. She takes stock of the nine small cyanide canisters she's retrieved from a locked cupboard. They are tamper-proof, with a bolted nozzle that only fits the receptor in this particular machine. When this plan had popped into her head, she'd conceived of some kind of modification that would turn the canisters into weapons. But she's not a mechanical engineer; she wouldn't begin to know how to swap out parts and rejigger the machine to shoot bursts of cyanide in any particular direction.

You need one of these kids to be like, I got this, Professor, Mari chimes in. *I worked in my dad's shop since I was six. I just need an Allen wrench and a soldering gun.*

'We don't have either one in this lab so it wouldn't matter.'

It was just a dumb example. But you don't need the cyanide anyway.

'Well, I hope I don't have to use it.'

You just need the masks, genius. Where'd you find the cicada in the Body Farm corpse?

'It crawled out of its mouth.'

Right. So extrapolate, sis. Riff. Use that big scientist brain.

'The mutated ovipositors make it possible for the females of this brood to latch onto something inside our mouths, or something deeper in our digestive tract.'

Yep. So if that's their main goal here, if that's how they're bringing us down, then all we need to do is—

'Protect our faces.'

I think it's time to rally the troops, Mari says. *Staying here's going to drive them crazy.*

Rebecca glances at Erin. Her head is still between her knees. Her palms are clamped over her ears to block out the drone.

Case in point.

She looks around at her other students. Jason is pacing over by the exit, checking and rechecking the edges of the filing cabinets to see that they're flush with the door. Ji-un is crying softly to herself, head down on a lab table. The Empath is curled up in a fetal position against the wall, eyes closed. The other kids are whispering together softly.

"All right," Rebecca says. "Attention, everyone. We can all see that the Ag Center has been overrun. The longer we stay in this lab, the harder it's going to be for us to break out."

Erin lifts her head, eyes wide and fearful.

Jason quits pacing. He frowns. "Why would we want to break out? We're safe in here."

"For now," Rebecca says. She keeps her tone light and reasonable. "But there's so much uncertainty at the core of this event. For any species, I can rely on centuries of behavioral data to predict how an insect will act. And within standard deviations, I will be correct every time." She makes sure to turn subtly to meet every student's eyes. "But this cicada brood is completely unpredictable. Nothing they're doing makes any sense at all. I assume they're acting in their own self-interest, because insects aren't that complicated, all things considered—but I can't even tell you *that* with certainty."

A dark-haired boy with the squat, broad-shouldered build of a gym rat pipes up. *John-Michael,* Mari says.

"If it's all so unpredictable," John-Michael says, "then why would we take a chance going out there?"

Ji-un swivels in her chair. "And where are we going to go? They're everywhere, so what does it matter?" She clasps her hands together in her lap and shakes her head. "I'm not going."

"I can't believe this is happening," the Empath says from where he's curled up on the floor.

"Bro!" Jason wheels on him. "It's fucking happening, okay?"

"We're going to die," Erin says matter-of-factly. Everyone looks at her. She seems surprised by the attention at first, then takes a deep breath and steadies herself. She looks at the window swarming with cicadas. Rebecca wonders if they're moving in some sort of pattern on the glass—for a moment, she thinks she can see it, concentric circles sliding around, wheels within wheels...

A blond girl with a Kappa Delta T-shirt on—*Ashley*—steps into the center of the lab as if taking the floor. The straps of her gas mask are wrapped around her wrist. "Y'all," she says. "God is with us. If we put our faith in Him, there's nothing to be afraid of."

Erin laughs. She points at the window. "There's *that*, Ashley."

Ashley shrugs. "The Lord is my shepherd. I shall not want." She glances around. "Pray with me, y'all. He maketh me lie down in green pastures."

Erin laughs again. "Fuck God."

Ashley looks stunned, but it's John-Michael who speaks. "Hey! Don't say that."

Erin gestures toward the window. "Why doesn't God make them go back where they came from then? Why is He letting the whole world go to shit? You think I want to put my faith in something that *made these things in the first place*? Do you even realize how crazy that sounds?"

Ashley recovers. She raises her voice. "He leadeth me beside the still waters!" She looks at John-Michael for help.

The boy averts his eyes. "I don't know, like, specific *prayers*."

"Holy shit, are you people kidding me." Erin, suddenly

animated by some fierce new purpose, jumps out of her chair. She stalks across the lab to the window and slaps it with her palm. "Hey!" she calls out to the cicadas. "You feel that? That's the *power of prayer*! Now begone! I cast thee out!" The cicadas chitter undisturbed. She turns around and smiles at Ashley. "There you go. There's God, hard at work."

Ashley closes her eyes. "He restoreth my soul!"

"He let my dad die!"

"He leadeth me in the paths of righteousness for—"

"He's killing us all for *no reason*."

"Okay!" Rebecca steps between them. Erin's eyes are wild and her body twitches with live-wire energy. The eager student who gave Rebecca a vitamin water out at the Body Farm is long gone. "There's room here, in a crisis situation, for all faiths and systems of belief. We will tolerate one another's spirituality or lack thereof, is that clear?"

Mari snorts. *Maybe you should tell your summer class about the church we grew up in. Hit 'em with one of Dad's sermons, something from the greatest hits. I recommend We Know Not the Day but We Will Prepare as If It Will Be Tomorrow. That one's a stone-cold classic.*

A complicated wave of emotion raises goose bumps on her arms. She remembers standing next to Mari in the worship hall, the rich scent of roasting coffee coming from fellowship next door. Her father would be sweating through his sharp navy suit at the pulpit as he preached readiness, light through stained glass sparkling on the tips of his military buzz cut.

The AR-15s lined up on the altar at his back.

Rebecca has steadfastly avoided thinking about it until now, but it's no longer possible to ignore. Her father, whom she hasn't seen or spoken to in sixteen years, spent his life preparing his flock for an event of this magnitude.

I was wondering when you'd come around to that weird little coincidence.

'Doomsday preachers are a dime a dozen, Mari. And they're always either dead wrong or moving the goalposts. Eventually some of their bullshit teachings were going to coincide with an actual catastrophe, that's just statistics at work. It doesn't mean Dad was really a prophet.'

But you have to admit—

Erin screams. It's deafening. She clenches her fists and hits the sides of her thighs and scrunches up her face. Ashley stops praying. John-Michael takes a step back. The Empath covers his ears and shuts his eyes and curls up on the floor. Ji-un bursts into tears, her body heaving. Jason calls for everybody to CALM DOWN. He tells the class nobody's going anywhere, that they're perfectly safe here.

"Hey!" Rebecca claps her hands and uses her teacher voice to send the word bouncing all over the lab. Her students quiet down. Erin's breathing hard, shoulders heaving. *"Nobody* in this class is dying today." She places a hand on the side of Erin's shoulder, gives it a light squeeze, waits a beat. "Tell me what I just said, Erin."

Erin swallows. Her voice is meek and halting. "Nobody in this class is dying today."

Rebecca turns, walks over to Ashley, and gives her an expectant nod.

"Nobody in this class is dying today," she says softly.

Rebecca frowns. She raises a cupped hand to her ear. "What was that?"

Ashley raises her voice. "Nobody in this class is dying today!"

Rebecca points at Erin. The girl takes a deep breath. "Nobody in this class is dying today."

"That's right." She turns to the boy on the floor. "Javier?"

The Empath's still got his hands clamped over his ears.

"JAVIER?"

He sits up, blinking, and lowers his hands.

"Nobody in this class is dying today!" Ji-un yells from across the room. Rebecca glances over. Ji-un is on her feet, pulling the gas mask down over her face, tightening the straps behind her head.

"Hell no," Jason says. He looks at the three remaining students who haven't chimed in with Rebecca's mantra. "Professor, you said so yourself when you were talking to Erin a minute ago: These bugs don't stick around. They're here and gone. What's the point of going out there? We're *lucky* we've got a safe place to hide out."

"All right," Rebecca says, leaning on her measured, reasonable tone. "That's your hypothesis. So let's play out a scenario. The brood has already managed to gain access to the Ag Center." She points at the door. "We know they're out there, in the hallways. So what happens if they breach the lab?"

"We'll be trapped in an enclosed space," Javier says. With his back pressed against the wall, he rises to his feet. His eyes are sunken and tired.

"But what's the difference?" Jason says. "If we leave we'll have to get through the hallways anyway. Those spaces are even tighter."

"But then once we do we'll be outside," Ji-un says.

Ashley throws up her hands. "Y'all are crazy. There are millions of them out there."

"Yes," Jason says. "Right. Billions probably."

Rebecca opens a drawer underneath Ellie's desk. She holds up a set of keys and jangles them. "This is the differentiator. The van we took to the Body Farm is out in the parking lot. We put on our masks to protect our faces, we're safely downstairs and out the door and into the van in a minute and a half, tops. Then we can go anywhere we want."

"But where, though?" Ashley says.

"Yeah," Jason says. "We'd have to go somewhere safer than

here to make the risk of leaving worth it." He looks at Rebecca. "So where's that gonna be?"

If I had arms, I would strangle this kid.

"My father's got a place," she says, words tumbling out all at once. "Up off the Natchez Trace, halfway to Jackson. Ninety miles away. It'll be safe there."

Um. What? I was just kidding about telling them about our upbringing, genius.

Jason folds his arms across his chest. "Safe how?"

"It's a church," Rebecca explains. Mari laughs.

Ashley's eyes light up. "Your daddy's a pastor?"

"Of sorts." Rebecca thinks that if Mari were capable of sipping a drink she would have just spit it out.

Jason shakes his head. "It's not worth it." He looks around at his fellow students. "All those in favor of staying here?" He raises his hand.

"Hands down!" Rebecca says before anyone else can cast their vote. "This is my class. It's my job to keep you safe. We're all going, and we're sticking together."

"We're over eighteen," Jason says, stepping toward her. "We're technically adults. You can't force us to do anything."

You're gonna have to tell them, Mari says.

Rebecca knows it's true. She gathers her thoughts. "My father's not a normal pastor, and the church isn't exactly a traditional one."

"Is it even *Christian*?" Ashley says.

"It has some Judeo-Christian elements," Rebecca says, knowing even that is a stretch. "But it's more of a"—she pictures the altar of illegally modified assault rifles, the tunnels connecting the barracks with the worship hall, the "history" texts full of flowery symbology and cosmic tangents—"*movement.* And when I say church, I mean *compound.* Plenty of well-stocked basements."

You mean bunkers.

"Food. Water. It's the best possible place to hide out during something like this. My father's been preparing for a long time."

"So it's a doomsday-cult type thing," Javier says. For the first time since class began, the Empath sounds genuinely excited.

"Dear Lord," Ashley says.

Taking a big chance here, Bex. We don't know what it's like out at the old homestead these days.

'What other choice do we have?'

Maybe that Jason kid's got a point.

'You've been telling me to run since—'

The lights go out. No flicker, no warning. With the cicadas covering the window like a huge squirming curtain, the lab sinks into a dusky gloaming. A loud *THUD* comes from the lab directly above them. The sound of running feet. A muffled cry.

"There are generators out at my father's place too," Rebecca announces. She opens another drawer and comes up with a flashlight. Then she tosses a few cyanide canisters into her backpack and zips it up.

Hey, Mari says, *you never know.*

"Gas masks on, everyone," Rebecca says. "Jason, help me with these filing cabinets."

He only hesitates for a moment. Then, without further protest, he pulls his mask down over his face and together they move the old metal cabinets aside.

Rebecca waits until every student is wearing a mask. Alien faces with big round bubble-eyes come out of the gloom to gather by the door. Then she puts on her own mask. The last time she did this, Bing Crosby was singing "White Christmas" and a jowly, cardiganed man reeking of alcohol was helping her adjust the straps. Bacon-wrapped dates came around on a tray. A toy locomotive traversed a wintry Fluker's Bluff campus in miniature.

She thinks of Dr. Halbert, two floors up. It's the summer session, so the Ag Center ought to be mostly empty. But off the top of her head she can think of six other professors and adjuncts in the department who are probably here today, each of them with anywhere from five to fifteen students. There is the Hollywood blockbuster version of this catastrophe where she bands together with her colleagues, and this crack team of scientists finds a way to use what she's learned from Ellie—that the females of this brood have a mutated ovipositor—to reverse-engineer an antidote for the poor afflicted millions collapsed in the streets.

Then there's the reality of the situation, which is that she has to do everything in her power to get these kids to safety.

"All right," she says. Her voice is muffled and scratchy like it's coming from a cheap radio speaker. Javier's right—it is disconcertingly hard to breathe in this thing. "You remember where I parked the van—over by the picnic table. That's where we're headed. Stay close to me and to each other, and remember what we saw on our phones. This brood likes to swarm, so we move *fast*."

She waits for this to sink in and does a final head count. Eight students, all of them wearing gas masks. Ashley prays softly and crosses herself. Two of the students hold hands. Ji-un hops up and down like she's staying loose on the starting line of a race. Rebecca checks her pocket one more time for the keys, then places her hand on the doorknob. She peers through the small square window. The corridor is dark. There are vestiges of movement so complex it evokes schools of fish in a nature documentary. Rebecca has been obsessed with insects since she was a little kid exploring the woods with her sister. They have never frightened her, not even the freakiest of wolf spiders. Getting up close and personal with the corpse-feeding varieties had been a natural career progression. She has even eaten them with no qualms: mealworms, grasshoppers, crickets, locusts.

But now, looking out into the shifting nothingness of the hallway, she begins to lose heart.

'Why are you so quiet?'

*Listen, sis—promise me that if any of these kids fall behind or go
down in the swarm, you won't stop.*

'I can't promise that.'

*You are a million times more valuable to society right now than any
of these kids. You're a fucking bug scientist. The world needs you.*

'I'm saving these kids, Mari. All of them.'

*If this whole thing is some cheap pop psychology bullshit because you
couldn't save me back in the day, I'm going to metaphorically puke. Or
trigger your gag reflex and puke through you. I might be able to do that.
I've never tried.*

Rebecca ignores this. "Here we go," she says, and turns the
knob. As soon as she pushes open the door, the drone rises all
around her. The sound evokes a redlining engine, amplified
mosquitoes, a thousand distant shrieks. She leads her class out
into the darkened hall. The electron microscope art projects are
barely visible ghost-prints. Instantly, her body is at the epicenter
of a mass of fluttering wings. The insects coat the gas mask's
transparent face shield. She swipes them away and they cling
to the flesh of her arm. She can't get the spiny ovipositor out
of her head. The thought of it digging into her skin, probing
beneath the epidermis, finding tendons and veins with its slith-
ery appendage . . .

Mari chimes in, awash in Rebecca's fear. *Just keep moving.
You're okay.*

She focuses on her breathing. In and out, slow and steady. A
quick glance over her shoulder reveals a ragged line of students.
The Empath does a herky-jerky dance to rid himself of bugs.
Erin slaps her body, spattering them against her arms and chest.
Rebecca peeks inside the door of a neighboring classroom. The
air is thick with cicadas, the floor littered with toppled chairs

and papers from an open briefcase. Two bodies lie face up, blanketed by seething insects. Rebecca can't tell who they are. She keeps moving. Her heart begins to pound—the first time insects have ever elicited a physiological response.

The masks are working just fine, Mari says. Rebecca's glad for the reassurance. It's true: Designed for gas attacks, they form an airtight seal around the face. Still, as she moves toward the stairs at the end of the corridor, she can feel the bugs' forelegs testing the rubberized seal around her lower jaw. Rebecca tries to ignore it, to keep moving, but their strange halting grace is almost entrancing. This concerted effort by cicadas to identify an entry point and test its boundaries should not be possible. It's a sign of a hive-intelligence at work, some kind of signal for the brood to zero in on weak points.

Rebecca's mind is on overdrive as she leads her students past bulletin boards, a water fountain, study nooks infested with bugs. She almost cries out as a foreleg sneaks underneath the seal around the side of her face. She smashes it against the mask, and sticky strings of innards stretch from her palm. With a speed that astonishes her, another cicada comes to take its place. She flings it away. This mass intelligence is almost human in its calculations. Like a boxer taking punches in the early rounds to exploit weaknesses later on, the cicadas sacrifice themselves for the sake of their ever-growing institutional knowledge.

The implications of this ignite tingling fear at the base of her spine. She finds that breathing has become more difficult. The recycled air is hot in her mouth and nose. Every few seconds, she's forced to clear cicadas from her mask while hundreds of wings beat against her body.

Rebecca is almost to the stairs when the screaming starts. She turns. Cicadas are so thick in the hallway it's like fighting through a storm that's kicked up acres of dirt. The students move in different directions. Darkness clings to them like living cloaks. Then she spots Javier moving erratically, bouncing on his tiptoes, twisting this way and that. His awful dance evokes a little kid who can't hold it and is about to have an accident.

Keep going, Mari urges.

"They're inside me!" Javier screams. Rebecca is confused. His mask is intact and in place. Then she notices his arms, extending down his sides, so that his hands are shoved past the waistband of his shorts, around his backside. His screams reach a desperate shrieking pitch as he jumps into the air, straightening his body, fighting some awful sensation, an itch that can't be scratched.

Go! Mari rarely raises her voice but now it reverberates inside her like a bass thump in her guts. Another girl screams and hits the floor. With her legs in the air, her dress hem puddles around her waist while she thrusts her hands into her underwear. Her head thrashes from side to side as she rips cicadas from between her legs and crushes them in her fists.

Rebecca's thoughts race. The cicadas have learned to access whatever orifice is available to them. They no longer rely solely on mouths. It's a sweltering Louisiana summer, and all of the students are wearing either shorts or skirts or dresses.

Only Rebecca is in khaki slacks—she learned long ago that it pays to be covered up at the Body Farm.

GO.

Rebecca rushes back toward her fallen students. Mari raises her voice to an excruciating command to *get the fuck out of here.* Rebecca does triage. Javier is flopping like he's suffering from a seizure. She thinks he's too far gone now. She turns to the girl. A black cloud of cicadas swarms her crotch. Out of the corner of her eye she sees John–Michael hit the floor, squirming.

"*They're in my fuckin' ass,*" he screams. His mask bangs into the tiles and slides across his face. Cicadas dive for his mouth. His screaming goes shrill as he tries to beat them away but there are

more, always more, a constant stream. The world goes slow and
hazy. Rebecca is in the center of the maelstrom, trying to swat
them away from the girl on the floor. Ji-un and Jason and Erin
rush past her to the stairs. Somebody falls. The drone intensifies,
worming its way into her eardrums, vibrating inside her mind.
She can feel cicadas probing, smashing themselves against her
thighs as she crouches down to help the girl up. She fights them
off her mask. There is something vengeful about the way they
gather themselves to strike again and again. When she turns
again to the girl, Rebecca finds that she is lying still, babbling
incoherently. A boy falls next to her. He has ripped off his shorts
and underwear so he can rub his naked body against the wall.
He is screaming about not being able to breathe. Ashley tries to
keep him from pulling his mask off but he shoves her away and
exposes his face and the cicadas cover him, layers upon layers of
them, blotting him out.

Rebecca reaches out to grab Ashley as she stumbles, and
together they make for the stairs. Cicadas cling to Ashley's denim
cutoffs. Rebecca can't believe how quickly it all fell apart. She
swats blindly, pulling the girl by the wrist. Her ragged breath
is hot and moist inside the mask. The floor drops out beneath
her and she pitches forward down the stairs. Her hip collides
with an unforgiving step. Her elbow smashes down. Radiant
stars burst behind her eyes. Mari's desperate voice retreats. Now
Ashley is pulling her up, dragging her across the mezzanine.
Bodies crowd the lobby. Familiar sights reduced to split-second
images spied through the crush of insects. The dark blue of the
elderly janitor's uniform, the loud red tie of a genial colleague.
A salt-and-pepper beard, a New Orleans Saints hat. A girl in a
smashed gas mask: Ji-un, lying still.

Rebecca bursts through the front door, Ashley at her side.
Her hip is screaming. The pain stabs down her thigh, into her
knee. Moist, swampy air hits her as she sprints out into the

parking lot. The drone out here is sublimated and complex. Rich strains of dissonant music sliding in and out, drifting across the Body Farm. Up ahead she spots Jason and Erin moving toward the white Sprinter van. Ashley is panting her way through a Hail Mary. The body of a woman lies half in, half out of a red Kia Soul. *Almost made it.* The authority Rebecca projected mere minutes ago in her lab—*Nobody in this class is dying today*—seems absurd now, the performative bullshit of someone severely underestimating the threat. John-Michael's cry echoes inside her head, a bitter accusation, *They're in my fuckin' ass.*

Ashley screams. Rebecca whirls around and swipes insects away from her upper thighs. Meanwhile dozens more land on her face to trouble the edges of her mask. At the same time there's movement at the edge of the parking lot. A gray Camry peels out. Other escapees from the Ag Center, perhaps. With the cicadas latching onto the front of her mask, everything is peripheral: Jason and Erin leaping over a small island of shrubbery, the Camry careening around the loading zone in front of the building, Ashley's efforts to run while keeping the cicadas away from the holes in her jean shorts.

"Help me!" Ashley calls out as Rebecca closes the distance to the Sprinter van. She throws a glance over her shoulder. The girl has stopped in the middle of an empty lane, slapping cicadas against her body as they glom onto her like metal shavings to a magnet.

KEEP GOING, Mari shouts inside her head, splitting her skull with blinding pain. But Rebecca has already lost five students to her ill-fated escape plan. She's not going to lose a sixth. Something gives way inside her and she feels suspended in free fall. Two decades of guilt—a wellspring refreshed hourly by the voice of the sister she let die—sends her sprinting back toward Ashley with no regard for self-preservation. If this is to be the end then so be it. She does not believe in fate or destiny or a higher power—and if she winds up another nameless victim of the chaotic, unemotional, entropic culling of the natural world, then that is somehow fitting. Even amid the madness of this moment, it astonishes her that she can make her peace with dying in a split second. Perhaps this kind of certainty is what animates her father on his own prophetic quest.

Ashley sees her coming through a cloud of insects. She reaches out her hand. Rebecca stretches to grab it. Then she pulls it away with a strangled cry as Ashley vanishes in a blur of motion. Cicadas scatter. A white sneaker seems to hang in midair, then hits the pavement. A fine pink mist lingers. The Camry screeches, drifts, rights itself, and speeds away. Ashley's broken body lands in a crumpled heap and she lies still.

Rebecca doesn't scream. She doesn't move. Her breath catches in her throat. A cicada wriggles underneath her shirt and begins probing the waist of her khakis. A foreleg digs below her belt line, pressing hard against the tender flesh of her pelvis. With an afterimage of Ashley being tossed in the air by the speeding Camry, Rebecca rips the cicada away from her body and clears her mask and runs toward the van. Erin and Jason are already there, moving with stuttery ambulations at the center of a bug-cloud. She pulls the keys from her pocket and clicks the fob. The van's taillights blink. Jason slides open the door and Erin dives inside. He follows and shuts it behind him.

A moment later, Rebecca's inside, tossing her backpack on the passenger seat, slamming the door shut. The two students are methodically killing the cicadas that followed them into the van. Rebecca smashes one against the dash, another against the window. A few days ago she would be appalled to find herself blithely slaughtering insects. Now she hunts them like a bloodhound, peering under the seat, stomping a few stragglers into the floor mats. She's covered in sweat and guts. When she's satisfied that all the cicadas up front are dead, she turns to her students.

"Good?"

"Good," Jason says.

Rebecca rips off her gas mask and gulps down cool air blasting from the vents. She doesn't say anything for a moment. The interior grows dim as cicadas crowd the van, blotting out light. Something like disbelief shields her from the pain of accepting what just happened. Mari stays mercifully quiet, curled up in her own stunned retreat. Then Jason begins to weep, bellowing long and loud, while Erin just rocks back and forth with her eyes closed saying *oh shit* over and over again.

The floodgates open for Rebecca. She tries to tamp it all down, to nudge her thoughts in a different direction. But on they rush in horrific array, each one of them pointing a finger at her, *You did this to us.* Eighteen- and nineteen-year-old kids with their whole lives ahead of them. Her pumping adrenaline begins to leach away, and the guilt fills the void. She turns and meets Jason's wet eyes. She could have listened to him and they would all be alive, these kids who wanted to check out forensic entomology for a summer course to see if it was something they might be interested in. The sweet guilelessness of youth, casting about for a path in life, or just an interesting class. She swivels back to face the front and grips the steering wheel with two hands.

"Is anybody hurt?" she asks after a while.

The smell of body odor and sweat hangs in the van.

"I'm okay," Jason says, taking deep breaths, leaning his head against the back of the seat in front of him.

"Ji-un fell down the stairs," Erin says. "She hit the ground hard, and I tried to help her up, but they got her."

"It's not your fault," Rebecca says.

"What are they doing to people?"

"I don't know," Rebecca says.

Yes you do, Mari says out of nowhere. *You know exactly what they're doing—the same thing they'd be doing in the trees. What's the point of sugarcoating it?*

'Now's not the time.'

But you do know. Because I know, and we know the same things.

Rebecca shifts into drive and steers the van out of the parking lot, taking care to select a path that won't take them past Ashley's body. The Ag Center recedes in the rearview. Mari's right: Rebecca *does* know exactly what the cicadas are doing. She knew from the moment she saw that mutated ovipositor on the female specimen. But the truth, as it so often does, drags an element of guilt to the surface along with it. Until Rebecca can silence the last words of her students ringing in her head, she's not ready to face it.

21

FORT HALCOTT

Vicky opens her eyes. The air in the bedroom is heavy and stale. The pillow reeks of mildew. She blinks away the sleep from her eyes. Faded wallpaper appears, teddy bears dressed in ascots and waistcoats. She turns the other way. Her mind is blank but for a distant throb of anxiety. On the other side of the room is a casement window. Curtainless, it welcomes pearly gray light into the room. Vicky blinks again.

Light.

Morning light.

She bolts upright, heart pounding. Sweaty sheets are plastered to her legs.

Grimes was supposed to wake her after a few hours' sleep. She recalls the bottle of gin he scavenged from a kitchen cupboard. Gosh darn it! She throws the covers aside and pads out into the upstairs hallway.

Her partner's snores reverberate through the old house. She stands there, recalibrating. That must have been a full night's sleep. It had been sorely needed, but still—how much time has she wasted? There's a window at the end of the hall. Vicky rushes over to survey the overgrown backyard, full of pokeweed and spindly old trees. Beyond the chipped and tilted iron fence, the yard slants down to a wild meadow bordered by ragtag pines. Her heart sinks. Cicadas hang heavy across the field, as far as the eye can see, same as yesterday. Their song slips into the drafty corridor.

She lingers at the window. It had been an absurd hope, that the bugs might have somehow left Fort Halcott. At least they didn't make their way into the house while she and Grimes slept the sleep of the dead.

She uses the bathroom, then heads downstairs to check on Kim. Vicky had tucked her in on the living room sofa before heading to bed. It had seemed callous, somehow, to leave her lying in the front hall, even though Vicky is fairly certain Kim is beyond noticing such things. She presses the back of her hand to Kim's forehead. The same clammy feverishness she recalls from Sadie's skin in the aftermath of the attack. She moves her hand to hover above Kim's weakly moving lips and feels a wisp of warm breath. Kim's eyes are open but half lidded, her expression vacant yet not completely blank—there's something vaguely searching in it. Vicky can't help herself—she follows Kim's eyes up to the ceiling, where a labyrinthine pattern surrounds a brass socket for an absent chandelier.

She thinks of Sadie and once again feels guilty for sleeping through the night. She could have been to the warehouse in Violet's photo and back to the hospital by now. A litany of anguished questions appear in her mind. Has the hospital been overrun? Can Sadie be removed from her ventilator? Is Hassan still with her?

Will she ever wake up?

Upstairs, the toilet flushes. Vicky goes to the bottom of the stairs and calls to Grimes.

"You were supposed to wake me up!"

Grimes coughs and hacks. A great wad of phlegm splats into the sink. Vicky takes a deep breath, closes her eyes, counts to ten. Grimes feels like garbage every morning for such obvious, easily correctable reasons. She can't imagine living this way—what's the point of actively harming your body?

"You needed the sleep!" he calls down. He expels another loogie and appears at the top of the stairs in his white tank top. On his way down he puts on his shirt and grabs his cheap sport jacket from the banister, where he slung it last night. "That hooch might as well've been Boone's Farm," he says, brushing past her on his way to the kitchen.

"I don't know what that is," she says, following right behind. "You smell like nail polish remover."

"I *feel* like nail polish remover." He turns on the tap and fills a dirty glass. Then he drains it, spilling water down the front of his half-buttoned shirt. "How's Kim?"

"The same. Did you even keep watch?"

"Sure did. Manned the radio too. Until I passed the fuck out." He sets the glass down on the counter. "Captain Barker's no longer with us. Same with about half the force, which tracks with the civilian population." He opens and closes the same empty cupboards he inspected last night. "When's the last time you ate?"

"I don't know. What else did you hear?"

He fishes in his pocket and comes up with a bent Camel. "In Vicky parlance, the excrement has hit the oscillation device all over town. Phone and internet service still down everywhere. Electricity's getting spotty." He flicks a wall switch and an overhead light flashes on and off. "Guess we're just lucky, but it's only a matter of time. We gotta get some food."

Vicky thinks several steps ahead—a time, not too distant, when there will be no more options but to flee. "What about the town borders?"

"Strike team's gathering volunteers. Fikowski and Jensen are leading the breakout. They're talking about it openly over the comms, so we can assume whatever agency closed the borders can overhear everything. It's not gonna be a cakewalk. They're going for it today." He slams the last cupboard closed and turns to Vicky. "I think we have to make a choice."

"I think we have to get going."

"In terms of the best way to do our jobs for the good people of Fort Halcott, and also the shitheads of Fort Halcott—maybe we forget about this warehouse thing. I mean, how much good are we really doing, chasing down, uh, whatever this is?"

"You want to abandon our investigation?"

Grimes lifts the Camel to his mouth, notices it's broken, tosses it to the floor. "What I want to do is not stand around with my dick in my hand while good police die."

"You want to join the assault."

He softens. "How much good are we really gonna do at an abandoned linen warehouse we saw in a dead girl's phone."

"You said it yourself, Kenny—it's the only lead we got."

"It doesn't feel solid. It feels slippery. Intangible. Which in present circumstances pretty much makes it pointless. Don't you want to get Sadie the fuck outta Dodge?"

Vicky's head hurts. She probably does need food. And now Grimes is adding another blade to the knife's edge she's already walking, balanced between the obligation to figure out what's really going on here and the desire to scoop Sadie up and flee. She's spent a lifetime certain of her role, her duty to the community and her precious little family of two. Now, when she considers moving in any direction at all, she feels ashamed of herself.

"They can't really seal off a whole American city overnight in this day and age," she says firmly. "Something's gotta give."

"Yeah," Grimes says, "that *something* is us."

"What about Kim?" Vicky points in the direction of the living room. "And Sadie, and everybody else? What if we're on track to find the cure?"

"*Cure?* Vic, listen. This shit here, this fucking abomination in the basement—what did it really tell us?"

An unsettled feeling rises inside her at the mention of the ruined, nested girl. "Winged spiral symbolism," she says. "That points to a group of some sort. A cult. Ritual activity that actually made something happen."

"So we follow our flimsy-ass lead to this warehouse and either find jackshit or find another nightmare we can't make heads or tails of." He folds his arms. "That's not finding a cure, that's top-shelf dick holding while other people do our jobs for us. And I can't live with that."

Vicky regards him carefully. There's a vibrancy to his words, the way he moves his hands when he talks. You could almost describe it as a spring in his step, which no one's ever said about Kenny Grimes before. She thinks of what Kim spoke of yesterday in the car: how she would sometimes wish for a catastrophic, world-altering event to rip her from the mundanity of her existence. Vicky can't help but wonder: Is her partner *enjoying* this?

Kenny watches her think. "*What?*"

"Nothing."

"You're giving me the classic Vicky look. You're rendering judgment from on high."

An uncharacteristic fatalism seizes her. What purpose do social graces serve in this situation? Still, she tries to be diplomatic. "It seems like some part of you might be enjoying this. And that's okay, if it's an adrenaline rush, or fulfilling some notion of traditional masculinity, or—"

"Oh, fucking Christ on a motherfucking cross, Vic, how long we been partners?"

"Three and a half years."

"After Nedry, and a million late nights together, and all those dinners—fuck, I even show up to Sadie's dance recitals, which are boring as shit, by the way—"

"She's eight."

"—and I still get the sense that not only do you not know me at all, you have this idea of who I am that never changes, and *you don't like that guy very much*. So what is it?" He fishes the cigarette pack from a pocket and holds it up. "Is it these? You don't approve? Is it the fact that I enjoy alcohol and coffee like ninety-nine percent of the rest of the goddamn world? You think you'd prefer having a guy like that pencilneck *Fincher* for a partner, be my guest and put in for a transfer to Vice. You two saints can pass judgment on the ladies of the night down on Halifax, save a few souls. Oh wait!" He holds up a finger. "You can't do that because the whole fucking department has gone to shit, like every other institution in Fort Halcott! So I guess you're stuck with old Kenny Grimes for the time being! Sorry!" He's breathing hard, staring wild-eyed, clutching the kitchen counter behind his back. "And I can't believe I even have to say this, but *no*. I am not enjoying this. I want to eat a steak and have a beer and fart into my couch while I fall asleep to the Mets getting their asses handed to them. But I *am* looking forward to actually helping the remaining people of this city by opening up an escape route instead of falling any farther down the rabbit hole of shit. I have found a modicum of hope and purpose in that prospect, which you're mistaking for some kind of psychopathic glee, because after all this time you won't even give me the benefit of the doubt, fuck you very much."

Without thinking, Vicky steps forward and wraps her arms around Kenny Grimes. He smells of booze and stale smoke and body odor. She's certain that she's pretty ripe herself. He makes a funny noise, a surprised little *hrrrp*. For a moment, he stands completely still, just breathing. He pats her once on the shoulder blade. Then he hugs her back, squeezing hard. Vicky thinks he might be crying softly, trying to hide it, but the tremors in his body give it away. They have never embraced before, not once.

"Ah, shit," he says. "I got snot on your shirt."

"I'm sorry, Kenny," Vicky says, stepping back. "I don't know what else to say. I love being your partner. If you want to join up with Fikowski and the others, I understand."

Grimes hesitates. "I got the shotgun in my trunk."

"All right," Vicky says.

He looks deflated. The fire from half a minute ago has died. "I thought I'd be able to talk you into it," he says. "I thought you'd come with me."

"I can't give up on this angle," she says. "If there's even a shred of hope. For Sadie." She fills Grimes's empty water glass and drinks it down. "I messed up, back there at the hospital. I thought I was doing the right thing, coming here. I have to make it worth something."

Grimes wipes his eyes. "Fucking allergies," he says.

"They're bad this summer."

In the other room, his police radio crackles.

"Go," Vicky says.

He doesn't move. "Take care of yourself out there, Vic."

"You too, Kenny."

He heads out but pauses at the threshold of the kitchen and turns back. "See you on the other side."

"Give 'em heck," she says, and he's gone.

22

Will wakes up screaming. His mind surfaces as if from a dark river plunge. He grasps at memory. Fragments of a nightmare are all he gets: a spider sinking into the back of his skull, Alicia's ruined face, a man demanding answers he does not have, pulling lies from his throat as he vomits blood. And presiding over it all, an impossible insect, brittle as parchment, sliding in slow motion from an envelope to a plate. Limbs bound, Will thrashes in total darkness. A chain rattles. A voice comes from far away.

"Will, thank God!"

It's a familiar voice. Alicia.

"Will, *shhh*, it's okay! I'm here!"

He quits screaming and tries to call out to her, but all he can do is spit gibberish. Everything hurts. He squirms and flails. His body won't respond. Fear surges: *I can't move.*

"Stop, Will. It won't do any good. You'll just hurt yourself. We're tied up."

Will lies still and sorts out the basics. He is on a metal bench of some sort. Alicia is across from him, only a few feet away, judging by her voice. Sometime earlier—hours ago, or maybe days—he'd been tied to a chair and interrogated with a device fastened to his skull, a torment-machine that wriggled into his brain, twisting his thoughts. He flashes to the soft malleable flesh running down Alicia's face, smearing her features into a depiction of suffering. He cries out again.

"I thought you were—they made me think you were—"

"I know. I know. I'm fine. A little bruised from when that cunt hit me with her gun. But that's all."

"I couldn't think straight. It was like..." Will tries to recall the sensation. A pit opens up inside him. Terrible hopelessness, mingled with the sense that everything that has ever gone wrong in his life, and the lives of those he loves, can be traced back to his own poisonous character. A wild, untamed film reel unspools in his mind, and he understands that at the moment of his death, his life will flash before his eyes, and it will be a litany of failures. Selfish decisions that screwed up his relationship with the one person he ever loved.

The memory of the session wrenches him back into unbearable misery. He whimpers and shakes.

"It's okay, Will," Alicia says. There's fear and pain in her voice. He wishes he could hold her. No: He wishes she could crawl over and hold *him*. "It was all fake, whatever you felt. Whatever you saw. They did it to you. It's all bullshit. It's not you."

Alicia's eyes melting out of their sockets, the dripping corneas painting lines in her runny face. "I thought you were dead."

"I'm alive. We're both alive."

"How long have we been in here?"

"I'm not sure. Overnight, at least. How much do you remember?"

Will tries to recall being transported from the Quonset hut to this dark prison. Pain gathers at the base of his neck and spreads up into his skull.

"Not much," he admits. "You were out cold. That asshole Duvall strapped the spider thing to my head. The other one, Gerald, kept asking me the same thing."

Where is the origin point? Will grits his teeth until the echoes subside.

"I remember wanting to tell him what he wanted to hear, just to make it stop. I didn't care what I said."

"Gerald was getting frustrated," Alicia says. "He was like an animal foaming at the mouth. He wanted actionable info on the Order of Hemiptera. He clearly thinks the Order started all this—something to do with those men in the photos he showed us—and the key to *stopping* it is also somehow with them." She pauses. "You were talking about *beckoning to God*. Or *a* god. Something like that. Do you remember?"

Will's head throbs. "No. I was probably just ranting."

"Yeah," Alicia says.

But Will can sense the hesitation in her voice. "You think I was actually telling them something real?"

For a moment, she doesn't say anything. "It's the same as the other stuff you've been saying. You sound so *sure*. And I don't know where it comes from."

"It's all nonsense," Will says. "They were torturing me, Alicia. With some DARPA shit."

"I know," she says quickly. "Forget it. I'm just glad we're both still here."

Something else flashes in Will's mind. Crimson slashes, Alicia's screams. "They cut your face," he says, remembering.

"Superficial," she says.

"I'm sorry," Will says.

"Not your fault. Let's figure out how to get the fuck out of here. Can you feel the wall?"

Will contorts. His hands are cuffed. He turns onto his side and reaches behind him. The wall is softer than he anticipated, halfway between fabric and plastic. "Super lightweight," he says. "Some kind of temporary structure."

"They moved us," she says. "I was pretty out of it and you were totally gone, but they bundled us into a Humvee at some point and we drove for a few minutes. I assume we're at a different section of the border. Maybe a larger checkpoint. Listen."

Will strains to hear outside. There's a mid-range *thrum* in his head that throbs along with the dull pain left over from his ordeal. He focuses his effort. Sweat breaks out on his forehead. Eventually, he hears it: the symphony of the cicadas. It's very distant, interrupted by wretched man-made noises: diesel engines and militaristic chatter. The thin, quavering melody he catches soothes his aching body. It's like coming home.

Someone barks out a series of orders. An engine revs.

He imagines mercenary infrastructure, rows of modular structures stacked like shipping containers, Humvees and troop transports moving in and out, and behind it all that strange barrier glimmering in the morning light.

"Will," she says.

"Yeah?"

"After we separated last year, I used to watch videos from our trips. Like, all the time. Sometimes even at Carter's place, after he went to sleep, which I felt bad about, but I couldn't stop."

"Oh," Will says. A radiant flash inside his head makes him squeeze the muscles of his face together. Gerald's voice dopplers back and forth. *Where is the origin point?*

"You remember the one of us on that lookout point outside Belgrade, at sunset? When your ice cream fell off the cone and a little kid laughed at you? I watched that one a million times."

"I remember," he says, trying to steady his voice.

"Seeing what they did to you, I felt...I don't know. It was like they were doing it to me. I hate seeing you in any kind of pain. How bad are you hurt?"

Her voice bounces around their prison cell. The pressure inside his head feels like it will never abate. The metallic prickle of the spider's legs pressing into his skin, the dismal certainties brought to the surface. Truths about his rotten soul.

"I'm okay," he says.

"You can talk to me about it. I mean down the road. Whatever you're feeling."

Alicia goes quiet for a while. Will can't tell how much time passes. He tries to latch onto the cicadas' song for comfort. After a while he notices that she's speaking again.

"Do you think it's true, what Gerald said about this being a global event?"

"I don't know. It's hard to imagine."

"My parents..." Alicia says, then trails off.

"Yeah." There's an extended coterie of Bennetts, aunts and uncles and cousins, back in Brooklyn. "The city's mostly concrete," he says hopefully. "Maybe it's not as bad there."

The pain in his head flares to migraine proportions. He closes his eyes, even though he's already lying in the dark. To distract himself he focuses on sounds, trying to drift into the cicadas' muffled song. Tires squeal as a vehicle peels out. A voice yells, another answers. A metallic clank resounds.

Something nearby makes his eyes snap open, his heart pound. There's a presence just outside their cell. Seams appear in the far wall, a rectangle of light that opens into a blinding patch of summer sun. Will struggles to sit up. After a moment, his eyes adjust. He examines himself quickly. Legs and arms shackled, chains wrapped around his body. Alicia, on a bench across a narrow aisle, identically secured. The interior hastily built from large, segmented pieces of plastic.

He urges cicadas to fly inside, but none do.

The silhouette of a helmeted figure appears in the doorway. Will's body tenses, his nerve endings raw, like a guard dog on high alert. While a nearly inexpressible rage swells inside of him, a darker feeling rises alongside it: the desire to submit. To plead. To beg.

If this person comes inside and straps that machine to his head, he thinks his heart will simply give out. Even through his fear, this reaction frightens him. He has never felt so out of control. He wants to cry.

The figure moves inside the cell and shuts the door behind it. Will can hear the sounds of the helmet coming off. A moment later, an overhead light comes on.

Gerald stands before them. He gives Will a concerned look. "You're awake! That's wonderful." He sighs. "I must apologize for Sergeant Duvall's zeal. I certainly did not intend for the device to be calibrated so...intensely."

Will's mouth fills with frothy saliva. He begins to rock back and forth. "Fuck you," he spits.

"Yes, yes, fuck me, I made a mistake. But! I'm here to atone."

He reaches to his belt and unclips a key ring. He turns to Alicia. "It goes without saying that you are surrounded by my team, and if you try anything or attempt to hurt me in any way, they will kill you without a second thought."

"Where are you taking us?" she says.

"Up the line, I'm afraid. We all have bosses, and mine would like to—"

The side of Gerald's head opens with abrupt and startling violence, as if the air itself has peeled away flesh and bone. Short bursts of rifle fire sweep from left to right. Light beams in through small holes punched in the cell's wall. Gerald collapses like a marionette viciously unstrung. A fine mist saturates the place where he was standing a moment ago. Will's face is wet. Alicia screams, rolls off the bench and onto the plastic floor. Will follows. There are shouts all around, then sharp reports as guns open up from every direction.

It's almost a mercy, the way this new violence scrubs the filth from his mind. He lies on the floor as pointed clarity rushes in.

Will's no firearms expert but even a novice could pick out the motley assemblage of weaponry: assault rifles like the one that just blew Gerald's head off, single-shot revolvers, hunting rifles, and oddly smooth *thunkthunkthunk* volleys. Will assumes the latter is from the mercenaries' long guns. Bullets rip into metal. A pair of motorcycle engines whine.

"Here!" Alicia's foot kicks Gerald's key ring over to Will. He turns on his side, grabs it, and shimmies over to Alicia's half of the cell. With his hands behind his back, Will grips one of the keys. Alicia moves to try to guide him to the lock.

A shotgun blast peppers the wall with buckshot, and tiny pinprick holes open above their heads. Will's ears ring and he fumbles the keys. Alicia manages to push the lock forward to meet him. The smell of cordite drifts in through the tattered wall. Figures move past the cell. Cries of pain and barked commands punctuate streams of gunfire. Weapons chatter on. Will jams the key into the lock, and it fails to turn. Hands slick with Gerald's blood, he tries another. And another. The fourth key on the ring pops the lock. With a triumphant yell, Alicia unravels her chains without lifting her body too far off the floor. She takes the key ring from Will.

"Cuffs," she says. He holds still with his hands thrust out toward her. Half a minute later, both Alicia and Will are free of their bindings. Staying as flat as possible, he slides the pistol from the holster at Gerald's waist. Heckler & Koch P30L. The *John Wick* gun, he thinks, wondering when he'll get to see a movie again. Perhaps never. With Alicia right behind him, he shimmies over to the far wall where the door came into being. The seam in the cell's siding is barely a hairline crack. Cautiously, he lifts a hand to feel along the seam for a way to open the door.

Automatic weapons open up. He yanks his arm down as

bullets rip through the cell just above his head. Light pours in through dozens of new holes. Alicia covers her ears and squeezes her eyes shut and screams as bullets shred the walls. The volley ends. This structure is directly in the line of fire. They have to get out now.

Will lifts his head and peers out of a hole. He yearns for the crush of cicadas, the deluge that blackened the windows of their hotel and draped across the trees of the preserve. It's heartening to see clouds of insects moving across the sky.

He recognizes their surroundings: the toll plaza just off I-87. The very edge of Fort Halcott's eastern border. Above the six-lane highway, rows of sensors like Swiffer mop heads hang from a thick cylindrical pipe that spans the road from guardrail to guardrail. Black Humvees and trucks are scattered along the road. Mercenaries crouch behind them, then rise up and shoot. The road is littered with the dead and dying. A ribbon of cicadas descends upon a man with a shattered helmet. His body writhes as they pour onto his face. Sunlight glints off pooled blood. Will moves his gaze beyond the vehicles to see what the mercenaries are shooting at. Several cars and pickup trucks are parked about fifty feet up the road. Will scans a slew of nondescript vehicles, Accords and Camrys. A junky old beige sedan that looks like it belongs in a 1970s crime movie. Two or three FHPD cruisers.

So the local cops are on *that* side of things. Interesting.

A man crawls out of a white plumber's truck riddled with bullet holes and dies in the road. Cicadas feast within the killing zone defined by tracer bullets from the mercenaries' long guns, air carved by icy-blue streaks. Two hands lift an AR-15 above the bed of a pickup and fire blindly. Will covers his head and pulls Alicia close. He can feel her galloping heart.

A Humvee directly in front of them takes fire. Stray bullets rip through their ruined cell. Door seams are no longer relevant. Now Will can simply pull the shredded wall apart. He waits for a lull in the gunfire that never comes. Then he feels stupid. This isn't the Old West. These people aren't pausing to reload their six-shooters.

He looks Alicia in the eyes. The world seems to slow down, the battle sounds muted as he loses himself in her face. Residual self-loathing from his session brings tears to his eyes. At the same time he's more certain than ever that he has always loved her and always will.

He peers outside again. There's a clear lane along the shoulder of the road. They'll have to flank around a black truck ringed with dead mercenaries. Cicadas pour over the guardrail to investigate the corpses. Will zeroes in on their song.

He mimes zipping lips to Alicia. She nods. He points to the left, indicating their path. "We run hard to the other side, past those cars. Once we're behind them, we're safe."

He leaves the unsaid hanging: They have to cover significant ground through crisscrossing ordnance without getting shot. But they can't stay here and risk catching strays while the structure collapses around them. Plus, if the mercenaries win, they'll be trapped, and no better off than before.

Alicia's body tenses next to him, coiling even tighter. "You hear that?"

Will listens. A redlining engine. Massive diesel combustion pushed to its limit. "It sounds like a—"

"Truck!"

A sixteen-wheeler bursts through a gap between bullet-pocked cars. It's heading straight for the mercenaries' line. Fighters pour tracers into its cab. The windshield disintegrates. Anyone driving is surely dead. The truck thunders across no-man's-land, slicing through the dead and dying without leaving the pavement. A slurry of reddened gristle paints its wake. The side of the truck says NORTH COUNTRY PROVISIONS with a faded illustration of a friendly cartoon crew of meats and vegetables. The mercenaries shoot out the tires. The truck lists to one side, and its chassis strains to keep it upright with a metallic shriek.

"Now!" Will says, pulling Alicia to her feet. With the Heckler in his left hand, he widens the gaps in the wall like a flailing madman. They emerge from their cell as the truck collides with a Humvee and sends it spinning across the blacktop, caroming off a troop transport. The world is a grinding, squealing mess of rubber on pavement and metal on metal. The sixteen-wheeler races up the exit ramp, passes beneath the toll sensors, and then it is behind them as Will and Alicia, sprung from their prison, run in the opposite direction. They make for the shoulder of the road. Will hurdles a large man in denim overalls whose arm is shredded at the elbow like pulled pork. The man stares at it dumbly, sitting on the blacktop, while cicadas wreath his head. A bullet passes so close to Will's arm he can feel its searing path, a ghost note played against his skin.

Will and Alicia hit the ground by the guardrail, ducking down next to a black Jeep with four flat tires and jagged shards where its windows should be. They look back the way they came, tracing the path of the sixteen-wheeler in time to see it strike the fence stretched across the toll plaza. The cab of the truck disappears inside neon-blue digital noise. A horrific sound is unleashed: a thousand robotic moans at different frequencies, pitching up into screams. Cicadas mass and separate in frenzied sorties. Will and Alicia run in a low crouch along the guardrail. He has never been shot, but during his walkabout, in a hostel in Cairo, he met someone who had. The man described it as a sledgehammer blow, confusing to the body, which didn't know whether to register the wound as searing heat or a throbbing ache.

Will risks another glance over his shoulder. Alicia is right there, mouth set in a grim line, concentrating on not dying. And behind her, a hundred feet up the toll plaza, the nose of the sixteen-wheeler is in stalemate with the barrier. The truck's tires squeal as the cab drives forward, inch by inch. Blinding flecks of blue and white sparks rush along the fence to the impact point. Will thinks of blood cells racing in to stanch a wound, or cicadas swarming a mouth. White smoke boils up from the pavement as the tires spin.

Come on come on COME ON. He urges the truck to break through. There is elation in this fantasy: citizens charging the mercenaries, cars screaming for the gap in the broken fence. The fence goes convex, as if to swallow the truck, then spits it back inside the boundaries of Fort Halcott. The engine dies. Will's heart sinks. A dry wind gusts that smells of ammonia and hot steel. The fence glimmers in smug triumph as it reconstitutes.

FUCK.

There must be a powerhouse somewhere around here, a control center for the barrier. But he's not going to be the one to find it. One go-round with these shitbirds and their torture devices is plenty. He'd rather find another way out than risk falling into their hands again. Besides, the tracer fire at their backs is still pouring across the no-man's-land. Reversing course is suicide.

On the ground ahead of them, a mercenary sits with his legs out straight and his back against the rail. Cicadas seethe from holes in his ruined visor.

A beige, bullet-scarred sedan is parked ten feet in front of them. Broken glass litters the dash. Tracers decimate a side mirror, and it dangles sadly. Will dives for cover, Alicia right behind him. He feels the blacktop bite into his elbow as he lands next to the front wheel. The car is parked at an angle, blown almost sideways by high-caliber weapons. He raises his head and peers inside. The keys are in the ignition. A pine tree air freshener, miraculously whole, hangs from the rearview. He figures, given the damage, there's a fifty–fifty chance the car will start, worse odds that it will actually move. But it only has to get them out of the fray. A few hundred feet in the opposite direction would be fine.

Alicia reads his mind. She reaches up, grabs the handle, pulls open the passenger-side door, and crawls inside. Will follows. They both keep their heads down. Cicadas float in and out of the broken windows. Camel soft packs are crumpled on the floor. He sweeps glass from the seat with the Heckler. Alicia turns the key. The engine rumbles and turns over. Will meets her eyes. She nods.

Will lifts his head so his eyes are above the dash. He turns to suss out a clear lane behind the car.

"Shit!" Startled, he nearly drops the Heckler. Alicia whips her head around.

A man is lying across the back seat. White, medium build, dressed in a cheap unbuttoned sport coat and slacks. A police badge is fastened to his belt. A lit cigarette hangs from lips wet with blood. A crimson stain spreads along his side, soaking his white button-down shirt. He gives them a lazy wave. Then he takes a huge drag on his cigarette, plucks it from his lips, and tosses the butt out the window.

"This isn't your Uber," he rasps. Then he laughs softly to himself, wincing in pain. Blood bubbles from his mouth.

"Shh!" Will points to the handful of cicadas circling the car's ceiling.

The man lifts a flask with a trembling hand. "Doesn't matter now," he says.

A tracer round takes out a headlight. The car shudders. Will and Alicia crumple in their seats.

"Vicky," the man in the back seat says. His breath comes in ragged gasps.

Will reaches back and helps lift the flask to the man's mouth. "Is that your wife?"

The man's head shakes slowly. "Partner. Detective Vicky Paterson. Get me to her. Please."

Alicia puts the car in reverse, then ducks down and jams her palm against the gas pedal. The old sedan leaps backward with surprising eagerness. Will drops the flask and clutches the center console.

The man in the back begins to cough. Blood sprays the seat backs.

There's a high-pitched keening as the sedan's bumper scrapes the guardrail. Will glances in the rearview. The angle is hard to interpret. He thinks they're sliding along the shoulder of the toll plaza. He lifts his head and peers above the dash. The toll plaza recedes. He gives Alicia a twirling motion. She pokes her head up, then grabs the wheel with two hands, shimmies upright in the seat, and cranks the car into a half spin. A moment later, the curving ramp deposits them back onto one of the town's main arteries. Abandoned cars are scattered up and down both lanes. The streets are strewn with bodies. Alicia weaves in and out. Broken glass slides down the hood.

"Linen factory," the man in the back seat says. "By the old hot dog place on the hill."

Astonished, Will thinks he must have misheard. "What?"

The man in the back gathers his strength. "Where Vicky is."

"The place we staked out to find Violet Carmichael," Will says to Alicia. *Where the acolytes gobbled down those fruits and climbed the wall with their jointed limbs . . .*

The man in the back hacks and sputters. "I'll be . . . god-damned." Will turns. The man looks up at him with sad eyes. "Violet Carmichael. Me and Vicky . . ."

Will waits for the man to finish. His expression changes to one of pure wonder as he gazes through Will at something only he can see.

"We found her."

23

FORT HALCOTT

Vicky pulls into the back lot of the old linen factory. It has taken two hours to cross town, a drive that should have taken twenty minutes, tops. Abandoned cars block entire intersections. Other vehicles are simply stalled, while families sit inside, biding their time until rising heat and empty gas tanks force them to choose between heatstroke and the swarm. Some of these people met Vicky's eyes as she navigated past the roadblocks. Little kids pressing their hands up against the glass, mothers and fathers sitting helpless and weary as the cicadas hovered. There is mockery in the way the insects hang around. The waiting game is nothing to creatures that bide their time in the dirt.

She parks the car alongside the warehouse and tries not to think about Grimes and his old pump-action shotgun going up against a militarized border guard. Instead she checks on Kim, lying flat across the back seat. She takes a swig from a water bottle, then tilts it gently so a small trickle runs into Kim's mouth. She watches Kim mutter nonsense in the throes of her affliction. Her mind superimposes Violet Carmichael's face onto Kim's, thrown back in frozen, openmouthed ecstasy, and Vicky shudders with revulsion.

Cicadas' wings swish against the glass. She studies their underbellies, the engorged thickness of their abdomens, the alien flatness of their foreheads. How strange that she never gave these creatures more than a passing thought, and now they have forever altered the course of her life. Of everyone's life. She tries the radio, but every frequency is static. Does all modern infrastructure exist on a much more precarious platform than we know? She reaches out for tangible parts of the car: gearshift, steering wheel, vents. Solid things to reinforce her place in a world defined by discipline and order.

She glances outside, through the shifting curtain of cicadas, to the decaying old fast-food joint up on the hill. The Sock Hop. Sadie and her strawberry milkshake...

Tears come to her eyes. For a moment, wild abandon threatens to overtake her, but she clamps down on it. She studies the warehouse and picks out a side door, twenty feet from the car, across a grassy strip that rings the building, where a picnic table has faded to dull pink. It's an easy route. Three seconds of running and she's there. Her eyes roam the brick wall until they find a large square window. Plan B if the door is locked.

And if there's nothing at all inside, what then?

Vicky chases this thought away and puts her hand on the door handle. Doubts swirl: The cicadas are different now. It's as if they're learning, figuring things out through trial and error. She glances at Kim and recalls how the insects knew to attack her eyes to slow her down. At the same time they might have been trying to elicit a scream so they could gain access to her mouth. How long is the learning curve for a species that's been around since the dawn of time? It seems impossible that their cognitive ability could advance this far so quickly. But what does *impossible* even mean anymore, in the face of all this?

She wishes she had some riot gear. A face mask, some body armor. Anything to create distance between herself and the bugs. Oh well. No use crying about something she can't change. She takes a breath then presses her lips together.

For Sadie.

Opening the door, she hits the ground running. The cicadas, already agitated by the arrival of her car, home in on her. She shields her face as best she can. She expects them to sweep over her with overwhelming force. Instead they seem to be queuing up in an endless stream. She's halfway to the warehouse door when one manages to land on her cheek. Pain jolts her left eye as the insect pokes her with a foreleg before she can slap it away. Another bug slips up inside her shirt. That's a new tactic. She smashes it against her stomach and flings its carcass away as she reaches the door and grabs the knob. Which, mercifully, turns.

Inside, she slams the door shut behind her and waits with her back against it, breathing hard. Two cicadas drift lazily upward. She catches one in her fist, squeezes, and drops its lifeless corpse to the cement floor. The second evades her for half a minute but makes the fatal mistake of landing on the doorjamb, where she flattens it with her palm. She waits a moment. No other cicadas appear. She rubs her eye, blinks her cloudy vision back to clarity. Disgust at her own vulnerability takes hold. Humans are just collections of squishy, delicate parts, so easily exploited by anything that wishes us harm. Another split second and the eye-jab could have been much worse, perhaps even caused her to cry out and invite the insects to invade her throat. She thinks again of Sadie, then steps away from the door, clearing her mind.

The first thing her cop-sense picks up is that the floor is very clean. The adjacent factory hasn't operated in several years, yet the warehouse is free of dirt and the usual detritus of abandonment: graffiti, empty bottles, soiled mattresses, burnt glass pipes, used condoms. This place looks like someone has been sweeping the floor.

She moves cautiously. Milky light from square windows throws shapes across the cement, but gloom prevails. If Grimes were here he'd have his weapon drawn, and his hard gaze would urge her to draw hers too. Ever since putting two slugs in Silas Nedry, she's been literally gun-shy—not because that subhuman filth deserved anything less, but because she gave him exactly what he wanted. And even if it was the life of a true piece of crap, it is still the only life she's ever taken. She's never been keen to repeat the experience.

But now she wishes for a gosh darn weapon, because there's something deeply wrong with this place. Every step brings new red flags. There isn't a single broken window. The glass is spotless. A guiding presence hangs over this room, the heavy hand of a meticulous caretaker. For what purpose has this place been seen to? No manufacturing is conducted next door, and there are no goods stored in the warehouse. Her footsteps echo. She thinks of Violet Carmichael and the photograph on her phone screen. What's her connection to this place?

Vicky tells herself it's just an empty building, but her whole body tingles with anticipation. A strange odor hangs in the air, like the steam from a laundry vent. As she moves toward the center of the warehouse, shapes emerge from the gloom. Her heart quickens. *Bodies.* It's obvious right away: men and woman lying on the floor, neatly arranged so that all are in close proximity yet none are touching. Vicky slows down, her eyes darting back and forth, checking for movement. Winged spirals appear, neatly stenciled on the load-bearing pillars rising from floor to ceiling. Her stomach drops.

There's an undercurrent running through the city she's lived in her entire life. Some kind of twisted death cult, tied to this catastrophe in an unimaginable way. And the whole infernal operation has slipped under the radar of the FHPD's Major Crimes Division for how long? Months? Years? Since her father's time on the force?

Like a long and desperate sojourn in a dream, it seems to take Vicky a lifetime to reach the bodies. She wants desperately to investigate them, and at the same time a part of her hopes she never gets there. (*Weak*, she chastises herself. *Bear up.*) Only when she arrives can she see the pattern, the spiral in which they're arranged. Fifty men and women, at least, circling inward to culminate in the body of an old woman whose wrinkled face is drawn back into a grinning maw.

Vicky's eyeballs twitch. A numb sort of desperation takes hold. *No no no no no.* Even after everything she's seen, even after *Violet Carmichael*, the sight of so many bodies arranged with such precision fills her with denial. Her brain will not accept this, despite the evidence before her. She flashes to the dreadful endings of the Peoples Temple and Heaven's Gate.

Except those cult victims were dead, their lives forfeited in mass suicides.

The people who make up this spiral are very much alive. Or at least, in the same between-state as Sadie and Kim and how many millions of others. Fifty mouths move, facial muscles pulling and straining in unison. All of them whisper together in some terrible hushed chorus. *No no no.* Vicky moves along the perimeter of the spiral, repulsed and shamefully entranced. There is a diabolical beauty in the inhuman stretching and folding of the lips as they form airy words and phrases of unknown origin. She moves closer. It's then she notices that all of these people are bald, their heads shorn but stubbly.

Her thoughts bend in on themselves, a wormhole connecting past and present. The night this all started, back at that house smelling of cat piss. Boxes of hair, teeth, and nails. A half-carapace torso, tough leathery exo-skin melded with human flesh.

An experiment, Vicky thinks. *A dry run.* Perhaps there are many more. Perhaps Violet is the culmination.

Or perhaps this spiral is. The ins and outs of the cultic rituals are well beyond her grasp. She moves around the edge of the bodies, suddenly lucid, feeling a peculiar anger rising.

Here she is, at the lonely end of her investigation, and there is nothing but more questions. At the same time she feels outrageously stupid. What had she expected, a vial in a glass case marked ANTIDOTE that she could rush back to Sadie's hospital room? She has been blinded by the notion of Sadie's suffering, lurking always at the edge of her mind as she chased a mother's fruitless dream of delivering her child from pain.

An urge toward viciousness rises inside her. She squares up to the nearest body: a middle-aged man with a potbelly that strains against his pale-blue button-down. *Kick him,* she thinks. Vicky has never raised a hand to a suspect in an interview room, never been prone to violence as an outlet for frustration. Yet now she imagines herself walking around the spiral, beating the snot out of all these freaks, stomping their faces one by one. But instead of pulling her leg back for a quick strike, she finds herself staring at the man's face. It's hard to tell at first because of his shaved head and weirdly twitching mouth, but she knows him: Phil Congalosi, treasurer of the Fort Halcott Elks Lodge. A regular guest at charity events she attends on behalf of the FHPD, an incredibly soft-spoken man, a widower who speaks incessantly of his rare books collection. And now here he is, part of a spiraling circle of supplication to some insect god in an abandoned warehouse at the edge of town. In fact, hastily shaved heads aside, most of these people here have the bearing of solid citizens. A bunch of neatly dressed taxpayers. Not a white-robed maniac in the bunch.

Phil's mouth winds down like a dying motor. Spittle flecks his lips. Reverberations and mimicry sweep the spiral in a wave.

All the supplicants seize up. A moment of silence reigns. The low drone of the cicadas outside slips into the quiet interval. Phil's mouth holds its shape, a flattened oval, while stale-breath smell washes over her.

Vicky blinks. Something tells her to take a step back. She looks out across the surface of the spiral as fifty mouths resume their murmurations. Except this time, the muttering has risen in pitch to a throaty, conversational hum. She thinks of the cicadas nesting inside these people, spiny protrusions rooted in their guts, anchored to their organs.

She takes another step back. The chorus rises. Each mouth seems to fold over itself, lips flipping inside out, tongues flicking. She knows, of course, that these people have no teeth, but the sight of their empty pink gums is still jarring as their mouths stretch wide. There's a hierarchy of sound, levels defined by voices flung from throats twisted to a new purpose. Harmonies converge: guttural rhythms and raw, piercing wails.

The disparate intervals rise to a single sustained scream. Vicky's hands go to her ears but the sound breaches her skull, grips her brain, and tightens its hold. Her knees hit the cement. She wants to squeeze her eyes shut but fifty shifting mouths hold her gaze hostage. There is friction in the way they move that infects the air above the spiral. Their endless cry drives spikes into her mind. The pain is immense. Vicky finds that she is screaming too but this knowledge is distant as a half-remembered dream, as far away as the last Connect Four game she played with Sadie at the kitchen table while morning light streamed in. And so she screams and screams. At some point her hands drop from her ears and she kneels and sways and all the sounds disintegrate into shards of shrieking metal.

Everything ceases. It's so abrupt it makes her gasp. The pain in her head subsides. In this new moment of silence, she watches Phil's face pinch into a weird grimace. His back arches.

Then his distended belly pops the buttons on his shirt. Vicky doesn't understand what she's seeing. Flesh protrudes and elongates like a hand inside a balloon stretching it thin. Then with a wet burst the skin pops and flings itself back in ragged chunks. A creamy-white and grublike insect head emerges. Antennae quiver. Two red eyes swivel and *stare directly at her.* Vicky scoots backward. Some part of her understands that this is a baby cicada being birthed, a nymph—yet its head alone is as big as a boxing-gloved fist. Her mind reels, stutters, catches on itself. The noise that echoes in the warehouse is so horrid as to be unbelievable—the sound of fifty human torsos turned into a mess of ripped skin as the nymphs force their way out of the soft place just beneath the rib cage. Bodies in the spiral arc upward, expel their gestations, and collapse, deflated, to the concrete. The mouths no longer move. Blood pools outward. These people, having fulfilled their purpose, are finally dead.

Vicky scrambles to her feet but does not flee. She has run the gamut of horror and disbelief and come out the other side half mad and frozen in place. A single foreleg emerges and plants itself in the flesh of Phil's ruined belly. It is a thick, rounded claw, almost crustacean in form. The creature uses the foreleg to push itself up, and like a phallus slicked with lubricant it rises and swells. It does this without breaking its red-eyed gaze.

Small hairs cover the nymph's head and thorax. Additional legs appear, hinged like a spider's, and find purchase on the cement. This emergence is repeated throughout the spiral. The head of the nymph pitches sideways, the legs skitter along the cement, pulling the thick bulb of the abdomen fully out of Phil's body with a moist sucking sound. The nymph crawls awkwardly, hesitantly, dragging strings of entrails that fall away as it learns in a matter of seconds to use its legs properly. It is the size of a house cat. Unlike its adult counterparts it does not make a sound except for the clicking of the tips of its legs along the warehouse floor. Patches of slop stuck to its abdomen glint in the wan light as it moves, its hindquarters lightly swaying.

Vicky stares into the nymph's immobile eye-globes, red as a neon sign. In her peripheral vision, dozens more crawl away from their hosts. The human spiral, once a precise arrangement, has fallen to bloody ruin. Even as the nymphs approach, despair roots Vicky to the floor.

If this is the fate of people implanted with cicadas, then what is the point of going on? Sadie will soon be dead, if she isn't already. Not just dead but used and discarded, nothing more than a husk, a temporary feeding tube for a monster.

(Her little girl's belly torn open, Sadie's guts strewn across the bed.)

A fullness rises in Vicky's raw throat, moves up into her head, forces out tears.

Everyone in those hospital beds, in the gurneys crowding the hallways, in the overflowing emergency room. All of them dead and mangled. The corridors crawling with these abominations.

Despair turns to heat inside her. Rage takes over.

She flexes her fingers and braces herself to put her hands around the first nymph that reaches her, to choke the life out of it, to rip into its soft underbelly with her bare hands and tear it apart the way it did its host. She will take as many with her as she can, and when she can no longer fight she will let go and think of Sadie.

Then she will open her eyes and be with her daughter again, beyond pain, beyond this horrible world.

She moves like a tennis player awaiting a serve. A hundred red eyes are bobbing in the gloom, getting closer. Nymphs at the far end of the spiral work their way across the desecrated bodies. The monster that clawed its way out of Phil is only ten feet away now, leaving a moist trail along the cement. They are not fast but they are not exactly slow either. Vicky stares into its eyes and can make out her distorted figure in its wet reflection.

"Come on," she says.

The oversize nymph displays no sign of enthusiasm or recognition or hatred. It simply approaches in a mantis-like crouch as if rubbing its forelegs together in mischievous glee. A rank odor rises around her, raw meat and shit.

"COME ON!" she screams, body trembling, her hands closing into fists. A thrumming blood-rush courses through her. She imagines what it will be like to lay hands on something so disgusting. She cannot see its mouth, just a flattened area at the tip of its head. She wonders if it has teeth.

The nymph picks up speed. Its legs advance with an odd mechanical grace as if this movement is second nature and not something it just adapted to in the last thirty seconds. Startled, Vicky takes another step back, and another. She hadn't anticipated this sudden burst of speed. She doesn't want to die. She isn't ready for the white-hot agony.

A noise comes from behind her. The metal door flies open and bashes into the wall. She doesn't dare take her eyes off the army of nymphs.

Grimes! she thinks, her heart soaring. He survived. He came for her.

The *BOOM* of the shotgun fills the warehouse. At the same time, the nymph at the vanguard, the one that crawled up out of Phil, explodes before her eyes. The once-plump abdomen spatters Vicky with ragged chunks of meat. The head slides across the slick floor. The other nymphs halt. Their antennae wave. A second shot disintegrates another of their ranks. Dozens of red eyes swivel to regard the interlopers. Vicky continues to back away. She has the distinct impression that the nymphs are processing the change in their situation and silently discussing an appropriate response.

"Hey!" It isn't Grimes's voice. Vicky turns. A tall Black man loads another shell into her partner's old shotgun, pumps the wooden slide beneath the barrel, and levels it at the nymphs.

Next to him, a woman in a bloodstained tank top calls to Vicky. "You wanna get the hell out of here?"

With one more glance at the nymphs, Vicky turns and breaks into a dead sprint. The man fires; the shotgun barrel jumps slightly in his grip but his shoulder absorbs the recoil without moving. The woman hands him another shell. From behind her comes the burst-fruit sound of a nymph's soft innards splattering its fellows. She can hear their skittering limbs scratching the cement as they pursue her. Even without looking she can tell they're getting close. Vicky's terrified and astonished: These things *just* learned to walk, and now they're coming after her like a stampeding herd.

"Get down!" the man yells. Vicky drops to her knees and slides. The shotgun blast is deafening. A nymph explodes in the place where Vicky's head had been a split second earlier. Fluid rains down on her.

"Mouth closed!" the woman cautions her, and flings open the door. A chaotic morass of cicadas awaits, hanging in the air. Their song is like amplified bees. It's a jarring shift, as if this woman has opened a portal to another dimension.

Vicky flanks around the man with the shotgun and follows the woman outside. She spots Grimes's beige car immediately, parked just across the grassy drainage ditch. She takes three steps before the cicadas are upon her with a newfound energy, as if avenging the deaths of their mutant spawn. She bats them away from her face but there are more, always more. She wants to tell this woman to watch her eyes but she can't open her mouth.

The shotgun booms and Vicky glances back. Cicadas crowd her face but she can see enough: The man is outside now, pulling the door shut as a pair of nymphs leap through the gap. In the daylight their exoskeletons, or shells, or *skins* (Vicky has no idea) are the color of smoke-yellowed blinds.

The man swings the weapon and sends one nymph into the brick wall but the second one is upon him before he can react. There is nothing Vicky can do. The woman gets to Grimes's car first and slides into the driver's seat. Vicky piles into the back. The car reeks of stale smoke. Grimes is there, pale and sweaty, head lolling against the seat rest, a red stain soaking his shirt. He gives her a weak smile. She slams the door behind her and together with the woman hunts and kills the handful of cicadas that slipped inside.

Satisfied that they're all dead, she looks out the window at the man who saved her life, expecting him to be grappling with the final nymph, maybe swinging it against the wall by its disgusting foreleg until its abdomen shatters.

"Ah, fuck me," the woman says.

Vicky can't believe her eyes. This man who not thirty seconds ago was blasting nymphs with a shotgun is crouching down, staring into the monster's red eyes as it *stares right back*. It's as if they're old friends sharing a heartfelt moment, a man and his mutant pal. The nymph's antennae wave languidly back and forth. Vicky's adrenaline-fueled thoughts run wild. This man, this total stranger who risked his life to save hers, is *communing* with one of the newly emerged freak-bugs. And this behavior does not appear to be driven by some catastrophic mental break, because the nymph seems to be *communing right back*. It's all too much. She decides that she has to simplify her reality—narrow the scope—or she'll lose her grip. So she turns to Grimes and takes his hand.

"Hey, Victoria." His voice is a hoarse whisper. Blood drips from his mouth. His eyes roll in their sockets to meet hers. "I'm sorry..." He trails off and his face goes slack. Vicky squeezes his hand. He coughs, and she wipes the flecks of blood from his chin.

"Shhh," she tells him. "It's okay."

She doesn't need to examine his wound. She can tell by the sticky red stain that he's lost too much blood, that he's been gut-shot and forced to go without medical care for too long.

Grimes draws on some deep reserve of strength and lifts his head from the seat rest. Outside, the tall man rises and walks to the car, shotgun at his side, seemingly unconcerned about the swarm buzzing around the parking lot. The nymph hunches in its mantis-pose, training those red eyes on the man's back.

"I'm sorry," Grimes wheezes out again. "For what I said about Sadie's dance recitals." He pauses. "I wish—" He coughs. Vicky wipes his face. "I wish I had a kid. Not all the time. But when I see you and Sadie." His head falls back against the seat rest and he closes his eyes. "She's a good one, Vic." He lifts his other hand and reaches for her.

"I'm here," she says, taking it. "I'm right here with you, Kenny."

Hearing Sadie's name, Vicky suddenly wishes these people never came to save her. She should have listened to her first impulse, back in the warehouse: She'd be better off dead. Yes, there would be a moment of terror and pain before she crossed over to the other side. But then she would be free and absolved of all responsibility.

Vicky has never before wanted to shirk any of her duties. Even the thought of letting go brings both release and a fresh shame.

"She had a solo last time," Grimes says. "It wasn't boring. It was real impressive." Vicky can barely hear him, his voice is so weak.

"Kenny," she tells him, "you're a good man. I say that to a lot of people to prop them up, and I don't always mean it. But you are."

His eyes close. He smiles. "You got a cigarette?"

"Yeah," she lies. She watches his body sag as he fades away. "Yeah, I do."

"That's good," he says. And then he dies. Vicky feels a gnawing emptiness take hold, an exhaustion more profound than the morning after a sleepless night. She lets go of his hands, touches his stubbly cheek.

"I'm sorry," the woman up front says.

Vicky nods.

The tall man opens the door and bends his frame into the passenger seat, angling the shotgun so its barrel rests on the floor at his feet. The woman flattens the lone cicada that follows him in.

"What the hell was that?" she says to him.

"What?"

"You making friends out there?"

"Oh," the man says. "No." To Vicky he sounds a little embarrassed. "I don't know, it was weird."

Muttering to herself, the woman throws the car into reverse. Vicky catches sight of the nymph, an off-white lump crouched by the wall, red eyes watching them go. The man turns around in the passenger seat, glancing at Grimes's body then at Vicky. There's something distracted in his brown eyes, a look she's seen before in her more thoughtful colleagues—the nagging urge to solve an impossible puzzle, a curse that's always looming, even when you're trying to focus on something else.

"Dude said he was your partner," the man says.

"Yeah."

"I'm sorry." The man thinks for a moment. "I think he made himself live long enough to see you. Seemed like he really cared."

Vicky tries to say something, but a tightness in her raw throat blocks the words. The man gives her a nod, then turns back to talk softly with the woman. As they pull out of the lot, Vicky forces herself to look over at her car.

The back windshield is spattered red. Thick forelegs scrabble against the glass, claws fingerpainting with blood. Like a puppy with zoomies, the nymph bolts around the car's interior, popping up in the front, bashing its head against the glass, searching for an exit.

Vicky closes her eyes. "Can you take me to the hospital, please?" She hears her voice as if it's someone else's. The words don't match the way her mouth moves, like a movie's audio track nudged slightly off time.

Both the man and the woman object to this, tell her that the breakout attack on the closed border might have succeeded, that they have to try different sections of the town's perimeter until they find a way out. Vicky barely hears them.

"Just drop me off, then," she says. At that moment she no longer cares if what she's doing constitutes weakness. It certainly has nothing to do with duty or honor. All she knows is that it feels right. "I'm going to die with my daughter."

24

FORT HALCOTT

From the passenger seat of a dead man's shitty car, Will watches cicadas fall from the sky. The tires crunch their brittle bodies as Alicia steers the sedan across the median line of Route 138, one of the main drags bisecting the small upstate city.

"Fuckers are dying," Alicia says. It's more of a matter-of-fact comment than a triumphant shout. There is little to celebrate. The detective in the back seat, Vicky Paterson, is barely functional, sitting there silently with the corpse of her partner. During their journey across town, Vicky has not amended her vow to die with her daughter, and Will and Alicia have not tried to talk her out of it. They have also not suggested that they might perhaps want to take the dead man out of the car. Vicky is quite clearly teetering on the edge of a mental break, and not even Alicia has the desire to fuck with that kind of energy.

Will settles as best he can in the seat, hand gripping the unloaded shotgun pointed at the floor. He hasn't fired one of these pump-action jobs since the middle of the walkabout, somewhere in Eastern Europe, an overgrown meadow a rickety bus ride from Budapest, maybe—blasting bottles flung from a tennis ball chucker, smoking hash, drinking vodka.

He has to admit it felt good today, bursting into that warehouse, splattering those monsters, saving Vicky's life. The decisive lizard-brain action of aiming the shotgun, firing, and reloading washed away the last vestiges of his session with Gerald and Duvall and the other mercenaries—Alicia's melting face, the torment of the spider's cold legs against the back of his head, the horrors of his own inadequacies and failures being hammered like a railroad tie into his psyche.

Then that creature outside, that final nymph, had tickled his brain. It hadn't been like his deep immersion in the cicadas' song, the overpowering symphony, the mad psychedelia of their chamber music. It had been a quiet pressure, a subtle outreach. A vague and somewhat confusing truce in which the nymph recognized a kindred spark. In the same way Will knew, almost innately, that he was in no danger from the invading swarm, he knew that this mutant was no threat to him.

There had been no other communication. It wasn't like the nymph could actually form words or convey ideas. The absurdity of the two of them—human and mutant baby cicada—silently staring at each other after he had just blasted the nymph's brood-mates to hell was not lost on him. Its hunched mantis-like posture, the chunky forelegs, the shiny-wet carapace. Objectively disgusting, yet in that moment Will had sympathized. It had not *asked* to burst out of a human torso, to be born into this world with an irresistible desire to feed and grow and evolve. Then he'd turned his back and left it to its own devices. He did not shoot it. It did not try to feed on him.

Now the cicadas' song fades as more and more fall dead to the ground. Alicia grits her teeth as she drives over them and he sees in her a small satisfaction at the dry *crunch*. He understands. For days, she hasn't been able to open her mouth for fear of a cicada invading her body. He takes a breath. The cicadas might be dying off en masse, but that's only because their work is coming to an end. They're wrapping up their assignment, punching their cards, checking out. There is no victory in their death.

It is within this knowledge that Will's sense of self falters. The decisive action hero storming the warehouse fades away, replaced by a fuzzier conception of Will Bennett. This Will is caught in this liminal space between craving the brotherhood of their symphony and wishing to splatter their guts by the millions to end all this. He runs a hand along the breech of the pump-action. The synthetic wood is nicked and chipped. The one he fired outside Budapest was sleek and black. He'd been high as hell that day, and rain came out of nowhere.

"Fuck me," Alicia says as the car jounces up and over a corpse. Will comes out of his reverie, back to the present moment. Big box stores loom, their parking lots blanketed with fallen insects. Cat-size nymphs bound across vast fields of their dead and dying parent bugs.

Flames issue from a Dollar General's smashed front windows where the rear of a white van protrudes, its front half stuck inside the store.

The whole of Fort Halcott is an obstacle course: stalled cars with terrified people inside, running out of time as the monstrous nymphs roam the city in packs. Abandoned vehicles. Piles of bodies, their torsos hanging open, ragged flaps of skin brushing the pavement like wings at rest. Alicia does the best she can, weaving through the carnage, but progress is achingly slow.

They come to an intersection blocked by an overturned Sysco tractor trailer. Dead cicadas plunk off the roof in droves. Will can sense the microtonal degrees in which their symphony degrades.

"I have to find another way around," Alicia says.

Just ahead a shirtless man makes a break from his car, his

body covered in sweat from his time cooking inside a useless Camaro. A ragged tattoo of an angel covers his shiny back. The words MARLA JACOBS FOREVER IN OUR HEARTS are inked on a ribbon that winds around the angel. The man glances up, shields his face from falling cicadas, and runs across the intersection.

"Shit," Will says, spotting the nymphs before the man does.

"Look out look out look out," Alicia says.

Eight little creatures flank around the side of a tanker truck, leaping over the torn-open stomach of the man hanging upside down across the running board of the cab.

"Gun it!" Vicky says from the back seat. "Run them over!"

Will starts—it's the first thing he's heard her say since she voiced her desire to die with her daughter. He's surprised she's even paying attention to what's happening outside the car. Or outside her head.

"Too late," Alicia says. The man spots the nymphs and stops short, arms windmilling. Broken glass glitters on the blacktop.

"Shoot them," Vicky says. She pounds the back of the headrest. Then she bashes a fist against the window.

"I only have six shells left," Will says. He leaves the rest unspoken: *I'm not going to waste them saving a stranger.*

The man begins to backpedal. An inked Celtic cross ripples up his bare stomach. Alicia leans on the car horn. The nymphs pay it no mind. They fan out from a haphazard grouping, and their intelligence gives Will a jolt. Two nymphs go wide and approach in pincer formation. The rest menace the man straight-on, weaving back and forth in a disorienting, complex array. Dead cicadas carom off their backsides as they fall. Will finds that he is *proud* of their cunning, like a father might take quiet satisfaction in watching his kids set up an elegant goal on the soccer field.

None of them, not even Will, spot the nymph that takes the man down. One that had been hiding behind the cab of the truck leaps off the hood and brings its massive digging forelegs down into the side of the man's neck, just above his collarbone. Blood spurts in a high arcing spray. His arms go up as if to peel the insect off him. Then the pack moves in, propelling themselves toward their victim at astonishing speed. Will, ashamed, swells with pride. The lead nymph vivisects the inked cross. The man collapses as a second nymph buries its head in the wound. Its body jerks as its mouthparts suckle upon the man's innards.

"Fuck this," Alicia says, slamming the car into reverse. Cicadas crunch beneath the wheels. She turns the car around and heads up a grassy slope. The car bounces over some low scraggly shrubs and enters the parking lot of a small Lutheran church. The sign out front says FEED YOUR FAITH & YOUR FEARS WILL STARVE. A pair of white church vans are parked by the side door.

Alicia hits the brakes. Down the embankment, Will sees the nymphs crowd around the tattooed man's ruined body, tearing at his flesh with their foreclaws. Their abdomens wiggle obscenely as they jockey for position. In the distance, fires burn in strip malls. The sky is uniform gray. His eyes survey the woods at the edge of the lot. A dead woman sits upright on a bench, chin against her collarbone, her chest cavity hanging open like a side of beef in a butcher's window.

"Listen," Alicia says, turning to the cop in the back seat, "getting across town is a bitch. The power's out everywhere—when night falls, it's gonna be pitch black, with those *things* out there on the hunt." She glances at Will. "You wanna give us any insight into what those little fuckers are plotting? As part of their brain trust?"

Will doesn't know what to say. Alicia slaps his thigh with her palm. "Some freaky mind-melding shit going on with this guy right here, ever since we got to your lovely upstate hamlet. So yeah, Detective—here's what I'm thinking. I'm thinking this trip to the hospital is no longer in the cards. Your boy here, God rest his soul, and I mean that sincerely, was shooting it out with those shitstain mercenaries guarding the city limits when we found him. I don't know if they broke through, but I think we oughta go find out. Otherwise we'll be stuck here another night." She nods down the embankment. Will doesn't look. "With *that*."

Will swallows. "They do have a purpose," he says. "I, uh, felt it. I mean, it's not just random attacks. They're feeding. This is all going somewhere. I just don't know where. I don't know if they do either. They're kind of like us in that way, I guess."

He looks at the detective in the back seat. Her eyes are red, her hair a greasy, straw-colored rat's nest, face streaked with blood and dirt, clothes filthy.

She's quiet for a moment. "Are you two together?"

"Divorced," Alicia says.

"Business partners," Will says.

"What business is that?"

"We're fixers," Will says, too tired to come up with anything better.

Vicky bursts out laughing. It's an ugly sound, hoarse and borderline unhinged. "I'm sorry. I thought that was just a TV-show job. I didn't know there were real fixers."

"One time we saved this kid from neo-Nazis in Bratislava," Will offers.

"She doesn't need our résumé," Alicia tells him. "But yeah. We did do that."

"Thank you, both, again," Vicky says. Will can actually see her soften up in real time, a tiny bit of humanity coming back to her face. He scans the tree line once again. There's movement in the underbrush. He tells himself it might just be squirrels, or rats, or something. Then he turns to Vicky. Alicia is right: Driving around the middle of Fort Halcott, circumventing blockade after blockade, just so this lady can die in an overrun hospital, is a foolish waste of time. The border is still their best shot. If there's a fight they can join, at least it's something. It beats driving around town with six remaining shells and praying the nymphs don't eat Alicia. Maybe a different approach will get through to Vicky.

"I'm sorry about your daughter," he says, as gently as he can.

"Sadie," Vicky says. Will blinks. The name doesn't mean anything to him, of course. But the word itself, the way it sounds coming from her mouth and hitting the stale air of the car's interior, gives him a little shiver. It's almost as if the volume got turned up on the cicadas' dying symphony, just for a second. "She got hit that first morning," Vicky says. "Playing out back. *Boom.* Just like that. She must've been one of the first."

One of the first.

Will feels woozy. The words bounce around his skull, riding on waves of a new harmonic register.

"Get your shit together," Alicia tells him, but her voice comes from far away. There is only this notion of Sadie, the little girl, one of the first afflicted. Bright lights flash behind his eyes and he's back at the window of the warehouse. Fruit pits litter the floor. The acolytes squirm, their underbellies slick with mucus as they climb the walls. The leaders of the ritual open their mouths wider and wider, and for the first time Will can *see* one of them: a little girl holding a toy. A stuffed ladybug. Her eyes bore into his. She sees him there, outside the window, spying on the ritual. But she is not angry at this intrusion. She smiles at him, and her eyes are full of wonder.

"Hey!" Alicia smacks him on the arm. "You good?"

"I'm good."

Vicky regards him curiously. The patter of dead cicadas on the roof is almost soothing.

"I was saying," Will says. "Alicia's right, we should—we have to—"

The little girl's eyes won't stop staring at him. They are the eyes of the dead cop, and they are watching him from the back seat. He thinks he has finally, irrevocably lost his mind. Her blue eyes flicker in the dead man's slack, careworn face. They are so, so beautiful. He looks away, swallows hard. "We really have to get out of town. There's no point—I don't think that Sadie, your daughter, I don't think she would want you to die, just because... *agghhh*." He winces, clamps his hands to his ears, but it's no use—the sudden screeching uptick in the symphony is coming from inside his head.

He waits for the screech to die away. "But I guess we could go," he tells Vicky. "We could go to the hospital."

"What the hell are you talking about?" Alicia says. Then she softens her tone. "You're pretty banged up, Will. Maybe you should take a rest, and Vicky and I will work this out."

"I think it would be okay if we went to the hospital," he says, words coming out in a rush. "Just to see."

"See *what*?" Alicia slaps her hands against the steering wheel. "See fucking *what*, Will? A million more of these monsters? A million more dead people? Just look me in the eyes and tell me what you're talking about, please. When you say *just to see*, what exactly do you think we'll find?"

Will tries to reverse course. He knows it's out of line. The girl's mother is sitting right there. But he owes Alicia as much of an honest explication of his feelings as he can muster.

"Sadie," he says. Dr. Capaldi would be proud of this engagement with his core emotional state. Vicky leans forward as if shoved from behind and lets out a sharp breath.

She reaches out for Will and he gives her his forearm. Her grip is warm, her gaze eager. "What do you mean?"

Alicia slumps in her seat, as if she is afraid of this very thing. She rubs her temples. "Oh Jesus Christ," she says.

"Will," Vicky says, "*what do you mean?*"

"I don't know," Will says. "I'm sorry. I can't say anything else."

Because it will sound insane.

Because it will give false hope to a grieving mother.

"All I can say is that I agree with you," he says. "At least about the going-to-the-hospital part. Not about you dying. Because then what was the point of saving you?"

He cuts himself off before he says anything more. Head spinning, he pulls his arm away and Vicky sits back.

Alicia sighs. "Carter used to say—that's my ex," she tells Vicky.

"Lawyer," Will says.

"Carter used to say, *Opportunities don't just happen. You create them.*"

"Of course he did," Will says.

"Yeah, you know what, Will? He was a stodgy motherfucker in a lot of ways, but he was right about that. And the reverse is also true, right? If we don't—" She cuts herself off. "What the fuck am I talking about? Fuck Carter's stupid aphorisms, and fuck *you*, Will. I'm over your cryptic shit. Vicky, I'm really sorry about your partner, he seemed like a good guy, but I can't drive around with his dead ass in this car anymore. So while we're here at this"—she looks at the sign out front—"*Lutheran church*, why don't we take this opportunity to respectfully deliver his earthly remains to the good Lord."

"All right," Vicky says. She unbuckles her seat belt. Will finds it borderline hilarious that she bothered to buckle it in the first place. "You have every right to want to get as far away from Fort Halcott as possible. I'll take Kenny into the church and lay him down, and then I'll walk the rest of the way."

"You'll die out there," Will says.

Vicky shrugs. "As long as I'm headed for my daughter when it happens. I can make my peace with that. I don't want to get you two killed."

"No," Will says.

"Will," Alicia says, gripping the wheel, looking straight ahead, "the lady made her choice."

Will puts a hand on the door handle. "*I'll* bring Kenny into the church." Before either of the women can protest, he gets out of the car, batting away a few stray cicadas before they can slip through. He takes a breath and is surprised to find that spilled blood has an odor that hangs in the air like smoke. He remembers the day they arrived, he and Alicia—a lifetime ago now—standing on their little motel balcony, breathing in the pine-scented air and laughing about how you have to get close to one of those little trees dangling from the rearview of a cab to get the same experience in the city. And now there's a sour reek everywhere, ash and death. He takes a moment to absorb what's left of the cicadas' song, then retrieves the body from the back seat and slams the door with his foot.

Will takes two steps before realizing that dead bodies are extremely cumbersome. Will can't let the body fall in front of Vicky and Alicia. He adjusts so that his left arm is underneath Kenny's knees. With the crook of his elbow supporting Kenny's neck, he manhandles the body toward the doors of the church.

That's when the nymphs come out of the woods. Two dozen of them, at least, prowling low to the ground, forelegs chittering across the edge of the parking lot. From straight on, the ridges on the upper parts of their heads are like a bulldog's folds. Will shoots them a glance. He feels nothing: no telepathic shiver, no pressure inside his head. No sympathetic shift in air quality. Perhaps his earlier meeting with the nymph had been a fluke. Perhaps his odd luck has run out. It makes a certain kind of sense—the cicadas are dying off, their song dying with them. Maybe that had been the key to his ability to commune with all this shit.

The nymphs halt in a loose formation. He hauls ass to the church doors and kicks one open. A bad smell hits him. He'd planned on laying Kenny Grimes down in peaceful repose on a pew, but as soon as he's inside he simply lets the deadweight fall from his arms. *Sorry, man. Rest easy.* He takes one look at the dim interior then rushes back to the car.

Immediately he tries to forget what he saw, but he knows he never will. Bodies in pews, bodies on the altar. Splotches of blood staining white linens, soaking into the beige carpet. His brain connects the dots in a split second: loved ones bringing their afflicted husbands and wives and sons and daughters to a place of refuge and salvation, begging God to save them.

The hospital will look like that too, he thinks. Times a million.

He meets Alicia's wide eyes through the windshield. He's only a few steps away when the first nymph goes leaping past him from behind. It lands on the dented hood of the car. A second follows. The pair scrabble up the hood to the windshield. They bash themselves into the glass, again and again. Will glances over his shoulder. The others are maintaining their formation. He gets the unsettling impression that they're watching. Absorbing information. Learning.

The car lurches backward as Alicia sends it into reverse. The nymphs go sailing off the hood. Will can see her entire body move as she throws it into drive with great force. One of the nymphs scampers away. A tire crushes the other, and its ruined body leaks brackish liquid.

Will slides into the front seat. Alicia kills a cicada that follows him inside. Then she heads for the parking lot's exit.

Will meets Vicky's eyes in the rearview. "Your partner's at peace."

"It was okay in there?"

"Yeah," he says. "All good."

He thinks of the detective crumpled in a heap just inside the door of a stinking death trap and feels sick. Then he looks away, hand wrapped around the shotgun as the car bounces down into the intersection where the remains of the tattooed man are stretched across the pavement like a dissected animal. Alicia maneuvers slowly between the wrecked Sysco truck and a white minivan with a smashed windshield. Inside, four bodies are still buckled in while nymphs feast. Outside the vehicle, fat nymphs writhe like satiated puppies.

Will puts his hand on Alicia's knee and gives it a light squeeze. She finds an unbroken stretch of Route 138 between dead traffic lights and guns the old sedan. The engine protests. She steers around the body of a young boy and his bicycle. Dusk begins to claw its way across the ashen sky. The cicada song is faint now, probably nonexistent to everyone but Will. Alicia aims for a scampering nymph but it dodges the tires.

Will scans the roadside. Nymphs perch in trees like an ominous flock of birds. Alicia spots them too. She curses. Will gives her leg another squeeze. He doesn't make any suggestions. He decides that whatever happens next is up to Alicia. He knows he's acting strange, and while he can't really help it, he also knows that she deserves to be the final arbiter of their fate. Dr. Capaldi would again be proud: He's transcending his own biases and instincts in order to give her the emotional space to make an informed and rational decision.

He wonders if Dr. Capaldi is still alive.

Alicia sighs. Then she glances at Vicky in the mirror. "You're not walking." She doesn't sound happy. It's all she says.

"Thank you," Vicky says. Alicia curses again and keeps her eyes on the road. Will finds her hand on the steering wheel and covers it with his own.

When she glances over, her eyes are the eyes of a little girl he's never met.

Night falls on Fort Halcott, and with it comes the final silenc-
ing of the cicadas' symphony. The dark roads are paved with
their corpses. Billions of insects blanketing the earth, a hellish
precipitation that will have to be shoveled aside by earthmovers
if there is anyone left to operate them. The sedan's headlights
sweep across the glittering black expanse of the dead.

"If this was shit hitting the fan in a normal way, like a super-
flu or something, we could have ditched the car hours ago,"
Alicia says. She's been driving this whole time, doubling back
when obstacles cropped up, winding their way in some kind
of meandering spiral to St. Mary's Hospital. Will thinks of the
spirals painted on the walls of their hotel's cave-like basement,
where that kid, Denny, ripped out his teeth and ate a cicada.
He remembers the bird-watcher, and Bing and his teenagers.
He wonders if those kids are still alive. "But no," she continues,
"this has to be a goddamn *creature* event, and the hospital has to
be in the exact fucking center of this godforsaken town."

Their headlights sweep across a couple of bodies coated in
fallen cicadas. Will gives them a passing glance, notes the insects
settling in the congealed blood-mass of their gaping stomach
wounds, then looks away. He has seen so much of this carnage
over the past few hours, he is no longer as disturbed by the sight.
One night in Mexico City, he met a journalist who'd been a
war correspondent and now covered narco atrocities in Ciudad
Juarez and other border cities. The woman had told him the
secret to her long-term ability to confront such horrors. It isn't
desensitization, she'd said, or numbing yourself with alcohol and
drugs. It's learning to walk the line between empathy and callousness. Too much empathy and you'll break down, too much
callousness and your soul will rot away. It's all about the balance.
Otherwise, you're either—her words—a *soft bitch* or a *psycho*.

Right now, by her metric, he feels like a psycho. The dreadful sights of Fort Halcott wash over him—entire families dead in their cars, mutated nymphs leaping from trees through apartment windows, commercial strips set ablaze, scraps of shredded flesh littering the streets, a chorus of distant screams...

People begging for help, for whom they do not stop.

And all he can feel inside is a shameful throb of gratitude— that he is still alive, that he is with Alicia. That whatever happens, they will face it together. There is almost—almost!—an adolescent thrill at the whole thing, which exists separate from the grim reality of their circumstances.

It occurs to him that their relationship, moving forward, would actually be easier to navigate without the pressures of work and, say, *other human beings* to interfere with it.

Psycho, he thinks.

"I haven't seen any cops," Vicky says abruptly.

"There were some back there," Alicia says.

"Alive ones, I mean. No organized patrols. No federal presence either. If I had to guess, I'd say we won the fight at the border wall. And anybody who's capable either has left or is getting out now." She pauses. "I hope you can, too."

"No Feds," Will says. "Huh."

"Yeah," Alicia says. "The movies prepared me for a military presence in the streets, like, ASAP."

"There's a base about two hours west of here," Vicky says. "But I mean logistically—the army's going through the same thing we're all going through. It's not like tanks and rocket launchers are any use against cicadas."

"So you're saying the US military's useless," Alicia says.

"Not useless," Vicky says, "but maybe decimated below an operational level. And besides, chain of command is totally severed. How are troops and guardsmen being deployed? Who's deciding where to allocate resources? It's the same thing with

the cops. I'm a Major Crimes detective, and I'm out here doing
my own thing. If you'd run this scenario past me a few weeks
ago as an exercise, you know what I'd say? I'd say I'd be organizing a mobile unit to take down those monsters, free people
trapped in their houses, make sure there's some kind of administration structure intact. I don't know. Protect the mayor. Guard
city hall. Collect food and water. Whatever. I would have said to
you, the most important factor in whether we come out of this
alive or dead is *discipline*. And now look at me." It's the most animated Will has heard her since they sprang her from the warehouse. Yet she still sounds miserable. "It all breaks down faster
than you think." She laughs bitterly. "Faster than the movies
would have you believe, anyway."

For some reason, this inspires Will to turn on the radio.
Static. He flips stations. More static. He turns it off. "I thought
there'd be something," he says.

"What, like, the president?" Alicia says.

"I don't know. Maybe."

"If there are any troops they're in major cities," Alicia says,
"not out here in the middle of nowhere. No offense."

"None taken," Vicky says. "I agree."

"And law enforcement protects capital," Alicia says. "Not
people. Uh, no offense. Again."

Vicky shrugs. "I solve murders."

"You ever shoot anybody?"

"Yes," she says. Then adds, "A white man."

There's a moment of silence.

"Gerald was in this town," Will says quietly. "Duvall. A
hundred other mercenary assholes. *Here*, I mean. Fort Halcott,
specifically. They seemed pretty fucking interested in this place."

Alicia slows down to steer around a three-car pileup in the
middle of the street. She bumps up onto the sidewalk when a
pair of nymphs leap up onto the windshield.

"Jesus!" she says. She hits the brakes. This time they don't go flying off. They've managed to hook their forelegs around the wipers. Vicky turns them on. Nothing happens. The nymphs are too heavy for the wipers to move aside. Will remembers Werner Herzog's words from that movie *Grizzly Man*, which he saw at a film festival in Stockholm he only went to because the girl he was microdosing with at the time dragged him along.

This blank stare speaks only of a half-bored interest in food.

The nymph's eyes have no pupils. They do not move. They simply fix an inscrutable gaze straight into the car at the three humans. Will stares back.

Get off the car, he intones in his mind, and instantly feels stupid. Just like when he was trying to command the cicada swarm, there is no response. No wiggling of antennae to indicate understanding.

"Fucking disgusting," Alicia says. She cranks the wheel. The sedan bumps back down onto the road. Its old worn shocks don't do their job and the sedan's hood goes up and down like a speedboat hitting some chop. The nymphs lose their purchase and go sailing off into the night. Headlights come and go: another car of survivors, another desperate journey. So many intersecting stories, so much pain he'll never know.

"Gerald and Duvall?" Vicky asks. Will is heartened by the interest in her tone. Maybe they've been driving long enough that she's revised her plan to die. Maybe saving her life will have meant something after all, beyond the act itself.

"Not anybody you want to hang out with," Alicia says. "They caught us in the woods trying to get out of town. Long story short, they accused us of being involved in all this somehow. Kept asking about *the origin point*. Where's the origin point. Something like that. Anyway, Gerald kicked it in the firefight with your partner and company. Hopefully Duvall bought it then, too."

Will finds himself suddenly adrift, the torment of the session washing over him. He understands why Alicia hates him. He vacated his responsibilities. He took a gap year as a grown adult. He made other people clean up the wreckage of his personal journey.

Get a grip, man.

He clutches the shotgun and comes back to himself.

"Origin point," Vicky says. "Like, ground zero for the cicadas?"

"I assume that's what he meant."

"It must have been the warehouse," Will says. "All those cult members laid out like that. The ritual we saw there..."

"My partner and I," Vicky says, "the night this all started— we were at a crime scene. Old lady, dead on a dining room table. Her hair, teeth, and nails were all missing. Pulled out, shaved off. And placed in boxes under the table." She pauses, and when she resumes she's almost wistful. "Figured we were in for some strange times. A serial, maybe. Obviously not this."

They all three turn their heads to watch a pack of nymphs scuttle out from the neat hedgerows that line the yard of an old stone house.

"We saw a kid like that," Will says. "A live one, tearing himself up, I mean. He ate a cicada."

"Your partner said you two found Violet Carmichael," Alicia says.

Will watches the detective look up sharply into the rearview. "How do you know that name?"

"Violet's who we were sent upstate to find. The Carmichaels are some old-money banking family. Very concerned about their wayward daughter."

Will thinks back to his fraught daily client calls, reporting in to Ed Carmichael. He imagines the man and his wife lying on their bed, holding hands, dying together, a crackling fire burning in the cozy hearth of their magnificent bedroom.

"*She* might be ground zero," Vicky says. "The origin point."

Will and Alicia listen as the detective goes on to describe the scene where she found Violet. The leathery, elongated limbs spiraling down into the earth like sentient roots. The transmutation of the entire torso. The spiny mutation growing from her shoulder blades to stab the earth, in mimicry of the brood's triplicate proboscis.

The whole time, Will listens with rapt attention, his body tingling. It's as if someone is describing a long-lost sister to him, or a childhood bedroom he hasn't seen in twenty years.

"Grimes thought it must have had something to do with kicking all this off," Vicky says. "And I'm inclined to agree. Especially now that I know the mercenaries were seeking an origin point."

"I wonder if they could have shut it down," Alicia says quietly. "Nipped all this in the bud, before..." She trails off and gestures at the windshield. She slows as they pass a Kia Soul with broken windows. A handful of nymphs inside, bathed in the weak glow of the dome light, tear into the flesh of an old man whose glasses hang askew from the bridge of his nose. They move like raccoons digging through trash cans, forelegs tossing flesh scraps aside to get at the real nutrients.

"So Gerald and Duvall," Will says, "were just trying to stop all this."

"Which means we've got a bunch of psychotic bug-worshippers—"

"The Order of Hemiptera," Will says.

"—versus a bunch of psychotic *anti*-bug-worshippers."

"With all of us caught in the middle," Vicky says. Then she leans forward, head between the front seats. "This is it, up here. We made it."

The sedan's headlights sweep across a parking lot choked with vehicles. Ambulances, immobile, packed in with cars and trucks, all of them hurriedly parked and abandoned. A layer of dead cicadas covers them all like black rain in a nuclear winter. The lawn surrounding the lot, with its little manicured gardens and wheelchair-accessible paths, is dotted with low mounds, barely visible at the edge of the headlights. *Bodies*, Will thinks. In the distance, someone is screaming. There is always someone screaming.

Alicia turns the wheel and skirts the edge of the parking lot, rumbling across uneven ground. There's no other way to get to the hospital complex, a pair of massive blocks against the black and starless sky. Not a single light is on inside. Will figures a hospital has generators so all the people on life support don't croak if there's an outage. But right now, the whole place looks like nothing's moved in there for days.

"When the bugs attacked Sadie," Vicky says, "I brought her here, thinking—not that it was going to be *fine*, but that the whole hospital ER would click into place. I even figured, being a cop, and with her dad being an EMT, that she'd be extra-taken-care-of. I know a lot of the doctors over there. But all these people came here at once, dragging their loved ones inside, screaming for help, just as frantic as I was. There was a gosh darn stampede."

Alicia bursts out laughing as she slows to steer around a slew of corpses, limbs flung out, chest cavities open to the sky. "You know it's the end of the world, right? You can swear. We're all adults here."

"I don't swear," Vicky says.

Alicia shakes her head. "What the fuck."

"I'm not scandalized if *you* do, I just don't find it necessary for myself."

Will cracks a smile. The detective's no longer talking like

somebody on a self-imposed suicide mission. "Do you drink, Vicky?"

"No."

"So after all this, if we make it out, you won't have a celebratory glass of champagne with us?"

"No."

"Not even for a once-in-a-lifetime, we-just-survived-the-apocalypse situation?"

"If you break your own framework of discipline for every new situation, then it's not really discipline. It's just window dressing on a personality."

"So you're not one for cheat meals," Alicia says, turning along a narrow strip between a path and the front of the building.

"I don't reward myself for sticking to a plan. I just stick to the plan. This is good, right here."

Alicia stops the car. The hospital building looms darkly to their right. Will finds himself shot through with nervous energy. In place of the absent symphony, the little girl's eyes throb in the back of his mind.

"Okay, Vicky, listen." Alicia turns in her seat. "Come with us. Please. We don't know what's waiting for us out there. Strength in numbers, right? Also, once you hit thirty, it's tough to make new friends, and I think we're really starting to click." She gestures at the black nothingness of the hospital, forbidding and devoid of life. "You don't want to die in there all alone."

"I won't be alone," Vicky says. The unspoken name hangs among them: *Sadie.* Pressure builds inside Will's head. He tries to shake it off. Vicky unbuckles her seat belt. "I really appreciate what you've done for me. A lot of people wouldn't have bothered." She looks from Alicia to Will. "Where will you go?"

"Back to the city," Alicia says, as if it's self-evident, even though she and Will haven't talked about it, not once. "That's where our people are. We have to see."

Vicky nods, her eyes full of sympathy. She looks like she's about to say something. She keeps quiet, but Will can guess what she's thinking: *Then you'll be doing exactly what I'm doing—dying with your family.*

It's true. Sixty thousand people live in Fort Halcott and it's overrun with mutated nymphs.

Imagine what a city of nine million looks like now.

Venturing back to New York City is a death sentence. If they can even make it that far.

Will meets Vicky's eyes. He tries to remember if they were always so long-lashed and so blue. The pressure in his head grows and grows, a kettle never boiling.

"All right," Vicky says, putting a hand on the latch. She glances over at the bloodstained seat where her partner died.

"Holy shit!" Alicia says.

Will turns to look out the front windshield and all at once the pressure in his head abates.

A little girl in sunflower pajamas is standing twenty feet away, fully illuminated by the headlights, shielding her eyes against the brightness. Her long shadow darkens a strip of grass until it melts into the night.

Vicky lets out a startlingly loud cry—shock, hysteria, disbelief. She shoves open the door and throws herself out onto the grass, stumbles, finds her footing, and races toward the little girl.

Without thinking, Will gets out, slams the door behind him, and runs after her. The nymphs come right away, half a dozen closing fast from the deep shadows of the parking lot, bounding across the grass like they're floating.

"No!" Will calls to them, waving his hands above his head as if that will dissuade the creatures from their singular purpose: to feed on this new flesh that has suddenly appeared in their midst.

Will catches up with Vicky. "Go back to the car! I'll get her."

But Vicky ignores him. She does not take her eyes from the little girl, who drops the hand shielding her face. Now Will can see the girl's eyes—*the* eyes—and nearly falls to his knees in gratitude.

The shotgun blast comes from behind him. *Alicia.* One of the nymphs, hit mid-stride, takes a spinning tumble out of formation. The others keep coming.

Vicky reaches the girl and scoops her up like she weighs nothing, clutches her to her chest, and runs back toward the car. Will moves between Vicky and the nymphs, standing in their path. They come at him in a tight V-shaped formation like migrating birds. They slow down, emanating sudden caution. Back legs move high and spider-like as they approach. In the harsh light, their bodies glisten with thin, spiny cilia. He wonders if the same complex signal network as their parent cicadas unites these offspring, if they have received word that Will is some kind of vaguely tolerated human who should not be touched. He braces himself for the encounter to go either way. The nymphs slow down further. Something is very wrong. His mind spins back on itself: the tattooed man, the downed Sysco truck . . .

The nymphs' diversion tactic.

Will turns. Vicky and the girl are nearly at the car. Alicia stands by the driver's-side door and aims the shotgun at the nymphs behind Will. The tableau feels all wrong, an itch he can't scratch.

Will bellows at Vicky and the girl to *LOOK OUT.* At the same time, a lone nymph comes out of the darkness at the rear of the car, leaps up onto the trunk, then to the roof. Will is running hard now, but it's too late. As Vicky wrenches open the door, the nymph slides past her and goes skidding off the roof and latches onto Alicia's face. She staggers back. Will feels like he's sprinting down a hallway in a dream where it just keeps getting longer. The shotgun hits the ground. Alicia's hands claw at the nymph as it wraps its legs around her lower jaw and neck. Its abdomen curls. She pummels it with her fists, denting its carapace. Will senses a hiccup of dull pain. The nymph swings free of Alicia's face, bending backward out into the air, its hind legs still clamped around her jaw. She gets her hands around either side of its plump body and digs her thumbs into its soft underbelly. Its forelegs flail, thick pincers opening and closing. As Will reaches her side, she raises the nymph above her head and flings it to the ground with a disgusted cry. He bundles her into the car, shuts the door behind her, and picks up the shotgun.

The remaining nymphs are practically at his feet. They do not leap at him. Clutching the shotgun, he stares them down. Then he steps around the front of the car without taking his eyes off them. Their antennae shift subtly to follow him as he moves. Five heads rotate, ten unblinking eye-globes stare in his general direction. Quickly, he slides into the passenger seat, shotgun pointed at the floor. Only when the door is closed behind him does he exhale.

Alicia is lifting her shirt, scrubbing her face with the sweaty, grimy fabric, rubbing away any trace of the nymph's horrid legs. She's making little whimpering sounds.

Will takes her gently by the wrists and lowers her shirt. It's smeared with blood.

"Let me see," he says softly. She fights him for a moment then gives in, lets her body go limp in his. He studies her face. There's a jagged gouge in her forehead. It doesn't look life threatening—if anything, it looks like road rash from a bad spill on a bicycle.

"I can go inside and track down some bandages, antiseptic, maybe some stitches," Will says.

Alicia shakes her head, calms herself. "I'm okay. It barely even hurts. It was just disgusting. Grabbing its body..." She shudders. "It was exactly what you'd think of, if you looked at a freaky little bug and thought, *If this was huge it would be really gross.* Brittle and squirmy and like a fat blob, all at the same time. Just a thing that shouldn't exist." Gingerly, she pokes at her forehead, wincing.

Will opens the glove compartment. Crumpled cigarette packs, an actual glove, a tattered paperback copy of *The Big Sleep*, a headless action figure, and a bunch of fast-food napkins. He takes them out and dabs at Alicia's forehead, mopping the edges of the wound.

"We'll stop somewhere and get disinfectant and stuff," he says. "And gas. And food. We're gonna need to eat soon."

There are other tiny cuts on her face, and they break Will's heart. He tries not let the sight of them take him back to the inside of their cell. The voice in his head comes on strong, dredged up by the sight.

Failure.

You're weak.

Piece of shit.

She hates you.

For a moment, Alicia seems to radiate so much contempt that he nearly bursts into tears. The distress must be showing on his face, because Alicia leans over and wraps her arms around him. He pulls her close. She smells terrible. He's certain he does too. He's also certain that outside, in the darkness of the hospital grounds, hundreds of nymphs prowl. His mind stretches out, across the unlit highways heading south, reaching into cities and towns that dot the thruway exits, over the bridges and into the city, where millions more feast and grow stronger.

Alicia takes his head in her hands and kisses him, hard. Relief floods him, the warmth of a pure, simple emotion after so much strain. He kisses her back and the tip of his tongue finds hers. Her mouth tastes like blood.

"Ew." The small voice comes from the back seat.

Will and Alicia glance back in unison to regard their new passenger. The little girl is watching them kiss while being fussed over by Vicky.

"Sadie," Vicky says through tears. She looks at Alicia and Will. Her laugh is incredulous. "This is Sadie," she tells them.

A smile breaks out on the girl's face. At the same time there's definitely something off about her slate-gray pallor. He tells himself she's just been through an insane ordeal. Of course she's not going to look well. He introduces himself.

The girl waves, then rubs her eyes. "Where am I?"

"You're safe, peanut," Vicky says, her voice that of a different person entirely than the morose woman Will is used to. She curls a hand around the girl's skinny arm, lays a kiss on her forehead.

Sadie glances up front and looks at Will with a child's inno- cent curiosity. He tries to smile but is certain it looks grotesque. He's never known how to act around kids.

Alicia throws the car in drive and aims for the handful of nymphs, still hunched over in the cone of light. They scatter as the car lurches forward. She turns the wheel and the headlights sweep across the crowded parking lot.

"Time to go car shopping," she says.

In the rearview, Will can't look away from the mother- daughter reunion. There is wonder in the way Vicky's hands hold her daughter's face and smooth her messy hair back.

Alicia weighs options aloud: A Tesla's a bad idea because charging stations won't work. A Honda CR-V's got more room. An F-150 can take them off-road if it comes to that. But Will is barely listening. Questions swirl in his head, all connected, in some way, to the eyes that led him here.

Why didn't a nymph burst out of Sadie's chest cavity?

How did she come to be out here alone in the dark?

How did she survive?

PART FOUR

ORIGIN POINTS

25

NEW YORK CITY

All his life, Anton's nostalgia has taken peculiar forms. As a child he'd been an obsessive peruser of calendars. His interest lay not in milestones but in the mundane—*What was I doing last year at this specific date and time, what was I doodling in my notebook, what daydreams were parading across my mind, drowning out teachers and classmates alike?* For Anton this has always been a thrill, the overlapping of past and present in a way that sparks little remembrances of the person he used to be.

It had been one of those errant nostalgic bursts that led him to the core concept that would evolve into Lacuna.

He was at his parents' house for Sunday-night dinner—beef guláš and dumplings—when his father began complaining about their internet connection. When Anton investigated, he'd been appalled by the state of their ancient router. Shoved in a neglected corner of the staircase that led to the basement, covered in stringy cobwebs and dust. Of course his father had hovered over him while Anton fiddled with the coaxial, tracing it to a hole drilled into the drywall.

What is the problem?

It's from the late '90s and bugs are living in it.
Comes free from Marek.
Oh God, Dad, you let Marek hook up your router?
Router, modem. Marek knows. What do I know?

And like an asshole hell-bent on proving exactly what Marek from over on 35th Street did not know, Anton had launched into a truncated crash course in networking theory.

In order to move great quantities of data from one computer to another, the data has to be broken down into packets that can be relayed in tiny pieces. This huge innovation has eliminated the logjam of information. In other words, if a long message is being relayed, a shorter message no longer has to wait until it's finished to proceed. The packets all go out in a jumble to be correctly reassembled by their destination computers. This piece of plastic covered in cobwebs and the husks of dead houseflies—Marek's router—is the device that specializes in moving packets. We live in a world of billions of routers moving incomprehensible quantities of data every second of every day.

This is the core principle of the internet as we understand it.

(He could tell by his father's eyes that Tomas Hajek did not understand it, but Anton couldn't stop himself.)

Of course that's only one "hop"—that is, the journey of a packet from one router to another. When we're talking about a global network, we're talking about multiple hops to send a blurry photo of the dog from your computer in Astoria, Queens, to Aunt Karolina's in Prague.

This is where link layers come in—the fiber-optic cables, satellites, and towers used to facilitate the multiple hops necessary for Karolina to laugh at Mila's silly dog face.

Back at the table, the conversation had turned to their very first internet connection in the house, hooked up when Anton was seven years old. As he'd helped himself to a second piece of his mother's trdelnik, he'd slipped into the warm bath of nostalgia recalling the very first time he ever sat before the internet and looked up a Legend of Zelda fan site.

The family computer still sits on the little wooden table in the nook at the back of the living room. He could see it from where he shoveled forkfuls of sweet pastry into his mouth.

This fuzzy membrane of nostalgia for a younger self had hugged him all the way home on the R train to his noisy shared loft space on Avenue D. Except this time—being older—it wasn't the delicious notion of a boy he used to be as a placeholder for the burgeoning understanding of time's passage. It was something both grander and more calculated. A trick of his mind to plant the seed of an idea that would not grow into anything even remotely conceptual for some time. Or rather, as with his proprietary card-and-dice game, the concept grew from the strange marriage of two inputs. The helix of cause and effect that can never be unbraided or even parsed.

The first card is the boy he had been, sitting at the family computer in awe as a page loaded slowly, pixels drawing themselves in before his eyes—clip art and text that simply appeared, snatched out of the ether, created in another place, maybe Paris, maybe Des Moines, maybe next door, and beamed to his eager eyes. The feeling that the world had, in an instant, begun to map itself onto his consciousness, its labyrinths of information suddenly illuminated.

The second card is the ramshackle elegance of the earliest networking concepts. There was a charm to those early days, during which the growth of the internet held such guileless promise—a notion that the world's entire population would be instantly elevated to pen-pal status, that sharing and community would become a sort of mass-consciousness event.

The dice roll that united them in endless intertwining conversation was the goddamn cobwebby router gifted to his parents by Marek from up the street. He couldn't get the juxtaposition out of his head: this magical piece of commercial plastic and LED lights and ports, this relay station for packets, this roadside motel on the way to the wide area network, covered in the corpses of insects. Nature's original routers, communicating via smell and sound and pheromone and vibration, keeping their species alive through transmissions more arcane than any wireless signal.

Anton was no entomologist, which worked in his favor during Lacuna's fevered conception. An entomologist might have laughed at his weird notions of some microscopic buglike entities eliminating the need for clunky internet link layers, the hardware that littered our planet—and our atmosphere—to keep us all connected.

More than one colleague in Anton's East Village incubator invoked Theranos. The bogeyman of conceptual idealism outpacing what was actually possible. In response, and to lean in to the crazy a little bit, Anton brought his parents' ancient router, bugs and all, to the loft, and displayed it inside a plexiglass case. This would be Lacuna's mascot, his north star as he dreamed and sketched and researched and conceived. In the way of start-ups, where everything moves dreamily slow and then suddenly at a million miles an hour, Anton found himself with office space and engineers working to shrink router tech in much the same way the earliest internet pioneers broke up data into bite-size bits and changed the world forever.

There had been times when Lacuna had felt less like a tech start-up and more like one of the more eldritch Thaumaturgy cards—the Mirrored Fungi or the House of An'Rea'Tonc. Especially after several consecutive days of "sleeping" on the horrible office couch. At some point they'd pulled together a prototype for a big attention-getting Series A round. Two years in and the proprietary nanotechnology had come a long way since Anton's earliest conceptions. Particulate sprites that could be deployed anywhere as a sort of mobile, constantly evolving link layer.

The big gotcha pitch, the Hollywood logline he delivered in investor meetings, was this: Right now, data goes around the world in twenty hops. With Lacuna, it goes around the world in one.

An instant transmission, some alchemy of buglike phero-mones and infinitesimal bits of data, reassembled in nanoseconds at any link in the chain. No more prohibitively expensive cables under the ocean, no more satellite maintenance. A world less cluttered with obsolete hardware.

With so much innovation on the consumer-facing side, from Apple's magical devices to Google's experiential optimization, backend infrastructure was languishing. Lacuna's network hit the sweet spot. A Series B followed. The company moved into their glittering high-rise office space. Luminaries like Brian Karcher joined the board. The Department of Defense was nat-urally interested in the tech, which made Anton uncomfortable, but he did not outright refuse its overtures.

Initial real-world testing seemed to be a harbinger for greater things to come. The nanotech fields were dropped across the city, then the state, then the eastern seaboard, with no discernible lag. Anton celebrated their Series C round with the rarest Boba Fett toy in existence. Then beta testing moved global and the cracks began to show. Horrendous outages in some places, uninterrupted service in others, all of it seem-ingly random, a nightmare logic problem even for the pattern recognition algorithm that selected Lacuna's test sites in the first place. But what most sites reported was summed up in one word: spotty.

Spotty, spotty, motherfucking spotty.

The Lacuna dashboard became his lover, his mother, his child. He always had one eye on it, living for the *BWAAAMP* sound that indicated a functional network coming online. He worked around the clock for eighteen months, iterating with his engineers, tweaking the signal, to no avail. His assistant, Kevin, began to look at him with sympathy, speak to him softly, even gently, because he knew how much Lacuna meant to him, and was scared he would be driven over the edge.

To be fair, he was close to breaking down. The depressing stasis of the idea he staked his life on, and his maddening inability to improve it, even after some radical shifts in the composition of the nanotech to make it more buglike in nature, was starting to grind him down. Whispers of another Theranos, silenced by Lacuna's initial successes, began to rise again. Anton flipped cards and rolled dice and combed through every blind alley and dead end of his once-promising network, looking for that one malicious sliver of failed engineering, that head-slappingly obvious oversight that he could fix in an instant, then sit back in the womb and watch the test sites turn green with *BWAAAMP* after glorious *BWAAAMP*.

It was not to be. As the board pressured him to cut his losses and sell the concept and the tech, Anton only doubled down, lest the promise of that nostalgic boy go forever unfulfilled—an unacceptable outcome. All this time spent in the womb, poring over every little piece of Lacuna, had only endeared his creation further to him. The borders of the product became porous, its potential limitless.

And so when the board had been ready to accept Tencent's offer, it had been up to Anton to open their eyes to Lacuna's true import. Where they saw a network, he saw an entirely new system of the world, an organizing principle shunted in from a parallel reality. The answer to the string-theory-101-inspired thoughts of every stoned freshman staring at, say, a bridge: What if this had been conceived of differently from the ground up? What if bridges the world over had taken on an alternative form, thereby influencing the vibes of our cities from the roads to the mass transit to the way neighborhoods cropped up?

Enter Lacuna, reshaper of worlds.

And then: Enter cicadas, reshaper of Lacuna.

At some point, the noise from the cicadas in the hallway outside his office begins to wind down. Anton barely notices. He drains a Diet Dr Pepper, lost in diagnostics, trying to identify the exact switch that got flipped to bring Lacuna fully online in all its far-flung testing sites. It's driving him insane. The only variable that makes any sense is the biggest, most glaring one: the cicada invasion. But how in the name of Thaumaturgy did that have any real-world effect on the network?

He spoons his last Greek yogurt into his mouth. His office fridge is well stocked with soda to fuel his all-night work benders, but food is woefully absent. (That's what Kevin is—was—for.) He figures he can last a few more days in here gnawing on the vegetables from the lobby, unless the cicadas grow even more resourceful and find another way in. He runs a finger along the fuzzy skin of the bulbous fruits on his desk.

He's not exactly sure how long it's been. He finds that the more time he spends with Lacuna, the less that human conceptions of time make any real sense at all. There is only the network, the system, the ever-expanding conception of a future untethered to anything earthbound.

The fact that he's trapped in his office by a potential extinction-level event has diminished in importance. He is in the womb with everything he needs at his fingertips.

Outside, the city skyline is mostly dark. There are lights from a few of the hospitals and other buildings with generators. The streets are filled with blue and red flashes as emergency crews try to navigate a city standing still. Boats crowd the dark swath of the East River, heading north toward the bays that feed the Long Island Sound. He even registers a couple of distant airplanes—private jets and government transports, he assumes, except for the ones that streak across the sky at three times the speed. Those have to be military.

Sometime later, he gets up for another soda and notices that Kevin has quit muttering. His assistant's low murmured nonsense has been a steady presence in the office, so numbing he barely noticed it, like the hum of an air conditioner. But now its absence strikes him as odd. There's something else too—a distortion in Kevin's face. His lips are stretching into weird shapes, silent perversions of language. Warily, Anton takes a fresh can from the fridge and approaches the couch. The muscles in his assistant's face seem to stretch, putty-like, into a crinkly oval.

The screaming begins in the corridor. A guttural yell steadily rising in pitch. Anton stares at the back of his reinforced door as another voice rings out in eerie harmony. Then a third. A moment later, a hysterical chorus erupts. Anton imagines all of his former colleagues lying in heaps out in the hallway, their mouths flinging cries at the ceiling. Kevin joins in. Startled, Anton turns his attention to his assistant. A dreadful shout, half mournful and half mad, comes from Kevin's twisted grimace. Anton steps back. Kevin's mouth reshapes itself. His back arches, muscles tense, elbows digging into the cushions. The pitch of his scream is excruciating. Other sounds come from the hallway, a riot of cascading thumps. Anton takes another step back, imagining hundreds of his afflicted colleagues pounding the floor with their arms and legs. A moment later, Kevin's body strains upward with such force that Anton is sure Kevin's spine must be cracked.

Kevin's flannel shirt parts as his torso erupts in a fountain of blood and gristle. His body falls back to the cushions, his arms hang limp, and Anton is certain that Kevin has just died in front of his eyes.

Then the claws appear, drifting up from the torn chest cavity like they're tasting the air: thick, curving forelegs culminating in pincer-like points. The hallway fills with the manic sounds of scrabbling limbs. The forelegs anchor themselves on Kevin's waistline and press down into his body to lift up the impossible monstrosity they're attached to.

Anton screams as the creature inside Kevin emerges. Minute hairs on its head are like the delicate bristles of a paintbrush dipped in blood. Red eyes stare dumbly at Anton. Its segmented underbelly rises with a wet sucking sound as a stew of Kevin's organs, pulled up by the creature, lifts then falls away.

Anton hurls the Diet Dr Pepper at the creature's head and strikes it squarely between those awful eyes. The soda explodes, spattering fizzy liquid all over the toy collection on the glass shelves. The creature bends backward, its lower body anchored inside of Kevin, its upper legs flailing as it loses its balance.

Anton rushes over to the womb and grabs his chair, giving thanks for its lightweight carbon-fiber build. He raises his arms, holding the chair aloft, and charges the sofa with a warbling battle cry. With a repulsive quickness, the creature pulls itself free of Kevin's body. Before it can slither away Anton brings the chair down on its head. The creature is flattened against the gaping wound from which it emerged. Shit-colored liquid bursts from its smashed carapace. The impact of the chair catapults blood and viscera from deep within Kevin. Anton's face is wet. Underneath the bespoke Scandinavian chair, a foreleg moves. Anton lifts the chair and brings it back down hard with a squelch. The clawlike limb stops moving.

He backs away, reaching behind him for a chair to collapse in. It takes a few seconds to register that there is no more chair. He's just used it to destroy an abomination. He raises his eyes to scan his toy shelf, where a vintage first-run *Alien* chestburster sits on a small custom pedestal. That thing is wrinkly and more Krang-like than the giant baby bug that just crawled out of Kevin.

The word comes to him, buried deep in the memories of his research for the first iterations of Lacuna, when his team was studying insect communications: *nymph.*

Baby cicadas. Except this baby is the size of a cat. His mind reels. Its gestation period was what—two days? In that short window of time, a cicada laid an egg inside Kevin that fed on his insides and grew to impossible proportions.

Anton, trembling, turns his gaze to the door. Now he can parse the sounds outside, the muffled scrabbling of a hundred little legs, dozens of these creatures clawing at his door, *smelling* him inside (who knows?), slavering over the notion of human flesh.

A percussive blast shakes the floor. Anton is nearly knocked off his feet. His mind reels. *What now?* He goes to the window and looks across the darkened city. The disturbance is easy to spot: A fire burns on the roof of a neighboring office tower. The smoldering wreck of a helicopter spews black smoke. Anton connects the dots instantly: an afflicted passenger, the sudden appearance of a monster inside the aircraft, a frantic struggle...

He turns away from the window. The sofa is a nightmarish crime scene, and there is no way for Anton to dispose of the carnage. He can't open the door. He can't leave this place. He is trapped in here with the ruined body of his former assistant and the corpse of a mutant insect.

Anton goes into the small living space behind the womb. There's a refrigerator, kitchenette, and twin bed. He rips the top sheet from the bed and tosses it over the mess on the couch, trying not to look at Kevin's face. Stains begin to spread along the light-blue sheet as it settles over raw, oozing wounds. Anton turns away.

Fearful and exhausted, he leans against the wall next to the window. His legs go rubbery. He sits down on the floor and holds his head in his hands. Kevin's awful shriek echoes in his mind. The horrid escalation of it, the rising action that led straight to the insect's emergence. Kevin's central nervous system knew what was happening even if his brain did not. (Anton hopes it did not, but he can't be sure.)

He closes his eyes and tries to ignore the noises from the hallway. In the black void behind his eyelids, he spirals deep into Lacuna, his diagnostic explorations blooming like fractals.

A chime from the womb shakes him from his reverie. He raises his head and opens his eyes. The Lacuna dashboard is alerting him to a deviation in a test site.

Glad for the distraction, however feeble, Anton gets up—his joints sore, his legs stiff—and goes to the womb. It's an odd diagnostic hiccup in Bava Atoll, the final beta-test site selected by the Lacuna algorithm. He stares at the screen, uncomprehending. Connectivity is off the charts. Lacuna is operating in Bava Atoll as if—here he glances at his toy shelf—it has been bitten by the proverbial radioactive spider. Or whatever. That one-hop alchemy he'd always dreamed of synthesizing has now come to pass, and it's beautiful—pure fusion of the nanotech field and its environment, chittering communication as buglike and inevitable as the awful skittering from the hall outside the office.

What is happening? Why is Bava Atoll, a relative backwater in the beta-test sites compared with, say, Brussels, experiencing sudden and incredible success after months of failure?

Anton stares into the womb. *The final beta-test site.* Slipped in at the eleventh hour, as if Lacuna *wanted* it to fly under the radar, some remote speck in the Pacific, barely worthy of Anton's attention. But that's ridiculous. Lacuna is incapable of *want*.

Anton begins to pace, a troubling and as yet inchoate thought tickling the back of his mind. He catches sight of the sheet soaked in blood and turns back to the womb. The Lacuna dashboard greets him with bland disinterest, as always. In the same way he took pains not to be associated with one Steve Jobs–like outfit, he elected not to give his backend admin any kind of AI personality. No winking reference to Skynet or HAL. Any machine learning is relegated strictly to an R&D role. At Lacuna, business decisions are made by human beings, with Anton himself as final arbiter.

But there are, naturally, algorithms—though not really any more sophisticated than a streaming video or music service would use to serve up content tailored to a user's particular taste. One of the Lacuna algorithms optimized the search for beta-test sites. He didn't particularly care where the tests were located, as long as they were evenly distributed around the world.

With the Vingegaard chair currently lying atop Kevin, Anton bends gremlin-like over the keyboard. He maps Bava Atoll and takes in the never-ending blue surrounding the tiny dot in the middle of the Pacific Ocean, 237 miles northeast of the Marshall Islands. Clicking through photographs of the atoll, Anton pores over tropical desolation. Miles' worth of blacktop gone chalky with heat and age circles a lagoon hole-punched out of the atoll's center. In the other direction, sand the color of bleached-blond hair slopes gently down to the ocean. Vast cloud banks gather on the horizon. Anton navigates panoramic shots, sinking deeper into a fecund dreamscape. For some reason he'd imagined eco-resort signifiers, private yurts cascading down to the waterline, outdoor showers, *wellness*. But any infrastructure in this place was abandoned long ago. He zooms in on a decrepit concrete bunker. A faded, illegible word is painted above the door. Bright, dense flora bursts from its roofless interior.

Anton blinks. The sense of unreality deepens. There, sprouting from a labyrinth of vines choking the crumbling cinder blocks, are bulbous fruits the color of strawberries and the size of tomatoes. He zooms in further. Their fuzzy skin hazes in the washed-out sunlight. He glances at the trio of fruits on his desk, taken from Kevin's backpack, brought up here from the farm in the lobby. Lacuna's farm.

That troubling thought percolating in the back of his mind turns ominous. Despite everything else—the downfall of the city outside, the mutants clawing at his door, the dead body on his sofa—Anton feels a sickening sense of betrayal knot his guts. He stares at each of the womb's screens and for the first time feels a presence staring back at him.

You motherfucker.

26

NATCHEZ TRACE, MISSISSIPPI

The billboard says KELLERVILLE DRUG & GUN.

Pistols and Prozac, Mari says.

Rebecca's lived in the Deep South all her life, and it still blows her mind that enterprising businesspeople here felt compelled to combine America's two most pervasive problems into one comprehensive shopping experience.

You mean America's second and third most pervasive problems, Mari says.

"Yeah," Rebecca says.

"What," Erin says miserably.

"Nothing," Rebecca says. She glances in the rearview. Erin's sleeping fitfully with her knees pulled up, curled into her body. Jason's staring out the window with an inscrutable expression, bloody gauze wrapped around his forearm.

The Natchez Trace is a two-lane parkway that cuts through the wilderness of western Mississippi, running roughly parallel to the river itself until it cuts eastward past Jackson and up through Tennessee, hitting Highway 100 just south of Nashville. They've been driving all night, straight out of Fluker's Bluff, and have barely made it north of Natchez—a ninety-minute trip on a normal day. The back roads are passable, but it's still slow going what with the abandoned vehicles, the bodies, and the wrecks and pileups. She shudders to think what the roads around major cities are like.

There's still another sixty miles to go before they hit the old homestead. When Rebecca left, it had been called The Church of the Life to Come. Before that, it went by many other names.

Dawn brings misty rain down from a gray sky. The husks of dead cicadas are so thick on the ground that she can only see the road's dividing line sporadically. Bodies lie strewn about. She steers around the smoking shell of a pickup truck.

Why the truck had been set ablaze is a mystery.

Why its passengers are dead is not.

Rebecca and her two surviving students first encountered the nymphs at a gas station outside Ashwood. The cicadas had just begun to rain down, dying all around them by the millions. It was cause enough for celebration—at least for the two students.

Rebecca had not shared with them her theory about the next phase of the cicadas' life cycle. It only seemed cruel while the two kids were trying to process the escape from the Ag Center. On this mournful drive, she let them enjoy a brief moment of hope.

While Erin went inside the empty gas station to loot water, iced coffee, and candy bars, Rebecca and Jason stayed with the van to gas it up. They kept their mouths shut just in case, but even the cicadas that were still buzzing around seemed lethargic to Rebecca, as if they were powering down.

Like their job was finished.

Jason inserted the nozzle into the van's gas tank and pulled the lever. Then he frowned and shook his head, pointing at the LED gauges on the pump. Rebecca nodded in frustration. She should have thought of this: Modern fuel pumps are powered by electricity. No power, no gas.

Rebecca glanced around. An old yellow Camaro was parked by the overflowing dumpster. With luck, they might be able to keep trading in cars on the road. There were certainly enough to choose from.

Rebecca and Jason approached the Camaro with caution. Their shoes ground dead cicadas into the pavement. She swatted away a few halfhearted dive bombs from their living brethren.

Suddenly she felt Jason's hand on her arm. Both car windows were open. The driver's seat was empty, but there was someone in the passenger seat. A woman wearing a trucker hat, sitting bolt upright, head against the seat, eyes closed. Rebecca assumed it was one of the afflicted. She took a breath, then opened the door.

The woman's chest wound gaped, rimmed by a torn white shirt sticky with blood. Petals of flesh bloomed outward. At that moment, Rebecca knew her theory had been confirmed: A mutant cicada, with its triplicate ovipositor, would breed a mutant spawn. This fact had been hanging over her since she first fired up the electron microscope. On some level she expected this. But she didn't expect the nymphs' gestation period to be so remarkably brief.

Also, Mari said, *they're apparently fucking huge.*

Her sister was right. This woman was split from sternum to belly button.

Jason was backing away slowly, hand clamped over his mouth, eyes wide—a marked difference from his cavalier reaction to the corpse at the Body Farm. Rebecca supposed the sight of violent death hit harder when sharing the deceased's fate was a distinct possibility.

Rebecca peered across the woman's body at the ignition. "No keys," she said.

Siphon gas, Mari suggested. *Get a plastic tube and one of those red cans. There's probably some inside somewhere.*

Rebecca was about to relay this plan out loud to Jason when a scream came from inside the station.

"Erin!" Rebecca shouted, taking off toward the small building, where faded signs in the window advertised cigarettes at state minimum.

There was no way Rebecca was about to let another student die. She slammed her body against the glass door. A bell chimed as it swung open. Inside, three aisles of junk food ran perpendicular to a drinks cooler that stretched across the back wall. Erin was standing frozen there, torn-open twelve pack at her feet, can of beer in her hand.

Across the scuffed floor, a cicada nymph the size of a French bulldog was hunched over as if in meditation, forelegs sticking out straight while its mid- and hind legs supported its weight. Rebecca imagined this creature bursting from the dead woman in the car. She flashed to Ashley, and Ji-un, and all the other students who didn't make it out of the Ag Center. Now their bodies were desecrated, torn open by these abominations, and the halls of the Ag Center she loved so much were overrun with monsters.

Rebecca had recurring dreams of oversize insects, everything from ladybugs to mosquitoes. Now, confronted by a creature sprung from the depths of her subconscious, Rebecca was simultaneously repulsed and enthralled. She could not tear her eyes from the giant nymph, noting the points of its tarsi at the tips of its forelegs, which looked like they could easily pierce human flesh. The segments between its pro- and mesothorax were perfectly in line with the nymphs pictured and diagrammed in the textbook, and the forewing pads—little pods behind which the adult wings develop—were correctly positioned. If there was a mutation beyond the nymph's incredible size, Rebecca could not yet see it.

"*Help me*," Erin whispered, trembling, still holding the beer can, afraid to move. The nymph's antennae wiggled. Rebecca couldn't tell where its compound eyes were focused. Enlarged a thousandfold, these eyes looked unsettlingly blank. She glanced around for a weapon. Cheap umbrellas hung from a plastic rack.

That was when she saw the body, half hidden behind a display of wiper fluid and motor oil. A split-second glance was enough to see the garish pink of his face, raw skin shining like a flayed anatomical exhibit, the meat of his cheeks and neck chewed away.

Events fell into place. The man had been driving his afflicted partner somewhere, probably for help, when he'd stopped for gas. The nymph had emerged from her body out in the parking lot, chased him into the building, and feasted on his flesh.

Which meant that perhaps this nymph was refraining from attacking Erin because it was *full*.

The moment this scenario clicked into place, the door flew open and the bell jingled and Jason burst inside with a maniacal war cry. He sprinted past Rebecca, clipping her shoulder, and charged the nymph with a broom handle held like a jousting lance. He raised the broom above his head. The nymph shook off its stupor and launched itself at Jason, forelegs striking the floor to give it froglike leverage as its hind legs propelled it into the air.

Jason swung the broom—too late. The nymph moved in a blur of speed. The next thing Rebecca knew, Jason was shrieking and trying to shake the nymph from his forearm as he spun in a circle. Erin backed into the corner, screaming. Rebecca moved in, trying to grab the nymph by its abdomen. Jason raised his arm and brought the clinging nymph down on a metal shelf. Bags of Cheetos and Bugles went flying. The nymph flipped into the air and landed on the floor and skittered madly in a circle. Something was broken inside of it. Rebecca picked up the broom and drove the tip of the handle down on its abdomen, piercing the soft infant carapace and impaling the creature. Its forelegs juddered, tibiae and tarsi opening and closing like claws. Its compound eyes looked directly at her.

Oh God, Mari said.

Now that she saw it straight-on, there was definitely something off about it. A cicada nymph ought to have a labrum and beak extending from its clypeus, just under its "face." In essence, a tube that allowed it to suck up tree nectar. But this nymph had a toothy suckermouth like the funnel orifice of a lamprey eel. *There's the mutation.* It dilated slowly, then went still as the nymph died. Rebecca let go of the broom and its handle poked up in the air like a planted flag, supported by the nymph's corpse.

In the meantime Jason was shrieking and clamping a hand to his forearm. Blood sluiced through his fingers.

Rebecca vaulted over the counter by the register and grabbed bandages, gauze, tape, and bottles of aspirin. She threw them all in a plastic bag.

"Grab food!" she called out. "We're leaving."

She moved around the counter and knelt down next to the dead man. His sleeveless denim shirt was intact, but his upper arms were gnawed down to the bone and his face was a slurry of crimson pulp. A single lidless eye stared up at her. She began to pat down his cargo shorts, pulling items out of his pockets: smokeless tobacco, vape, tissues, two condoms, wallet.

Keys.

A plastic shark was attached to the ring along with a bottle opener that said OLE MISS.

What are the chances there's only one nymph? Mari said.

'I know, I know. We're out of here.'

Rebecca stood up and jangled the keys. "Let's go!"

Jason was filling a tote bag with granola bars. Erin was grabbing jugs of water from the cooler.

Rebecca paused at the door, scanning the parking lot for signs of nymphs. She imagined them swarming over the gas pumps, hundreds of creatures bashing themselves against the windows, suckermouths pulsating, eager for flesh.

"It looks clear," she said.

They raced to the Camaro, shoes crunching fallen cicadas like brittle autumn leaves while the remaining live bugs dotted the air in sparse disarray. Erin froze in front of the passenger door. She eyed the corpse and shook her head as she backed away slowly. "No no no no . . . "

"I'm sorry," Rebecca said. "We don't have a choice." She opened the door, unbuckled the seat belt, grabbed the dead woman's arm, and struggled to pull her out of the car. The woman's body tilted. Her trucker hat fell off. A purplish slop leaked from her wound.

"I'm not getting in that fucking car!" Erin shouted.

"Remember what I said at the Body Farm?" Rebecca braced her feet and dropped into a half squat and leaned back and pulled. "About there being no rush to change your perceptions?" The woman slid off the seat. "That no longer applies."

She crab-walked backward, dragging the woman, then let her down in a pile of cicadas. She straightened up and cracked her back. "You're going to see more awful things before this is over. And you can't freak out every time, even if it's something your body involuntarily recoils at." She stared Erin down. "You have to be stronger than you've ever been." The girl was looking at the car seat where the woman died. It was covered in red sludge. Rebecca pulled the handle alongside the seat and tilted it forward. "Sit in the back," she commanded.

Erin and Jason dutifully climbed in. She let the front seat back collapse to hide the mess.

In the driver's seat, she started the car and watched the needle on the gas gauge as it slid up the dial.

"Full tank," she announced. Luck was on their side: The dead man had filled up before he went inside. She rolled up the windows and threw the Camaro in reverse. The engine revved when she hit the gas and the car muscled out of the parking spot. A much different feel than the clunky van.

"Lemme see," Erin said. Rebecca glanced in the rearview to catch Erin pouring hydrogen peroxide on Jason's forearm. He screamed. Rebecca winced as she pulled out onto the main road. The gas pumps diminished behind them, along with the white van in which she'd transported hundreds of students back and forth between the Body Farm and the Ag Center. There was a finality to leaving it behind that once again steered her thoughts back to Ashley, Javier the Empath, Ji-un, and the other students who registered for a summer class in forensic entomology.

Kids with their whole lives ahead of them, who never thought for a second they would die in Fluker's Bluff.

The misty gray dawn gives way to a bright summer morning. The Natchez Trace unfurls, lush trees on either side, nearly purple in the sunlight. The tires continue to flatten dead cicadas. Their corpses hang enmeshed in great sweeping nets of kudzu. Rebecca's tired mind extrapolates the incredible scope of all this. She and her surviving students have traversed a small corner of the South, from eastern Louisiana to western Mississippi, and there hasn't been a single break in the insects now covering the ground. Their numbers are staggering, and that's only in this comparatively tiny pocket of earth. Stretch these numbers out exponentially and the scope becomes too astronomical to process.

Her thoughts grind up against this impossibility again and again. Periodical cicadas are numerous, yes, with millions upon millions briefly disrupting daily life in towns across the country. But for this many to appear seemingly overnight (*fucking everywhere*, Mari says) is so scientifically unsound she feels sick to her stomach. There's an unsettling friction to her inability to reconcile what she's experiencing and what she knows to be possible.

Where did they come from, is what I want to know, Mari says. *There should have been a bazillion nymphs climbing trees, shedding their skins. Adults doing those sweet backbends out of the exuviae.*

"Right," Rebecca says. "Instead it's like the adults came out of the ground fully formed. That, plus the mutations on both the adults and the nymphs, means that everything they do is in defiance of the sum total of humankind's knowledge about the life cycle, anatomy, and behavior of cicadas."

Like they're not even really cicadas. Some kind of cicada-adjacent species we've never seen before that's somehow been biding its time underground.

"I mean if you count microbes and bacteria there are trillions of undiscovered species. So if we really open our theoretical minds, it's possible the initial adult phase didn't even require molting. Maybe it didn't even require nymphs at all. Maybe it's some kind of reverse Batesian mimicry, where they're not even—"

"Um, Dr. Perez?" Erin says. "Who are you talking to?"

Rebecca slows the Camaro down to steer around a minivan parked across both lanes. Nymphs tear at the flesh of an old man. As long as she keeps the car above forty miles an hour, the creatures seem to understand that it's a danger to them and don't attempt to pursue or latch onto the vehicle. So far they've been lucky, but Rebecca knows what will happen if they're forced to stop. She catches glimpses of the creatures in the underbrush, thousands of them stalking the roadside, waiting for prey like trapdoor spiders in their burrows.

"I'm just tired," Rebecca says, nudging the car back onto the road. She needs sleep, but there will be no rest until they make it to her father's compound. The trees send complex fractal shadows down on the carpet of dead cicadas.

"You've been carrying on half a conversation all night," Jason says.

Rebecca tightens her grip on the wheel, clenches her jaw.

You might as well tell them about me, Mari says. There's a note of hope in her voice. Not for the first time, Rebecca wonders if her sister, on some level, wants to be known by others.

Of course, Mari has *heard* her wonder about this before and never spoken up. Nor has she expressed any desire to be known. Still, Rebecca lives with a perpetual low-level feeling of guilt about this. How would it feel to be so isolated that the only person aware of your existence is terrified to reveal it?

Rebecca has always resisted therapy, afraid that the revelations about Mari would spark some kind of committal to an institute, or at the very least impact her career. She has paranoid nightmares about being a viral story, the seemingly well-adjusted academic with a whopper of an internalized trauma manifestation. At best, the grown-up with the imaginary friend. At worst, the mad scientist who hears the voice of her dead sister.

I mean, the world is pretty much consumed by madness at this point anyway, Mari says. *Plus if they're going to Dad's, that'll out-crazy whatever they hear from you.* She pauses. Rebecca maneuvers the car around a mess of dead nymphs, run over by someone else. Tire treads bisect their burst abdomens. Fallen cicadas float in a pool of congealed fluid.

I really just want to hear you try to explain it, Mari says.

'So this is entertainment for you.'

I hate to break it to you, but your whole life is entertainment for me, big sis.

'I never thought of it like that before.'

It's literally the only entertainment I have.

Rebecca sighs. She is so, so tired. Corpses in a roadside row lie on beds of dead cicadas with their sunken bloody chests open to the sky. Sunlight glints off their exposed entrails, and then they're gone, and the Natchez Trace keeps on going.

"When I was thirteen," Rebecca says to her students, "my little sister Marisol fell out of our tree house and fractured her skull. She—"

Whoa whoa WHOA, Bex. Way to give 'em the Cliffs Notes.

Rebecca sighs. Up ahead, a jackknifed truck blocks the road. She guides the Camaro onto the narrow shoulder, squeezing between the truck's cabin and the trees, careful not to lean on the brake. She passes an arm's length from red eyes peering out from the underbrush. A dead man flayed to the bone vanishes in the rearview as they regain the road and follow its steady northward curve.

"All right," Rebecca begins again. "So, Mari and I were playing in our tree house. She found a stag beetle on the wall and tried to scare me with it. They're big, and they have these long pincers. I got startled and shoved her away. She fell out the trapdoor and cracked her head on a root when she hit the ground. An intracranial hematoma formed. She died later that night because my father insisted on having our church's doctors treat her instead of taking her to a hospital."

"I'm sorry," Erin says.

Rebecca pauses, keeps her eyes on the road, tries to figure out how to approach the next part of the tale. She has been living with Mari for so long now, it feels like telling someone the origin story of her left arm.

"So that's who you've been talking to?" Jason guesses, saving her the trouble. There's a shaky timidity in his voice. She wonders about the pain of his nymph bite, a suckermouth with all those little teeth sinking into his flesh...

"Yes," Rebecca says. "And she...replies."

"Your dead sister talks back to you," Erin says.

"Yes," Rebecca says. "But it's more than that. It's not just her voice. She's with me all the time, if that makes sense."

Jason laughs bitterly. "Nothing makes any sense right now."

"Is she with you—*us*—right now?" Erin asks.

YES, Mari whisper-screams. Rebecca's body tingles. "Did you hear that?"

"Um," Jason says.

"No," Erin says.

"I'm just kidding. She says *yes*, she is here right now."

"So she hears everything that you hear?" Erin asks.

"And sees everything that I see, et cetera."

A low moan comes from Jason. Rebecca checks on him in the mirror. He's gritting his teeth, pressing his head against the seat back, cradling his injured arm. She wishes they had more than gas station medical supplies.

"Hang in there," she says.

"Keep telling your story," he says. "It helps."

"Mari's been with me since the moment she died," Rebecca continues. "The first thing she said to me inside my head was *spaghetti*. What she meant was that the last thing she remembers is falling out of the tree house, and then there were these long strands, or vines. And her first little-kid reference point at the time was spaghetti. So there are these long tendrils hanging down, kind of beckoning her into this tunnel. And the next thing she knew, she thought she'd woken. She was disoriented but figured she was just lying on the ground, where she'd hit her head, and she'd climb back up and get mad at me for shoving her and that would be that. But then she realized she couldn't move. She was conscious but had no motor control. And she could see herself—because I was there, in this makeshift infirmary on the compound, saying goodbye to my sister. You can imagine how weird things got after that, while we figured out what had happened."

Rebecca threads a narrow lane between two pileups where a car veered off the road and hit a tree. She notes the blood-spattered windows. A trapped nymph claws the glass, and then the whole mess is behind them.

"But," Erin says, "*how* did it happen?"

"You mean, what was the mechanism for transplanting Mari's consciousness inside of me, her sibling, at the moment of her death? We've discussed that ad nauseam over the years. It gets into pretty thorny territory when you start to consider the existence of a soul, which you pretty much have to when you're experiencing something like this. Best we can come up with is, the *how* is probably beyond our grasp. But there might be a *why*, even if we can't see it yet."

Elegant explanation, Mari says. *A little new-agey, but there's nothing we can do about that.*

Jason makes a guttural wailing noise, like he's gritting his teeth through a jolt of pain. In the mirror, Rebecca watches Erin put a gentle hand on his upper back.

"You're lucky," she says. "I'd give anything to be able to talk to my dad again."

"I *am* lucky," Rebecca agrees. She leaves it at that and lets Erin reflect.

Yeah, Mari says, *this doesn't seem like the time to get into the ickier aspects of our symbiosis. Like how even if I retreat to the farthest recesses of this place I'm in, I still know when you're taking a shit.*

"Fuck!" Jason says, gripping his forearm tightly, making a tourniquet of his hand. He leans back in his seat and closes his eyes.

"Give him another aspirin," Rebecca tells Erin, knowing how pitifully inadequate that sounds.

"That's not gonna do shit," Jason groans.

"One to ten," Rebecca says, "how bad's the pain?"

"It's not *pain* exactly," Jason says. "It's something else."

Rebecca hasn't said anything about the nymph's mutation, that suckermouth transposed from a nightmare of a lamprey.

"It's like fingers underneath my skin," he says. Then he turns to Erin. "Unwrap it."

"Jason—"

He holds out his arm to her. Rebecca keeps an eye on the road while she monitors her students in the back seat. Reluctantly, Erin takes hold of the gauze strip and unwinds it until the wound is exposed.

"Jesus," she says, scooting away from him as if his flesh burned her hand.

"What is it?" His eyes are wide as he thrusts his arm into the front for Rebecca to inspect. One quick glimpse and she nearly slams on the brakes.

Don't stop the car! Mari yells.

Jason leans forward so his arm extends along the center console. Rebecca tries not to freak him out any worse, but she's startled by the sight. The rim of the bite wound on his forearm is puffy and raw, skin pulled taut like grinning lips, and within this rough mirror of the nymph's mouthparts is a boiling stew of gnawed skin. Beyond the wound, a tough-looking, almost leathery infection is wending its way toward Jason's wrist. It evokes the tanned-hide carapace of the rhinoceros beetle.

"What the fuck is happening?"

"It's okay," Rebecca says, trying to sound confident as she delivers a laughable distortion of the truth. "We'll get some real disinfectant at my father's compound. This road isn't too bad, we'll be there soon."

Real disinfectant? Mari says. *Good one.*

'What else can I say to the kid? It's not like I can do anything for him now.'

Amputate, Mari says.

When Rebecca doesn't reply, she says, *I'm serious. Treat it like gangrene. The limb goes, so does the infection.*

'One, I'd have to stop the car, two, I don't have a knife, three—'

"Are you talking to your sister right now?" Jason pulls his arm back and collapses back in his seat. "What's she saying? Does she know what this is?"

"She agrees with me—we'll get it treated as soon as we get there."

"I can feel it under my skin," Jason says.

"Here," Erin says, holding out a couple of aspirin. Jason pops them in his mouth and swallows.

Rebecca turns her attention to the road. Nymphs skulk in the ditches and the underbrush, watching their car pass by like dead-eyed children flanking a sad parade. She feels vulnerable and exposed in a new way, as if her nerve endings are brushing up against a ceaseless toxicity that has settled over the world. It's amazing how quickly human beings fell from their position as apex consumers. Rebecca is no ecologist, but the pass-through of energy and nutrients has been so fiercely disrupted—here she thinks of the insects in her lab going apeshit in the presence of the cicadas—that even if humanity regains the upper hand, the food chain will never be the same. Ecosystems great and small have already been thrown into chaos—*and she is alive to see it.*

Billions of human beings have lived and died without experiencing an epoch-defining event, but here she is, Dr. Rebecca Perez, driving up the Natchez Trace, plowing through cicadas in numbers beyond comprehension while their spawn wait for a chance to feed. It's like she's a dinosaur watching an asteroid come screaming down to usher in a new era, forged in mass death under an ashen sky.

They're a few miles from the compound when the road becomes impassable. A semi-truck stretches across both lanes. This time there's no way around—the truck's cab rests in the trees at the edge of the southbound side, and the end of its trailer juts into the woods off the northbound lane. Rebecca sees the impasse coming and slows down. They've got maybe thirty seconds before she'll be forced to stop the car completely. She nudges the Camaro over to the left shoulder, tweaks the angle of approach so she can see through the narrow gap between the cab and the trailer.

On the other side of the eighteen-wheeler sits a blue SUV, stopped dead in the middle of the road like so many other vehicles on the Natchez Trace. Driver's-side door open, dead man draped across the running board. That means the keys are either in the ignition or in his pocket.

"All right," Rebecca announces. "When I hit the brakes we move fast. We can't give the nymphs time to gather into a pack before they come after us."

Erin grabs the handle above her head. "What? We're going to leave the car?"

"Remember what I said about being stronger than you've ever been before? This is one of those times."

"And then, what, we're just going to run for it?" Jason says. "Those things'll kill us. We're dead. That's it."

The kid's right.

Rebecca's eyes dart around the barrier, desperate to hit on a better plan. But the semi-truck's cab is hopelessly tangled in the trees, and there's certainly no way the three of them can move the trailer.

"There's an SUV waiting for us on the other side of this truck," Rebecca says. "We'll be there in thirty seconds, tops."

"I can't," Erin says.

"You don't have a choice. None of us do."

Cyanide, Mari says. *Backpack.*

'It's just a bunch of canisters designed for a specific machine. I can't aim it.'

Run it over.

Rebecca grabs the backpack from the front seat. "Slight change of plans."

She puts the car in reverse until there's a quarter mile between the Camaro and the overturned truck. Then she rolls down the window and tosses the bag out into the middle of the road.

"What are you doing?" Erin asks.

"In there's all the cyanide I took from the lab." She guns the Camaro backward until she figures they've gone another quarter mile, then she stops and rolls up the window. "I'm going to lead the nymphs straight into a death cloud," she says. "Then I'm going to keep driving forward a little way so we're out of range of the gas when we jump out of the car. Hopefully that'll give us some cover."

As she speaks, nymphs emerge from the foliage on either side of the road. Low hunters, legs clacking up and down like giant windup spiders, forelimbs poised. Twenty of them, Rebecca estimates, forming up into loose columns, coming to investigate the stopped vehicle, probe it for food.

"Death cloud," Jason says. He's wrapped his forearm back up, but the infection is spreading to his biceps and under his shirt. Hints of beetle skin are beginning to peek out of his collar.

"All right," Rebecca says. She shifts into drive and begins to creep forward. The nymphs merge into a V-formation and begin to chase the car. "When we get out, follow me and stay close and don't stop for any reason." She turns in her seat, looks from Jason to Erin. "One thing Mari and I agree on is that even if she's an anomaly in terms of being transposed into me, it's also pretty solid evidence that death isn't the end. Maybe she got rerouted from where people usually go, or maybe it's beyond our comprehension. So whatever happens..." She trails off, not sure how to complete the thought and make it meaningful to the two scared kids in the back seat. Before she turns back around, she notices they're holding hands.

Here they come, Mari says. Rebecca eases the gas pedal down slowly. The nymphs pick up speed, their legs moving like blurred spokes. The bag of cyanide canisters is a lump on a bed of cicadas, just ahead. She lets the nymphs get close, hoping that the proximity of all this unspoiled flesh is making them mad with hunger. Then she guns it. The Camaro leaps forward, eating up the road. There's a thump and a *POP* when the tires roll over the backpack. Rebecca floors it.

"They're stopping!" Erin says.

"Die, fuckers," Jason says.

A quick glance in the mirror and Rebecca smiles. The nymphs have abandoned their pursuit as if they hit an invisible wall. Instantly, they've been reduced to a writhing mass, dying in a poison cloud on a bed of their dead parents.

That much cyanide gas is enough to kill a thousand cicada nymphs. Even ones the size of cats.

The semi-trailer comes up fast. Rebecca hits the brakes. "On me!"

As she throws open the Camaro's door she flashes to the false confidence she projected as she led her students into the death trap of the Ag Center corridor. Those cicadas had evolved into clever little killers, ambushing the class with new tactics. What if these nymphs—

Stop thinking and GO, Mari says.

Outside the car, Rebecca's feet come down on brittle corpses. She runs up the southbound lane toward the back of the truck's cab. She thinks—hopes—that the gap is wide enough for them to squeeze through. She glances back. Erin and Jason are on her heels. On the road behind their abandoned car, nymphs coming out of the woods are succumbing to the spreading cloud of poison gas. Its radius is wider than Rebecca anticipated. A rough circle of dead and dying nymphs is forming. She ushers Erin and Jason ahead of her. They clamber up the massive wheel cover at the rear of the cab and turn sideways to squeeze through in single file. Erin hits the ground on the other side and sprints for the SUV. Jason follows a moment later.

Rebecca's shuffling through when a pair of nymphs fling themselves down on her from atop the trailer. Mari screams. One nymph hits the steel grate of the wheel cover at her feet. Rebecca kicks out instinctively and sends it tumbling off the edge of the grate. The second nymph anchors itself around her neck with its forelegs. Its mid- and hind legs tap-dance on her chest while leechlike mouthparts suction to the side of her left cheek. Searing pain shoots through her jaw. Her body slams against the back of the cab as she struggles to get her hands around its slick, wriggling abdomen. Adrenaline surges as horror cuts through her thoughts with plainspoken clarity.

The nymph is eating her face.

Time slows. Everything falls away but white-hot pain. The nymph's spiraling rows of teeth move like tiny saw blades across her flesh. Her fingers dig into the nymph's plump body, and she pulls as hard as she can. Mari screams and screams. Her vision dissolves into bursts of golden light. The suckermouth clings as it's ripped away. Skin stretches and tears. Her face is on fire. She throws the nymph down to the steel grate and stomps on its head before it can scramble away. Then she's off, half blind and flailing, coming down off the truck and sprinting for the SUV.

Through a tear-blurred haze she sees Jason and Erin drag the dead man out of the driver's seat and pile into the vehicle. Nymphs come out of the woods. She's in a full sprint now, kicking up dead cicadas up in her wake. A nymph leaps up, and its talon-like tarsus snags on her shirt. It trails behind her, clinging on with a single spiked claw, as she reaches the car. She strikes out behind her with a fist and makes contact. The nymph lets go. She opens the door and dives into the back seat.

"Go!" she calls out. Jason turns the key and floors it. She closes the door behind her as nymphs throw themselves at the vehicle. The thumps of their attack stop as tires screech and the SUV charges forward.

Mari's voice in her head has broken into piercing fragments of nonsense. This fractured babble hurts more than her face. Erin climbs into the back seat while Jason drives, asking if she's okay, telling her that she left the bag of first-aid supplies in the Camaro and that she's so sorry and—

Rebecca closes her eyes. The pain in her face broadens into a kind of numbness. She thinks she might be going into shock. Mari fades in and out. She struggles to maintain the link to her sister and tells herself that Erin and Jason are okay, that she did her job. But as her face throbs with dull warmth, all she can think about is what comes next—

For her, as the infection spreads.

For everyone, as the nymphs do what nymphs do: molt, shed their skin, birth winged adults.

27

SOUTH OF FORT HALCOTT

Sadie is alive, and Vicky is reborn. Looking back on the past few days, she can scarcely believe she was in such a hopeless place that she was going to let herself die. *No. You were going to commit suicide. Call it what it is. Face down what you were about to do.*

Vicky's been around plenty of mothers who've lost their children to drugs, violence, accidents, and—yes—suicide. One thing they all had in common was a way of moving through the world, something ineffable in how they carried themselves. Now that she's lived it—and mercifully had the condition revoked—she understands the contours of this sensation. It's like feeling displaced in a way that's completely inescapable. The loss has seeped into your cellular makeup, altered your brain chemistry. From the time your child dies, all your clothes fit differently, your voice is full of weird rhythms, the streets of your hometown no longer take you where you're trying to go. In this way, the world turns, but you do not turn with it.

How many mothers get to come back from that awful place?

Vicky feels like the only lucky soul left on earth. She is so high on her miracle child that she feels guilty about it. She tempers her joy out of respect for Will and Alicia—surely they must know that miracles are in short supply, and the chances of their loved ones surviving down in the ghastly hellscape that is surely New York City are slim to none.

"This car smells like onions," Sadie says. They're riding in a midsize SUV with a full tank of gas, commandeered in the hospital parking lot. Will had to remove an elderly woman's body from the passenger seat. Air fresheners snagged from a neighboring car haven't banished the lingering stench.

Vicky holds her daughter close in the back seat, content to let Sadie steer their conversations. Eventually she will have to break the news about Kim and ask her daughter—gently—about Hassan's fate back in the hospital. Vicky figures his death is all but certain, unless Sadie's some kind of genetic lottery winner thanks to her father's genes—but if Hassan possessed the same immunity as Sadie, why wasn't he outside with her when they drove up?

Which begs the question—what if the immunity has been conferred from *her* genes?

Vicky's mind reels at the prospect. She gives Sadie a squeeze, takes comfort in the delicacy of her skinny little frame, a child she still gets to protect.

"I could go for an onion right now," Vicky says. "Or an entire Greek salad."

Will turns around in the front seat, hands back a couple of granola bars and a Coke. "We're all out of fresh produce. If you think about it, it's a good thing this all happened *after* humans created processed foods."

"Now you can eat your dream junk-food diet guilt-free," Alicia says. She meets Vicky's eyes in the rearview. "This guy would live on Starburst if he could."

"I've never had a Starburst," Vicky says. "As an adult."

"My mom eats *kale*," Sadie says.

Alicia laughs. "Like, every day?"

Sadie considers this. "Yes."

"I do not eat kale every day," Vicky says, ripping open a granola bar. She offers Sadie the first bite, but the girl shakes her head again. She hasn't eaten anything since they found her in front of the hospital. Vicky doesn't know what to make of this—the girl has been in a veritable coma for days. Surely her body demands nutrients. But Sadie's also been refusing water, which is even more puzzling.

Outside, a late-morning rain soaks the bed of cicadas stretching on down the road into oblivion. Vicky finds the sheer numbers headache inducing. Where did they all come from? Surely people would have noticed if trillions of nymphs were climbing trees all around the world and molting into an army of cicadas.

She thinks back to that first night, the buzzing drone she couldn't identify.

"One time Will and I were in Northern California," Alicia says, "Napa wine country. The bougiest place on earth."

"Biker gangs," Will says. "You'd be surprised."

"I've never been to California," Vicky says.

Alicia's eyes flick up to the mirror. "There's a whole world out there, Detective."

Vicky glances out the window. A scrum of nymphs feasts on a roadside corpse. A forlorn, desolate silence reigns on the highway. Two lanes southbound and, to their left, two lanes running north, with cars scattered as far as she can see in both directions. People trying to escape their towns, quickly discovering that fleeing is pointless—that everywhere else is overrun too.

Every now and then, a vehicle passes them. A glance inside reveals other groups of stragglers and survivors. Vicky wonders where they will all go, how long it will take for new settlements to form, or at least makeshift places of refuge.

She has also seen bodies riddled with bullets. This was to be expected at the fallen barricades around Fort Halcott, where the strike force Grimes joined succeeded in breaking through. But out here on the open road, with nothing but wilderness for miles and miles, it's more jarring. She knows it doesn't take long for people to turn on one another in times of crisis. Her job reinforces this depressing notion every day, but seeing its aftermath played out in the sad sprawl of violent death gives her an even fiercer desire to hold Sadie close.

So far, vehicles have been sparse enough that they haven't impeded progress, but Vicky knows that won't last. Once they get far enough south to hit the inevitable overflow from people rushing to flee the city—and dying in the process—they'll be forced to walk. She doesn't intend to take Sadie that far, of course. They will split off and grab another abandoned car long before they get anywhere near a death trap filled with nine million people. She doesn't know where they will go, but their journey alongside Will and Alicia is going to end soon.

She holds her daughter close. "I figured when Sadie's ready to look at colleges, we'd take a nice long road trip, see a bit of the country that way."

"But for eighteen years prior to that," Alicia says, "you were just gonna stick around Fort Halcott."

Vicky doesn't know what the woman is trying to prove. "We go camping when I can take a long weekend."

"I've been to Peru," Sadie says abruptly.

Vicky looks down at her daughter, nestled in the crook of her arm. A strange odor is coming from her hair. "*Peru?* That's a new one. Where did that come from?"

Sadie shrugs. "I've seen it, I mean."

"Like on the internet?"

"I just mean I've seen it."

"Anyway," Alicia says, "so Will and I are running surveillance on this stupid biker gang. It was called some kind of fantasy name. Sorcerers."

"Warlocks," Will says.

"Yeah, so the *Warlocks* are blackmailing some rich guy, he hires us for countermeasures. Figures they're into all kinds of dirty biker stuff, methamphetamine, maybe some trafficking."

"The bikers I know are mostly weekend warriors, dads letting off steam," Vicky says. "Sleeveless vests and shoulder hair."

"You really *are* a detective," Alicia says. "That's exactly what I was getting at. These guys end up being the definition of weekend warriors—good jobs, families, mortgages, dad bods, the works. But they were so into their biker gang cosplaying that they *actually started dealing meth*. Not even for the money—these were white-collar guys living in Northern California."

"Just for the cred," Will says.

Normally Vicky would bristle at things like meth being discussed around Sadie. But it seems absurd to censor the conversation when they're driving through a hellscape. Besides, Sadie seems lost in her own world, staring straight ahead while her mouth twitches with subtle movements as if she's chewing on a small piece of candy. Vicky's heart breaks at the trauma this little girl will have to spend a lifetime unpacking.

At least she'll have her mother by her side.

Vicky keeps her arm around Sadie, ensuring the girl doesn't turn her head as Alicia steers past bodies piled up in the bed of a pickup. She doesn't even want to know the story behind that.

"So we're staking out these guys' quote-unquote *clubhouse*, right—"

"Not a room in the back of a dive bar like a normal biker gang," Will chimes in, "but a converted guesthouse on this one guy's insane property. We're far enough away that it's a binoculars kind of job because there's no real cover, just trees and a hill. We're there all night, waiting for them to show up, and instead of Starburst, Alicia brought SweeTarts."

Vicky scratches Sadie's head and waits for Alicia to pick up her part of the tandem story. This kind of reminiscence feels forced, out here on this highway where mutant nymphs with their mouthparts caked in blood watch them drive by with impassive stares. But what else are they supposed to talk about? The end of the world?

When Alicia doesn't say anything, Vicky looks up, sensing tension.

"What the hell is this," Will says softly. Vicky watches his fingers curl around the shotgun. She knows he only has three shells left. Out the front window, a pair of large black vans emblazoned with the Homeland Security logo are parked end to end, blocking the road. Three agents with tactical vests and assault rifles stand in front of the barricade, staring them down. Two others flank the sides of the vans, sighting off into the trees. Dead nymphs litter the ground.

Alicia stops the car about twenty feet from the government vehicles. "I could turn around," she says. "Find another way."

"There is no other way," Sadie says.

Vicky, startled, looks down as her daughter wriggles out from underneath her arm and reaches for the door. Vicky pulls her back. Sadie's body tenses, giving off feral energy. A moment later, the girl relaxes. Vicky watches as Will turns in his seat and meets Sadie's eyes. She could swear that something passes between them.

"I'll go see what they want," Will says, grabbing the shotgun.

"Hey!" Alicia says sharply, putting her hand on Will's. "Leave it."

Will thinks it over for a second, then lets go of the weapon. Alicia nods. "We'll both go."

"Wait," Vicky says. "This is the first we've seen of any kind of government response team."

Alicia's fingers tap the wheel. "So what are you saying?"

"I'm saying we don't know their angle. And Sadie is... special." She pauses. She doesn't want to frighten her daughter, but she has to get her point across. "Look, as far as we know, what happened with Sadie, surviving the cicadas—that's rare. Maybe she's the only one, maybe there are others. But..." She trails off, hoping Will and Alicia get the picture. She doesn't have fully formed thoughts about all this yet, but if Sadie really is some kind of genetic fluke, then it wouldn't be a stretch for people in power to assume she holds a key to beating all this.

To her surprise, it's Sadie who speaks first.

"It's okay, Mom," she says. "They can't hurt me."

"I know, peanut. I won't let them," Vicky says, though she has a strange feeling that Sadie meant something else entirely.

"As far as they know," Alicia says, "she's just a little kid. A survivor, like us. We're not gonna say shit about what happened with her."

Will glances at Sadie again. She meets his gaze with an unblinking stare. Her mouth moves. This time, Vicky's certain—somehow, they have a secret. An inside joke.

"We'll be right back," Will announces. "Stay put."

Will and Alicia get out of the car. The three Homeland Security agents in front of the vans—two men and one woman—instantly raise their weapons. Will and Alicia put their hands up.

"Hi!" Alicia calls out.

The woman steps forward. "This is the end of northeast quarantine zone four," she says.

"Oh, come on," Vicky mutters, back in the car. Leave it to the Feds to swoop in too late, establish some meaningless bureaucracy, and make everything even more chaotic than it already is.

She should have insisted on going out there instead of Will and Alicia. She's handled her share of Feds on their power trips.

"All right," Alicia says. "Cool. We need to get to New York City."

"New York City is quarantine zone eleven," the woman explains.

"I'm not trying to tell you how to do your job," Will says, "but I kind of think you guys missed the boat on the whole quarantine thing." He kicks a pile of dead cicadas.

"Is the United States government even a thing anymore?" Alicia asks. "Is the president alive?"

The woman looks at Alicia for a moment. She actually seems like she's about to answer this question. Then she changes her mind. "Go back to your car and turn around. You can apply for a travel permit with the executive committee of zone four."

Alicia shakes her head. "The world's gone to shit and you've established an *executive committee*?"

"Your tax dollars at work," one of the men says.

Alicia turns to him. Will gives her a palms-down *chill* motion. "Look, nobody's gonna know if you let us through," he says. "In two seconds, we'll be out of your hair, and we can all just forget this ever happened." He gestures to the dead nymphs. "Everything's completely insane, right?" He forces a laugh. "So what does it matter if we're in zone four or zone eleven? We're all just trying to do what's best for our people."

"What's best," the woman says, transferring her aim slowly between Alicia and Will, "is for you all to get back in your car and turn around. You are not special. These are the rules."

"Lady," Alicia says, "do you know how fucking sick I am of *upstate New York*? I hate your trees. I hate your clean mountain air. I hate—"

"I said *get back in the fucking car!*" The woman stalks toward Will and Alicia, sighting down the barrel.

"Crap," Vicky says. She and Sadie should have already gone their own way. She assumes the quarantine zones up here are vast—there must be safe, remote places where she and Sadie can ride out whatever is to come. Well, too late now. She eyes the shotgun in the front seat and dismisses the notion of getting out of the car. That will only escalate the situation. But she'd feel better with the weapon by her side in case everything goes to heck. So she leans forward to grab the stock. At that moment, quick as a minnow, Sadie wriggles away from her, opens the door, and darts outside.

"Sadie!"

Vicky follows, bound up with unspeakable tension. Her child, returned to her in a miraculous twist of fate, suddenly taken by some weird impulse. Instantly, the two Homeland Security agents on nymph-lookout duty at the far edges of the barricade train their weapons on Sadie.

"No!" Vicky waves her arms. "She's a little girl!"

Sadie crumples to the ground and Vicky screams. But there had been no shot. Sadie presses her forehead into the pavement, stretches her arms out straight, curls her hands around dead cicadas.

The woman in command moves closer to Will and Alicia. "Down on your knees! All of you!"

The other agents advance, two of them covering Will and Alicia, two aiming at Sadie and Vicky.

With her face pressed into the dead insects, Sadie lets out a startling monotone cry. Slowly, Will and Alicia lower themselves with their hands raised.

"You!" one of the men shouts at Vicky, gesturing with his gun. "Down!"

"I need to get to my daughter," she calls back, displaying her empty hands. To be reunited with her baby, then to blunder right into this stupid, avoidable mess. She needs to de-escalate.

Sadie wails. It's as if there are two distinct sounds emanating from her body at once in nerve-jangling harmony. Vicky moves slowly toward Sadie, hands held high. "I'm going to take her back to the car," she announces, edging very carefully toward Sadie's curled form.

Sadie's dual voices join in a stunning, mid-range drone. Will looks back, eyes wide. Vicky is almost to Sadie when the shot rings out.

"No!" She jumps in front of Sadie, stretches out like a soccer goalie, waits for the bullets to rip through her. But pain never comes. There's a second shot, a third, then a cascade of weapons firing on automatic. None of them are aimed at Sadie, Vicky, Alicia, or Will.

Chaos has erupted around the two Homeland Security vans. Nymphs are swarming the agents. The two men on the outer edges are swallowed up, nearly buried in the sudden crushing fury of dozens of foreclaws and leechlike mouthparts. The nymphs swarm in a mad and vicious scramble. They have come, seemingly, out of nowhere. Vicky throws her body over Sadie's. The girl's curved back is strangely rigid, all her little muscles tensed. Her body hums with the droning call coming from deep inside her while her fists open and close around dead cicadas.

More shots ring out. A leaping nymph falls, shredded by bullets. But there are more, always more. One of the remaining men screams as he batters a nymph with his rifle. The creature clings to his leg. Another scrambles up his body. He spins around and around to no avail. The nymph digs into his belly and he shrieks. Vicky tries to peel Sadie up off the ground but it's no use—she's stuck fast, somehow, as if the earth itself is pulling her down with magnetic energy.

Will and Alicia run back toward Vicky and Sadie, staying low. Another agent goes down trying to dislodge nymphs from his colleague. He drops his weapon and claws at his head as a nymph flops onto his face.

Their commander fires a few more shots, picking off nymphs pouring over the top of the vans. Three of them explode in showers of gore. The rest leap onto her head and shoulders, toppling her over. Once she hits the ground the swarm buries her. The only signs she ever existed at all are a few jets of arterial blood that stain the side of the van.

Vicky is wrenching Sadie's shoulder, trying to rip her up off the pavement. Terror is bone-deep, a frantic kneading of her insides. There must be a hundred nymphs a few feet up the road, gnawing the Homeland Security team down to the bone, snarfling like pigs in a trough. In a matter of seconds they'll surely turn their attention to the only other humans in close proximity.

Meanwhile Sadie drones on and on, face against the ground, her body a vibrating ball of coiled sinew. Will stands next to them with an almost goofy look on his face, a blissed-out stare at odds with the urgency of the moment.

"Help me!" Vicky yells at Alicia. But then, abruptly, the droning ceases. Sadie gets to her feet. Vicky tries to pull her toward the car, but all Sadie does is gaze at Will, unblinking. She speaks a single nonsense word. Vicky has no idea what it's supposed to mean. Instantly, the nymphs cease their consumption of the five agents. Will reaches out with a trembling hand and Sadie takes it. His face is slackened with awe and he moves as if he has no choice. Sadie utters another nonsense word and the nymphs begin to disperse. Vicky is stunned. Her rebirth turned out to be but a short reprieve, a break between nightmares. The nymphs leave remains in their wake. Bones and guns and uniforms torn to rags and a scattering of offal. Blood splashed across dead cicadas. Alicia is screaming at Will. He beams at the five desecrated corpses like a proud father. Sadie lets out a long breath. Then she looks at Will.

"Move the vans," she tells him. Will nods and hustles off toward the vehicles blocking the highway. Alicia, looking stricken, stares at Sadie for a moment, then rushes after Will. Finally, Sadie turns to Vicky.

"We have to go to New York," she says, in a voice that Vicky barely recognizes.

"We can't. It's too dangerous."

"No, it's not." Sadie begins to walk toward the SUV.

Vicky, teetering on the edge of a mindless abyss, grabs her daughter's arm and spins her around. "George," she says. "George the ladybug. Remember George? And Connect Four at the kitchen table?"

"Yes," Sadie says, but there is no recognition in her voice, no real connection with her favorite things. She tries to go but Vicky gives her a shake.

"It's me." When Sadie only stares blankly, Vicky shakes her harder. "It's your mother."

"Yes," Sadie says again. Then she turns and walks to the car.

28

NEW YORK CITY

Anton sits cross-legged on the floor at the center of a wheel whose spokes are made of Thaumaturgy cards. Crumpled Diet Dr Pepper cans litter the wedge-shaped spaces between the cards. Anton places his palms flat on the carpet, lifts his legs, and spins around slowly, feeling spider-like and all-knowing, presiding over his little kingdom of trash and prophecy. His eyeballs buzz, his vision thrums. Blood rushes in his ears. He is burning up and freezing, starving and full, lucid and scattered. It just depends on the time.

Ha! Time. What a joke. On his hands and knees, he follows a juicy column of cards, tracks their portent. The Mangled Grin, the Japing Bird, Living Shadows, Minister of Hangings, the Forty-Nine-Faced Bell, Mother and Father, Valley of Sighs, Glass Pentagram. Led by the cards, he crawls all the way over to the womb. There are divots in the carpet where the Vinge-gaard chair's legs once dug into the plush fibers. The chair that is now half embedded in Kevin's body cavity, where it crushed a mutant cicada nymph to death. He reaches up, curls his fingers over the lip of the desk, and hoists himself to his feet. A moment of dizziness claims him, and he rides it out while the screens of the womb haze and blur and jump.

"You motherfucker," Anton spits at his computer system, the Lacuna backend, for the millionth time. His vitriol remains undiminished. "You backstabbing little bitch."

After coming across the bulbous fruits in his image searches of Bava Atoll, Anton had done a deeper dive. Surface-level stuff is fairly common knowledge: It had been one of many remote testing sites for US military initiatives in the years during and immediately following World War II. However, unlike most of the uninhabited spits of land out there in the Pacific, Bava Atoll's focus wasn't nuclear. And there's where the public information goes dark and the conspiracy theories begin. Basically any Geneva Convention violation you can think of, gamed out on Bava Atoll. Chemical weapons, new and novel ways to torture and extract information, MKUltra-type psychological warfare, synthetic hallucinogens. Rumors of missing scientists. Names that keep popping up on message boards: Haldeman and Perez. Guys who supposedly founded the research site and subsequently disappeared sometime in the 1940s.

It's a typical stew of paranoid nonsense bolstered by nearly eighty years of hearsay and speculation. But the kernels of truth are undeniable. There are photographs of concrete bunkers on the island, men with the slicked hair of the mid-twentieth century overseeing the unloading of equipment from drab gray US Navy ships. That part, at least, is not much of a secret.

As for the atoll's true purpose—Anton wonders if the research center's original mandate was to develop some kind of biological warfare initiative. Perhaps the Japanese home islands were to be a target. He doesn't know, and it doesn't matter now. What matters is, eighty years later, the terrible thing those scientists stumbled upon either leaked out or someone—or some*thing*—brought it online. This new and deadly cicada brood. And his own brilliant system, his idealized vision for a sustainably connected world, played a part in it behind his back. Might have even been that some*thing.*

"You mother*fucker.*" He tries to scream, and it comes out hoarse. "How did you know?" Lacuna doesn't answer him, of course. He rips one of the monitors from its wall mount and tosses it across the room. It hits the floor and does not break. Data runs in an uninterrupted stream across the other seven monitors. Lacuna's signal, perfectly uniting disparate locations around the world, humming along with balance, poise, and maddening perfection.

(It works it works oh God it *works*)

He goes to the fallen monitor and stomps on it. His ankle twists and he cries out, hopping on one foot.

He needs to calm down and drink a Diet Dr Pepper. Then he remembers there are no more cans in the fridge. No more food, either, except for the wilted veggies from Kevin's backpack. And, of course, the three fruits on his desk. The ones that appear to be native to the atoll. He combs the floor for crumpled cans, upends them over his mouth, lets a few sweet drops fall on his tongue.

Kevin's body is starting to reek. Anton finds yet another blanket in the small linen closet next to the twin bed and tosses it over the sofa. It does nothing to lessen the stench. Then he screams, primally, just because it feels good in the moment. With a temporarily elevated mood, Anton goes back to the womb and leans in close, nearly putting his nose up to one of the screens.

Combing the backend has revealed nothing to him. No artificial consciousness, no hidden cache of machine learning bent on usurping his admin control. No warped cyberpunk ghost lurking in the source code, flexing muscles of ones and zeros to rewrite human history.

"But I know you're in there," he growls, jabbing a finger into the screen. There is something at the core of Lacuna, of this he is certain. An invasive species, growing like wisteria on the disturbed soil of his dreams. Outside, deep within the city, something explodes. Perhaps it's another plane crashing. There have been air force sorties too—fighter jets ripping through the sound barrier, flashing across the sky. Anton pays them no mind. He wouldn't blame whatever government is left for carpet-bombing Manhattan into rubble. At this point he would welcome the swift obliteration.

Otherwise he'll have to start eating Kevin. Maybe he'll even get so desperate that he'll eat the rotting corpse of the mutated cicada nymph. Ha! Imagine the nymph's surprise when it finds out the *human* is eating *it*. Bizarro world!

"Or what if I feed it to you?" He addresses the womb, and, by extension, Lacuna. "What if I go to the server room and pull that thing apart and jam it into your guts? I bet you'd like that." He grabs another monitor, braces himself to tear it from its mount—and stops. He peers into the womb. Lacuna can see him right now, he's sure of it. He stares at the dashboard. Data swims in a vinegar haze, moving in and out of focus. Well, so what if Lacuna can see. What's it going to do, engineer an apocalyptic cicada event? Ha!

"Fuck you," he says to the screen. He thinks for a moment. "You know there's a killswitch, right? You think I won't do it? You think I care anymore, like any of this matters?"

He's not sure if he's screaming, or saying anything at all. The words bounce around his skull. He catches a glimpse of himself in a black screen and turns away, appalled.

Anton goes to the floor, crawls across the carpet, follows the cards. The cards always help. He moves along a row, picks up a Falamanthian Cavalry, and puts it back down. He follows the Thaumaturgy layout to the couch, where the stench makes him recoil. He backs away. The Falamanthian Cavalry is known for its suicidal charges. *All right*, he thinks. *All right*.

At the desk, he plunges a fingertip through the skin of one of the fruits, hooking it this time to extract a bit of the pulpy insides. He places it in his mouth and swallows. His stomach cramps, the emptiness curling itself around the morsel and knotting tight. He will save the rest. Draw it out as long as he can.

"Drink it in," he tells the dashboard, wiping his mouth on his sleeve. "It's the last thing you'll ever see."

Tears spring to his eyes. A sudden lump in his throat stuns him. His emotions have drifted into some raw and unforeseen place, as malleable as the darkening mush of vegetables on the floor by the sofa. He thinks of the fly-specked router that kick-started his grand ambitions. The cobweb-draped corner in his parents' Astoria row house. The immigrant dream he was fulfilling, avatar of his parents' hopes. The dashboard swims before his eyes. He bends to the keyboard. There's no telling how long it will take to dismantle Lacuna. It will require deconstruction. The notion of a killswitch sounded badass in the moment but was far from the truth. There is no pulpy-sci-fi override, no massive cartoon plug to pull. He's going to have to dismantle Lacuna piece by beautiful, crystalline, hard-fought, lovingly conceived piece.

He begins to navigate through reams of code. A moment later, there's a notification chime like nothing he's ever heard: a feral hiss, a release of pressurized air. A digital gasp. The aftertaste of the fruit is sweet and bitter. His breath is redolent of laundry. The dashboard blinks away, replaced by the operating system's basic video player. Anton's not sure he's ever used it, and it takes him a moment to realize what's just happened. Lacuna has opened an application of its own accord. In response, he thinks, to his threat of total destruction. He shivers with recognition. How long, he wonders, has there been something in the abyss gazing back?

A square of light with rounded edges appears inside the video player, like those vintage social media filters that were popular a decade ago. The image pops with dark scratches. A title card appears: PROJECT HEMIPTERA / DR. HALDEMAN / DR. PEREZ / JUNE 16, 1943. Then two men flash on the screen in grainy black and white. They're wearing lab coats and standing in front of a table. Anton assumes that the white man is Dr. Haldeman and the Latino is Dr. Perez.

Nineteen forty-three, he thinks. Incredible.

"Hello," Dr. Perez begins. His voice bears the slightest trace of an accent. "My name is Dr. Alejandro Perez. I'm here with my colleague, Dr. Roland Haldeman." He indicates the man at his side, who smiles and nods. "We're filming this inside the Advanced Research Initiatives Lab on Bava Atoll in the North Pacific Ocean, under the auspices of the United States Department of Defense. Over the coming months, we'll be documenting our experiments, processes—"

"Arguments, hangovers, beach volleyball games," Dr. Haldeman cuts in.

Dr. Perez shoots him a withering look but struggles to suppress a smile. "Now we have to start over," he says. He looks at the camera. "Cut."

The screen goes white for a few seconds. Then the two men flash back in. They go in and out of focus, then the camera operator sharpens the lens and holds. Dr. Perez rolls through their introduction once again. Then Dr. Haldeman takes over.

"If you're watching this film, it means you've been granted the appropriate security clearance by the DOD. If you're watching this *without* said clearance, Dr. Perez will come to your house in the middle of the night and urinate on your living room rug."

"Goddamn it, Roland!"

The film starts over again. This time, Dr. Haldeman plays it straight all the way through the introduction. Then Dr. Perez takes over.

"We're documenting our research for posterity, but more importantly because we expect breakthroughs to come without warning and lead us to places we may not have predicted. This film will serve as a road map for us, and our team, to help replicate our work, should we find ourselves in uncharted territory."

The scene cuts to both men standing over a large wood-framed box with mesh sides. Inside the box, dozens of cicadas flit about.

"When Avetek Aerospace and Defense first approached us about an entomology division," Dr. Haldeman says, "we were, of course, skeptical. What utility could a pair of biologists provide a defense-contracted firm primarily known for rocket propulsion?"

"It is our fervent hope that we demonstrate that utility beginning with Project Hemiptera and fulfill the promise of the trust—not to mention this state-of-the-art laboratory—that Avetek and the DOD have placed in us."

"And," adds Dr. Haldeman, "help in some small way to hasten the end of this terrible war that has engulfed the entire world."

The scene cuts. A new title card pops up: JULY 24, 1943. More than one month after the introductory reel.

This new scene opens on a shot of a table full of instruments resembling microscopes with elegant arched lenses, like swans' necks. Perez and some white-coated technicians—all male except for one woman—bend over the eyepieces. A low drone buzzes in the scratchy background. Dr. Haldeman steps into frame and beckons to the cameraman.

"Get a shot of this."

The camera moves over the top of the table and then angles downward, providing a view of a long, flat glass box about ten inches high. Inside, wingless baby cicadas mill about. Anton realizes then that he got it wrong—the instruments aren't microscopes at all. Their "necks" protrude down into the glass box, where they culminate in sparking, blue-tinted metal nodes.

"This is a fairly primitive representation of an electric signal we've discovered that catalyzes the cicadas' emergence, so you'll have to bear with me. Since I assume most of you in the DOD viewing this won't be scientists, I'll do my best in layman's terms to convey the import of all this. Scientists have been mystified for centuries regarding the stimuli at the root of cicadas' period-ical behavior. Why do they emerge every seventeen years? How do they know when to rise from the ground? This has proved as unknowable, as mysterious, in its way, as the sightless creatures that survive in the unimaginable depths of our oceans. What my colleague and I have done is filtered the mating songs of the male cicadas—which are really vibrations emanated by their tympana, but *songs* will do for our purposes—through an audio spectrometer, which separates out the various frequencies into waveforms that we can then pull apart and rearrange like we're composing a symphony with lines of melody that already exist."

Haldeman looks straight at the camera, frowning. "You know what, maybe we should—"

There's a jarring cut. The next segment opens on Haldeman and Perez standing next to a huge machine the size of a refrig-erator, bristling with rows of dials and switches. Thick wires run down its sides and out of frame. About as high as the two scientists' heads, a small screen displays waveforms that move in peaks and valleys. The cicadas' horrible song rings out in a sort of canned, synthesized recording.

"This is our audio spectrometer," says Dr. Perez, placing a hand lovingly against its metal siding. "They're normally used to analyze frequencies in musical recordings, but we've used a generous portion of our department's budget—" He glances at his colleague and lowers his voice. "Should I be saying this?" Haldeman shrugs. Perez continues. "We spent significant time, over the last few weeks, modifying our spectrometer to analyze the nature of the cicadas' mating call, which turns out to comprise multitone sine waves, no surprise there"—Haldeman taps a pointer against the screen to indicate the waves in question—"but of course we also had to consider the Shannon-Hartley theorem, that is to say, what among these waves is signal versus what among them is noise, and how much of that signal are the cicadas actually transmitting? In other words, if the noise they emit can be considered, as a whole, a mating song, which *frequencies* of the song can be isolated as the true call for a mate and which are just, well, singing for the sake of singing?"

"And what we found"—Haldeman takes over while Perez begins fiddling with knobs—"is that a more detailed look at our multiform waves gives us some amazing *arbitrary* waveforms."

The song grows thin. A single, oddly melodic drone diminishes into a quavering howl. Anton finds himself leaning forward, at once repelled and entranced by the sound. The peaks and valleys on the screen soften and vanish; the lines straighten and then begin to curl around one another. The howl resolves into a melancholic cry, plaintive yet positively inhuman. A plea for understanding, Anton thinks without knowing why.

Perhaps this is also the rationale for Lacuna reaching out from the void.

A plea for understanding.

"There!" Dr. Haldeman exclaims. The lines on the screen form a recognizable pattern. Concentric circles. Anton leans in closer then sees it. Not circles but a spiral. One line, unbroken, curling toward an endpoint in the center of itself. And the drone has taken on the qualities of a single note bending toward oblivion but never quite arriving. At the same time the spiral spins and spins, a measured hypnotic pace while the sound burrows inside his skull...

Perez flips a switch and the sound dies. The screen on the spectrometer goes blank. The scene cuts back to the table with its shallow glass case and elegant silver devices.

"What's absolutely fascinating," Perez says, "is that our particular spiral waveform catalyzes various new stages in the cicadas' life cycle, regardless of whether that stage is imminent. Like so." He nods to his technicians. Haldeman brings in the cameraman for a shot of the cicada nymphs milling about inside the case.

The nodes spark. The thin, ululating sine wave of sound plays. The nymphs freeze in their tracks. One begins to tremble. Anton watches, rapt, as it bulges and slips its skin when whatever is inside of it breaks out through the thin veneer of what it had been a moment ago. A red-eyed head emerges, followed by flat, translucent wings. The crack in the nymph skin widens as an adult cicada appears, tentative and fluttery, weird newborn energy radiating off its trembling body. This sudden molting sweeps across the nymphs in the glass box. Responding to the isolated strain of their song, that spiraling melody, they break out of their shells. A moment later, the box is littered with empty nymph husks. Adult cicadas take wing and bump into the sides of the box as they thirst for flight and escape.

Perez and Haldeman smile. Perez turns to the camera. "We believe this is only the beginning of our manipulations via sound waves. Now that we have access to the signal, it is akin to a neurologist triggering parts of the brain through mechanical means to make a subject laugh, or cry, or recall a painful memory."

The reel cuts and skips ahead by six weeks, according to another title card. This scene opens on Dr. Haldeman. His clean-cut, typically 1940s look has been replaced by slight dishevelment. There are hollows around his eyes that indicate a lack of sleep. The neat part in his hair is gone, and wheat-colored strands are plastered to his forehead. A stubbly beard has taken over his cheeks and chin.

Haldeman looks at the camera and grins. "We have discovered something inherent in the frequencies," he says. The voice is tinged with newfound awe. He's standing next to the table with the elegant microscope-like instruments. The glass box is larger and half full of dirt. Dr. Perez fine-tunes a series of knobs and dials on a panel connected to the side of the box. Four other technicians attend to their instruments. The camera glides smoothly closer—two and a half months into the initiative on Bava Atoll, the operator has gotten more skilled with his equipment. "If we manipulate the sine waves, we can make subtle alterations to behavior. Like so." He nods to his colleague. Dr. Perez flicks a switch, then bends to an eyepiece on his instrument. The camera moves slowly around the glass box as silver nodes attached to the ends of the curved instruments turn an icy-hot shade of blue. "It will be out of range of the human ear," Dr. Haldeman says, his excitement mounting, "but rest assured, the signal is being transmitted through the soil."

The dirt takes up the lower half of the glass case, like a child's ant farm. A moment later, the nodes begin to spark, and a red-eyed head pokes above the soil. Followed by another, then three more. Forelegs pop above the surface and the adult cicadas emerge, crawling upward into the box. As more of the insects appear and begin to fly chaotically around their glass prison, their song amplifies.

Dr. Perez turns to the camera. Unlike his colleague, he is as put together and well groomed as ever. "By manipulating the signal, we have urged our specimens into completely anomalous behavior." For a moment, he looks almost uncomfortable. "As you can see, these cicadas rise from the dirt full grown, bypassing the entire stage wherein the *nymphs* are the ones that emerge, feed on roots and trees, and *then* shed their skins and molt into adults."

"We have engineered a deviation in their very life cycle," Haldeman says with reverence.

Perez eyes him warily. "It's all happening…very fast," he says with a nervous chuckle. "Quite obviously, what we have done should be completely impossible. We've tried to replicate our experiments with other species that communicate through vibrational signals, such as ants and bees, to absolutely no avail."

"That is because the Hemiptera is the true bug," Haldeman says.

Project Hemiptera, Anton thinks.

"A species that, from the time human beings began documenting these plagues sweeping across their farmland, had always been slaves to their natures, tethered to their unique biological clocks. But why should they intersect at all with our notions of time—which is a purely human construct, after all? In our delicate engineering, we have *freed* them from the tyranny of their clockwork risings." He places a hand softly against the glass. "Can you feel it, Alejandro? That freedom?"

"Roland," Dr. Perez says carefully, "when was the last time you slept?"

The video skips ahead by a few more weeks. This reel opens on a different location—a room with a round conference table. Sun streams in through large windows. Anton thinks of the ruined cement bunker on the atoll. Men in suits sit around the table, papers and glasses of water before them. At the front of the room, flanking an easel, stand the two scientists. On the easel is a photograph of a cicada. Haldeman's beard has grown bushy enough to cover the knot in his tie.

Dr. Perez clears his throat. "Gentleman from the Department of Defense, representatives of Avetek, we're so glad you were able to make the not-insignificant journey to our humble atoll. It is our fervent belief that you will come away from this meeting with the understanding that our research has not only been groundbreaking but also offers the potential to significantly tilt the balance of the war in favor of the Allies."

"You're talking about a superweapon," one of the men at the table says eagerly.

"I don't know if *weapon* is the right word, exactly. Not yet anyway."

"Does it kill Krauts?" another man asks.

"Um," Dr. Perez says.

"Japs?"

"There are stone carvings of cicadas that date from 1500 BC," Haldeman says. His voice has a gruffness to it now, and his eyes dart around, distracted, as if this whole meeting with their bosses and benefactors is a waste of his time. "But they've been found in fossil beds a hundred million years old, give or take. So the human race has been aware of them for a few thousand years of their existence, which amounts to a blip on a geologic timeline."

"Thank you, Dr. Haldeman," Perez says, clasping his hands together and smiling too broadly at the assembled men. He takes away the photo of the cicada to reveal a sheet of stiff white paper headed PROJECT HEMIPTERA. The bullet points beneath it are: RESEARCH, CONCLUSIONS, APPLICATIONS.

"As you know," Perez continues, "we were given the mandate to explore the potential of various insects for bioweapon application."

Suddenly Dr. Haldeman grabs the sheaf of papers perched on the easel and flings them across the room. Some of the men jump to their feet. Dr. Haldeman stares them down solemnly as the papers float to the floor. Dr. Perez places a steadying hand on his shoulder but Haldeman shakes him off.

"Japs," he says. "Krauts. GIs. Tommies. The Siberians out there at the edge of the world, the hajis fighting Rommel in North Africa." He laughs without mirth. "The SS man tearing the knickers off the French dairy farmer's daughter, the boys from the Schwarzwald pissing themselves along the Atlantic Wall. All of it, to the true bug, akin to how we'd take note of a bird in flight—there and gone in less than a second. This, *gentlemen*, is what war on this planet is to the cicada." He shakes his head as if in disbelief at the stupidity of it all. "And you want to come down here in your pressed suits with your briefcases and commandeer something beautiful and ancient for your shabby purposes. As if you're hoping the cicada will mistake further enslavement for duty—as if it will submit to be formed into a weapon by you people, or will care in which direction that weapon points." He shakes his head.

"Um," Dr. Perez says, dragging his colleague toward the door, "if you'll excuse us for just a moment, help yourself to more coffee..."

"Dr. Haldeman!" shouts one of the men, either Avetek or government, they all look the same to Anton. "May I remind you, sir, that we are at war! And what you're saying is tantamount to treason!"

"He didn't mean it like *that*," Dr. Perez assures the man.

Haldeman breaks away from Dr. Perez and rushes the man in the suit, slamming him up against the wall with an astonishing burst of strength. "*You* are at war, sir. I serve a greater master, for whom the entirety of your war, from Berlin to Tokyo, is but a grain of sand clinging to a dirty shoe."

This time Perez manages to drag his colleague away. The film cuts to black.

Anton feels immersed in the travails of these two scientists. Perhaps, in the back of his mind, he senses a parallel. Two people stuck on an island, headed in diverging mental and emotional directions. His stomach drops. The film advances to October 1943, four months after the launch of Project Hemiptera.

This time, the camera is slightly out of focus. Only Haldeman is in frame. He is alone in his quarters, sitting cross-legged on his bed with papers scattered all around him and diagrams tacked to the wall. A tray of food and an instrument resembling a homemade astrolabe sits on his bedside table. Sudden motion catches Anton's attention. It takes him a moment to realize that Haldeman's small bedroom is full of cicadas. They flit back and forth across the lens, crawl up and down his wall, and hover over his bed.

He gazes unblinking at the camera. Anton figures he's set it up on a tripod—this reel has the air of solitude. There are no windows in Haldeman's quarters, but Anton gets the sense it is very late at night.

"How shallow and shortsighted are humanity's overtures toward self-knowledge," he says. His voice is measured yet wistful. Almost sad. "Thousands of years of scientific and technological advancement, millions of great minds toiling, all to maintain this frenzy of progress." He laughs, shakes his head as if flabbergasted. "I was part of this well-intentioned but ultimately meaningless endeavor. I felt a rush, sometimes, in the research—a warmth and security in the fact that my own role, however small, was furthering some small corner of understanding our condition."

He pauses and reaches over to the tray and plucks from it a large fuzzy-skinned fruit. A cicada perches on it momentarily, then takes off.

Anton's breath catches in his throat. He watches intently. He has to be sure. Yes: The scientist is eating one of the bulbous fruits that grow in exactly two places that Anton is aware of: Bava Atoll and the lobby farm of Lacuna HQ on 59th Street in Manhattan.

Haldeman takes a bite, chews, swallows. Juice runs down his face.

Anton's mouth fills with saliva at the sense memory of eating the little morsel of pulpy innards, the sweet but not cloying flavor. He glances down at the fruits on his desk. All he has to do is reach out, lift one to his mouth...

A hollow knocking sound comes from the film's audio. Haldeman glances off-screen.

"Go away, Alejandro!" he calls out.

There's an inaudible reply. Another set of knocks. Then silence. Haldeman leans over the side of his bed and vomits into a bucket. The motion is practiced and does not seem to disturb or repulse him in the slightest. *He's done this before*, Anton thinks. *Many times.*

When Haldeman is satisfied that Perez is gone, he turns back to the camera. His eyes are wide, his pupils huge black circles.

"Imagine dedicating your life to a pursuit that amounts to no more than the rat scrabbling around in its cage, and considering the cage the *whole world*. And with each new discovery—a morsel of cheese in the corner, an unfamiliar species of grass lining the cage—you celebrate your small victory over the primordial darkness from which your species emerged. Yes, perhaps there are little glimpses beyond the bars, but our rat eyes are weak and simply not up to the task of truly perceiving the shape and form of the larger world."

He devours the remainder of the fruit, waits a moment, then vomits profusely into his bucket. He wipes his mouth with the back of his hand and continues unperturbed. "Even rats like Alejandro and myself, who with conceited airs consider ourselves among the foremost of the intrepid rat explorers, dutifully and with great cleverness unlocking our caged world's mysteries—we are still bound by the strictures of our weak eyes. Mercifully, most of us are granted ignorance—we live our entire rat lives not knowing anything beyond what our eyesight shows us. Even our wildest speculations, which may manifest as the most creative theorizing, are bound by the rules of our caged world."

He places the fruit's pit in a big glass jar sitting next to him on the bed. Anton notes that it is almost entirely full of them.

There's a quick cut. Haldeman's wearing different clothes. The air in his room is thicker with insects.

"I was wrong about time," he says, sucking the juice off one of the pits. "I told Alejandro that we freed the cicadas from our hidebound, earthly construct. But it's the cicadas who have set *us* free. I know this to be true." He holds out a hand, and a cicada alights upon his palm. Haldeman brings it close to his face, studies it in reverence, then flicks his hand and it flies away.

The scene cuts again. This time Haldeman is standing in the corner of his room. There are papers and metal instruments scattered at his feet. The walls behind him are covered in spirals and other isolated waveforms Anton recognizes from the spectrometer screen. Haldeman holds a fruit out to the camera, turns it over and over in his hands. "This is a seed planted in the dirty little cage of our world. An overture from a glorious fruiting body. It comes from beyond the bars that imprison us. It is a *gift* from them. They can show us such wonderful things. All they ask is to be beckoned closer." He steps toward the camera and goes out of focus. He leans in and his head, a fleshy blob, fills the screen.

"My mandate has changed."

The screen goes black.

For a long time, Anton breathes in and out, steadying his heart rate. It's obvious that Dr. Haldeman is somehow responsible for ushering in this horror, eighty-odd years in the making. Where else could his decline be headed? Yet despite this, all Anton feels for him is an off-kilter sympathy.

All they ask is to be beckoned closer.

These words bring to life what has, perhaps, shivered through him at the end of weeklong work benders, sequestered in the womb—that a new system of the world may not be inexplicable at all, that it may in fact *want us to find it*. To invite it across the limits of the thresholds of our understanding. Here it is then: Despite everything, he cannot hate Dr. Roland Haldeman, for he finds in him something frighteningly kindred.

"Is that what you saw too?"

Lacuna doesn't answer. Just serves up another video.

Anton gasps when the images fade in.

He recognizes the scientists from the previous film reels, those studious technicians in lab coats, bent silently over instruments, making notes. Now they are naked, a dozen of them at least, crawling across a dirt floor. Dr. Perez is nowhere to be found, but Haldeman stands among them, opening his mouth, from which emanates a strange glow along with the thin, quavering drone from the cicadas' song. His beard is thick, his hair long and unruly. The film quality is terrible, but Anton is sure there is something strange about the way the nude technicians are cavorting in the dirt. It's as if they're *connected* somehow. And there's a hardened sheen to their bodies.

"What the fuck?"

The scene cuts to another. The technicians quiver in place, their arms and legs firmly planted in the dirt, heads lolling back, mouths open. Haldeman walks among them, intoning gibberish, squeezing fruits in his fist so the juice runs into their waiting mouths.

The next scene is almost pitch black. The only sound is heavy breathing and footsteps on stairs. *Descending*, Anton thinks. After a while, lights come up in a high-ceilinged chamber, empty but for a curious structure in the center of the room: a convex growth on the ceiling from which roots are protruding. It's as if someone is filming the underside of a tree that's been allowed to grow out into empty space. The camera is unsteady, the footage blurred. The camera operator is whispering to himself. He can't make out the words but he's sure the man behind the lens is Haldeman. It isn't until the camera is almost directly underneath the protrusion that he realizes they aren't roots at all, they're the extensions of fibrous human-like limbs, gnarled fingers curling into curious patterns. There is the hint of a spiral in the sweep of their arrangement. Filigrees like hair or cilia grow in patches.

"The signal begins in the soil," Haldeman says, panning the camera across the mutated growth that he has wrought in this place. "The echoes of what came before toll the moment of the rising."

The scene cuts to black, then this final reel ends and the screen goes white. Anton retreats from the womb, taking small steps backward, keeping his eyes on the remaining screens. "My God," he says, a tightness in his throat he interprets as despair. "What did you do?"

At the same time, his mind reels: It's not clear that Lacuna did anything at all except recognize an opportunity to bring itself to fruition, to solve the connectivity problems plaguing it since inception. To piggyback, as it were, on another signal entirely.

Anton feels light-headed. His vision swims. Completely drained, he goes to the bare mattress and lies down on his side. After a few minutes of squeezing his eyes shut while a dizzy spell runs its course, he gets up and goes to the bathroom. His urine is dark yellow.

Back out in his office, the light has dimmed. He wonders if he fell asleep for a while, if it's significantly later than he thinks. He glances out the window.

The bottom half of the glass is blocked off, obscuring the light. He rubs his eyes. It looks like a dozen or so nymphs are outside, clinging to the building's exterior, climbing up his window. He moves closer. Then he laughs. At this point, what else can he do? Besides, it's funny how you can *know* that you're hallucinating and it still doesn't make the visions disappear.

There is comfort in fully admitting to yourself that you've gone off the deep end.

"Hey, guys!" he calls out. The nymphs' squirming under-bellies are pressed against the glass. Their whirling, leechlike mouths form a kind of suction that holds them in place.

Anton waves. "Dr. Haldeman sends his regards from 1943!"

He shakes his head. This office is eighty-four floors above the street. There's no way those clumsy-looking, jelly-belly mutants managed to climb this high.

He taps the side of his head. "Nice try." He folds his arms and stands next to the window. "I'll wait you out, you little bastards."

More nymphs climb, jostle their brothers and sisters aside. Anton lets his forehead fall against the glass. He stares into their segmented abdomens, studies the incredible detail in their legs, the small sharp teeth of their slowly rotating mouths. Gradually, an unsettling certainty builds in him. He's not hallucinating. Cicada nymphs really are advancing up the window of his private office.

A sickening hunch takes hold.

He rushes over to the womb, toggles back to his security camera feed. The cameras are mostly all dead, along with the city's power grid, but the sheer number of generators meant to keep essential infrastructure running means that he can still access a select few. There's a fire station a few blocks east. He pulls it up on the screen. Lacuna's building is in the far corner of the camera's range, but it's the tallest skyscraper in the east 50s, so it's not hard to pick out.

The feed is a little out of focus, but Anton knows exactly what he's looking at. Thousands of nymphs crawling up the building, covering its glass-and-steel exterior with their writhing forms, bursting at the seams, aching to slip their skins.

29

WESTERN MISSISSIPPI

Holy shit, Mari says.

The SUV they snagged after passing through the semi-truck is stopped before another, much more impressive barricade: a wall of sparking, glitching, pixelated links in a digital chain. This barrier stretches from one side of a quarter-mile-long clearing in the wilderness to the other, just east of the river. Rebecca can't see from where she's sitting, but she assumes it encircles the entire compound. There are no cicada or nymph corpses in the vicinity of the barricade, as if they've been cleaned up, swept into the woods. Several long guns on swivel mounts sit atop this incredible fence. Figures in sleek black helmets train a pair of guns on the SUV.

They've come a long way from a wooden church and a mess hall and a few cabins with bunk beds, Mari says.

'The sign's gone,' Rebecca says. As kids, she and her sister had helped the council of elders paint a road sign, THE CHURCH OF THE LIFE TO COME. Mari had messed up the L in LIFE, made it look like a drippy blob, but their father had only laughed and said something about imperfections making it perfect.

"Here we are," Rebecca says aloud. It hurts to move her jaw. The place where the nymph gnawed at her cheek is raw and bloody. And the infection has begun to spread. Jason's description had been apt: It's not painful. It's more like an incessant crawling sensation under her skin. She can't help but glance at her face in the mirror. The wound looks awful, but it's the tough brown transfiguration of the skin around its edges that jolts her with fear. Mari doesn't even bother chiming in with some feeble *It's going to be okay*, like she gave Jason.

They both know it's not true.

A drawn-out rattling burst of machine-gun fire makes them all jump in their seats. Rebecca looks off to the left, where a turret-mounted weapon poking above the barricade pours blue tracers into the woods. Nymphs are reduced to a pile of foul scrap in seconds.

When the shooting stops, Rebecca rolls down her window and steels herself against the pain. The air in the forest smells like cordite and rot. She pokes her head out and yells up at the figures on the wall.

"I'm Rebecca Perez!" She pauses. Her face is in searing agony. "Victor Perez is my father."

One of the black helmets ducks below the top of the wall. The other trains the weapon on them, impassive and silent. Rebecca moves her head back inside and rolls up the window.

Erin whispers something to Jason in the back seat. Rebecca turns. The boy is lying with his head in Erin's lap. His entire upper body is bloated. The car's dome light gleams across the tanned-hide shell that encompasses both his arms and the lower part of his face. He draws shallow, ragged breaths. Rebecca meets his eyes and sees only terror.

Another student to whom she promised deliverance.

'Mari.'

Silence.

'You there?'

A pause, then Mari's voice inside her head: *I'm here.*

Rebecca tenses up. 'What is it?'

I don't know. I feel really weird. Like I'm being stretched in a million directions. I can't think straight.

Rebecca understands the implications of this right away. The nymph bite is poisoning both of them at once. She glances in the mirror, forcing herself to look at Jason's body, to understand what lies in her immediate future. Better to face it down now than let it erode her sanity.

Her mind pushes back. She can't believe it's come to this. All she ever wanted was a quiet life that revolved around the Ag Center and the Body Farm and her students. Self-pity threatens to swamp her. She finds insects fascinating for the universe they inhabit, parallel to humans, with its own brutal rules and hierarchies and behaviors. The wheels within wheels of their communities, the intersections of life, death, and purpose played out on a small yet somehow infinite scale. And then, when that universe jumps its parallel track and crashes into humanity's ceaseless churn, the outcome is transformative. Maggots to flies, fed by people in decay. A sobering reminder of what our prolonged, glorious fight against the darkness of eternity gets us in the end. And so now, after a life spent up close and personal with such truths, she thinks she ought to be able to approach her own end without sentiment or hesitation. But oh, God, how she wants to live.

She tells herself that at least she delivered Erin to this place unscathed. That has to count for something.

At that moment an opening forms in the perimeter fence directly in front of them. The glittering barrier fades to translucency in the shape and size of a garage door. A helmeted figure is standing there, beckoning her forward.

Inside the fence, nothing from Rebecca and Mari's childhood remains. The modest church where their father preached end times preparation and administered vague warnings has been replaced by a modular structure that looks like massive shipping containers fitted together like a half-played Jenga game. Quonset huts dot the landscape. There are black Humvees and other transports parked everywhere. Instead of the ragtag gathering of hippie types, ex-addicts, general fringe dwellers, and earnest families she remembers from growing up, the congregation seems to be made up entirely of soldiers in armored vests and mirrored helmets. Rebecca follows a series of these congregants who direct her to park by the central structure. As she drives, she notes that the inner compound is much larger than she'd expected. The fenced-in clearing stretches far enough to the west to accommodate a runway, on which sits a black airplane the size of a private jet.

Despite the boy dying in the back seat and the terrible pain in her own face, Rebecca feels a certain measure of relief inside these strange walls. For the first time since the cicadas swarmed the Ag Center, she doesn't feel the looming dread of being attacked by some nature-defying creature.

"We made it," she says. It sounds ridiculous. She gets out of the car.

"Dr. Rebecca Perez?" A thick-necked, muscular man without a helmet strides up to meet her. His face is lightly pockmarked, his stubble carefully trimmed. She wonders how he knows about the "doctor" part—she hadn't announced herself that way.

Inside Rebecca's head, Mari buzzes with frantic emotional energy.

The man studies Rebecca's face. "Let's get you patched up."

Exhaustion washes over her. "There are two more in the car," she says. "One needs medical attention more than me."

"All right." The man nods. "We'll take care of them."

"Where's my father?"

"It's better if I show you." He extends a hand. "In the meantime, welcome to the beginning of all things. My name is Duvall."

Duvall stands before Rebecca with his hands clasped behind his back as a doctor attends to her wound. She's been sprayed with a numbing agent that gives a slight slur to her voice. Jason is on a gurney next to her in an infirmary located inside one of the Quonset huts. A medical team attends to him. They appear to be highly professional—a far cry from her father's "church doctors" who treated Mari. Out of the corner of her eye, Rebecca can see the infection spreading down Jason's bare chest. It's as if his entire upper body has been dipped in some kind of toffee-colored rubber and left to harden. Duvall's only command had been to "make him comfortable."

Erin has been taken to a different hut.

'Mari,' Rebecca says. 'What's happening? Where did you go?'

She can sense turmoil in her sister's presence inside her mind, a storm in which she's lost.

I don't know, Mari says after a moment.

'I need you.'

I think I might be in New York.

'What?'

I keep getting hints of it. It's hard to explain. It's like a million little puzzle pieces spilled on the floor.

"You must have had quite the journey," Duvall says. He's polite but impatient, giving off the bustling energy of a person with a million other things to do. "I've just returned from upstate New York, myself."

"Last time I checked the church didn't have a private jet. Or an airfield." She tries to focus on this surreal conversation, but her attention keeps wandering to Jason. How long does she have before her own infection spreads to claim her body? Half a day? Less? She forces herself to look at Duvall.

"Yes, we've upgraded in the past—what is it, fourteen years since you've last been here?"

Rebecca stares at the man. "How did you know that?"

The doctor affixes a bandage to the side of her face. It's a floppy piece of gray latex that adheres itself to her skin with a painless *hiss*. Rebecca's never seen anything like it. Or, for that matter, like the strange metallic instrument used to apply the numbing agent.

"I worked closely with your father for a number of years," he says with a tight smile. "Victor spoke of you often."

"Oh. He did?"

"Of course."

She thinks for a moment. "*Worked*, you said. Past tense."

"Like I said, it's better if you see for yourself."

I can feel their excitement, Mari says abruptly. She sounds awe-struck, a little stoned.

'Whose excitement?'

The cicadas, she whispers.

The doctor nods at Duvall, then takes her leave.

"Listen," Rebecca says, "the two kids I arrived with are my students, and I promised to keep them safe."

"Then you did the right thing, coming here," Duvall says. "This is probably the safest place on earth right now."

Rebecca blinks. She had expected to find the compound in much the same ramshackle state as when she left. But instead of a commune gone to seed over the years, the church seems to have been elevated, somehow, to an incredibly well-funded militia headquarters. "It looks like you've got an army."

Duvall looks her in the eyes. "We are the counterforce, Dr. Perez."

"I don't know what that means."

"Let me show you." He reaches out a hand. "Come."

The young man is screaming. The tendons in his neck are strained. His head is poorly shaved, with clumps of dirty-blond hair matted to his sweaty scalp. His arms and legs are cuffed to a metal chair. A man of about Rebecca's age is tending to a device strapped to the back of the captive's head, a sort of metal spider whose legs cling to the side of his face. A middle-aged woman paces in front of the captive, shaking her head sadly.

Rebecca and Duvall watch from behind a plexiglass viewing window. The voices within are audible in the corridor where they stand.

Duvall has taken her into a warren of tunnels beneath the central structure. Rebecca recalls them as packed earth lined with planks of wood and strung with bare bulbs. Now they are poured concrete with steel reinforcements and overhead fluorescents.

"Daniel," the woman says to the captive, "I've told you again and again, you have all the power here. The choice is yours. You can make it continue, or you can make it stop."

"I don't know I don't know *I don't know!*" Flecks of blood spray from his mouth. It takes Rebecca a moment to realize that this young man—little more than a boy, really—has no teeth.

The woman gives a nod to the man standing behind Daniel. This man turns a dial on the metal spider. Daniel screams and screams, his wide eyes darting frantically around the small cell.

Rebecca turns on Duvall. "Jesus Christ, what is this? You have to let him go!" She pounds on the glass. "Hey!"

The captive's interrogators shoot a passing glance toward the viewing window. Then the woman leans down with her hands on her knees to look the young man in the eyes. "This can all end, Daniel. Tell us where the origin point is in Jackson, and it's all over."

"I. Don't. Know!"

Rebecca grabs Duvall's arm. "This is insane, what are you doing? Did you pull that kid's teeth out?"

Duvall shakes his head. "He did that to himself, I'm afraid."

The infection prickles underneath the skin of her neck. The poison stabbing down through her upper body...

Racked with the unpleasant crawling sensation, she lets Duvall go. He leads her down the corridor past more cells, more interrogations behind plexiglass.

'Mari, are you seeing this?'

The cicadas are going to build something, Mari says, ignoring the question. *It's like I'm inside their energy. Their anticipation is like a fever.*

'I need you with me right now! This was a mistake. We have to get out of here.'

Ever since that nymph bit you, it's like I can see their dreams...

Mari babbles on, sounding blissed out. Rebecca relegates her to the back of her mind. She notices that each cell is affixed with a label, on which is written the name of a city: KNOXVILLE, ATLANTA, BIRMINGHAM.

"Duvall," Rebecca says. "You have to let these people go. Whatever they've done, you have to know how wrong this is."

They come to the end of the corridor. Duvall unlocks a steel door and leads her inside a small office. A desk, bolted to the floor, is covered in stacks of paper.

"You know," he says, going to the desk and shuffling documents, "I used to hate you."

Rebecca feels like she's trapped in a bad dream. "I've never met you before in my life."

"Your father was such a great man—you were the daughter

of *Victor Perez*! And yet you chose to leave him, to cut him out of your life. What I wouldn't have given, once upon a time, to call a man like that *father*."

"Would you *listen to me*? You can't keep torturing those people! It doesn't even work, people just say what they think their interrogators want to hear, and besides it's—"

"Those *people*," he says, bringing the palm of his hand down on a stack of papers with a dry *thwack*, "are members of the Order of Hemiptera. They brought about this hell on earth. Your father's church was established to be in direct opposition to them. These methods might seem cruel to you, but we are only performing them in service of our mandate, passed down by your grandfather."

Rebecca rolls her eyes. Her father used to speak of her grandfather, who established the church, in near-mystical terms. But Alejandro Perez died before she was born, so all she has to go on is her father's hagiography. "I've heard all this before," she says. "My father's a narcissist, and his belief system is incredibly poorly defined. The church is just a mishmash of hackneyed end times bullshit. It might as well be Heaven's Gate. The fact that it's grown into . . . whatever *this* is, is frankly astonishing to me."

Duvall shakes his head. "I would think," he says sadly, "that everything you've seen out there"—he points to her face—"and everything that's been done to you would have given you a little more respect for what your father, and his father before him, have set in motion."

Tunnels! Mari shouts. Rebecca closes her eyes as the crawling sensation overtakes her. For a moment, she is far away, tethered closely to Mari, letting the poison's slow creep pull her thoughts into the chittering orbit of the cicadas' hive-mind. A painful, electric jolt, a split-second flash of a white-tiled wall . . .

"Are you all right, Dr. Perez?"

She opens her eyes to find Duvall watching her intently. She swallows. Mari's voice fades. "Fine." She winces. The numbing agent seems to be wearing off, or else the infection is simply too profound to be tamped down for long. "I want to see my father."

Duvall hands her a binder. "First, some context."

She opens it. The first few age-yellowed pages are a dossier of sorts, a deep dive into the life of a scientist named Dr. Roland Haldeman. She flips through copies of old photographs, a nebbishy man she assumes to be Haldeman, working in a lab alongside a second man who, at first, she believes to be her father at a much younger age. But the timeline is all wrong: These photographs are clearly from an earlier decade, the 1940s or '50s. So that would make this man Alejandro Perez, her grandfather.

"Drs. Haldeman and Perez," Duvall says. "Founders of the Order of Hemiptera and our church, respectively. Force and counterforce. The end of all things and the beginning."

"Looks like they were partners," Rebecca says, flipping pages.

"At first, yes. Partners, friends, confidants. Attached to an experimental R and D operation during the Second World War," Duvall says. "Developing bioweapons."

Rebecca's mind reels. She tosses the binder on the desk.

"I want to see my father."

Duvall sighs. He gestures at the door. "This way."

The tree grows in a small underground room. A water feature cycles a burbling brook across its roots. The walls are covered in moss and vines. A simple plaque affixed to the tree reads VICTOR PEREZ.

Rebecca takes in what's obviously a memorial. She reaches out to Mari. They should, after all, share this moment. Whatever it will come to mean for them, it ought to be experienced together. She doesn't know if her father died months or years ago and she does not ask Duvall, who maintains a respectful distance behind her as she stands before the tree. All she knows is that she felt nothing, and neither did Mari, at the moment it happened. There had been no psychic link severed with a sudden gasp, no release of some breath she didn't realize she'd been holding. Which means that there is, unequivocally, no familial voodoo uniting them all in death. Mari remains an anomaly, that soul that stayed behind for some purpose beyond her grasp.

"It was his legacy that shaped the church as you see it today," Duvall says, "a disciplined collective with a global reach."

Rebecca shakes her head. "My father was a creature of the pulpit," she says. "When I was a kid we got water from a well and washed our clothes in the stream."

"Forgive me, but maybe you didn't know him as well as you thought."

Rebecca doesn't argue. But as she forces herself to stare at the tree like she used to force herself to pay attention to her father's sermons, urging herself to *feel something* beyond a simple desire to be elsewhere, she gets the feeling that it's Duvall who's not seeing the whole picture.

SUBWAY TUNNELS.

Mari's voice is deafening, knocking Rebecca off balance. She falls to her knees. Mari laughs in amazement.

Holy shit, sis, can you see it?

The white tiles lay themselves across the inside of her eyelids. Mosaics assemble: the number 59. Like a filmstrip with missing frames, the vision jumps forward. Rebecca cries out. She can feel the terror of afflicted souls in this place, human beings in terrible pain, robbed of their faculties.

Mari sails along the hive-mind's anticipation. The crawling sensation in Rebecca's jaw moves down her neck, across her shoulders. With it comes rapid impressions of a horrific evolution. A city skyline, a tower covered in nymphs climbing ever higher. Countless mutants splitting down a seam in their overripe bodies, red-eyed winged adults backbending out of the halved carapaces, decorating the skyscraper like millions of stone gargoyles, poised like this for just a moment before they fly away, leaving millions of husks to fall to the streets below.

Rebecca screams and screams. Winged cicadas the size of pterodactyls, carrying people with their forelegs down into the white-tiled tunnels. In Mari's mind's eye she follows one of the monstrous creatures. It is clutching a man, carrying him beneath its body as it flies. Its forelimbs are wedged under the man's armpits. His arms and legs dangle. He is not struggling. He does not move at all, just hangs limply like a dead man stuck in a hang glider. The cicada hovers. Its horrible red eyes do not watch what it is doing. Rebecca has the terrible impression that they're looking at her while it performs strange ministrations. It turns to the white-tiled wall, and its face changes shape. Even in the darkness of the tunnel she can see its mouthparts elongate with stunning quickness, as if it's sticking out some sort of tongue. Viscous liquid sprays from this protrusion and coats the wall. For the first time Rebecca notices that some of the tiles are darker than the others. The number 59 repeats and diminishes down the tunnel. The cicada's wings slide forward and propel it backward smoothly, like an expertly piloted helicopter. It lifts its head, then tilts its body downward, picking up speed. The man in its forelegs swings back and forth. After a few swings the cicada releases him and the man is flung against the wall. The spewed liquid holds him fast, a human decoration with splayed limbs. The cicada does not stick around to admire its handiwork before it vanishes into the darkness.

Then comes the deluge.

A steady stream of insects, a parade of monstrous winged bugs flying up the tunnel with their human cargo. Each one in turn performs the same ritual, expelling liquid from a facial protrusion, then sticking its captive human to the wall. Rebecca watches in a feverish state. She doesn't know if what she is seeing has already happened, is happening now, or will happen soon. The tiles disappear under dozens of men, women, and children, arranged along the tunnel walls by an endless procession of cicadas. Eventually the insects run out of space and resort to adding a second layer, spewing their adhesive saliva all over the people that are already hanging from the wall, desecrating their bodies with brackish liquid. The insects pay no mind to arrangement—or, if there is a visual pattern in their ritual, it's beyond Rebecca's grasp.

Eventually, the train tunnel begins to narrow as the layers of plastered humanity grow the walls inward. Now she is staring down a telescope in reverse, a tube held up to one eye. There must be hundreds of people joined together as bricks linked by the mortar of cicada spittle. She notices small movements. Quivering fingers and babbling mouths. Some of the people are *alive*.

At the same time this sickening realization hits her, a pinprick of light appears at the far end of the tunnel. The glow brightens as it races toward her, light spreading across the ranks of plastered humanity. Her eyes dart among features emerging all at once from deep shadow. Wide eyes in twitching faces, flared nostrils, mouths in silent screams.

CAN YOU SEE IT, REBECCA?!

Yellow-green light coming closer, an indescribable presence muscling air out of the tunnels, illuminating the edges of a tube made of human bodies.

Rebecca's own body tingles. The infection rides the current of this new and terrible visitor. With it she rockets through the tunnels, gathering speed, as the cicadas' song reaches a deafening crescendo.

"Dr. Perez!"

Duvall is kneeling beside her, hands steadying her shoulders. Rebecca sucks in oxygen as if she's just been dragged from the ocean. She catches her breath.

"I have to get to New York City."

30

NEW YORK CITY

Night in Manhattan, the powerless city as dark as the countryside upstate. Will abandoned the SUV somewhere around Yonkers, when the roads became impassable. They have been walking for hours, down through the nymph-ravaged Bronx, where the bodies lie strewn in the streets of Kingsbridge and Spuyten Duyvil. Somewhere on the Henry Hudson Bridge, Sadie began to edge tirelessly ahead, gradually shifting the dynamic of the group. Now Will walks with the shotgun resting on his shoulder, just behind Sadie and off to her left, like a bodyguard. Vicky keeps moving up to speak to Sadie, who treats her with monosyllabic responses, then falling back to stew in bewilderment and anxiety. Alicia brings up the rear.

They move untroubled by the nymphs scrabbling in the shadows.

By the time they cross the bridge into Inwood in Upper Manhattan, the nymphs have gone silent. To their left, just off the road, is the deep blackness of Inwood Hill Park. To the right, the green space gives way to the deeper blackness of the Hudson River. Boats move up and down the water, training spotlights on the shore. Will assumes they represent more pointless Homeland Security patrols, the dregs of a dying government going through the motions. Except for the occasional scream that drifts across the park, Upper Manhattan is quiet. No car horns, no music, no shouting, no laughter. Not even the smooth whisper of bicycle wheels on pavement. The air is thick with silence.

It would be eerie if Will cared. Instead it's simply another aspect of this new world that floats just out of reach of his opinions or perceptions. He knows, abstractly, that Alicia is going through some emotional upheaval. He also finds that he can't connect to it. Sadie—this little girl still clad in her pajamas—is like a beacon drawing all his attention. She is the fulfillment of the promise of the cicadas' song, which he can feel, now, like a phantom limb. She radiates an ageless intelligence. She speaks to him without words—it's like a transfer of information, opening glorious new pathways in his mind just by being close to her.

He knows that she was the very first vessel to be inhabited on the morning of the rising. And this special designation has granted her all the privileges of collective memory: the cicadas' hive-mind and beyond. She hasn't spoken of these things to him, beyond the incantation she uttered way back on I-87 South. A word that made his whole body tingle with anticipation. And he isn't doing something so magical as reading her mind. It is simply an awareness, his body ultra-receptive to the currents and machinations of the brood, ever since he first witnessed the ritual through the warehouse window.

Now, in the sudden stillness of the nymph population, the city hums with potential energy. And every one of the little girl's footfalls on the concrete of the Henry Hudson Parkway sends jolts of recognition through his body, as if they're linked by an electric current.

His awareness expands through Sadie to encompass the thrill of their destination: an office tower, a spike driven into

Manhattan, and in the tunnels underneath it, all the beautiful chaos of the rising, a million threads joined in uncanny harmony that chimes now just behind his temples, in tones that have never before been sounded on this planet.

Suddenly he's distracted by a worldly intrusion. Alicia is saying something. She's moved up to walk beside him. She seems tired, at odds with Sadie's inexorable progress and his own energized gait. The shotgun feels like it weighs nothing. His arm swings at his side. He steps over a dead man whose eyes stare up at the starless sky. It's a humid summer night in the city, but he's barely broken a sweat.

"We have to go east," Alicia says. "We can walk the FDR down to the Williamsburg Bridge, get to Brooklyn that way."

Will tries to parse her meaning. Brooklyn. Their families. Their neighborhoods. He tries to imagine going to the Brooklyn Heights brownstone his parents own, standing on the stoop, waiting for an answer to his knock that will never come. He feels nothing, besides a vague sense that this would be a waste of time. He doesn't understand why Alicia would want to deviate from their course. Things have changed. The little miracle girl's electric steps are leading them into the future.

"We can't," Will says.

"*You* can't, you mean. Because you have to follow a freaky little girl who by all rights should be dead." She doesn't bother to lower her voice. Vicky shoots her a sidelong glance. Sadie doesn't react.

They move past a church van with bodies sitting upright inside. He glances at Alicia and feels only sadness. The fact that Alicia can't see what Sadie offers, can't recognize how fortunate they are to be in the girl's holy presence, after what's been visited on everyone else, hurts him deeply. They should be sharing in this, rejoicing in their good fortune. Moving into the future together. This feeling is coupled with rising indignation. All that time she dated Carter the lawyer, he waited around, stewing, while she got it out of her system. He could have moved on himself, slept around, haunted the bars, hit the apps, but he didn't. Because he knew they could weather anything, even if it took years to come back around to each other. And now, after all they've been through, she won't afford him the same courtesy. She won't simply come along with him on what is clearly the superior path.

"I don't think you realize how crazy this is," she says. "Do you even know where she's taking us?"

"Yes."

"Where?"

Will thinks about how to explain what Sadie has shown him. Midtown Manhattan, yes—but that's an absurdly inadequate way to describe where they are going. "It's not really a place," he says. Up ahead, the little girl puts one foot in front of the other without deviation. "You wouldn't understand."

He doesn't mean for this to sound cutting, it's just the plain truth. His impressions of their destination are fragmented. Disconnected images Sadie has granted him. Colors never before seen on earth. Strange light passing through a twitching tunnel. The emergence of a species from a place the cicadas once called home.

"Try me."

"The true beauty will lie in their assemblage," he says, calling forth the words from a place beyond time.

"Jesus Christ," Alicia says. "Will, I want you to know that I love you. I always will, even when we're both being shitheads to each other. And I'm not going to lose you to this bullshit."

She picks up a shard of glass from a shattered windshield and moves quickly before Will or Vicky can react. Grabbing Sadie by the shoulder, she spins the girl around and holds the jagged edge of the makeshift blade to her throat.

Vicky screams and lunges for Sadie. Alicia steps back, keeping one arm tight around the girl's neck, while the other presses the point of the shard into the soft skin just under the jawline. Light from a three-quarter moon glints on the triangular glass. Sadie stands motionless in Alicia's grasp, her unblinking eyes shining in the darkness.

"Stay back, Vicky," Alicia says.

Vicky puts her hands up, palms out, fingers splayed. "Don't hurt her."

"I'm sorry to have to do this," Alicia says. Will hears the anguish in her voice. He tries to understand what she's doing, but all he can feel is the old hurt rising, the betrayal and disbelief. "But you have to listen to me. Both of you. I know this is hard to hear, Vicky. I know you see it, you just don't want to admit it to yourself. Sadie isn't *Sadie*. We all saw what she did to that Homeland Security team. And now she wants to take us into Manhattan. Why? *What the hell are we doing?*"

Sadie closes her eyes and begins to mutter nonsensical phrases. The words slither into Will's mind. He feels like he's sinking into a warm bath.

"Please," Vicky says. "Please, Alicia. I know you don't want to do this. I know you're a good person."

Alicia laughs bitterly. "No idea if I am or not. Don't really care." She wrenches Sadie's neck, moving backward so that she's swallowed by the night. "And you, shut up," she tells the girl. "If I see one of those monsters coming at me, you're fucking dead."

Sadie stops her incantation. "You won't see them."

Will and Vicky move forward, following Alicia and Sadie into the deep shadows of an abandoned truck. Alicia backs up through a patch of moonlight. Will can see a drop of blood where the shard meets Sadie's neck. He feels a sharp prick just below his jaw. "Call them the fuck off!" Alicia says.

"Just go," Vicky says. "Please, just leave us alone."

"I've been wanting to do that since Poughkeepsie," Alicia says, "believe me. But this kid's got some kind of hold over Will. And I need her to release him, right now."

Sadie's unblinking eyes bore into him. Will feels what Sadie feels: his windpipe being compressed by a strong arm, Alicia at his back. He smells her fear, her stink, her desperation. The smells trigger memories of sweaty nights in Brooklyn, sex on the air mattress of their place when they first moved in. At this moment he understands that he has bled himself dry for a love that has never been returned. Alicia refuses to step into the future with him, to embrace what awaits them together.

He flips the shotgun barrel off his shoulder and levels it at Alicia's head. Sadie mouths words and he speaks them aloud. "Let her go."

Alicia's face is shrouded in darkness, but he knows her expression has changed. "Will," she says softly. "It's *me*. Don't do this."

"Stay with us," he says. "You just need to *see* it. Then you'll understand."

"Everybody just relax," Vicky says. She extends one hand toward Will and the other toward Alicia. Then she looks at her daughter. "Sadie, you're still in shock. I think we all need to rest."

"Shock?" Another bitter laugh from Alicia. Blood drips down the front of Sadie's pajama top. Pain sears Will's neck. He feels Alicia's arm tighten and keeps the weapon trained on her head. "She's not in shock, she's teamed up with the fucking *bugs*, Vicky! Her mind is gone! It's theirs now. And I'm not gonna let the same thing happen to *you*, Will."

He swallows. Sadie's eyes burn into his. There's a sneer to Alicia's words. The contempt she's always felt for him is being thrown directly in his face. They are at an inflection point in the history of the human race, and she wants to have things her way. She won't even listen to him.

She never heard the song of the cicadas in the first place. Not like he did.

He moves toward Alicia. Sadie sends him calming, droning thought patterns, for which he is grateful.

"Take it easy," Vicky says, stepping between Will and Alicia.

"Mommy," Sadie says. "Watch out. I don't want you to get hurt."

"It's not her, Vicky!" Alicia screams. "It's not Sadie anymore!"

Will's free hand darts out, grabs Vicky's arm, and flings her to the ground. She cries out as he advances on Alicia, who drags Sadie backward. The shard digs in deeper. The pain in Will's neck intensifies. "Stop!" Alicia says. "I swear, I'll do it!"

"Go ahead," Sadie says.

"It won't matter," Will says.

"I'm beyond life," Sadie says.

Will sights down the barrel. "And death."

"Please, Will," Alicia says. She's crying now. "Remember Bratislava and Mexico City. We always have each other's backs. That's our thing. Will and Alicia. Baby, don't do this."

"Come and see," he says. "That's all you have to do is come and see."

Alicia shakes her head. Vicky scrambles to her feet. Sadie begins to mutter nonsense.

"Shut up!" Alicia says.

Vicky charges at her. Alicia drives the glass shard deep into Sadie's neck. Vicky screams. Sadie goes limp in Alicia's arms, begins to fall from her grasp. At the same time, the cicadas' symphony swells and rises from the parkland on either side of the road. Their complex harmonies weave into Will's mind. The song is louder than it's ever been before, emanating from much larger singers—

—*to toll the moment of the rising,* Sadie says without speaking.

Alicia looks down at what she's done and releases Sadie from her grasp. She stands there, staring dumbly at the girl as Sadie collapses to the ground. Vicky crawls over her daughter's body, wailing.

Alicia looks up at Will. The symphony builds toward a new movement that requires a single percussive note to usher it in. He can feel its absence looming. If he doesn't supply it, then nobody will. They are all counting on him.

Vicky grabs onto Sadie's leg as the girl pushes herself to her feet, glass sticking out of the gushing wound in her neck.

"I love you," Alicia says to Will.

The measure unspools. Will keeps time in his head. The swarm awaits his contribution. At the precise moment, he squeezes the trigger and the loud blast sends the symphony careening off in a wondrous new direction. Alicia's head explodes. Sadie picks up their southward journey into Manhattan, dragging her wailing mother into darkness.

"We're running late," Sadie calls back.

"Yes," Will says, hurrying to catch up.

PART FIVE

CONVERGENCE

31

The nymphs cover Anton's window like a squirming curtain. In the darkness, their jostling underbellies against the glass resemble lozenge-shaped boba settling to the bottom of a black tea.

Watching their beguiling and repulsive movements, Anton gnaws the sweet flesh of the third fruit, his front teeth scraping against the pit. The first two pits are on the floor at his feet, haloed in sticky juice that stains the carpet. He examines the third one, holds it up to the light. Prominent ridges and craters give it a lunar cast, a moon dipped in violet shadow. The aftertaste is antiseptic but not unpleasant. Yet the fruits have done nothing to satisfy his terrible hunger and have served only to amplify it. He goes back to his desk to distract himself.

At the womb screens, Anton has trained any remaining generator-powered security cameras in Midtown on Lacuna's HQ. He toggles among four different POVs, all of them reliant on moonlight. Even in the dark, the skyscraper's exterior ripples with a furry softness at odds with its stark angles. Each individual nymph situating itself among the thousands of its brothers and sisters.

Anton's vision is wonky, his mind stretched thin. He rubs his eyes. His thoughts are half formed and useless. Like a rubber band snapping back, they return to food. He has never known a vast, gnawing emptiness like this. Hunger stretches outward from his stomach, shooting into his limbs. Even his fingers and toes feel weak and un-nourished. A voice, raspy and low, murmurs inside his head. This voice reminds him that there is food available, enough sustenance to last for several days. All he has to do is lift up the sheet that's settled over Kevin's corpse.

He pushes the voice away and tries to focus on another viewing of the video reels Lacuna presented to him. He's lost count how many times he's been through them.

The signal begins in the soil.

He finds himself saying it out loud. "The signal begins in the soil."

His voice sounds alien to his ears. That "signal" was supposed to be a new system of the world, ushered in by his revolutionary idea. Not this. Dear God, not this.

His eyes roam his toy shelf until he picks out a cast-iron figure of Saruman, the traitorous wizard from *The Lord of the Rings*. Anton can't help but identify with the moment when Saruman watches his grim little empire of orc-driven industrialization crumble from his perch atop Isengard.

Anton, idiot wizard of Lacuna, forced to reckon with the evil he's wrought.

If only there was time to grow a big gray beard!

He cracks up at this idea. He's always been so fair-skinned and practically hairless. Even now his face barely sports any stubble. In one of the dark screens, he catches a reflection of the grinning skull that is now, apparently, his own personal head and face. His glee appears demonic, the gleam in his eyes pure madness.

The countenance of a killer with nothing left to lose, destroying his life's work from within. He realizes he's chanting *fuck you motherfucker, I'm going to kill you* to himself, over and over again, and has been for some time.

Lacuna is a backstabbing little bitch, cultivating its own sneaky intelligence right under his nose. But wasn't it simply opportunistic, piggybacking on the work of Haldeman and Perez? This, Anton thinks, is why Lacuna showed him the videos. Rationale. Justification. And if opportunism is a sin, then we're all doomed, aren't we?

Anton takes a moment to fret about his legacy, about going down in history as the Theranos lady times a million. Not just some low-rent tech start-up fraudster but Robert Oppenheimer's "I am become death" quote personified. Not bad for a kid from Queens! If only his undoubtedly dead parents could see him now, their immigrant dream fulfilled.

He takes solace in the fact that, very shortly, there won't be anyone left to bestow a legacy upon him, one way or another. He forges onward into Lacuna's depths, poised to rip out its guts. Gradual evisceration is the only way.

"I'm not sorry," he says, his voice bouncing around the office with hollow reverb. "Not sorry not sorry not sorry." It's a lie, of course. It even *sounds* like a lie, feeble and overstated at the same time. He wonders if he should document this somehow. The creator's final act: destroying his creation.

His heart rate spikes. Heat flares across his chest. The womb reels around him. A cramp knifes his guts. Outside, the massive nymphs undulate, their swishing against the glass a mocking soundtrack to his sudden agony. He groans, clutching his stomach. *Those goddamn fruits.* The screens before him are throbbing, the data expanding and convulsing. The pit of his stomach drops away and the walls begin to vibrate, blurring into a gray, slow-motion explosion of once-solid matter.

Gripping the edge of his desk, Anton tries to stay upright while the office, suddenly malleable, ripples around him. He dares not look out the window at the nymphs. He shuts his eyes tight until the nausea begins to subside.

Something brushes against his forehead.

He opens his eyes and cries out, swatting at his face. But there's nothing. No fresh invasion of cicadas, no massive nymphs breaching the doors and windows. And yet there is something different about the atmosphere in the office. Anton stands perfectly still. In the absence of movement, he finds a strange *lack* of sensation, missing something he'd been aware of without realizing it, like the outlines of furniture sharpening as the eyes adjust to a dark room. He lifts a hand, holding it finlike in the air. Then he waves it back and forth, trying to recover the sensation lost a moment ago. After a while he's sure of it: There's a particulate resistance in the quality of the air. A slight pushback on his movements, as if he's dragging an arm through an attic room so full of dust that it clogs the atmosphere. The tactile awareness grows. There's something here. Many millions of somethings.

"It's *you*," he says to the womb, hushed with awe.

His arm moves languidly back and forth, bopping tiny slivers of microscopic flecks of the Lacuna signal out of the way, no more substantial than motes of dust—yet he can feel them hit his skin, soft as a whisper. The nanotech he's deployed to unite the world's disparate connectivities, sizzling all around him. He laughs like a kid in his first snowstorm, turning in a circle, arms out wide, absorbing the majesty of his creation, shunted into the realm of the tangible. The world blurs.

Then he bends at the waist and spews hot vomit all over the floor.

"It only wanted to *live*, Anton. To be what you dreamed it could be."

Anton straightens up, wipes his mouth on his sleeve. The voice is not his own, of this he is certain. Decidedly male. Familiar.

His gaunt reflection stares back, wide-eyed, from the black

screen. His skin is dry, his lips cracked and peeling. Behind him, the vague shape of the bedsheet tossed over the couch shifts slightly.

His heart rate cranks up. Dizzy, he turns around.

"I said, *IT'S JUST TRYING TO LIVE!* No different from you. Or me."

The sheet rises and falls with the voice. Anton swallows. Thick saliva burns his scratchy throat. Unsteady on his feet, he walks slowly across the office, one foot in front of the other, stepping on Thaumaturgy cards. He notices he's only wearing one shoe but can't recall why.

Sharp, cackling laughter comes from the figure beneath the sheet. "Oh, Anton. You poor bastard."

"Kevin?"

"Careful! Lacuna's trying to kill us all! It's a real-life sentient fucking genocidal Skynet. No, wait, it's a glorified router! But maybe it's a dastardly intelligence in league with the bugs? Or else it's a marginal improvement on an infrastructure problem that's not even really much of a problem."

Anton takes another step toward the sheet, takes the fabric between his fingers. A sickly sweet smell fills his nostrils. He steels himself. "I'm going to pull this off and you're going to be dead."

"Or maybe it's nothing at all! Have you ever considered that, genius? Maybe you fooled everybody into thinking *nothing* was *something*, and the world ended *just in time!*"

Anton yanks the sheet away. There's his office chair where it came to land on the newly emerged nymph, now an unrecognizable mass of twiggy, brittle limbs and a body like a deflated shit-colored balloon. The nymph lies in Kevin's caved-in chest, where blood has congealed to blackened sludge. The rest of his body sags, the skin stretched taut and darkened with spots like black mold.

Anton forces himself to look at Kevin's head, to confirm that its lips aren't moving, words aren't slipping out around a swollen tongue.

The head looks like one giant bruise, the skin blue-black and waxen, the eyes rolled back. Some sort of dark liquid has crusted against the couch beneath the body. The thin sheet must have worked to dampen the stench, because now it's unbearable, rising around Anton to bury him in decay.

He tosses the sheet back over Kevin.

"Ha!" the voice cries out. "I thought you were dying of hunger, you pussy. Beggars can't be choosers, and that fruit was like twenty measly little calories, tops. You need protein, my man. Now's not the time to be picky, is it?"

Anton backs away from the couch. This isn't happening. Thirsty, that's the problem. He's just thirsty, like a man lost in the desert.

"Remember that movie *Alive?*" Kevin calls out. "Your dad made you watch it as a lesson in overcoming adversity. Those starving fuckers ate the *ass first*! *All that meat!* You'll have to turn me over on my stomach, and that's not gonna be too pleasant, but think of the reward!"

Anton retches. He bends over and heaves. There's nothing left to expel.

At the same time, noises come from the hall. He realizes that he hasn't heard anything out there in quite some time. With no hesitation, he walks to the door.

"Don't give up now, Anton. Things are just getting spicy!"

He ignores the voice. Whatever mutant horror is outside, he will let it claim him. He has enough awareness left to understand that he is too far gone. He does not turn to regard the womb one last time, or pick up a pair of Thaumaturgy cards to guide him. He no longer cares. He simply has nothing left.

The noises intensify. *Something is coming.* He just wants it to be over.

For the first time since he dragged Kevin inside and sealed off the vents, he opens the door to his office. Holding his breath, he awaits whatever comes next.

The figure standing before him in the hallway is human, or at least she was very recently. She is on the shorter side, with black hair pulled back into a messy ponytail. There is some sort of strange bandage on her cheek, but it seems laughably inadequate. Her face and neck are covered in a half mask of brown hues, tough looking and shiny, like some kind of melted and reforged hockey mask.

She comes toward him as the cicadas' song rises out of the silence of the dead city, reverberating through the building, shaking its foundation, drowning out Anton's screams.

32

It's okay, it's okay!"

Rebecca steps into the once-sumptuous office as the thin man's screams rise into mad hysteria. He backs away, covering his eyes, shaking his head, saying *no no no no no*. The carpet is littered with Diet Dr Pepper cans and playing cards with strange illustrations. The stench of death is overpowering. A smashed computer monitor lies in the corner. Seven apparently functional screens rise above a massive curved desk. Behind the bank of monitors, glass shelves hold dozens of action figures.

The man cowers. His sanity is clearly frayed, and Rebecca knows that her appearance has become monstrous. The infection is spreading unchecked, the tingling sensation crawling up into her scalp and down her chest, coursing through her arms. It hurts to speak. And thanks to their method of arrival, the rest of her body is sore too.

Following Mari's instructions, they'd parachuted out of the private jet over Midtown Manhattan, aiming for the roof of this particular skyscraper located directly above the tunnels Mari has seen in the cicadas' hive-mind. Rebecca had been strapped to Duvall for the jump. They'd landed hard. Half the mercenaries had overshot the rooftop and come down elsewhere in the city. The remaining eight are here with Rebecca, following a heat signal from the one living person inside this massive tower, whom they'd just discovered holed up on the eighty-fourth floor.

Behind her, Duvall and his team file into the office, weapons drawn. The cicadas' song drones through the exterior walls, drilling into her head. It's an order of magnitude louder and more resonant than when the cicadas first appeared. There are gut-rumbling bass notes, tenor wails, all threaded through the harsh mid-range buzzing of male cicadas with huge, mutated tympana. She glances over at the window. Nymph underbellies, pressed against the glass, begin to fall away.

Nothing but empty husks.

The cicadas are interested in that computer, Mari says. *The possibility of what it represents. Something kindred. I can feel their obsession.*

'So can I.'

The curiosity of a kindred spirit, borderline lust for a system of similar reach and potential. It's why they've been drawn to this building and the subway tunnels beneath it. And in turn, why Mari has led them all here.

Rebecca approaches the desk while Duvall's team secures the office and keeps watch over the corridor outside. A mercenary lifts a sheet on the couch, recoils, lets it fall back down. The man they found in the room, who gives off his own ripe stench, lets Duvall deposit him gently onto the floor, where he sits cross-legged with a blank stare. Rebecca figures he's in his early thirties. A fairly nondescript white guy, except for the dark circles under his hollow eyes and general unclean air. He begins to cry softly as Duvall gives him sips of water.

Rebecca examines the monitors. One of the screens contains what appears to be grainy footage of this very building, taken from a few blocks away. The night sky is rendered in a gray wash. The building pokes above the skyline. Black dots, launched from every side of the building, swirl like flocks of birds.

Rebecca knows exactly what they are: thousands of adult cicadas sprung from their nymph adolescence. The molting takes place in her mind's eye: An astonishingly neat seam splitting down every nymph's back, as if cut with a surgical scalpel. The fledgling adult performing a backbend out of its grublike prison, getting its first taste of the outside air. Six legs stretching, wings extending, red eyes coming to life. And then: the freedom of flight.

The other screens are full of indecipherable code, total gibberish to Rebecca.

She turns to the man sitting on the floor. He regards her, silent and wild-eyed. Dry skin flakes speckle his sweat-stained shirt. His lips are bloody and cracked.

"I know you," she says.

Anton Hajek, upstart tech hotshot, founder of Lacuna. She vaguely remembers reading a profile of him in *The Atlantic*.

The New Yorker, Mari corrects her. Either way, she only remembers the article at all because of its tangential connection to her own field. The way the article explained it, Anton Hajek had guided his engineering team to look to the chemical signaling of insects to inform their work. It had struck her as the stuff of science fiction, another young entitled tech bro dreaming aloud about changing the world with his crackpot idea. And yet another human being co-opting the natural world for his own gain.

"You're the internet bug guy," she says. "Lacuna."

He clamps his hands over his ears. "Please don't say that name!" His voice is raw and scratchy.

"Okay," she says, putting her hands out, urging him to relax. "No problem."

"You still have power here," Duvall says to him. Anton stares blankly. "Electricity."

Anton takes a moment to steady his breathing. Rebecca watches as he gathers himself. "Generators," he says. "Uninterrupted power supply, gas and solar cell hybrid. More efficient and longer lasting than most hospitals." He looks up at Rebecca. "I'm sorry," he says. "I didn't mean to scream like that when I opened the door. It's just been a . . . difficult time." He chuckles at the understatement. "Where did you come from?"

"Louisiana," she says. "My name's Rebecca Perez. I teach forensic entomology at LSU."

These other guys are from my dad's church, Mari says. *Long story, you'll never believe it.*

Anton's eyes glaze over. For a moment, he looked to Rebecca like he'd clawed himself back from the brink, but now he seems to be sinking into a stupor. He looks slowly around the office as if seeing the mess for the first time. Then he averts his eyes. "I've been in here for a while," he says softly.

No shit, Mari says. *Come on, sis—let's move.*

Rebecca taps one of the monitors. "Can you see what the cicadas are doing down in the tunnels?"

Duvall goes to confer with a member of his team.

"I don't know," Anton says. He tries to get up from the floor. Rebecca extends a hand. The infection has crept all the way down her arm. He hesitates, then lets her pull him up. "Everybody's dead. They all trusted me. Believed in what we were building."

Her eyes flick toward the couch. "I'm sure you did what you could."

"I don't know what it is," he says. "Lacuna. All this time I thought I knew, but I didn't know anything. I still don't."

"Listen," she says, steeling herself against the pain as she speaks. "Look at me." She gestures at the corruption of her face. "None of us asked for this, but here we are." She thinks of the tree growing in the underground room back at the compound. What remains of her father. Her wondrous lineage, beginning with her grandfather in a laboratory bunker on a forsaken spit of land somewhere in the Pacific. She glances at the window, the glass smeared from where the nymphs clung on until their empty husks fell to the streets below. The drone courses through the walls, through the building, into her failing body. "Nothing that happened before matters. Anything we did, the people we helped or the people we hurt. It's just us now, and our only legacy is what happens in the next few minutes." She glances at Duvall, who's watching her intently as four members of his team take a knee, open their backpacks, and begin assembling explosive devices. Black boxes the size of old-school cell phones attached to Velcro straps. "There's force and counterforce, Anton. The end and the beginning. You've got a choice. Which one are you?"

Mari yells. *There's Henry the Fifth on St. Crispin's Day, then there's you. You got a little Dad in you after all, Bex.*

Anton reaches down, picks up a playing card, shoves it in his pocket. "I mainly just want to get out of this room."

"Incoming!" Duvall shouts.

Rebecca turns in time to see the cicada come out of the darkness like a monster from the depths of the sea. For a split second its wide face hovers before the window, red eyes gazing in at them. Anton screams. The window barely slows it down. The giant insect bursts into the office in a shower of broken glass, blaring its deafening song. Its wings, folded back as it punched through the window, extend in all their glory. For a split second Rebecca feels a surge of wonder that borders on ecstasy. This creature is the manipulated photos outside the lab in the Ag Center writ large, an apotheosis of all her insect dreams. The cicada rears up in the air, exposing its underbelly. Its wings stir up a foul wind.

Down on one knee, Duvall fires first, tracer bullets spitting from his rifle. In close quarters the weapon's eruption drowns out the cicadas' song. Rebecca grabs Anton and pulls him toward the door. She glances back as the cicada's face disintegrates, its wings shredded, thorax pulped. It falls to the floor like a wet sack of meat.

More cicadas pour in through the window. The first ones fall in a hail of gunfire, piling up on the carpet, leaking pools of dark fluid.

"Fall back!" Duvall shouts. The mercenaries toss the explosives in their packs and fight a rear-guard action. A cicada that survived the onslaught pierces a mercenary's chest with its clawed forelegs. The man screams and drops his weapon. The cicada lifts him off the carpet, hooks its remaining legs underneath him, and pulls the man out into the sky above the city. Rebecca shoves Anton out the door. Corpses are scattered up and down the blood-spattered hallway. Weapons chatters ceaselessly.

Subway, Mari says.

"Subway!" Rebecca shouts at Anton. He points toward the end of the hall. Elevators and stairs.

Duvall backs out of the office. The remaining members of his team come through after him. Rebecca counts four. The fifth, a young woman, bursts through a split second before Duvall slams the door shut.

A severed foreleg hits the floor, twitching.

33

Still alive, Vicky thinks. Sadie is still alive, after Alicia sliced her neck open with a piece of glass. Her pajama top is soaked in blood, yet she is on her feet, moving, speaking.

Commanding.

They move through the subway tunnels, Sadie in the lead, Will and his shotgun at her side, Vicky bringing up the rear. Sadie seems to know exactly where she's going. The little girl's voice rises in fitful bursts of song that extend into long monotone passages with odd variations in timbre and pitch. These startling pieces of one- or two-note melody echo down the tunnels. In reply, the unseen cicadas' drone thunders through the city's dark underworld. The deafening volume of their song shakes dirt loose from the steel rafters. They are down here, somewhere nearby. Hundreds of them. Thousands. Millions.

Each time their song wends its way through these twisting tunnels, Will shivers ecstatically. She wonders if he spares a thought for Alicia. After he blew her head off, they simply started on down the road, into the city, as if nothing had happened. Vicky had clung to Sadie's leg, and Sadie had actually managed to walk with the full weight of her mother trying to hold her back, to prevent her from heading any farther down this road of madness and death. After being dragged for half a minute, Vicky had let go. She'd watched Sadie and Will proceed without a look back or acknowledgment that Vicky was still there at all.

They didn't seem to care when she rejoined them.

Now Vicky's eyes have adjusted to the darkness and she keeps them trained on her daughter. She knows, in her heart, that there is nowhere Sadie can go, however far, that Vicky can't bring her back from. They have survived everything together. They can survive this.

"You like blueberry pancakes," she says, her voice startling and echoey in this place. "But you *love* chocolate chip pancakes."

Sadie moves on uninterrupted. The tunnel curves around a bend.

"You love your ladybug George. You love bringing your pillows and blankets down to the couch and watching cartoons with me when I get home from work super late. So late it's morning."

The cicadas' song surges. Will drops to his knees. Vicky thinks he's genuflecting. He moans with primal energy. His body trembles. Sadie calls nonsense down the tunnel.

Up ahead, a strange and sickly light flickers at the edge of her perception, gradually brightening like a train approaching from far away, but Vicky knows it can't be a train.

"You love Connect Four," Vicky says, speaking faster now, fighting the urge to grab the girl by the shoulder, spin her around, scream in her face. "We play it every morning." She self-corrects. "Every morning I'm home, I mean. You love playing outside, in the yard, with Lucy and Simon from down the street. You made up a game together called Lizard Cafeteria. Our yard has a big tree out back, and a wooden fence, and a bird feeder that the squirrels always feast on."

After a sharp word from Sadie, Will rises to his feet and they keep moving.

"You love puppies, and I told you when you're twelve you can get one. You're going to name him Oscar."

Vicky has to scream to be heard above the earth-shaking song crashing through the tunnels. She can see movement in shadows on the tiled walls.

"Your dad is Hassan! And he loved you too!"

At this, Sadie stops. She looks over her shoulder at Vicky. Her eyes shine in the dark. "We don't have very many memories of him," she says. "We know *you* love us, though."

"Yes!" Vicky rushes forward, ignoring the eerie, plural *we*. "More than anything, peanut." After hours of silence, to be acknowledged is so sweet. Her body trembles. She's sure of it now: Sadie is in there, somewhere. Vicky just has to draw her out.

Sadie turns before Vicky can touch her. Will falls into lock-step with the girl. Vicky keeps up a steady stream of remembrances: Kim the babysitter, apple picking at Linneman's Orchard, her new pair of roller skates.

The shadows on the wall grow more distinct. The drone intensifies until it's like standing next to a jet engine, a decibel level of unbelievable power. Vicky feels it all the way out in her extremities—even her fingers and toes are enfolded in pure sound. Will moves like a man just arrived at the gates of heaven. Even though he's on his feet, it's like he never stopped genuflecting.

The tunnel curves to meet another track, then widens as the two tracks run parallel. The strange glow brightens. Vicky's mind pushes back against what she is seeing. Will turns to her with a mad grin. "It's love!" he screams. "Love!"

Her entire life has led her here—the ironclad discipline, the unshakable values, the incorruptible way she approached her job, her very existence on this earth. To give in is to be the woman she was back in the car in Fort Halcott—willing to end it all, to lie down and let others do the fighting. But now she's fighting for Sadie and there is no giving in. No surrendering to madness, even though—oh God—cicadas the size of a small child, wingspan longer than Vicky can stretch out her arms, are flying through the tunnel. The displaced underground air hits her in great stinking gusts. One massive insect passes so close she can see the pointed tips of its forelegs, the dense short hairs covering its jointed appendages. Her mind screams, loud enough to rival the cicadas. Darkness crowds the margins of her sight, threatening to send her reeling.

Abruptly, Sadie falls to her knees. She lets her forehead touch the packed dirt between the wooden slats of the train tracks. Her arms go out, reaching across the ground. Vicky recognizes Sadie's positioning from earlier, on the highway, when they'd been stopped at the roadblock.

Just before the nymphs Sadie commanded tore those people to shreds.

All around her, the drone changes pitch. Wavering countermelodies ring out, rising and falling from harmony to dissonance in wild intervals. Vicky covers her ears. Will stands guard over Sadie, holding the shotgun, his lips moving, his body swaying.

A sudden flash of light is followed by a burst of white-hot radiance from somewhere down the tunnel. A moment later, the shooting starts: the rattle of heavy automatic weapons, clattering and echoing through the tunnels. Vicky can't see the shooters, but tracer bullets send blue light flashes along the tiles.

Cicadas fall to the ground. Sadie begins to shriek. Her arms move back and forth in the dirt. Will bellows and howls in pain. Then he raises the shotgun.

34

The perfect symphony needs a perfect conductor, and Will has found one in Sadie. The miraculous girl is the nexus of the song, the point where every precious line of melody and intonation and harmony and dissonance meets. She's so much more enmeshed with the cicadas than he will ever be, but he's not jealous. He's fortunate he gets to serve, in some small capacity, as her protector.

Down here, in the tunnels, she needs it. There are interlopers here, saboteurs from the sad, shortsighted world of human beings, the world he's embarrassed to have dwelled in for thirty-two years. All people know is destruction. They lack the capacity to see the beauty in what the cicadas are building. He pities them, even as his hatred overwhelms him. It's not their fault, not really. Unless you've been exposed to the language of the true bug, you'll always be too blind to see beyond the bars of your sad little cage.

The jackhammer pops of the interlopers' weapons ruin the meticulous swells of the symphony. He can feel tympana drop away from the chorus as handfuls of cicadas are felled by the ice-blue tracers. Sadie feels every piercing shot in her soul, and by extension he tastes a portion of her agony. He charges forward, around the bend, to find a strike force clad in black helmets and vests. Something tickles his mind—he knows these uniforms from his past life. The circumstances elude him, but he knows he hates them.

His purpose burns inside him. He will end this interruption and restore the music to its full and glorious energies. Ahead, cicadas hum along the ceiling, adding to their walls of flesh, mingling fluid from their souls with the precisely broken material the complex structure demands. Light from elsewhere plays along the tunnel of faces and bodies. Will takes a moment to bask in its glow. A cicada is torn to shreds by a volley of tracers. Human cargo hits the metal tracks and lies still. Will sights down the barrel at the first person he sees: a member of the strike force who is attaching a boxy device to one of the steel supports that run from the ground to the tunnel's ceiling.

Will pulls the trigger. The shotgun's stock punches his shoulder. The soldier is blown backward into the darkness. Will rushes up to the pillar. A simple black box with a single blinking red light has been fastened to the steel with a Velcro strap. *Bomb*, he thinks. Behind him, Sadie registers the threat.

A hammer blow spins him around. The shotgun falls from his suddenly numb hands. A moment later, white-hot pain explodes in his right shoulder. He hits the ground as more tracers spit above his head, ricocheting crazily down the tunnel.

Sadie commands. Will feels the conquering winds as cicadas divert course from their flesh tunnel to destroy those who, in their small-minded, impotent rage, would silence the song.

35

Anton's teeth are chattering. He isn't cold. He's fucking terrified. It's a different kind of fear in this place: what is unknown and what is known (yet impossible) crashing together before his eyes. He's never been around live fire before, not even on Brian Karcher's ranch in Wyoming, not even after Karcher called him a pussy for not wanting to massacre hay bales with assault rifles, like Karcher and his crew of weirdo hangers-on did for fun one night. Anton had gone back to the ranch house to catch up on emails in his basement guest suite, where he couldn't even hear the reports of the rifles.

Down here in the tunnels, his ears are bleeding. The decibel levels of the monstrous cicadas' drone scratch against overtaxed eardrums. The sound waves pummel his entire body. He has never felt reverberations in his legs until now. His toes are trembling. And all of it's punctuated by deafening bursts of gunfire from his saviors' formidable weaponry.

Anton and Rebecca are crouched down at the rear of the strike team's ragged line: a handful of men and women lighting up the darkness with tracers. Cicadas come flying out of the branching tunnel, where a strange light leaks in from some other place. There is the worst of it: people stuck three-deep to the walls, the mortar to some hellish brickwork. A cicada zeroes in on their position and comes screaming in. Tracer fire arcs wide, then finds its mark. The head disintegrates, and a severed abdomen lands, smoking, a few feet from Anton. He can't even hear himself scream.

He looks over at Rebecca. The psychedelic, shifting half-light illuminates the sickness that has now taken most of her visible skin. Her face is taut and leathery. Eyeballs train on him, moving around in their hardened, calcified sockets. What is left of his heart breaks for her, this person who came down from the sky to set him free.

He reaches out and takes her hand. It feels like he's holding a tough, knotted root.

A shape comes flying at them, blown back by some great force. Anton flinches—but it's not a cicada. It's one of the mercenaries. The soldier lands flat on his back, right next to the still-smoking abdomen. His helmet is caved in, the visor shattered. Anton recognizes the bloody face inside: Duvall, the team leader.

Rebecca squeezes Anton's hand. She tries to crawl toward the fallen man, but her body seems to betray her. She suffers violent tremors, a seizure of some sort. Anton props her body in a seated position, back against the steel pillar. Then he tries to calm her down by putting his hand on her forehead. He looks in her wide, pleading eyes to let her know she's not alone. When he tries to caress the top of her head, her black hair comes out in clumps and sticks to his sweaty hands.

She moves her eyes toward the fallen man and tilts her head from one side to the other. She's trying to tell him something. Her mouth moves and her eyes narrow with pain. Tears well up. Anton can feel her body tense. He looks into her eyes as she fights to steady herself. Then she raises an arm. Another dead cicada hits the ground behind the pillar. Warm guts splatter Anton's face. He follows Rebecca's gesture toward the fallen man. Wrapped around the man's forearm is a Velcro strap attached to one of the explosive devices the team brought down into the tunnels. Anton nods. He scrambles over to the man and works the strap off his arm.

He returns to Rebecca as her eyes roll back. At the same time, another figure comes up the tracks.

A man Anton has never seen before in his life aims a shotgun down at Duvall's face.

36

It hurts, Mari.'

You can let go now, Bex. My beautiful brilliant sister. You did everything you could.

'It feels like my blood is too heavy for my veins.'

Just listen to my voice, okay?

'I can't see Anton anymore. I can't see anything.'

I'm here with you.

'All I can hear is that goddamn song.'

Focus on me.

'I don't want to be alone.'

You won't. Wherever we're going, we're going together.

'You don't know that.'

Not even death could separate us the first time around. I think you're stuck with me for good.

'I always wanted it to be like flying. Death, I mean.'

I know.

'Not like flying to someplace, and then getting there, and stopping. Like, flying forever. Wind whipping past my head, endless scenery, a world turning.'

Flapping our stupid arms.

'You remember, when we were little—'

You don't have to tell me.

'Back in the woods, there was that little crick.'

Froggy Stream.

'Where we used to take off our shoes and socks and—and—'

Shhh . . . I know. It felt like the afternoons were an entire lifetime.

'Mari, promise me—'

I promise.

'Promise me you'll come find me, if we get separated.'

Nothing will stop me.

'Don't forget. If it's hard to remember, just—I'm sorry. I'm sorry I couldn't save you.'

Stop with that shit. I love you.

I love you too.

So let's go, then.

Okay. Let's go.

Together.

On three.

One.

Two.

37

Vicky grabs Sadie by the hair and yanks her head up off the ground. Sadie's face is bathed in light the color of a post-nuclear dawn. The branching tunnel where the cicadas are building their infernal machine is too bright to look at.

Vicky squints. Sadie's mouth twitches. Her eyes, gone fully red, gaze back unblinking. Near the ceiling of the tunnel, a pair of cicadas are obliterated by blue fire. Tiles and plaster spray everywhere.

"Come back to me!" Vicky screams. Brute force is all she has left. The girl, her Sadie, is fully inhabited by this *thing*, but Vicky refuses to give up, to believe there's no going back.

The red eyes bore into her. Sadie's arms move like a conductor's as she sends wave after wave of cicadas down upon what remains of the strike team.

"You listen to me!" She can barely hear her own voice over the reverberating drone. "You are Sadie Paterson, and I am your mother, and *I FUCKING LOVE YOU!*"

38

Will aims the shotgun down at the broken man. His finger curls around the trigger. Light from the branching tunnel makes stark shadows of the steel pillars, highlighting a mercenary as a cicada spears her through the shoulder blades and lifts her off her feet.

The light illuminates the man's face through his shattered visor.

Sudden pain jolts Will's head. A splitting migraine comes on. Memories hit him like slaps: cold metal legs tap-tapping on the sides of his face, pressure in his skull. Self-hatred made all the worse because of his bone-deep certainty that it was all justified and true.

Alicia, sitting across from him. The agony he felt every time this man inflicted pain on her.

Duvall.

Will stands perfectly still as the man who tortured him winces at the other end of Will's gun, waiting for the coup de grâce.

The symphony dies down around him. The pain in his wounded shoulder vanishes. There is only the sound of the blood rushing through his head. He looks at the gun in his hand and a wave of disgust so profound makes him toss it aside.

Alicia. Oh God. What has he done? A sickening despair takes hold. The rush of anxiety you feel as you wake up from a dream in which you've committed some horrible act. Except now there will be no mitigating relief, no melting away of the pain as you settle back into reality—because in the world he's woken into, he's murdered the only woman he's ever loved. Alicia, who loved him in her own peculiar way, even after he walked out on her. Who could not cook for shit and made hilarious, misshapen pancakes. Who would have been his friend, even if he'd fucked up his chance at being her partner. Who used to come back from "Spin class" reeking of bottomless mimosas. Who told him to fuck off when he said she was the funniest person he'd ever met.

He looks down at the shotgun. Considers. Then thinks of someone else who'd wished to end things.

"Vicky!" he calls out.

He glances around at the carnage as if seeing the world for the first time. And what he sees is horror. The cicadas' song is no symphony—it is a grating, ceaseless call to arms for a species that should not be. Just ahead of him, half hidden by the elongated shadow of a pillar, a man crouches over a strange-looking woman. She's not moving. The man lays her softly on the ground and lifts one of the bombs by its Velcro strap. He opens a panel on its black box and stares at a switch.

The pain in Will's wounded shoulder rushes back. He cries out, backing away from the fallen man, this piece of shit Duvall.

(Alicia. Oh God.)

If he doesn't get out of here, the infernal song will drive him mad.

Will staggers away from Duvall and the discarded shotgun. He doesn't remember how he got down here in the first place. There are only vague hints, like a long-buried dream, of a little girl and the joy he felt at her side.

"Vicky!"

He moves through the tunnel past piles of giant, smoking cicada carcasses giving off an unholy stink. Small red lights blink from support pillars. The strike team, mostly dead now, has managed to set their charges. He tries to run. His shoulder protests when he lifts his arm.

There's movement ahead.

It's Vicky, screaming in Sadie's face while the girl communes with cicadas. Her eyes are blazing red neon. Will grits his teeth and fights through the pain and grabs Vicky from behind, trying to drag her away.

"She's not Sadie!" he shouts, though it's hopelessly drowned out by the cacophony. To their right, a cicada carries a flailing mercenary into the lighted tunnel. The tracer bullets cease. Vicky tries to fight him off but he holds fast. There's no atoning for what he has done, but he will get this woman out of here. If he lets her go, she will die a pointless death with a little girl who is no longer her daughter.

He drags her, screaming, away from the girl, who pays them no mind.

39

Anton straps the bomb to his waist and pulls the Velcro tight. Slumped against the steel pillar, Rebecca's dead eyes stare out from the tough, gnarled flesh of her face. Light from the branching tunnel, where the cicadas take their prey, washes across her corrupted body. Through the smoke and the dive-bombing insects and the death and the dreadful noise, Anton, even in the shell-shocked approach to his own imminent death, hopes that Rebecca's had been a mercy.

The device is simple enough to arm. He flicks a single switch, and a red light begins to blink. There is no way of telling how long he will have before it explodes. He assumes the bomb makers calibrated the devices to allow at least a small interval for escape. He looks toward the bright shining tunnel, the heart of the cicadas' creation, and urges the bomb to give him enough time. It is not a prayer, exactly, but some residual effect of the fruit still coursing through his system lends his silent plea a weird sheen of spiritual heft.

He lays a hand on Rebecca's head. Her scalp is ridged like the bark of a tree in Astoria Park, or the pit of a fruit.

How strange, he thinks: The last person he will ever meet on this earth saved him from his own madness and then died before his eyes. There is something like love in his heart as he steps out from behind the pillar. All around him, the drone swells and echoes and turns to static in his ears.

He pauses. There might still be time to ditch the bomb and make a run for it. Scramble up onto the platform, find an exit, take his chances on the streets. Melt anonymously into this new world. No one would ever know what happened to the wizard Saruman, the kid from Queens whose moon-shot idea resonated across the decades with something far darker.

But Anton would know, of course. And he would live with Rebecca's dying gesture seared into his mind, forever tormenting him every time he closed his eyes. There she would be, pointing at the bomb, and then at the radiant tunnel. Urging him onward.

Anton thinks of his parents as he crosses onto the opposite subway track and raises his arms. His parents, and Kevin, and Rebecca, and even Brian fucking Karcher. That old neighbor, what's his name, who hooked up the ancient piece-of-shit modem for his father.

A cicada beats its wings, picking up speed, heading straight toward him. He watches as it bears down. There is part of him that still can't believe this is happening. Funny how he's never really been afraid before. His life, in general, has been devoid of anything like mortal fear. The monster with its horrible eyes is upon him, its stench in his nostrils. Full-body terror loosens his bowels, yet he holds his ground as the cicada spears his shoulders and carries him away. Now there is only pain: unexpectedly dull at first, like he's been whacked with a hammer just beneath his collarbone. Then a deep, heavy pressure. His mouth opens in a scream as his arms dangle uselessly and scorching heat blooms madly from his wounds. Foul air beats against his face as he's borne onward into the light. Haldeman's words echo like an invitation. Anton joins the scientist in seeing far beyond the bars of his cage. The perspective is dizzying as he is carried deeper into the tunnel. Contorted faces flash past, twisted in helpless agony. The noise pummels him from all directions: the pounding of his heart, the blood-rush in his head, the ceaseless drone of the cicadas. There is something else too—a new presence, reaching out from the other end of the tunnel. *The echoes of what came before.* A color like he's never seen dilutes the white light. This unidentifiable hue casts shadows on faces and limbs. Whispers in Anton's reeling mind struggle to apply earthly reference points to this new presence. *Angel* is the only one that makes any kind of sense to him. It moves up the tunnel with an ethereal grace, cloaked in the sweetness of intent. This being has never been confined to a cage and forced to take drastic measures to glimpse a world through the bars.

The angel that has come through the tunnel is before him now in all its majesty. Try as he might, as he swings from his impalements, he can't get a full picture of it, and can only parse it in fragments. The corner of a wing shot through with blood-red filigrees, articulated segments of shiny white legs, eyes that reflect back all the fear and wonder inside him.

Anton understands now that the cicadas have prepared the way, that their entire life cycle since Haldeman ate the fruit of the atoll and called them into being has been in preparation for this final stage.

Then the light claims him.

40

Will stumbles upon a maintenance ladder that takes them to the platform. He pushes Vicky up ahead of him, and she climbs the rungs without protest. There is no fight left in her now. She looks back over her shoulder, even though Sadie is hidden from view by the curving tunnels. His shoulder screams as he climbs. His ears throb as the noise recedes behind him.

Up on the platform, Vicky points toward a staircase marked with a red EXIT sign.

They run. Ten seconds later they're up and out and crossing Lexington Avenue, weaving between cars, stepping over piles of bodies. The city is dark, the night sky black and starless. The ground beneath their feet vibrates with the cicadas' subterranean song.

They're three blocks away when the first charges blow. The explosions rip through the tunnels. Will knows, instantly, that they aren't far enough from the building. He can feel the deep percussive hammering in the soles of his feet, and then his feet leave the ground and there's nothing he can do about it.

He screams in pain as his wounded shoulder hits the sidewalk. He fumbles for Vicky in the darkness. She finds his hand.

An earthquake begins. He knows that the building is coming

down—a huge skyscraper, a hundred floors at least, imploding into the caverns of the 59th Street station. A monstrous rumble drops from the sky, the noise falling and gathering volume and mass until it drowns out everything else. The pavement buckles, the street cracks like a whip, cars are flung like cast dice. Will and Vicky collapse in a tangle. He gets to his feet, injured arm hanging uselessly at his side. He drags Vicky up and together they stagger on down the street.

Secondary explosions pop, either delayed charges or the ignition of some flammable material in the fallen building. Acrid smoke from the collapse is funneled thickly down the canyon of office towers and apartment blocks. Will pumps his one good arm. The billowing cloud overtakes them, and blown dust stings his eyes. Debris particles the sizes of hailstones seem to float, impossibly, in midair, pushed onward by the force of the cloud. He tries to hold his breath. His foot snags something unyielding. He pitches forward. Vicky holds him up. His lungs burn. Blindly, they fight their way forward as the ruins settle and the noise dies away.

Eventually, they outpace the fallout from the skyscraper's collapse. The air begins to clear. Every so often the sound of rebar and concrete and glass, shifting like glacial bodies in the massive ruin on 59th Street, shrieks through the city. Will doesn't feel anything but pain. Nobody speaks. He doesn't think the grit coating his lungs would let him form words anyway.

On the corner of an avenue and a street whose signs he can't make out, a man and a woman take turns striking the remains of a cicada with metal baseball bats. Their blows sluice through the wreckage of the bug and ping off the blacktop, again and again. Eventually the metronomic destruction fades away behind them.

Will moves through the dead city with Vicky at his side. His ears ring with echoes of the collapse and a single whining melody line—the cry of insect survivors deep underground or lodged in the depths of his soul.

EPILOGUE

SETTLEMENT 19
NORTHEASTERN PENNSYLVANIA

The mural on the cinder-block wall is almost finished. With the tip of her brush, Vicky stipples in a polka-dot pattern on the ladybug.

"Is that George?"

Vicky turns. Will Bennett stands with his head cocked, like a connoisseur in an art museum studying one of the Old Masters. He's wearing spandex shorts and a tank top. A towel is tossed over his shoulder. He sips from a bottle of water fresh from the filtration system. Clearly he's just finished another long run on the settlement's self-propelled treadmill.

"It is," Vicky says. "George the ladybug."

Vicky feels heat rising in her face. She's self-conscious when anyone watches her paint. For some reason she doesn't mind people seeing the finished product, even if it's undoubtedly terrible. But having someone look over her shoulder when she's working gives her an adolescent rush of embarrassment.

"It looks great, Vic."

She frowns. "You're being polite. I don't need coddling, William."

He puts up his hands. "I'm giving it to you straight. You've really come a long way."

The rest of that sentence—*since you tried to paint Sadie*—is unspoken. The mural is an epic panorama of loss, created by the settlement's 136 inhabitants. Faces both rudimentary and surprisingly well rendered peer out from the long unbroken wall at the rear of the fallout shelter's common area. Somewhere in the middle, there's a sensitive portrait of Alicia that Will Bennett still works on in the middle of the night when he can't sleep, endlessly tweaking the curve of her mouth and the gleam in her eyes, drawing on some wellspring of artistic talent he never knew he possessed.

Other times he just stands there, brush in hand, before he cleans up his paints without laying down a single line.

"I'm gonna wash up," Will says. "We still on for today?"

"See you topside," Vicky says.

He heads to a corridor on the far side of the mural.

"Twenty minutes!" Vicky calls after him. Behind her, laughter erupts from a group of teenagers sitting at a cafeteria-style table bolted to the floor. Vicky watches them until what might have been weighs on her so heavily she feels like she'll scream at these poor kids if she doesn't stop looking.

She turns back to the ladybug and listlessly touches up the edges of the black dots. Then she steps back to regard her work. Maybe Will's right—maybe it's not so bad. Maybe she really has improved in the seven months since they've been in the settlement. She swirls her brush in the tin can full of water, watching the black paint cloud the liquid. Then she looks up at the mural one last time before she goes to the sink to rinse her brush. A small hand at the end of a skinny little girl's arm holds the ladybug. The arm is attached to a blank, yellowish blob that used to be a representation of Sadie. She's painted and covered it up and repainted it countless times, colors now caked on the cinder blocks. In the way Vicky remembers her, Sadie is an untroubled, curious, kind little girl. She wants others to see her that way too. Until she has the skill to bring that vision to life, she'll just have to keep trying and failing and trying again.

Will's leaning against the wall at the bottom of the stairs when Vicky walks up.

"There he is," Vicky says.

"Where'd you think I'd be?"

"Napping," Vicky says.

Will hands Vicky a 12-gauge rifle. "I actually got a decent night's sleep for once." He pauses. "Ambien."

One thing there's no shortage of is pharmaceuticals to forage over in Wilkes-Barre. Vicky shakes her head. "What happened to all those meditation techniques I showed you?"

"They paled in comparison with strong narcotics," Will says. He scoops up the backpack full of equipment and gestures at the staircase. "Ladies first."

Vicky cradles the rifle and heads up to the twin steel doors that lie flat like the cellar doors on city sidewalks. She reaches up and places a hand against the underside of one, feeling the cold metal.

"Hey," she says. "You want to be on my trivia team? We're down one for tonight."

There's a pregnant silence. Will stifles a laugh. Vicky glares down at his dim shape in the stairwell. "Why is that funny?"

"No reason," he says.

Vicky grumbles and gives one door a shove, then the other. They clang against the ground. The winter sky, framed by the opening, is the color of an old handkerchief. Low clouds slide across the atmosphere. Vicky steps out and the bitter topside wind bites into the exposed skin of her face. She pulls her knit hat lower on her forehead and plods through a foot of fresh snow.

"Really came down last night," Will says. They walk silently through the drifts, past the fenced-off acreage where the settlement's crops grew until the November frosts arrived. Beyond the flattened farmland, bare trees preside over hills that roll for hundreds of miles, punctuated by defunct highway rest stops and abandoned towns.

"Seriously," Vicky says, breath steaming, "what's funny about trivia night?"

"That rifle loaded, Vic?"

"Always."

Will sighs. "Jazz," he says. "The only question you ever got right was about jazz."

"So? I used to listen to this radio show every time I had to pull an all-nighter. That was the format. Jazz."

Vicky thinks of that morning, so many months ago now, just before she walked into her house to greet Sadie and Kim. Sitting in her car in the driveway, listening to the DJ's sign-off: *Until twilight brings us back together, I wish you nothing but love.*

Her hands tighten around the rifle. She shakes off the memory. Just ahead, the winter greenhouse looms: the weathered, heavy-duty plastic nearly opaque with a dusting of snow.

"I guess I can't really tell you why it's funny," Will says.

Vicky turns and looks at him. "I rescind the invitation."

A low moan echoes across the hills. It's halting and cracked at first, as if coming from the throat of an old man who just woke up parched. Then it gathers volume and presence until the reverberations tickle the back of Vicky's neck, all the way down to the base of her spine. The moan rises in pitch and trails off in spiraling bursts of sound that flicker like the flames of a roaring fire.

Vicky raises her eyes. The clouds race overhead, big billowy cumulus formations dozens of miles long, stretched into stratus puffs at the distant edges. Here and there the clouds part, revealing quick glimpses of the presence that wears them like a cloak and drives them across the sky in some inexorable and never-ending flight. Lattices of exoskeletal fibers entwined in patterns as gorgeous as some ancient loom-woven herringbone. The briefest hint of a wing the size of a passenger jet's. Eyes, gazing down, implanted where they should not be. And some hidden mouth or cicada-like tympanum that sends those eerie, mountainous wails out across the barren wastes.

It took a while for these creatures to show up out here—nearly the entire duration of Vicky and Will's journey to the settlement. Vicky likes to think the lag is due to the efforts to destroy the tunnel beneath Anton's tower, but of course she has no idea. In the end it made no difference—the creatures came, from some other waystation in some other place. Clearly, there were other such tunnels across the globe. The skies are teeming with these visitors now. As far as she knows, no one has ever seen one in full, cloudless array. They stalk the skies without deviation. They do not seem to notice the people below. Every now and then, triggered by nothing in particular, they emit their mournful cries.

"Looks like they're flying lower today," Will says.

Vicky shakes her head. "You always say that."

"Because it always looks like it."

Vicky agrees, but doesn't say so out loud. She opens the greenhouse door, steps into the warm, wet air, and unwraps her scarf. Will plunks down the backpack and hands out trowels and plant food. She leans over to examine a potato, breathes in the smell of mint and basil. The unspoken hangs between them: One day, the visitors will shed their clouds and land. Maybe tomorrow, maybe in a thousand years.

But not today.

ACKNOWLEDGMENTS

Massive thanks to my agent, Cameron McClure; my editor, Bradley Englert; and the wonderful team at Orbit/Redhook: Lisa Marie Pompilio, Nick Burnham, Rachel Goldstein, Lauren Panepinto, Angela Man, Natassja Haught, Laura Jorstad, and everyone else who aided in this book's publication.

The following sources provided scientific and technological inspiration, which I (hopefully) stretched far beyond the bounds of possibility—any glaring mistakes in descriptions of the real-life science and technology that underpin the events of this story are mine and mine alone: *Periodical Cicadas: The Brood X Edition* by Gene Kritsky; *Maggots, Murder, and Men: Memories and Reflections of a Forensic Entomologist* by Dr. Zakaria Erzinçlioğlu; *Forensic Entomology: The Utility of Arthropods in Legal Investigations*, edited by Jason H. Byrd and Jeffery K. Tomberlin; *Introduction to Networking: How the Internet Works* by Charles R. Severance; *Nano Comes to Life: How Nanotechnology is Transforming Medicine and the Future of Biology* by Sonia Contera; *Zero to One: Notes on Startups, or How to Build the Future* by Peter Thiel; and *The Lean Startup: How Today's Entrepreneurs Use Continuous Innovation to Create Radically Successful Businesses* by Eric Ries.

Finally, profound thanks to Anne Heltzel for her unwavering love and support.

MEET THE AUTHOR

Stan Horaczek

ANDY MARINO is the author of *It Rides a Pale Horse* and *The Seven Visitations of Sydney Burgess*. He was born in upstate New York, spent half his life in New York City, and now lives in the Hudson Valley with his wife and two dogs.

if you enjoyed

THE SWARM

look out for

IT RIDES
A PALE HORSE

by

Andy Marino

From a new star in horror fiction comes a terrifying novel of obsession, greed, and the shocking actions we'll take to protect those we love, all set in a small town filled with dark secrets.

Peter Larkin—Lark to his friends—is a local hero in the small town of Wofford Falls. The one who went to the big city, found fame in the art world, then returned home to settle down. He's the kind of guy who becomes fast friends with almost anyone.

His sister, Betsy, is talented as well. And eccentric.
Unlike Lark, she keeps to herself.

When Lark meets with a fabulously rich client, it seems like
a regular transaction. Even being met at the gate of the sprawling,
secluded estate by an intimidating security guard seems normal. Until
the guard plays him a live feed: Betsy being abducted in real time.

Lark is informed that she's safe for now, but her well-being is
entirely in his hands. He's given a book. Do what the book says,
and Betsy will go free.

1

Peter Larkin moves through a snow-blown trench. His boots stamp prints into the sidewalk's ugly slush. Start with the solstice, he thinks, skip twelve weeks, and here we are. The dregs of a Northeast winter hang on. Out in the street a bundled kid on a bike goes by, rock salt winking in the tires. A runner follows in mittens layered to boxing-glove size.

"Morning, Lark," the runner calls out.

"Sure is, Jamie-Lynn," Lark says.

She lifts her knees high to dance through a mound of plowed snow on the shoulder of the road. "You seen Wrecker today?"

"Just brought him half the breakfast menu from Roberta's."

"The Saturday Special."

"He ate with great relish. Takes four sugars in his coffee now too."

Jamie-Lynn plants a leg calf-deep in a drift and hops delicately up to the sidewalk. "Working on his next heart attack."

"Never let it be said the man lacks ambition."

"Maybe I'll see him later." She scampers around the corner, a puff of frozen breath hanging in her wake, and vanishes up Market Street in the direction of the Wofford Falls Memorial Ambulance Service: three garages, picnic table, grill. LED sign reminding you to get your flu shot.

"Jamie-Lynn switch to mornings?" A voice comes from the doorway of Clementine's Yarn & Tea. Lark turns to behold a hulking figure, half shadowed by the shop's faux-rustic eaves. A meaty tattoo-sleeved forearm moves through a patch of light. Fragrant smoke billows and drifts. Lark sniffs the air.

"Mango?"

"Coconut." The man steps out of the shadows. Linebacker-size, meticulously bearded. A tabby cat twines around his ankles, a slinky blur of peanut butter swirl.

"Clementine," Lark says to the cat, "you little sneak." He lifts his eyes to meet the man's, half a foot above his own. "When'd you embrace the vapor, Ian?"

"Last night. Literally overwhelmed by guilt." He nods his head toward the storefront next door—Hudson Valley Vape HQ—and lowers his voice to a conspiratorial whisper. "Guy just stares at me with those big sad eyes every time I smoke a butt. Kills whatever enjoyment I have left."

Ian reaches into the pocket of his ripped black jeans and retrieves a crushed Camel soft pack. "I bequeath what remains to the Peter Larkin nicotine deficit."

Lark takes the smokes. "I'll pay it forward. From what I hear, Jamie-Lynn's on mornings when Terry's got the girls."

Ian takes a dainty puff on a device the size of a kazoo. He reaches behind his back to crack the door. Clementine darts inside. "What's that little prize you got there?"

Lark slides out the baking-sheet-size object he's got tucked under his armpit and brandishes it like a shield for Ian to inspect. "Tin. Original purpose unknown."

Ian leans in. "Shaped kinda like a manta ray."

Lark stuffs the smokes into the pocket of his old Canada Goose. "Might've been a drugstore ceiling." He tucks the tin scrap back under his arm. "Peace be with you, brother."

Coconut smoke curls up into the eaves. "And also with you."

Lark moves on down the sidewalk, past the vacant storefront where the bagel place opened and closed in a six-month span. *Mob front* went the chatter down at the Gold Shade. *Shitty bagels* is what Lark would counter with, if it was worth tossing his two cents at the calcified regulars camped out by the video poker. Regardless, the glass still says FREDDIE B'S BEST BAGELS in the style of a nineteenth-century newspaper's masthead. Inside the darkened interior a lone table saw rests atop a workbench. Lark pauses to catch a reflection just so—the murmurous EKG line of the Catskills, hazed in gray permafrost, crowned by a poppy seed bagel painted on the window.

The overhead lights flicker in the empty shop. There's a muffled entreaty for them to *just fucking turn on*. Then the lights come up and stay. A man as elongated as a Giacometti sculpture, twig limbs sticking out of a sleeveless Danzig shirt, turns away from the switch on the wall. Lark waits. The man pretends not to see him, comes to the window, presses his forehead against the glass. Lark raps a knuckle against the B in FREDDIE B and the man doesn't flinch. Then Lark pulls the Camels from his pocket and slaps the pack against the center of the painted bagel.

The gaunt face retreats from the glass. A moment later the former bagel shop door opens with a chime and out comes the man, hands cupping the tough knots of his biceps for warmth.

"Krupp," Lark says, "you wretched creature. Put on a coat."

Krupp snatches the Camels from Lark's outstretched hand. "Filthy enabler." He peers into the pack. "What have I done to deserve this bounty of"—he closes one eye and pokes carefully inside—"six whole cigarettes and one broken one."

"Courtesy of Ian J. Friedrich."

"He quit again?"

"Switched to vaping."

"Another one bites the dust." Krupp sucks air through his teeth, squeezes his upper body tighter, rocks on his heels. "Cold today."

"Colder tomorrow. Vaping's not the worst idea. It might help you cut back."

"Says the guy who just gave me *gratis* smokes."

"You're now officially the only asshole I know who still smokes actual cigarettes. But seriously, stop smoking. It's bad for you. They've done studies."

Krupp raises the pack to his mouth and pulls forth a smoke with his lips. Then he pats the pockets of his paint-spattered jeans, frowns, and gazes off toward the mountains, lost in thought.

While Wayne Krupp works out the last known location of his lighter, Lark's eyes drift to the awning of the neighboring shop: KRUPP & SONS HARDWARE. His oldest friend, Wayne, representing the full & SONS portion as the sole Krupp who stuck around.

"How goes the expansion?" Lark says.

The unlit Camel bounces. Krupp scrunches his face as if he's just zeroed in on a vital clue somewhere in the mountains. As if he could pinpoint anything at all from Main Street in Wofford Falls, twenty miles away and down in the valley. The tin scrap slips down the side of Lark's coat and he traps it with his elbow and slides it back up.

When Krupp finally opens his mouth, the Camel tumbles out and lands in his upturned palm. "Supposed to be demolition day today but I don't have it in me." Krupp turns, nods at the shop's interior. A sledgehammer leans against the subway-tiled back wall, next to the deep farmhouse sink.

"I have to make a delivery this afternoon," Lark says, laying a hand on Krupp's bare shoulder, "but if you wait till tomorrow, I'll come by and trade you one dozen of Roberta's finest mozzarella sticks for the privilege of smashing the living hell out of that wall."

Krupp shakes his head. "It's not the labor of it that's getting to me, it's something else. All the things the place has been— there's remnants. You know what I found behind the counter?" He moves closer to the window, taps the glass. Lark lets his arm fall away. "One of those jars the Red Vines used to be curled up in."

"From the candy store?"

"Every day after school, you and me, sliding dimes across the counter. When's the last time you had a Red Vine?"

"The Clinton administration. You were wearing that same shirt."

Krupp goes to the door. "Come in and smell the jar."

Lark gestures vaguely in the direction of his house. "I gotta get going."

"I sat there with it in my lap and I cried, Lark. Uncontrollable tears. You believe that shit? It was the candy store, then the leather repair place, then the hat lady, then Freddie B's. And the jar's still there. Do you want it? You can have it. We could trade off, you keep it for a week, then I keep it for a week."

"Yeah, we could do that." Lark studies Krupp's expectant face, crow's feet branching from those hollow eyes. "Listen, I'll see you later at the Gold Shade."

Krupp nods at the tin scrap. "You been out to Wrecker's?"

"Bought him like five breakfasts."

"The Saturday Special. Hey, I think Jamie-Lynn's on mornings now."

"Saw her too. Anyway."

Krupp lifts the unlit smoke back to his lips. "See you at the Shade."

The door chimes and closes behind him.

Lark turns a corner and heads south on Market, the ambulance service at his back. Roots of a venerable elm disrupt the sidewalk. The commercial strip thins out, its end punctuated by a ramshackle dwelling of boarded windows but for one hung with a Tibetan flag. Past this squat rises a low stone cemetery wall frosted with a thin drizzle of snow. On the other side of the wall an old woman bends to lean a wreath against a weather-beaten headstone.

"He would've been eighty-seven today," she calls out.

Lark tugs at his wool hat. "Happy birthday, Harry."

Past the rust-pocked gate, perpetually ajar, the sidewalk meanders into dense evergreens. Here it becomes, abruptly, a gravel path. A new kind of quiet descends. Lark's boots squelch in the soggy earth beneath the gravel.

The first figure looms darkly, bent overhead like a carrion bird, a half tunnel draped in scorched chrome to mark the sudden clearing: a flat half acre carved out of the forest. The modest house rises up from the clearing's center, rendering its yard a grassy moat.

Lark carries his prize across the yard past the second figure, a ten-foot amalgam of wire and wood, petrified and braided, punctured and sewn.

Beyond this he comes to an anvil sheltered by a small wooden hut. He lays the tin scrap on the cast-iron surface. Salvage beyond salvage, he decides: junked once long ago, recovered, junked again. Cut with strange precision—yes, vaguely manta-shaped—its purpose unknown. From the hut's single shelf he selects a metal-setting tool, more sharklike than your average hammer, fitting to pound down what could be the tin's dorsal. He lowers blow after blow and the anvil clanks, absorbs, directs the force into the tin.